HIDDEN PASSION

A NOVEL

R. D. HATHAWAY

RD Hathaway Books

Cast of Major Characters

Rennie Haran . . . . Reporter for the *Des Moines Record* newspaper in Des Moines, Iowa

Bud. . . . . Rennie's Editor

Angie McGrady . . . . Chief Librarian and Archivist for Simpson College in Indianola, Iowa

Professor Matthew Justus . . . Archeologist specializing in the Near East retired from teaching and ad hoc staff at the British Museum

Professor Alistair
Thorsten Snapper . . . . Friend and professional associate of Professor Justus

David Justus - . . . . Theoretical research physicist and grandson of Professor Justus

Charles Sfumato - . . . . Wealthy collector of ancient artifacts, primarily Christian

Michael - . . . . Position unknown; assists Rennie in emergency situations

Rafael. . . . . Old boarding house owner on Island of Ischia

The Vatican:

Father Angelotti . . . . Secretary for the Propagation of the Faith; assisted in organizing of the grand exhibition of the newly discovered letters of Jesus

Abbess Serena Magdalena . . . General Affairs Assistant to His Eminence, the Secretary of State of the Holy See; an American and lawyer by training

Father Joseph . . . . Assistant to Abbess Serena

Sister Katherine . . . . Served two previous popes; now
in general service

Father Daniel . . . . Secretary for the Cardinal of the
Congregation of the Oriental
Churches; an American and
lawyer by training; investigator
of recent deaths of religious
figures

Francesco Busca and
Paolo Scarpia. . . . . Associates of Father Angelotti

Sister Angelina . . . . Assists in the escape of Rennie
and David

Archbishop Barberini . . . . Secretary of the Office of the
Supreme Tribunal of the
Apostolic Signatura, (the
Supreme Court of the Holy See)

Italy:

Lieutenant Borromeo . . . . Police official in Naples, IT

Topkapi Museum, Istanbul:

Aslan Yilmaz. . . . . Director of Antiquities and
Museum Operations

Yusuf Pashazade
Mustafa . . . . Chief Archivist

Chetin . . . . Archival Intern working for
Yusuf

Turkey:

Umit (Demir)
Yildirim . . . . Security Official, Government of
Republic of Turkey

Prologue

hen people make their way through international airport terminals, their focus on finding a gate or a restroom deadens their senses.

Blazing lights and an array of signs that blur past the eye conceal the tearful sadness of a woman in rough clothing saying farewell to loved ones, while nearby a man yells in Arabic into his mobile phone. Few notice the two female flight attendants walking past with grace and speed down the concourse.

That well-dressed man walking slightly behind you is invisible to your challenged awareness. He too speaks into a phone, but he's watching you. Is his gaze casual, appreciative, or something you'd rather not think about? You don't see. You don't know.

Heathrow International Airport
London, England

Her eyes hidden by sunglasses, a beautiful young woman with rhythm in her walk and a sly smile on her lips should capture the interests of many. But in the early morning, she was almost invisible among throngs of confused travelers.

For the third time in eighteen months, the heels of Rennie Haran's boots knocked on the white tile floors of Heathrow International Airport. Days of meetings with experts and officials at the British Museum for the exhibition at the Vatican were finally done. There was nothing more for her to do; no decisions to be made, no stress to bear.

Relaxing, elegant parties in fine houses cushioned her heartache of leaving old Matthew on his sickbed. He said she should go to Rome without him. He would be okay, and this was now her time.

"Besides," he said, "a man nearing ninety might get in the way of a good time."

She protested, of course, but she had to go.

The last reception was behind her and the first glimpse of Italy was only a few hours away. This day and those ahead were going to be hers. No more chaos. Just fun and possibly, hopefully, pleasure were on the horizon.

Her confident stride declared her to be invulnerable.

The well-dressed man walking a little behind her had other ideas.

PART ONE

London, England
Heathrow International Airport
Present Day

I / 1

Rennie stood next to her assigned seat in first class and breathed in the luxurious moment. She was ready to get away. *Here we go, girl!* Her tall, slender frame and lustrous dark hair flowing over her shoulders often attracted the eyes of men, and the well-dressed guy three rows back in coach, aisle seat, clearly had his eye on her.

Colorful scenes of the days in London flowed through her mind. Discussions with eminent staff at the British Museum focused on arrangements at the Vatican. A private gala in the home of a member of parliament with celebrities and members of the ultra-wealthy offered unexpected fantasies. Everyone wanted to meet her to hear how she did it.

Her investigation into the death of Professor Matthias Justus led to her accidental discovery of the most profound ancient treasures in Christianity. Then there was an exhausting year of political games, publicity, and petty administrative hurdles. Now, she could relax and begin her personal celebration as she traveled for the grand exhibition. A sense of pleasure curled the corners of her lips into a grin.

Polite instruction with crisp consonants from a flight attendant speaking "proper English" on an intercom rose above the background noise in the aircraft cabin.

"Welcome to British Airways Flight 548 to Rome, Italy. We will soon prepare for takeoff so please take your seats. If you need assistance with baggage in the overhead compartment, please let us know. Smaller items are best placed under the seat in front of you."

Quiet moments sitting with good old Matthew were difficult although he remained full of spunk despite his frailty. They celebrated the excitement of the discovery, escaping the grasp of dangerous people, and revealing the precious artifacts to the world. They mused about the overwhelming wonder and delight of how Matthew's father, Matthias, must have felt when he first discovered them ninety years earlier in a British Museum storehouse.

Then, the antiquities disappeared until Rennie found them. She and Matthew spoke of the frustration Matthias must have felt with not being able to tell the world of his discovery, especially to his new and true love Priscilla, before he was murdered.

Another crisp announcement interrupted the moment. "The captain has asked that all passengers please take their seats and prepare for takeoff. Please observe the screens for our presentation. An attendant will assist you with any questions."

Rennie settled into her seat. Her mood shifted back to the thought of Matthew, so weak, but still so full of life. He teased her with the suggestion he would join her later in Rome to protect her from the men who would be chasing her.

Rennie looked at the open seat next to hers. It would be convenient to set things there. She pulled her backpack from beneath the seat in front of her then noticed an elderly nun in traditional attire hurry onto the plane, show her boarding pass to the attendant at the door, and turn down the aisle. With a sweet smile but clearly confused, the nun stumbled forward, looking at each row number until arriving next to Rennie.

"Excuse me, do you speak English?" the nun asked.

"Yes, of course, I mean, yes. Is this seat yours?" Rennie gestured to the seat.

"I guess so. I'm sorry, I've not been on many aircraft."

She observed the old woman fumble about as she settled into what must be an unfamiliar place. Buckling the seat belt seemed unduly complex despite its commonality, so Rennie offered appropriate advice. When she finished, the nun issued a gushing exhale suggesting this was indeed all new and uncomfortable.

Quiet filled the cabin as a video presentation with a bouncing melody guided the passengers through routine safety procedures, to which no one paid attention. The engines came to life and seized everyone's attention as a rumbling motion led to acceleration and a leap into unknown space.

Once aloft and awaiting the beverage service, the nun turned to Rennie. "This is all much nicer than I expected. One hears of the ugly aspects of flying, but I'm quite delighted."

The lilt of her voice whispered a delicate innocence that drew Rennie in with a loving embrace.

For Rennie, it was time to escape the burdens of her phenomenal discovery, including responsibilities to classic institutions, publications, and even fame. The presence of this nun felt like a highlight to the start of a well-deserved victory journey.

"Well, sister—may I call you that?—this is the first-class section. I usually sit in the back, and it isn't anything like this."

"I see, I'm sorry I didn't introduce myself. I'm Sister Marjorie. I had no idea I would be riding up here or even be on this flight. It's a bit embarrassing. But then, Jesus did say the last shall be first, and those who sit in the back will be called to the front, so I guess it's true!"

Rennie laughed, "Marjorie, I'm glad you joined me. This is also my first flight in first class, and it does feel special. My name is Rennie Haran."

"Ah, Miss Haran. What an interesting name."

"Thanks, I'm not sure where it comes from. My dad is a professor of religious studies and he dabbles in old languages."

"Well, I wondered about that. Your last name is also the land from which the Patriarch Abram, or later Abraham, came at the bidding of God. Very interesting. Have you also come at His divine request?" She flicked her eyes upwards to the heavens, indicating just who she meant.

"That's a good question. I never thought of it that way, but I guess if we're both going to the Vatican, we might have received the same call."

Sister Marjorie's old eyes squinted as she looked at Rennie, a tilt of her head gaining a different perspective. She sat back and seemed to be in thought, and then again expressed interest. "Miss Haran, I recognize that name. Are you the person who found the letters of our Lord Jesus?"

Humility flushed through Rennie and her throat became dry, surprising her in response to what had become a routine inquiry. The question had been tossed to her a hundred times, but this felt different. She sensed no arrogance or adulation coming from Marjorie.

"Yes, I found the letters written by Jesus. I wasn't looking for them and was on a different mission. It was an accident, and in truth, I re-found them. I wish I could have met the man who made the original discovery a long time ago."

"But you revealed them," Marjorie whispered. "You could have done so much else. Your humility kept you in the background. I followed the story with great interest. Miss Haran, you were the one chosen to find them."

This perspective of destiny was uncomfortable and raised questions she tried to avoid. Rennie didn't like the "puppet" concept where the Almighty pulls the strings and humanity dances or even dies. Yet, the unique conditions and situations that occur in life and happened in finding the letters can be looked at from the predestined angle.

"Sister, I'll admit the idea of 'chance' driving events, like when two people meet who are perfect for each other or someone misses a train that's then derailed, can be looked at as too unlikely to have happened without a 'hand' directing those activities. Still, my perspective doesn't allow such 'God management.' Unpredictable free will is the core of how I see people operating. The two approaches can't easily coexist. But my accidentally finding the letters raises this challenge of ideas. Now, I've had found a life of peace, and I want to keep it."

"That's a worthy goal."

"However, it all came about, I'm very grateful for the friends who stepped up to help me when I needed them. I stumbled into treasure and they helped me deal with it."

"Did it all go well?"

"There were problems with some people wanting the documents for their own purposes. One guy, by the name of Galila, thought the letters could harm Christianity. We heard he was ready to do whatever he could to get them and destroy them. Another guy, Charles Sfumato, is a wealthy collector and broker of Christian antiquities. He wanted the letters because he figured the priceless nature of the writings would make him even wealthier. The letters would never have become public or be released to scholars."

"So, like a quest, you had some serious obstacles to overcome. Were you in danger?"

"The first guy, Galila, who wanted to destroy the letters, apparently had a novel technique of getting rid of his enemies by shoving stones down their throat. Luckily, he didn't get close enough. This was partly due to unknown assistance I got from the second guy, Sfumato. He wanted the documents for himself and not destroyed. So, my throat is untouched, and the letters are available to the world."

"Miss Haran, the peace I sense in you was probably a valuable resource to help you succeed."

Rennie began to chuckle. "I'm sorry, sister, that's a new and untested quality for me. Before this, I was all passion in my projects and probably a lot of trouble. I had little patience and should have thought first before I took action. I'd like to stay in this happy, peaceful place from now on."

"Given what you've been through, you may be on a path that will again cause you to do something very special, so be alert to that opportunity. But it can bring more danger. The unexpected will always happen. Staying in touch with that place of peace instead of your old approach will be better for you."

The thoughts offered by this fragile, non-threatening little woman caused unexpected anxiety to roll through Rennie.

"Thank you, sister, but I'd like my name to now fade into the past and get on with life. I hope the choices I have in the future only involve selections of food and wine."

Their flight attendant asked for beverage requests and offered them warm, moist towels. Rennie and Marjorie took them with delight and joked about their possible uses. The attendant returned with a glass of red wine for Rennie, and for Marjorie, a bottle of water with a glass of ice. Rennie began to make an excuse for asking for wine in the morning, but Marjorie interrupted.

"My dear, you know the first miracle of Jesus was to make the best wine. I would not criticize your choice."

"I'll drink to that," Rennie responded with a lifted glass.

"May I ask you about them, the letters?"

"Of course."

"I've seen and studied images of them, but you touched and handled letters written by our Lord Jesus. Were you aware of that? Did it change you?"

"I've been asked that, and I've wondered if I changed, and

what it first felt like to have the letters in my hands. I see it from too many perspectives to know for sure, and I second-guess myself. For one thing, I'm a journalist at heart, and an investigator. I've always had this need to know the truth. I get anxious, excited and maybe erratic—and possibly just a tiny bit afraid—when faced with the unknown. My passion for shedding light on mystery is satisfying to me. At the same time, I don't like risk and somehow manage to overcome it by always moving forward. Like others in my business, I may be more individualistic, and even cynical, than other people.

"Were you always like that?"

"Before the letters came along, I was okay with being alone and was probably not a nice person. In fact, there was a time when I was pretty bad. My teenage rebellion years lasted a long time—way past adolescence. But, I evolved, and after the discovery, I felt that peace you mentioned, like I belonged to everyone in good ways, and everything was connected."

Marjorie sat back and nodded to some line of inner thought, her thick eyebrows dancing with each insight that passed by.

She leaned onto the armrest between them and said, "Miss Haran, in addition to the letters, you discovered the central and most overlooked feature of the teachings of Jesus. Christian doctrine highlights sin, forgiveness, love, and other qualities, but few ever speak of what is perhaps most important: belonging to one another."

Rennie reflected on the thought. "I can share this with you, since we're speaking in confidence. Or is that only with priests?"

Marjorie chuckled, "Your thoughts, my dear, will be held in sacred confidence."

"Well, after finding the letters, all the PR and stories, the public interest, the analysis of academics, even the love letters from strangers, all that noise, I just want it to go away. I'm ready for privacy, fun, and —" Rennie dropped the volume of her voice to a saucy whisper "—maybe a little romance."

They quietly laughed as Marjorie covered her mouth, pretending to be shocked.

"Miss Haran, who knows? It may be that your trip is also preordained for that special intention. But it can be risky! Ha! There are things in heaven and on Earth we will never understand. You may discover that on this trip."

"Well, sister, I'm thirty-two years old and I think I'm just beginning to understand a few things. Understanding men, however, is one topic that's a complete mystery and perhaps always will be!"

"My dear, I've not had to deal with the complexities of romance, but I do know that real love is different. People can't love one another unless there's a sense they belong with one another."

The flight attendant stopped again to offer a selection of comforts and a refill of Rennie's glass, allowing moments of distraction and quiet. When Marjorie said *belong to one another,* Rennie thought of her previous relationships with men and how they too often dwelled on doing things instead of just being with each other. This guy liked camping, and that guy liked dancing, and that guy was into literature, and that guy was into much more intimate adventures. But she ultimately found the "doing" was a distraction from knowing the deeper personal connection her soul needed for the now and the forever.

"Marjorie, enough about me, please tell me about you and your trip to the Vatican."

"Well, it's quite fortuitous for me. I've done advanced studies in ancient Greek and even Aramaic, so at times our bishop has asked me to clarify scripture passages by looking at the original languages. When the revelation of the letters released that amazing text to the world, we spent a good deal of time reviewing them. Miss Haran, they offer powerful, fresh insights on where

He went and the people who shared His mission work. I know you're modest about your role, but I'm confident those letters have touched the lives of millions of people in wonderful ways. Have you wondered what new accidental discovery awaits you?"

"No, and I'm happy to leave that to someone else. I did my job."

Rennie enjoyed another sip of wine as a reflective mood warmed her thoughts and mingled with her gratitude for friends and family when they protected and supported her through unprecedented media demands and personal pressures. The discovery transformed what was hard and distant into a new person who was soft and welcoming.

"Miss Haran, did people tell you how their lives were changed, by the letters, I mean? I'm sure there were many, and you are the source of their blessing."

"Thanks, but others were involved. Some key friends were at my side all the way. My buddy Angie is the chief librarian at the college in Iowa where Professor Justus was, back in the 1920s, and her presence was like bedrock for me, especially when we went to London. My editor at the *Des Moines Record*, Bud, assigned me to investigate what happened to Professor Justus. Then, he stepped up and helped convince the paper's management to do the right thing and publish the story of how we found the letters. People aren't aware how reluctant the paper was to do that."

Rennie gently elbowed the nun and said, "And then there's Matthew, who is the son of Professor Justus. He's a little older than you, but I know he's single."

Marjorie slapped Rennie's arm and pretended astonishment.

"You'd like him. Matthew became a professor and also served at the British Museum in the same field as his father. He's now about ninety but was the most critical resource in helping me and then validating the letters. Together, this little group became my family and inspired me to reconnect with my own family and friends."

"Miss Haran, I'm happy for you and I'm not surprised your life is full of goodness."

"It is, sister. I'm sorry, I might have interrupted you when you were talking about you and the bishop and going to the Vatican."

"Well, the bishop was planning to attend the exhibition at the Vatican and had a seat booked for the trip. But he's become quite ill. As a special gift to me, he arranged for me to take his place. I must say, I feel overwhelmed with the opportunity. I'm sure you'll be consumed with more significant matters, but I hope I'll see you there."

"Let's plan on it."

Turbulence shook the plane. The women pushed back into their seats and tightened their belts.

Rennie muttered, "I hate flying."

I / 2

A priest instructs his secretary, *"Julia, per favore.* I must take a call in the office. I'll need a few minutes. *Grazie."*

In the privacy of his office, heavy drapes hang shoulder to shoulder in front of windows ten feet high. Their bulk can't shield the interior from the noise of delivery trucks and expressive voices of Italian men outside in the streets below. The priest's fingernail taps a beat on a leather desktop matching the quick clicking of a ringtone on an unanswered phone.

The priest grows impatient and wonders if the number he called was the new cell phone number or the old. His work requires diplomacy, and the rails on which he rides are subtle communications with firm action and accountability. The second hand moves smoothly around the dial of his watch, each segment of time building frustration inside him. This always happens when he calls Turkey. Finally, he hears an excited breath responding. The priest sits up.

"Turk, is that you?"

"Yes, yes. Sorry, I'm in a hurry. Forgive me, Father."

The priest blurts out a laugh. "You're asking for forgiveness?"

The heavy voice of the Turk joins in. "Ha! Now, I must laugh. Should I say, 'for I have sinned?'"

"That's good. A Turk asks a priest for absolution of sins."

"My friend, at least I'm a believer and not one of those intellectuals with maggoty thoughts about the Almighty."

The baroque, golden splendor of a desk clock reminds the

priest to press on. "You said you're in a hurry. Are you in Istanbul? Is the business taken care of?"

"Yes, I'm here." Background shouts in Turkish highlight the statement. "The job is finished. The Greek infestation is gone."

"Did they find what you needed?"

"Nothing. A diary but no documents. The diary had nothing, so they left it."

Stroking the crucifix hanging around his neck, the priest closes his eyes. This poison in the church has been gurgling since the beginning of time, but now they are finally close to a solution. Yet they must rely on goons to get the job done. He doesn't know what to say or whether to trust the voice at the end of the line. He does know there's a chance that the prize they seek could be found and not reported to him but delivered to others for selfish reasons. His motives and those who are with him are, with certainty, pure and devoted to the sanctity of the church's origins and mission. The purposes of anyone else in the game are easily suspect. His people must not be careless. The church cannot afford it.

"Turk, do we know why this Greek was there? There were rumors of him meeting with someone, and their location is significant in our traditions. People said he knew the location of the documents. Was this true?"

"No documents. The men learned of no one else. They asked around. A few strangers were in the area, probably tourists or archaeologists."

"And your people left nothing for others to follow?"

The rough voice from Istanbul is more emphatic. "Of course not! They made a mess in the process, but no one will understand it. It had to be dramatic."

"Turk, this drawing of blood is a powerful message. Those above me here in Rome like the idea. They are traditionalists. It also tells the deceivers we're serious."

"Have the higher-ups said when we can go after the leadership?"

"It's coming, very soon. This action with the Greek is a test of the waters, you might say."

"Well Father, the water is redder than it was yesterday."

For a moment, the priest has a moment of insecurity— not regarding their venture but in not knowing who to trust among his own web of devoted conspirators. Some are fervent and others simply obedient, following the orders of a contact they respect or need. No one even knows all who are involved. He has worked too hard to achieve the position he's in, and despite his passion for their cause, a mistake by anyone could not just end the current mission but terminate every privilege he has and ever will have. He looks into the distance.

"Those of us in Rome stand with you on this field of battle. Our time has come. The deceivers in the church will finally be destroyed."

The military metaphors come easily in this pursuit. Just as the top officers in any campaign reside in comfort far from the action, he enjoys the luxuries of his roles; secret and public. A satisfied look around his office confirms that.

More Turkish voices burst in the background.

"Sorry, Father, there's much happening here. My friend, the terrorism that grips Turkey and the rest of the world is a perfect distraction for suspicious eyes. Refugees have flooded Europe and Turkey, and the police and intelligence agencies are overwhelmed. No one will care about our surgical dissection of an old institution."

"Our plans are ready, and I'll let you know more. Action is coming."

"Here in Istanbul, things are becoming intense and it serves our cause. Perhaps we will meet someday. That will allow our unveiling. I'm sorry, but I must go now."

"God be with you."

"And also, with you."

The priest slips his phone into a pocket and tilts back into the soft leather cushion of his desk chair. The thought that the world will someday become aware of his role in returning true glory and reverence to the Creator brings him a shiver of near ecstasy. The passion of power is so much better than the passion of flesh. His mind races.

God is indeed with us. Why else would our situation be so good?

Authority, comfort, and independence are his, but soon the ultimate victory will come. A deep breath exudes confidence and his eyes close.

Now, it begins.

Naples, Italy

I / 3

Forty minutes after arriving in Rome, Rennie found herself on a helicopter with a serious and unexpected change in plans. Her autumn complexion, warm with the residual kiss of summer, was now pale with winter tones, and her white-knuckled grasp of the arm rest and her heart thumping against her blouse suggested intense stress. She never liked flying, and an unexpected helicopter trip was worse. The fact that this was the pope's helicopter didn't help.

Across from her, the wide, plush chair reserved for the pope was draped with a purple ribbon of velvet edged with gold. Above her and through her bones the dull humming of the chopper's engines pulsed a steady rhythm, cushioned only a little by the luxury of the cabin. She tried to put a positive spin on the situation. *If only Angie and Matthew could see me. And what about Bud? Mr. Catholic!*

The thought almost helped erase her anxiety when a laugh nearly popped from her mouth. She held it back so the young priest in a seat nearby wouldn't notice. Rennie tried to understand why her journey had taken a sudden turn toward Naples? The priest at the airport in Rome spoke little English. He didn't mention any change in plans. Her thoughts drifted along a current of questions, as she passed through the diplomatic access at the airport to an awaiting helicopter.

The exhibition should be ready at the Vatican, and she should be there. Her conversations by phone and email with Father Angelotti, the Vatican contact, had been smooth. Now this? Questions of trust churned in her belly.

The helicopter turned, then leveled. She stiffened against the seat back. Rennie had been full of confidence after finding and revealing the letters written by Jesus. But now, with another angled turn of the aircraft, her throat was ready to heave the airline food she forced down for breakfast. She gasped deep breaths and gazed through the large, tinted window at the green fields and busy roads below. She tried to think of her home in Iowa and how similar people and places seem when you look at them from a distance. She tried to focus on that thought.

Rennie noticed a reflection of herself in the window. Her lustrous, thick hair appeared more auburn in the sun than the dark chestnut color it appeared indoors. She slid her fingers through the natural wave that accented her strong cheek bones. Satisfaction eased her tension and calm returned to her belly.

The young priest sitting next to the pilot was primly upright. He was kind of cute and childlike, yet he was uncomfortably frivolous and distracted. She wondered how Catholics feel calling kids like this "Father," and if the irony of a celibate young man being given that title ever occurs to the faithful. She realized the cynicism that dominated the "old Rennie" in that thought so she guarded herself to stay centered and at peace.

The priest turned and told her they would soon land in Naples. He actually said *Napoli* of course, but his English was strong enough to convey his meaning.

"Father?" she asked. He must not have heard her. "Father!"

He looked back, eyebrows arched high. "*Si?*"

"Where are we going? Where's Father Angelotti?"

"*Napoli*. Good, yes? *Napoli,* not *Roma,* better." He turned to the pilot who ignored him.

She tapped his shoulder. "At the airport, did they get my luggage? Is it on board?"

"*Si,* yes! All is here!" He seemed to be having a good time.

"One other question, Father. Did they mistake me for

someone else?"

"No, no! Only you, our special guest. You found the letters of our Lord!"

The raw uncertainty in the situation renewed the fears and anger of her "old" self. The "new" Rennie that blossomed from her discovery had no tested depth or practical tools to guide her when danger was sensed. She crossed her arms and slumped into the seat, extending one leg and putting her foot on the pope's chair. Her black boot heel pressed into the soft leather.

The helicopter turned, and the gaping mouth of the volcano Vesuvius appeared outside her window. Rennie's large eyes grew even more. This vast, black hole that had spewed instant death on Pompeii sucked on her soul. Thousands of people were living ordinary lives and then death swept over them. No mercy. No justice. Darkness prevailed. Darkness and evil, always there, hidden and ready.

The aircraft swung around in a wide arc at a steep angle. It paused and dove, slowly drifting to the ground. Rennie pressed her back against the seat and locked her fingers onto the arm-rests. A drop of sweat slipped down one temple.

As the craft settled onto a concrete pad at Naples Airport, two motorcycles, a black Range Rover, and a sedan appeared. The doors of the helicopter opened, and hands lunged toward her.

"Back off!" she yelled.

Men shouted as the blades of the chopper whoosh-whooshed above. Rennie took a deep breath, released the seat belt, and tilted forward. Her arms jerked as they grabbed her jacket and pulled her from the cabin.

She threw her hands in the air and commanded, "Stop! I'm not going anywhere without some answers!"

The priest from the helicopter stepped up beside her. "Signora Haran, please forgive. I'm sorry. We take our time now. Padre Angelotti waits for you. Almost there."

He looked innocent and she wanted to hear more. Instead, he turned to the men and calmly directed them in Italian. As the support team returned to their vehicles, the young priest winked at her.

"*Prego,*" he said with a soft wave toward the Range Rover.

The motorcycles led the way with lights flashing but no sirens calling out.

What the heck is going on? Somehow, she was now part of it.

Sitting in the back seat next to the young priest, she turned to him. "Why is Father Angelotti in Naples?"

"*Che?*"

"Father Angelotti. Why here?"

With a proud look, he cooed, "Special project. Want you here. *Bene.* Okay?"

He seemed harmless, and maybe this adventure might go somewhere. So far, no real harm had been done.

And riding in the pope's helicopter was pretty cool.

At the airport fence, the caravan approached a gate where uniformed armed guards stood watch. The driver and a guard exchanged angry words, but the gate opened and the motorcade burst into traffic.

The air in the SUV was heavy with the musk smell of working men. It was quiet in the big vehicle, but outside the windows, the city looked angry. The buildings were dismal, the traffic chaotic, and even the people seemed covered with drab distress. Pedestrians dashed through traffic. It was dangerous, but it worked.

She had heard this part of Italy was notorious for crime families and corruption.

Crime and corruption. Damaged souls. The pope has his hands full.

The motorcycles leading their short procession swerved between warehouses, piercing and separating a line of trucks entering the harbor's loading area. The vehicle rumbled over heavy old planks.

Rennie's breathing became shallow and quick.

The priest pointed, "Almost there, Signora Haran. See there, Padre Angelotti."

Throngs of workers, men in uniform, diving seagulls, hanging nets, and stacks of crates filled the chaotic scene. A small man in a priest's traditional black cassock moved quickly through the mélange. He nodded and gestured as he encountered people, sliding among them and moving to a small clearing on the wharf. A black cape hung on his back.

The motorcycles pulled aside but the car continued through the throng to where Angelotti stood. As it stopped, the priest next to Rennie jumped out and ran around the vehicle to open her door while two of the security personnel took positions on each side of the car. Father Angelotti spoke quietly to the driver.

Rennie felt her coat pocket to confirm her phone was there. Focused and motivated, she whispered, "It's time." With a quick turn and a push, she was out of the SUV.

The horns of ships and noise of the workers hit Rennie as she stepped down. Angelotti approached, offering his hand and a warm welcome. "Signora Haran, this is a great honor. Thank you for coming. I'm sorry for this diversion. I hope the ride in the helicopter was okay?"

In their correspondence and calls leading up to the exhibition, Angelotti had been dry and reticent. But here he's expressive and gracious. More doubts flowed in her.

"Yes, Father, it was okay but unexpected."

At five feet nine, Rennie was comfortable being able to look many men in the eye, but this guy was short and thin. His closely cropped black hair had a hint of gray along the temples. He seemed too small.

"I'm grateful you have come, and I wish we had more time in Naples. It's a city with a big heart. Not so, shall we say, formal, like Rome. If you please, we must take a short ride in a boat."

"Father Angelotti, what does this have to do with the exhibition? Why are we here?"

He drew a deep breath. His eyes flicked to the side where an Italian police boat was docked; a sleek craft, large enough for a small wheelhouse at its center. He glanced up at her. "I'm sorry, Signora Haran. A tragedy has occurred. I must attend to it, and I could use your assistance."

"What happened?"

"A priest was murdered. They say it's an awful sight. He was lashed to a slab of wood and set adrift at sea. Birds and fish got to him. I only hope he drowned first."

Rennie held her breath. Evil was present.

Angelotti covered his eyes with one hand. A long moment passed. "Signora Haran, this is an awkward time for the Vatican. The priest is Greek Orthodox, and you know His Holiness has tried to restore the difficult relationship with our brothers in Greece. We have a serious diplomatic problem. It's a complex and possibly dangerous situation for us. You're an investigator, and I'd value your thoughts."

A cool breeze slid around her neck. Rennie tugged together her open jacket. The tight, hip-length style was fine for a business meeting but would be a challenge on the open water. The wind teased her face with her hair and wisps of it clung to her long eyelashes. She wasn't ready for this.

"What do you mean dangerous?"

Her tone was flat and restrained.

"It's not a personal danger, only a challenge to the church. I had to come to Naples and must now report on this to the highest levels of the Vatican. This evening we'll be in Rome and this ugliness will be gone. Your investigative skills are deeply important to me."

She studied him as her curiosity blossomed. This trip might

be more of an adventure than she expected.

"I guess we can discuss the exhibition tomorrow. Now what?"

"*Grazie*, Rennie! Now, we go."

With a quick, gangly turn he motioned to the boat. His hand flung into the air. "Lorenzo!"

A uniformed man onboard shook his finger at another. He swung around and motioned to Rennie and Father Angelotti to come. He turned back to the subordinate and barked another order.

Rennie followed the Vatican emissary along the uneven planks of the old wharf while seagulls screamed far away. A shiver ran up her back as she imagined the birds landing on a man's face. A pungent mixture of diesel odor and fish drifted over her.

Behind them a sudden rumble was accented by men yelling. A horn blasted through the crisp air, causing an instinctive jerk in Rennie's shoulders. People on the dock leaped to the edge as a black Alfa Romeo sedan suddenly appeared at their heels. Angelotti grabbed Rennie's arm to move her to the side.

She pulled free from him as the car blew past her pant leg. The sleek beast was accented with a red stripe, and the word *Carabinieri* blazed across the doors. Figures hid behind the dark windows.

Angelotti was suddenly in her face. "I will handle this. Do not speak. This is *Raggruppamento Operativo Speciale*, ROS. They are military intelligence. They can do whatever they want."

He was tense. His cold eyes beamed into hers. Then a toothy smile swept across his face, and he turned.

"*Bello vederti, Capitano,*" Angelotti called out as two men casually exited from the back of the Alfa Romeo. Their dark blue uniforms held massive red epaulets, gold collars, and stacked ribbons on the left side of the coats. They feigned indifference to the priest's greeting.

Rennie stood her ground. Her nostrils flared as her doubts about Angelotti grew again. She slid designer sunglasses from her jacket pocket and slowly positioned them on her nose. Her mind raced through their conversations for a reference that would help her understand and deal with him. Now military intelligence is involved? Cold energy grew within her.

Father Angelotti's cape lifted behind him as he raised his arms and he seemed to glide to the officers. One of them gave him polite but restrained attention. The priest's head bobbed, and his arms churned the air.

She surveyed the scene at the wharf. A couple of young men at an adjacent dock called to her in a soft, pleading way. They were easy to dismiss. Mystery and investigating a death came first.

The priest was again at her side. "It's all okay. This matter apparently called away our military friends from attending some nonsense ceremony, so they weren't happy. But now they know they are not needed."

As the black sedan backed up, Angelotti waved at the windows. The car's horn sounded loud and long as it disappeared into traffic.

Angelotti gasped, "So, now the boat." He took a step toward the naval craft.

"Father, what was their interest and why aren't they needed?" Rennie asked.

The priest swiveled. "Everyone is interested in this unfortunate death. The ROS is concerned with state security. Italy is dealing with massive numbers of refugees and even criminals who continue to come to our shores, so the military is on alert. It's best they are not involved in this matter."

"Father, what exactly is this matter?"

"We're not sure." The priest's expression was blank. His eyes didn't blink in the breeze. "There's an early report that the poor fellow who died in the water is Father Ioannis Anastasios. He's an Orthodox priest and a renowned authority on the early church. He's from Greece. Well, recently from Turkey. No one knows how he entered the country. He was found several hours ago."

He stared into her sunglasses. "Will you join me, Signora Haran? This sad situation is on a beach a short ride out of the harbor."

Questions raced through Rennie's mind as they boarded the boat. She locked onto every movement, noise and smell. Shapes and sounds had edges. She reminded herself to be centered and clear, but suspicions lingered.

Refugees. Terrorists. Military intelligence. Murder.

Even if nothing else happened, she would already have quite a story for the readers in good old Des Moines, Iowa.

The small naval craft powered its way into Naples Harbor where the chaotic activity resembled the streets of the city. Boats and ships cut through the waves in angular paths like the motorbikes, cars, and trucks racing between random gaps of fearless pedestrians. Angelotti and Rennie huddled in the cockpit of their craft to escape the blowing wind.

He shouted, "Signora Haran, did my assistant help you make the connection in Rome for the flight to Naples?"

"Yes, when I arrived he escorted me to the car that took me to the helicopter. He said nothing."

The boat slid sideways as it gathered speed. Sailors shouted at each other. Rennie grabbed a handle on the wall and flexed her knees to not be thrown by the pounding waves.

Angelotti raised his voice again as wind and thudding sounds of waves on the hull filled their senses.

"This unfortunate death raises questions and risks for us. It could be more than a murder. It might be an attack on Christianity itself."

He leaned toward her. "Signora Haran, there are dark forces at work. They've always been there."

Naples, Italy
Present Day

I / 4

Adventure splashed over the bow of the boat sending sparkles of foam into the air and across the small cabin in which Rennie and Angelotti huddled. She clutched a chrome bar for support as another wave hit the boat. Her imagination was dazzled with thoughts of military and intelligence agents guarding the coastline as criminals and refugees slipped onto the beach. Death floated in, joining the unwanted in the form of a murdered priest. They said he was a threat to Christianity and suspicions were rampant. Sister Marjorie was right, the unexpected will always happen.

The boat came around a point to a small bay. On the shore, Rennie could see groups of men and a large, brown slab of wood with a bulging tarp covering what she assumed must be the deceased. Five men in police uniforms stood around the tarp, two priests in flowing black cloaks clung to each other nearby, and two men in suits had an animated discussion away from the scene. One of the suits was a thin fellow who carried a thick file folder. The other, who filled his suit with muscle, didn't look happy.

As the boat turned and accelerated directly for shore, Rennie braced herself. The versatile craft slid smoothly over the rocks, avoiding boulders, and pulled up onto the sand.

The two priests stumbled across the rugged beach as they hurried to greet the Vatican emissary. They glanced at Rennie while trying to wave to Father Angelotti, cross themselves, and clasp their hands in prayer at the same time. Their ankle-length garments caught their feet and knees and the rocks around them.

A tall police officer with gold braid on his shoulders moved away from his group accompanied by the thin man carrying the files as they stepped quickly toward the new visitors. They all arrived to meet Angelotti and Rennie at the same time.

"Greetings, Excellency," shouted the police officer to Angelotti.

He touched his cap as a salute to Rennie and offered a hand to assist her in stepping from the craft.

The priests gathered to help Father Angelotti step down before then falling at his feet. He laid his hands on their heads and murmured for them to get up. Helping the priests to stand, he suggested they talk for a moment. They glanced around and stumbled away, mumbling apologies and again crossing themselves.

Rennie found smooth footing and waited, scanning the surroundings. Barren slopes rose to a thick grove of pine trees. About a hundred yards away, the high walls of an ancient ruin rose above the shoreline. Across the bay, a castle-like structure jutted from a long causeway. A dry air current flowed from the land to the sea.

The police officer scowled when the angular man carrying the fat folder of paper stepped in front of him. The other, thicker stranger in the civilian suit arrived and greeted Angelotti. His face was rough with life.

"*Bello vederti, Padre.* Signora Haran. I am Paolo Scarpia. I'm here to assist Padre Angelotti." His voice rumbled a low tone that commanded one to listen. "My associate here is Francesco Busca. He is taking notes for the record."

He turned to Angelotti, "Padre, may we speak privately? *Mi scusi,* Signora Haran."

Scarpia and Busca walked with Angelotti toward the crime scene, whispering along the way.

Rennie broke a moment of awkward silence with the police

officer.

"Do you speak English?"

"*Si*. Yes, a little."

He glanced to where the others had gone then offered his hand to Rennie.

"I am Lieutenant Lorenzo Borromeo. Our district is responsible for this investigation. Others, of course, became involved." He swiveled his commanding presence in the direction of Father Angelotti.

"Officer, who are those other men?"

"They are—how shall we say?—connected with the church. They are private but carry authority."

His voice was comforting.

"Signora Haran, this is Italy, and everyone here has a special position. It's a mess sometimes, but this may be one reason for a long history of our wonderful country. Too many people get involved in everything, so maybe that keeps things going."

He bowed his head, said, "*Permesso*," and hurried away to where the other officers stood around the slab of wood.

Rennie felt driven to follow him. She nimbly cruised over the rocks and quickly passed Father Angelotti, Scarpia, and Busca. Riding a crescendo of energy, she hurried toward the crime scene until the rancid stench of death stung her nostrils.

Turning away, she removed a white handkerchief from her pocket and held it to her nose. A swirl of wind lifted a corner of the tarp revealing what she guessed was a bare human foot and lower leg. From what she could see, the body parts were bloated, ruptured, and hardly recognizable. Between the open wounds on the skin, the flesh reflected a shiny, almost khaki coloration. A burgundy stain ran across the exposed wooden plank.

Rennie gagged but motioned to the tarp.

Lieutenant Borromeo began to say "Signora, we cannot—" when Scarpia growled as he approached.

"*Si!* Show her!"

A policeman knelt on a rock and grabbed a corner of the tarp and jerked away a stone that held the corner in place.

"*Prego,*" Scarpia responded.

The policeman flipped the edge of the tarp and spun around, retching and crawling away. A seagull screeched as Scarpia and Rennie saw the corpse.

Heat flushed through Rennie's body and filled her face. She glared at the human-like head on the body. It was puffed up to a ball-shaped mass of matter invaded with crimson pockets. One eye bulged open as if surprised. The other was gone, leaving a small hole filled with water. A fat tongue stood between huge, swollen lips. Patches of hair were gone from the scalp and gray beard.

Scarpia placed his hand over his nose and mouth and pulled the cover over the body. One of the local priests hurried to where shrubs grew above the shoreline and fell to his knees. The other priest held his face and stumbled away from the scene. A policeman stepped quickly to grasp the priest's elbow to guide him.

Father Angelotti motioned to Rennie to follow him higher up the beach. As they approached a line of sea grass and brush, Borromeo dashed to meet them.

"Signora Haran, we have a small office up there, at the *Veduta.*"

The tall officer pointed to the ruins beyond the trees. "*Per favore,* please, let us go there."

All eyes gave attention to the ancient gray walls of the ruins above them, accented with arched openings, sculptures, and columns. Angelotti shrugged and nodded.

The lieutenant displayed a full smile and enthusiastic greeting, "*Grazie!* We'll have coffee and discuss things."

He and Scarpia quickly turned, taking long strides up to

smoother ground as Rennie and Angelotti followed.

Angelotti touched Rennie's sleeve and stopped. "I must say something to the priests. Follow the officer and Scarpia, but slowly. Please heed my instruction until we get to Rome. *Per favore.* We don't know how the local authorities want to proceed, but the military must not get involved."

She heard each consonant. "What's this *Veduta?*"

"Oh, *Veduta* is like the view from a place. Above us is a park, an archaeological site. There's an ancient amphitheater and buildings. It's another place for tourists. I will join with you in a moment, but go slowly."

He gathered up his garment and hurried to where the priests consoled each other. They cried out with his arrival. His arms opened to them and all three talked at once until he took command. Angelotti leaned in and spoke to the priests, punctuating his comments with sharp hand gestures.

Rennie walked up the slope to a nearby pine tree and closed her eyes. *Quiet, be mindful,* she reminded herself as she counted her breaths flowing into her and pouring out again. Her focus shifted to her surroundings and senses where she reconnected with the present.

Father Angelotti's sudden return didn't surprise her; he was just part of the environment.

"We shall see," he remarked without reference, "we shall see. You have a noble character, Signora Haran. I can see why God chose you for the revelation of His letters. Now, it appears you have a new mission."

"What shall we see?"

"I was thinking ahead. When we meet with the lieutenant, please follow my lead. I'm not certain of his intentions. It may be nothing."

They worked their way up a well-worn path toward the old ruins. A breeze blew through the tall greenery, gently waving the branches that lined the rising trail through a thick grove of pines. Gravel crunched under her boots.

They paused up the slope where the shrubbery opened to reveal a view of the sea. Vivid blue water reflected a gray shore on the other side of the small bay. Rising with vertical walls from this foundation stood a granite mountain, forbidding yet stunning.

Angelotti sighed, "Signora Haran, life might seem to be a journey, but it's only moments in hope of a destiny. Creation is truth and the presence of the divine."

"*Ciao! Salute,*" Lieutenant Borromeo called down the path as he marched toward them. "Everything okay?"

"*Bravo, eccelente,*" Angelotti announced with a wave of his hand toward the sea. "Glorious beauty! God is good!"

Rennie felt a subtle push on her back as the priest whispered, "We must move ahead."

She was ready and waved a friendly greeting to the officer. A game was at play, and it was time to get in. With her jaw set firm, she extended her hand.

"Lieutenant, with handsome men in such a wonderful place, I think I might never leave here."

"Ah, Signora Haran, please stay. Another thirty meters, please. I will guide you to our temporary office."

Scarpia stood at the top of the hill, the sun behind him; a dark, indiscernible figure.

PART TWO

Naples, Italy

II / 1

Rennie could see ancient ruins behind modern buildings as their trail up the hill reached a parking lot. The lining of her nostrils felt like parchment in the dry air high above and away from the sea. Dust rested on all things, knowing it would always win. Dust to dust; life and civilizations all gave way to dust.

Following Angelotti and Lieutenant Borromeo to what she hoped would be a place of understanding, Rennie noticed the contrasts of plain frame buildings against a backdrop of classic, eternal architecture. Somehow, all of history blends together then repeats itself with no concern for the players or the place.

They approached a beige stucco building connected with covered walkways to two similar modern structures. Signs on one said "Information" and "Museum," and on another "Information" again. Small clouds of sunbaked dust swirled off the parking-lot gravel. No staff or tourists could be seen. It didn't feel right. Where was everybody?

She followed Borromeo through a doorway into a plain room as Angelotti stepped aside. Two wooden chairs were in front of a cluttered desk and a few old, framed photographs and posters of Greece hung on plaster walls. Shiny marble floor tiles helped brighten the dull setting.

Rennie's mind raced through suspicions and strategies. These hours of dramatic changes in plans were difficult to process. The ache of travel and stress had soaked into her muscles.

This wasn't just a visit to a crime scene to help Father Angelotti understand the situation and report to the Vatican, and this police officer was not happy with it. Rennie was now in the middle and had to figure a way out.

Despite his early cordial manner, Borromeo assumed a different attitude. He motioned to the wooden chairs with a flip of his hand while settling into a tall cushioned seat behind the desk.

Scarpia stepped into the room. His tight, rumpled black suit made his presence more powerful in this setting. Rennie discreetly watched him as he went to a wooden bench by the wall. He was quiet but imposing. She could see Borromeo's eyes follow Scarpia as he moved across the space and sat down.

Father Angelotti slid forward in his chair. "Lieutenant, the church is pleased for you to allow us to be aware of this sad event. I must now return with Signora Haran and deliver a full report to our people. Prayers will be said to assist you in solving this terrible crime."

Rennie saw a pulsing vein in Angelotti's temple. *Can Borromeo see it?*

Borromeo smirked and opened a thin file of paperwork.

"We will handle this the Neapolitan way. This isn't Rome," he said with a staccato beat.

"To complete these papers, I must ask a few questions. It's for these papers."

Angelotti glanced at Scarpia, shrugged his shoulders, and turned back to the police officer. "What do you need? We're here for you."

Borromeo flipped a couple of pages in his files. Forms, written notes, and a checklist could be seen. "Padre, how did you know this poor Father Anastasios? What were your contacts with him?"

Angelotti's voice took on a musical tone. "I only know of him as a name, an authority on obscure church matters. I had no contacts with him."

Borromeo scribbled a note on a pad. "I see. So again, Padre Angelotti, what contacts did you have with him, perhaps through others?"

Borromeo's eyes shifted from Scarpia to Angelotti and then at Rennie.

Angelotti continued with innocence, "None that I know of. He was a scholar they say. I'm no scholar. I serve God as a clerk. I help with modest business affairs."

Angelotti turned to Rennie and tried to look humble.

Borromeo laughed loudly, "Yes, the world is full of clerks. Like me, too!"

The lieutenant reviewed his notes. His pen remained ready to write. "Yet our Holy Father in Rome and the powers of the Vatican have sent a clerk to this tragic situation. It must be important to them, and to you. In what ways?"

Rennie could sense this policeman was building a trap.

Again, a musical response.

"Well, Lieutenant, I don't know. I'm not aware of why decisions are made. I was directed to come. That's it."

The priest gazed up at the fan on the ceiling. "Could we have the fan on? The air is getting warm."

Borromeo sat back in his chair and stared at Angelotti. He tapped his fingertips together. "I have many years in this police business. It's best that you tell me now how you might be involved. Other agencies will not be so understanding."

Angelotti's chair creaked as he sat more erect. "As I said, this is outside of my understanding. Whatever happened with poor Father Anastasios was done by evil men. You will not find them at the Vatican."

He gave a quick nod as if to accent his firm statement.

Borromeo continued to stare before shifting his gaze to Rennie. "And you, Signora Haran. How did you know this poor fellow Anastasios?"

Rennie was startled. "I didn't know him, or of him, until this day."

"I see. You did not know him, but we need to know of what contacts you had with him. We're trying to finish this matter. All information is necessary. This is police business."

"I'd like to help, Lieutenant, but I've had no contacts with Father Anastasios. Is that his name?"

She turned to Angelotti.

Borromeo leaned forward and began to scribble more notes. "Miss Haran, why do you suppose this poor priest knew your name, but you did not know his? It's quite a mystery."

Father Angelotti suddenly stood up. "*Scusi,* Lieutenant, there is confusion here. Miss Haran knows nothing of this. We need to return to the Vatican for important church business. I'm sure you understand. As you need information, please let me know."

He pulled at his collar.

The lieutenant tapped his pen on the file papers. Rennie noticed a subtle hint of confidence in his bearing. "*Patriarca,* another moment. My deepest apologies for this delay. There is some confusion, one might call it. Please know I'm humble to the will of the church, but for now, we must do what is right."

Angelotti leaned forward, resting his hands on the desk. Slowly, he sat down. Again, he looked up at the ceiling fan.

Rennie followed his gaze. She wondered what was capturing his attention. Her anxiety and suspicions shifted into an ice-cold, defensive drive. She felt an impulse to be proactive.

"Lieutenant, how did the priest die? Do we know how he was killed?"

The officer squinted at her.

Rennie continued, "As an investigative reporter, I know the solution of any crime is best solved when all the facts are on the table and good minds, like ours, team together. I'm happy to offer whatever I know, but I can only help you if you share with us all you have at this time.”

Borromeo said nothing. He reviewed his file again and flipped over a few pages.

Rennie felt pleased. In her side vision, she could see Angelotti staring at her, his mouth slightly open.

The lieutenant slumped back into his chair and again tapped his fingertips together. “You saw him, and we know you knew him. You tell me the manner of death. That will help close this investigation, Signora Investigator.”

Rennie sat forward. “I didn’t know him.”

“How did he die?”

“*That*, Lieutenant, is what I asked.”

Borromeo wagged his head. “I don’t feel much cooperation from either of you. Maybe this can be handled in other ways.”

Scarpia loudly cleared his throat. It sounded more like a growl with gravel in the mouth.

Borromeo glared at him then turned back to Rennie. “How did you know him?”

Years of challenges by bosses, lawyers in depositions, and people behind scandalous stories she investigated prepared her for this. A clever distraction of his thinking would help her pivot the challenge back at him.

“Lieutenant, I’d like to help, and I need your help, but don’t kind women often go unrewarded?” She paused. “Again, I will say that I did not know this poor priest. Why do you think I knew him?”

Lieutenant Borromeo’s eyes seemed to bulge.

He blurted out, “The priest’s journal was discovered under the bed in a room he had been in. Signora Haran, your name is in that journal. Other interesting information is also in that journal. All information is being gathered. Your words are now needed. Father Angelotti, I expect your cooperation.”

His intensity grew with each comment.

No one moved. Scarpia rose quietly from the side bench and stood. Everyone noticed. Finally, he said, *"Permesso,"* and with a slight bow, left the room.

Rennie ignored the departure. She would not be distracted or intimidated. She was focused on Borromeo.

He again mounted his demands. "I need answers, now."

He pounded the desk. "Signora Haran, we have a serious problem here. Father Anastasios mentions you in his belongings, several notes of your name. Why would that be? You were clearly involved."

An idea came to her. Rennie relaxed. "Well, Lieutenant, that is easily explained. I discovered something wonderful not long ago: letters written by Jesus Christ."

The lieutenant and Father Angelotti crossed themselves.

"I have traveled here to Italy to arrange with the church the display of these letters, so people can see them and believe. Certainly, Father Anastasios, who I'm told was a scholar might have come to Italy to see the exhibition of the letters and he knew my name because of this."

Borromeo suddenly appeared pleased if not delighted. "Ah, ha!"

He slapped the file folder. "*Si*, this must be it! Signora Haran forgive me. I'm a country person. I do not know these things. This is of great help. Letters from our Lord! Amazing! Father, you and the church must be very excited!"

"Yes, of course! This is why we must return to Rome."

Pressure slid away from Rennie's lungs. A fresh breath flowed in. "Now, Lieutenant, could you share with me the cause of death before we leave?"

His eyebrows wrinkled, and a grimace emerged on his face. He checked his file and turned a page. Finally, he looked up.

"Father Anastasios probably died from a wooden sword

stabbed into his heart. The handle of the sword was found on him and secured by the ropes that held him to the door. The door came from a small hotel in Ventotene. But, before we conclude this, I must know more about the letters you found."

Rennie's energy soared through her. "Yes, of course. A wooden sword? That's odd, we didn't see one on the body. What did it look like?"

Borromeo stared at her. "What do you mean? Why is this important? We have the weapon and photos of it."

"That's good. Lieutenant, please forgive me. What did this sword look like? Do you know where it's from? May I see the photo?"

"It's the weapon that killed the priest. That's it."

Father Angelotti put his hand on Rennie's arm. "Lieutenant, I know Signora Haran is trying to assist us."

Borromeo closed the file. Silence filled the room like the rising heat.

She wondered, *Did I push it too far? There's no reason for this. Stay strong.*

The lieutenant reached into his jacket pocket and removed a cell phone. He touched it a few times then turned the face of the phone toward Rennie and Angelotti. A photo of the body of Father Anastasios was displayed with something lying across the lower part of his chest.

"Here, see it."

Rennie reached for the phone and the officer placed it in her hand. Angelotti leaned over as Rennie adjusted the photo for more close-up detail.

"A crosier," Angelotti whispered.

"What? A crosier?" She replied.

"Sorry, nothing." Angelotti sat back.

She set the phone on the desk. "This is helpful. You know the cause of death and the weapon. I'm sure your skilled team can question those in the area and test the wood of the sword, as well as find the sources of the ropes that held the poor man. Lieutenant, based on my experience, which is far less than yours, you are well on the way to solving this."

Borromeo didn't move except for a slow turn of his eyes from Rennie to Angelotti and back.

"Signora Haran, you are correct. But more questioning is needed. You were on your way to Rome, but you are here. Both of you are here. What is the cause of this coincidence? We in Napoli might seem less sophisticated than those in Rome, but we know the ways of the world. We have a noble history and we will not forget it."

Angelotti responded, "My dear friend, you are on the front lines of the war against evil and we support you. If you need us to return, that can easily be arranged. Just between us, I must say that I enjoy this part of our country and its dignity more than where I'm from. I would be happy to see you again. For now, the Holy Father expects our return."

Borromeo didn't move. "Let me advise you." His eyes narrowed to slits. "You are lucky the body arrived at this place and not a little further away. Over there is *Maricomlog Napoli*. That is a place for the Ministry of Defense. ROS has an office there. Military people handle things quite differently. Maybe not so nice. Here at the park, it is my place. However, I could let them deal with this. Full cooperation in disclosing all knowledge of this matter is needed if you want to work with me instead of them."

Naples, Italy

II / 2

A quiet group of anxious young men milled around a scenic turn-off in *Parco Virgiliano*. A flaming cigarette butt bounced off one man's rough boot, but he didn't notice. The mobile phone pressed to his ear shielded his senses from the world around him.

One of the men elbowed his partner.

"His head is in the clouds again."

They laughed.

Stuffing the phone in his pocket, Peter gazed at the distant sea but no plan or solutions could be seen in the distance.

The others gathered around.

"What are we doing, boss?"

"Michael says we need to pick someone up and take them to safety. I'm sorting out where they are and what obstacles might be there."

"Boss, for us there are no obstacles. We can handle it. Where do we go?"

"Over there, the archeological park. It's just a few priests and local authorities. The timing is important, though. It's not clear what's happening."

"Do we need help? We can get more guys. We could use the old decoy approach, send a guy in who appears innocent. Our van won't stand out."

"That's an idea."

Peter zipped up his jacket.

"Joe, you and Tim drive by there and scout what's up—make sure to include the vicinity. Every detail. Be back here in thirty minutes. I'll call you as I get more information. No one sees you, okay?"

"Got it."

The two men climbed into the cab of the van and kicked up gravel as they turned onto the pavement. Blowing past other vehicles, the van slowed to a crawl when they got close to the target. The surveillance was easy—no traffic, limited access, the sun high, nothing moving. Half a block from the entrance, the van stopped. Tim slung an old backpack over his shoulder and got out.

"Tim, use a British accent and fake a little Italian like a tourist would do."

"Jolly good!" he said with a shake of his head.

As Joe eased to the side of the road, his partner ambled across the parking lot and acted confused, wandering toward the buildings.

A policeman appeared from one of the buildings and yelled in Italian.

Tim waved. "Uh, do you speak English? *Prego?*"

He did his best to appear stupid.

Another policeman came out and whispered to the other.

The second one asked, "Why you here?"

Tim pointed to the road and took a map from the backpack.

"The bus stopped here. Is this place open? It's an old ruin, right? Can I see it?"

The guards conferred. The new cop took charge. "Not now. Not open. Next day, okay?"

Turning the map and swiveling his head, Tim continued his act. "Say, could I get some water? It's been a long day."

Another minute of discussion by the police prompted another policeman to exit a building. All three talked and argued as Tim listened, understanding everything. They discussed who was there and what was going on.

Idiots, he thought.

Finally, the third police officer went back inside and returned with a plastic cup of water. "Go now."

"*Grazie*, old chap!"

Tim downed the water and returned the cup. He stuffed the map into a pocket and wandered back to the road. He checked the map again, pointed down the road, and walked out of sight. Moments later, he was back in the van. Joe backed up and turned around.

"What have we got?"

"There's an officer interrogating a priest and woman. A couple other guys—more priests—and no more than four cops right now."

"What happened? Priests and a woman?"

"Unknown. It might not have been questioning. Maybe there was an accident. The cops seem annoyed. No *carabinieri*."

"If we have to go in, what would you do? You know Peter will ask."

"Two vans, fast in, guns out. They'd put up no fight. I doubt they could find the guns on their belts. We yell some references to the Camorra, grab the people we need, and go. Let one van stay an extra minute to hold them down. Different paths back to a meeting point. Drop the vans a block from each other, get new cars, and we're gone."

"Hmm, he might go for it. Damn, what's that? Was that a ROS car that went by? We've got to turn around. If they're involved, that changes things."

A quick turn into a driveway and then a slow drive-by past the entrance to the ruins revealed their concerns.

"Slow down, way down. Don't let them see us. If they're going to the target, there's no hurry."

"Lean down. They know you."

Tim tilted over.

"Okay, we're past."

"What's up? Who was it?"

"A couple of higher-up cops. Not *carabinieri*. This must be important for the locals. It's like they're bringing in support. That changes things. Let's tell Peter."

II / 3

A young police officer cautiously entered what was now an interrogation room and motioned for Lieutenant Borromeo. The lieutenant said, "*Scusi*," and stepped into a hallway. Rennie could hear them whisper before stepping away from the door. She tried to hear where their footsteps went. Her thoughts scanned through a hundred risk scenarios and a thousand arguments to defend herself, all the while encouraging herself to be strong and to try and unravel this bizarre situation.

Father Angelotti leaned over. "Listen to me. Listen. You must do exactly as I say. Also, do as our priests here tell you. This must be done. The authorities become more dangerous when they say we are safe. ROS might be behind this."

She glared at him and started to say, "What—" But Borromeo returned.

"Lieutenant," Angelotti began, "Signora Haran has faced many stresses and is in need of a rest. Given what we've all been through, may we all take a short break? Forgive me, *signora*, our stay has been an inconvenience to you. Lieutenant, where might the facilities be?"

The officer drummed his fingers on the desk. He stopped and yelled, "*Pietro!*"

As a policeman hurried into the room, Lieutenant Borromeo shoved the file folder to the side.

"Signora Haran, you must not only have a break but coffee or water also. I am foolish in my manners. Please, this officer will guide you."

Angelotti stood and gave an awkward salute to Borromeo.

"*Grazie,* Lieutenant. Perhaps one of the local priests could attend to Signora Haran. A nun is here with them. She could best assist Signora Haran."

"*Si, si,* go," Borromeo replied with a flip of his hand.

Rennie noticed a priest, a heavy old man in a brown habit, peer around the edge of a doorway.

"Wait here," Angelotti whispered to Rennie. "Then, come when I give the signal."

He hurried to the exit, glancing to see if Borromeo noticed. The lieutenant became busy in quiet conversation with two policemen.

Rennie's body shivered with anxiety. Something was in play. Trying to be casual, she got up, stretched her limbs, and strolled away from the desk. As she moved, tension formed in her upper body and her vision shifted from observation to glare. She looked away from Borromeo to avoid his seeing her growing intensity. She needed a break and time alone. Nothing that anyone did or said made sense. She thought there were only two options: confrontation or escape.

As she viewed a framed photo of the ancient amphitheater, she saw a reflection of Angelotti waving to her in the glass. A burst of adrenaline ran through her. Angelotti waved again. She moved swiftly to the hallway where Angelotti and the plump priest nervously waited. The priest held a bundle of folded, black cloth under his arm and nimbly turned when she arrived. They hurried into an outdoor corridor of stone columns that carried a high, arched portico. Across the parking lot, Rennie noticed a few police officers talking with what might be a tourist.

The group made a turn down another corridor and went to the end of the building. Father Angelotti followed behind. Pausing at a door, the priest twisted the door handle to release the catch and motioned them to enter.

Rennie stopped a few paces into the room. It was a small

storage space with a single faucet over a utility wash basin. Mops and brooms and various bottles of chemicals lined one wall. A rough worktable filled the middle of the small open space.

She spun around. "This is no restroom!"

Angelotti didn't respond. He closed the door and took the cloth bundle from the priest.

"Signora Haran. You must leave here immediately. Put on these garments, now. Brother Vittorio here will take you to a car as soon as you are dressed. Do exactly as you are told. I will deal with our friend Borromeo. God be with you."

Rennie's frustrations burst as Angelotti went to the door. She threw the bundle to the floor. "What are you doing?" she demanded.

"*Signora*, these are our ways, not yours."

He turned and was quickly out the door.

"*Fare presto*, you do now," urged Vittorio.

He lifted the bundle from the floor.

Rennie felt numb. "What?"

"*Cosi*," he said again, flailing his arms as if pulling something apart. "*Presto*," he said, placing the material on the worktable.

He opened it up. Part of a flat, white hood appeared when the folds of cloth separated. Rennie realized this was a traditional nun's habit. Her mind raced.

Am I to wear this? Does he expect me to be a nun?

As she held up the black gown, Vittorio became animated, almost gleeful. He motioned for her to put the gown over her head.

"Vittorio, you've got the wrong girl for this. No way."

Rennie went to the window and peeked past the curtain. A couple of cops stood guard in front of another building. Anger burst through her. She paced around the workroom and grabbed a mop with two hands as she went by.

"I will *not* be framed with this murder and go to jail like that college girl did," she said, slamming the mop to the floor. She turned to him, her fists tightly clenched. "*No!*"

She moved back around the room with ferocious energy.

Vittorio stepped back.

Seeing a pained look on his face, she closed her eyes and shook her head. "I'm sorry, I know this isn't your plan."

Rennie looked out the window again. "What do we do now, *padre*?"

"*Presto*, go now. Okay?" he said with caution.

Rennie returned to the worktable and stared at the tunic. Finally, she lifted the material and slipped it over her head, pulling it into place. It felt rough and had a faint chemical odor. She looked down and saw it was about a foot too short, clearly revealing her polished, black leather boots.

"This will not —"

The sound of a car outside made them freeze. Her eyes met those of the priest.

"*Fare presto*," he pleaded.

She grabbed the white coif and pulled it on. She did her best to stuff her hair back and smooth it out under the hood. The priest grabbed the overlying veil and fit it to her head. Rennie picked from the table what appeared to be a woolen belt and tied it around her middle. She turned to the priest.

"So, am I a nun?"

Vittorio removed a rosary from his belt and hung it on her belt. Finally, he took the black apron and tied it around her, slipping it under the belt. He stepped back and considered her appearance. His face screwed up with doubts, but he shrugged tacit approval.

For a moment she felt amused and wondered what her friend Angie would say if she saw her. *Trick or treat?*

There was a soft knock on the door. Rennie turned, ready for combat. The priest hurried to the window near the door and peered between the curtain and the window casing. He spun around and motioned for Rennie to come to the door. As she arrived, he opened it to reveal Scarpia.

Rennie stopped so fast she nearly fell forward.

Scarpia stepped in and handed car keys to the priest. "Signora Haran, the priest will get you out of here. There's no time to wait. I'll stay here to help Padre Angelotti. You must go, now."

His growl carried an ominous authority.

The priest peeked out the door and trundled to the driver's side of a blue Fiat. As he was getting in, a police sedan drove up to another building. It slowed down as the driver observed the priest and the car.

"Wait," Scarpia said to Rennie. "When those men enter the office, you go to the car."

Her mind raced and her throat was tight. She was about to become a fugitive. But she was ready.

Scarpia stayed far from the window, studying the policemen. "Now," he said. "Go."

Rennie gathered and lifted her tunic with one hand and burst across the portico to the car. The moment she was in and closed the door, the priest shifted into low gear and drove across the dusty parking lot toward the street.

"Go, Vittorio. Go!" Rennie urged.

Naples, Italy

II / 4

From the storage room window, Scarpia watched the car carrying Rennie and the priest until it disappeared down the road. Across the parking lot, he noticed one of the policemen that had arrived. The officer stepped from a doorway of the administration building, observed the car's departure, and returned inside.

Scarpia checked his watch, scanned the workroom for leftover items, and slipped out the door. He hurried down an outdoor corridor and around the far side of the building to a hallway near the office. He pulled a cell phone from his jacket pocket and made a quick call. Pleased with how events were proceeding, he strolled into the shade of the portico and lit a cigarette.

Father Angelotti came around the corner and nervously looked back and scanned the area. Even from a distance his face seemed to twitch. Angelotti noticed Scarpia in the shade of a pillar and beckoned for him. Scarpia stamped his cigarette into the gravel drive and strolled along the walk.

When they met, Angelotti whispered, "*Sono andati?*"

Scarpia nodded. "Yes, they have gone."

Angelotti gave him a pat on the arm. "And, Busca?"

"I just spoke with him. All is ready."

Angelotti pivoted into a brisk walk along the portico, his arms swinging freely.

Scarpia followed him into Borromeo's temporary office. Angelotti paused at a tray holding a pitcher of ice water and an old, green insulated pot that showed coffee stains down the front. Pouring water into a plastic cup, the priest sipped it, and refreshed the cup with more.

Scarpia studied him with a quiet sense of raw power. He was ready for the confrontation he knew was coming. Angelotti checked the thick buttons on the front of his cassock and slid his hands down his chest to his legs in a smoothing motion. Taking a deep breath, he retrieved his cup of water, and gazed out the window. He spun around when Borromeo entered the room and sat down at his desk. Angelotti approached the lieutenant, who was now reviewing the files scattered in front of him.

He said, "Lieutenant, I've sent for the priest and the nun to see if Signora Haran can now return to finish this. We need to return to Rome and give our report. The preparations for the exhibition of the Lord's letters must be completed."

"I don't care about Rome. We're dealing with a murder. I'm sure you know there are others concerned with this matter. ROS is applying pressure and we don't want national intelligence agents getting involved. With refugees pouring in, they're alert to everything. The Camorra is also interested in these things. Father, you might not be familiar with them, but I can tell you that when a murder occurs, the Camorra acts like any crime family. They think it's another turf war. We don't need more of that in Naples."

Borromeo settled into the desk chair. "*Padre*, I must get some firm answers here. People will be more interested in how Signora Haran relates to this crime than whether your show happens on time. That's why good answers are needed. Where is she? Is she coming?"

He turned a page in the file.

Angelotti went to the doorway and glanced in both directions. The boots of policemen who had just arrived in the police car could be heard clicking down the hallway. The Vatican priest turned away and stuffed his hands into pockets of his cassock. He told Borromeo he'd go find Rennie, nodded at Scarpia, then breezed past the arriving policemen and hurried down the colonnade.

A few minutes later, Lieutenant Borromeo stepped from the office into the hallway to speak to the police officers who had just arrived. Scarpia could hear the men exchange words. The lieutenant glanced back at Scarpia, slammed the door casing with an open hand and then glared at the two officers. Borromeo lunged from the door and hurried down the hallway yelling, "*Patri-arca.*" Scarpia followed to see where he went.

Borromeo took a few steps in one direction, raced a dozen steps the other way, spun around, and yelled again. At the end of the building, Father Angelotti ran across the portico into the open air and yelled, "Miss Haran!" He appeared to listen and called again. He turned, saw Lieutenant Borromeo across the courtyard and stomped across the gravel, slamming dust into the air with each step. He pointed at Borromeo and yelled in Italian.

"Where is she? What did you do? This is an outrage!"

Scarpia had followed orders well and could now enjoy the improvisation Angelotti was performing. He waited in the shadows for the next act.

Angelotti and Borromeo hurried toward each other, meeting on a small patch of grass between the driveway and the building. The tall authority figure of Borromeo glared down at the little priest. They hurled questions and arguments at each other with increasing energy.

Finally, Angelotti threw his arms into the air and shouted, "What happened?"

"You tell me!"

"That woman is a guest of the Holy See, of the Supreme Pontiff, our Holy Father! If your people took her, release her now and I will not speak of this!"

"What are you saying? My men have now informed me they went to the women's toilet and found a priest standing at the door. They demanded entry and when they went in, she was not there. The window was open. They searched the area. She's gone! You said that nun was going to be with her, but the nun left with the other priest. What's going on?"

Scarpia moved closer. The situation seemed to need intervention, physical intervention, and he was ready. Busca appeared in another hallway. They nodded a greeting. Their position was now strong.

Father Angelotti's head seemed to vibrate with intensity. "You spoke of the Camorra. Could this be their doing?"

"Why would they take her? She's nothing to them."

Borromeo saw the police officers standing in the shade of the portico.

He turned and leaned over Father Angelotti shouting, "This is your doing. There will be serious consequences!"

Suddenly both men pivoted to look in the same direction shading their eyes as they squinted at the horizon. The police officers stepped from the portico into the sun. Scarpia waved for Busca to come. They met and exited the shadows into the open air, tilting their heads for the strange sound in the distance.

"What is that?" Father Angelotti asked as he stepped forward.

"It sounds like locusts."

He pointed into Borromeo's face. "It's a curse! The swarms of locusts that have swept across northern Italy are now coming here! We've lost Signora Haran so now we're cursed with locusts!"

Borromeo's eyes blinked as he stared in the direction of the buzzing sound, growing louder and evolving into a thumping beat. Scarpia and Busca ran to the side of Father Angelotti.

A flash of reflected sunlight appeared above the tree line. It was a helicopter, emerging over the hills and forests and coming directly at them. It swung sideways, revealing the papal seal on its side.

Busca lifted his chin high with accomplished arrogance. Scarpia elbowed him.

Father Angelotti turned to Lieutenant Borromeo. "It's his Holiness, our pope."

He crossed himself.

"Quickly! Prepare yourself and your men. Go to your office, and I will await him!"

Borromeo's mouth opened but he said nothing. He studied the approaching helicopter and stumbled in the direction of the other policemen near the portico. Angelotti, Scarpia, and Busca hurried to the other side of the parking area.

The helicopter carved a slow circle above the open area. Whirlwinds of dust grew out of the gravel and chased each other around the parking lot. All the men retreated from their positions as the aircraft descended. The wheels delicately touched the ground, rose, and finally settled on the earth.

Lieutenant Borromeo and the other policemen could be seen crossing themselves. They watched as Angelotti, Scarpia, and Busca ran to the opposite side of the helicopter, out of their view. The craft roared into the air, tilted its nose down, and shot over the buildings with a graceful turn.

Looking back, Scarpia could see Borromeo and his men wander into the parking lot waving their hands in front of their faces to blow away currents of dust in the air. As the aircraft gained speed, Scarpia relaxed with a snort of a laugh watching Borromeo fade into the distance, his fist pumping at the departing visitors.

Rome, Italy
The Vatican

II / 5

Father Joseph's natural complexion had a plump, pink tone, but when he was with the Abbess Serena Magdalene, he felt his flesh go cold. Her incisive, calculating manner demanded the precision he normally appreciated, but with her he felt fear. His Teutonic determination could only stumble forward, guessing at what she might want next.

He studied her as she gazed down from the tall windows of her office on those walking in the peace of a warm afternoon. The second floor of the classic old structure in the midst of the Vatican offered a chance to observe people without being seen. The privilege went with the authority. Joseph knew that as an abbess, she was in service to those with power, and those she worked with were at the top of power pole. As a key member of the staff of the secretary of state, authority drifted upon her. Joseph was well aware that her consummate success in serving his needs for coordination of diplomacy, and even special tasks for the Holy Father, cemented her prestige with anyone who dealt with her.

Joseph could feel it, and his respect for authority made him obedient. Still, the way she carried it wasn't comfortable for him. He preferred a more expressive, physically commanding countenance. She strolled away and settled into a chair as he waited for instructions. When the phone rang, he hurried to answer it. He spoke in the expected Italian, although it wasn't natural.

"Abbess Serena, Father Angelotti is calling for you." Joseph held the old phone handset off to the side as if it smelled. "He's arriving soon from Naples and needs to speak with you."

His native German tongue gave speaking Italian a slow, unfamiliar rhythm.

Except for her vivid white face and hands, the abbess' attire blended her figure into the black velvet cushions of an ornate chair. Brass buttons around the edge of the chair's back provided a halo effect to her presence. She didn't move. Her profile remained fixed.

"Padre Angelotti is on the line."

The pupils of her eyes appeared as black as her cloak in the dim light.

He put the phone to his ear again. "Yes, padre, she will be here. I understand."

A soft snarl escaped from her as she jerked a glance at Joseph. Rising slowly, she smoothed her skirt and marched to him taking the phone without comment.

"Good evening, padre," She cooed into the phone.

Her Italian was also not native.

"I hope your trip was a success. How is the helicopter ride? Two cardinals of the Curia have asked me how this matter was handled. We in General Affairs for the Secretariat of State are always concerned with the church's relationships."

Her pleased look would not offer comfort to anyone. "Will you be able to brief me this evening? They'll expect an update in the morning. So, where is Signora Haran at this time?"

She listened for a moment.

"Hello, hello, can you hear me?"

The abbess stuck the phone toward Joseph. He took it from her hand, laid it in the cradle, and stepped back.

Her eyelids narrowed to slits. "Joseph, arrange a meeting as soon as possible for me to see the cardinal prefect of the Apostolic Signatura. As soon as possible. Right after that, I need to see the secretary of state."

"Yes, Sister."

He approached the door to her office but waited. She grabbed the phone and pressed four buttons in the base.

"Hello, Archbishop. This is Abbess Serena. When you hear this message please call me or send someone and I'll come to you. I'll brief you on a diplomatic issue I'm following."

He waited to see if she needed him until a flick of her fingers suggested he leave. Joseph remained standing outside the door, listening. His cheeks again flushed red with anxiety. When he heard the handset return to its cradle, he hurried out of the office and down the hall. He made a turn, pulled his cell phone from a pocket, and tapped a number as he opened a door and went down a stairway. Holding the railing with one hand, he skipped down the steps and stopped on a landing waiting for an answer. His thoughts raced through options and risks of the larger mission he knew was in play. Hearing an answer message, he said in German to contact the housekeeper, and have her call him. Joseph ended the call and felt good, confident he was still a step ahead of the bureaucrats.

Arriving on the main floor, he slipped the phone into a pocket and calmly greeted others as they passed in the wide, central gallery. An arched ceiling, heavily decorated with vast, gold accents and ancient people in colorful robes caught his attention, prompting a contented sense of belonging in this place of power. Long ago he had let go of the shame of his father's role as a Nazi officer in World War II and accepted the ideas of purity and glory to be achieved by those with high ideals. Like his father, he too, could be a small piece in a disciplined system with aggressive goals for a better world order. Excesses were always possible but dismissible for those on noble missions.

Joseph turned into a small office where a young woman in a pink, satin blouse sat staring blankly at a computer monitor, mindlessly sliding a mouse back and forth. He walked past her but stopped to gaze over her shoulder to see into her cleavage.

His blood warmed as he appreciated the low V-neck of her top. He stepped back, appreciating the indulgence.

A deep breath filled her chest and prompted a loud yawn. Oblivious of him, she pushed the mouse to the side, stood, and stacked some papers together. She bent over the desk and a soft shriek emitted from her skirt, followed by a foul odor. His face shriveled into disgust. Joseph retreated to a partitioned area down a short hallway. Before sitting, he glanced back to see if anyone was close enough to hear him as he reached for the desk phone.

A woman with a strong voice answered his call. In passable Italian she said, "Hello, Sister Katherine here."

Joseph responded in German, "*Schwester*, let's meet to see what needs to be done next."

"The usual place, twenty minutes. Are things going well?"

A broad smile spread across Joseph's face, puffing up his cheeks. "Yes, the sanctuary is secure."

"I'll see you."

He sat back, satisfied. *We will clean up the pests. Soon!*

He thought about the abbess and her beloved hierarchy. *They can try to protect their meaningless positions as they tolerate heresy, but they will fail.*

Joseph knew it was time for the guardians of the true faith to stand against those who satisfy their desires while heresy breeds across the globe. He jumped up renewed, his mind racing. He was among the elite, a warrior for God. It was good the many didn't care. *Those who take action are the only heroes.*

At the appropriate time, he trotted down marble steps into the setting sun, eager to hear Katherine's plans. Would this be when they finally eliminate those so-called Christians who deny the sanctity of the cross? The best hearts and minds of the saints defined God rightly and placed Him in heaven. The ideas of divine beings roaming about the world, or the cross as a symbol of joy, were cancer among true believers.

He arrived in the secluded garden early, but Katherine was waiting. For him, her presence was heavenly, always disciplined, serene, and wise. He was inclined to kneel before her, but he didn't. He sat a respectful distance from her on the stone bench.

"Peace be with you," he said in German.

"And, also with you, brother."

"*Schwester*, our dear abbess is reporting to her benefactors the meaningless actions of Father Angelotti. It's amusing to see them playing their games. Is there any progress in finding the American?"

"Of course. Our friends in the ROS keep us informed."

Katherine's nostrils flared as she turned and peered into his eyes. "Let's not be distracted. She's nothing. The Vatican will deal with her and she'll run in circles. Galila should have dealt with her when she was in London, but he's weak. He plays with stones. We must extinguish the Arian followers now that we have them excited. Killing the Greek brought them out of their holes."

Joseph looked away, humbled in the presence of one with such powerful determination and clarity of vision. "Do we know who did it?"

"It doesn't matter. We'll find out and reward them. Joseph, is there any progress in finding the letters? We must get to them first."

"The letters? Do you mean those of our Christ, the ones the American found?"

"Of course not. The letters of the women who worshiped St. Paul and his fantasies. Stay on top of it. Once those letters are gone, there will only be legends for the heretics to embrace."

"I will. I'm on it."

His chest swelled with a sense of glory. "One other thing, *Schwester*, the abbess wishes to have an immediate audience with the cardinal prefect of the Apostolic Signatura. Then, she wants to see His Eminence, the secretary of state. Can you have that arranged and calls from their secretaries to confirm times with the abbess?"

He sensed he had overstepped his role, but she seemed amused.

"Yes, Joseph, it's become entertaining to watch them dance for us."

Without another word, Katherine rose from the bench and glided away.

Joseph waited, as if for instructions. Realizing there were none, he hurried back to his office.

PART THREE

Naples, Italy

III / 1

A layer of fine dust coated the car as it left the parking lot and clung to it as the vehicle shot down the street. The priest worked the gears, clutch, and accelerator to swiftly get them away. Rennie jerked the seat belt across her body and punched the buckle into the lock as he accelerated around corners.

Despite the confusion and fury of the escape, she felt focused and powerful, but alone. The priest was quiet. The calm on his face suggested he was enjoying this adventure. She studied him as he checked the mirrors and continued through the gears of the little car as it sped downhill.

A three-foot wall of stone bordering one side of the street became a blur. Dense, green forest and thick shrubbery filled the landscape beyond. Continuous buildings and walls stood tall on the edge of the other side of the road. Motorcycles and scooters burst into the road, wove through traffic, and buzzed away. Two lanes of oncoming busses and cars challenged opposing vehicles in the narrow street.

As the car flew forward, Rennie saw a road sign that read "Discesa Gaiola." She grabbed the hem of the nun's tunic with both hands and pulled it up past her seat belt. The priest glanced at her as she reached into her jacket pocket and removed her cell phone. She needed to know where she was and get outside help.

Vittorio downshifted to take them around the next hairpin turn. A quick heel-and-toe method on the clutch and accelerator with another gear change sped them forward. A sly grin appeared on his face, suggesting another side of this humble man of God.

Rennie checked her phone for reception. It was good enough. The ability to connect with friends to let them know her situation brought comfort. Her new sense of belonging with them needed reconnection. She reviewed her favorited contacts and touched the name of "Angie." She thought through the time difference between Italy and Iowa— it should be all right, early morning there. She might be at home or on the way to work. Rennie listened for her friend's voice but closed her eyes in disappointment as Angie's voicemail message sounded.

"Angie, this is Rennie. Call me. I'm in Naples, not Rome. I'm in trouble and need help. Please call Matthew and ask him to call me. A local priest is helping me get out of here and back to Rome. Please call. Thanks."

She looked out her side window at the hard faces of the drivers passing by. "Don't panic," she whispered. Rennie thought of the student Amanda Knox, who had been accused of a murder in Italy and jailed for years.

The road became wider and busier, but the priest went faster. Pedestrians added to the jangle of humanity rushing in all directions.

Rennie considered her options. She wondered if the police were searching for her. Had Father Angelotti calmed things down so everything was now okay and her trip could continue as planned, or should she be heading to an airport to take the next plane home? A truck turned onto the highway in front of them, so the priest hit the brake, and swerved.

"Padre, easy," Rennie yelled. "This isn't Formula One."

Vittorio nodded and seemed to relax as he slowed their pace.

Rennie opened the map application on her phone. She waited for the cursor to show up, indicating her location. She pinched the screen to zoom in for more detail. Street names appeared so she could finally get a sense of her location in Naples. She looked for a street sign or other marker to help her. Her gut begged for information.

Another street sign came up: "Via Alessandro Manzoni."

Okay, now we're cooking.

Rennie studied the map on her phone. *Are we going east, northeast? That's not right. Naples is southeast of Rome!*

She stared out the window, searching for a map of Italy in her mind. "Padre, is Formia ahead?"

He frowned.

She repeated, "Formia?"

He seemed to shiver a positive nod of the head.

"*Si,* Formia."

He waved at the windshield.

That wasn't clear. Rennie had doubts about her ability to communicate with this guy but still felt safe for the first time all day. She leaned back in her seat. Her memory raced through images of sitting in the helicopter, the ride in the SUV, the face of the dead priest. *That face!* She sat up and turned on her phone, reviewed her contacts for Matthew's name, and touched the icon. She poked it hard. Rennie listened to another voicemail message, then blurted her call for help.

"Matthew, hi, this is Rennie. I'm in a jam in Italy, actually Naples. Please call as soon as you get this."

She ended the call.

She called him again. "This is Rennie again. Have you heard of a Greek Orthodox priest by the name of Ioannis something? I was told he was an expert on early church history. I figured you'd know. Somebody killed him. Call me."

Rennie saw the power level on her phone was low. She squeezed the power button off and stared at a black screen.

A sickening sadness swirled through her. The road ahead became a routine suburban gathering of cars, scooters, vans, gas stations and small stores. Another sign came up: Posillipo.

A moment of desperation swept into her. *Where are we going?*

The ringtone for Angie blasted away. Rennie dropped the phone on the floor between her feet and scrambled to pick it up. The priest was so startled, he slowed down and pulled to the side of the road.

"Hang on, girl!" Rennie pleaded with the phone.

She swiped the face and pushed it to her ear. "Angie, are you there?"

"Rennie, hey, I was in an early meeting. What's going on? Are you okay?"

"Angie, it's been crazy. I'm in Naples or a town called Posillipo. I think the police are after me. It's complicated. I'm trying to get back to Rome. I need help, but I don't know what."

"What?" Angie shrieked. "The police? What happened? Rennie, are you in a safe place? Should I call the American Embassy?"

"No, they might ask the police for help. I can't trust anyone. Angie, call Matthew. I left a message for him. That dear old man is so sick, his health —"

"Rennie, listen. You are your own best resource right now. You can trust you. I'll talk to Matthew. Bud might have ideas, too. You can do this, and you know we'll help."

"I'm tired. I've got to go now."

"Get some rest and be safe. You'll be okay. We've been through more than this. Oh, my God. The police?"

"Angie, tell my mom I'm sorry. She wanted me to settle down, be normal. I've screwed it all up."

"What are you talking about? She thinks you're amazing. You're strong and decisive, and she admires that in you. So do I. Do you remember when my boyfriend ditched me because he got a better job? I went a little crazy but you stepped up. You were the calm in my storm. You didn't need to think about what to do.

You just did it. Do that now."

"Yeah, you were wild. I've never seen someone trash their own office!"

They shared a laugh.

"Rennie, how can I reach you?"

"If you have any ideas, just call me. My phone is dying. I'll check in later."

"Okay, we'll fix this. Remember who's on your side."

"Yeah, I know. Angie, I might be in over my head this time. I'll call you later."

Car horns blared around them as the car slowly cruised forward. Rennie turned the phone off and held it to her chest.

"Go, go please." Rennie urged the priest.

Easing the little car back into the stream of traffic, the priest murmured in a steady accented tone, "Okay, okay."

Rennie's mind jerked through ways to get help, questions about Angelotti, whether Lieutenant Borromeo was in a car chasing them, and even where her luggage might be. She sensed a familiar swirl of confusion and anxiety building within her. *No!* That's what would happen to her old self before finding the letters. She wouldn't let that emotion-driven Rennie take over. The new Rennie, based on peace and principle, had to prevail.

She felt the warm sun heat the heavy, black cloth of her disguise and realized there was nothing to do at this point. Her eyes fluttered, trying to stay open as the stress in her body slowly slipped away. The cocoon of the car and rhythmic purr of the engine numbed her senses. A soft, empty darkness filled her eyes, pushing aside her thoughts, and flowed down through her body. The world went away.

Ten minutes later, the car turned, and Rennie's head fell to the side. Light flickered into her awareness. A snort of needed breath jumped into her nose as she thrust her hands out.

She shouted, "Where are we?"

The priest made another quick turn.

"*Che?*"

"Where are we?" she demanded again. "How far have we gone?"

He pointed at a passing road sign that displayed "A56." Rennie's hands fumbled in her lap for her phone and turned on the map feature. She found the slow-moving arrow that showed her location. "Pozzuoli? Where's Pozzuoli?"

He flicked his finger at the windshield. "*Si, Pozzuoli.*"

As he said that, a white utility van in the center lane slid close to them. It had a long, sliding door on one side with no window and no markings. The front door windows were dark. The priest moved the car to the right, nearer to the edge of the road. He scowled and shook an open palm at the van. The van moved closer again so the priest downshifted and accelerated to get ahead of the truck. It matched his speed. A car behind them kept pace, too closely.

Rennie shot glances in all directions to see what was around them. They were getting trapped. Fury flushed through her.

"What's going on? Do something! Take the exit ramp!"

Rennie pointed at the approaching departure lane.

Vittorio checked his mirrors, glared at the broad side of the van closing in on them, and swerved at the last moment onto the exit road. The car slowed as it journeyed up the hill into a long curve. Another car darted from a side road ahead of them and rolled to a stop.

"Go around that car!" Rennie shouted.

The priest jerked the steering wheel causing it to skid. He braked then accelerated, driving off the side of the road, spitting gravel until spinning to a halt. He yelled and threw his hands in the air. He opened his door and released his seat belt. With unexpected agility, he was out of the car.

Two men exited the vehicle that had cut them off. Dark

blue jackets and aviator sunglasses presented them as a force. The priest stepped back. As he did, the sound of another vehicle driving into the gravel crackled behind them.

A stab of cold fear hit Rennie between the shoulders. She flipped open the door and took a few steps down the slope away from the road. Options flowed through her. This was a good time to play the nun role. She straightened out the habit and veil, and surveyed the scene, hoping for emergency help or an escape route. Nothing was obvious. She was ready to run.

The vehicle behind them was a brown utility van, similar to the one that drove them off the road. This was no coincidence, well planned, and it felt personal. She knew they weren't interested in the priest. They wanted her.

Three men got out of the van and walked toward the car at a casual pace. One waved at Rennie. He wore khaki slacks, brown loafers, and a polo shirt with the collar turned up.

"Hi, Miss Haran, we're here to help."

"Who are you? How do you know me?"

He sounded and looked American. There was no hint of him being anything else.

"What's important right now, Rennie, is that you come with us. The police are up ahead waiting for you. The priest followed orders, but Scarpia's plans were shortsighted. We need to take another route."

He continued his stroll toward her.

Rennie studied him as she stumbled up the slope to the car. "I asked who you are."

"My name's Michael. Call me Mike. I'm supposed to take you safely back to the Vatican. Since your luggage was on the helicopter, we have a change of clothes for you and will get you to a place of rest while the security forces are on the hunt. Hey, Peter, we need to go now."

Rennie noticed that the men who were with Mike and the

two from the first car gathered around the priest. They acted like old friends. Vittorio's mood was jovial and expressive. He turned to Rennie and nodded with enthusiasm. He gave her a thumbs-up and said, "Okay!"

Doubt soured her flesh. "So, Michael, how can the police be waiting up ahead?"

"Well, if you made any phone calls, you can believe they were listening, probably the ROS and NSA, the National Security Agency. They have an operations station in Naples. It wouldn't matter. They listen to everything, and they'll be in touch with ROS. You've become a person of interest to them. Assume they know where you are, how you're traveling, and where you're going. We're changing that. But we need to go."

He gestured toward the van. "Please come with us. You can take the nun's outfit off in the van." He chuckled, "— Unless, you like it."

He seemed to know what he was saying. The possibility of the police lying in wait for her on the road ahead and taking her to prison for more questions was frightening.

"Give me a second."

She walked down the slope again. The beauty of tall, dark-green Cypress trees scattered along a fence line under a soft blue sky gave her some peace. She took a long, deep breath then turned and marched up to the road. Mike was gazing at the sky.

"Let's go," she said. "Thanks, *padre*," she called out to Vittorio.

He flicked his hand in a quick wave and returned to the Fiat.

The men in the first car returned to theirs. As soon as they drove off, the priest revved his engine and kicked up loose gravel as the tires gained traction. Mike, Rennie, and the two men returned to the van. Mike helped her into the side door as the others got into the front seats.

"I'm afraid we have to make ourselves comfortable back

here," he said. We don't want anyone peeking in to see you. We'll be at our destination in a few minutes. Feel free to take off the nun's thing now if you like."

He turned on a light in the rear compartment.

Rennie's doubts about this guy were running high.

Nun's thing? That doesn't sound like what someone with the Vatican would say.

She decided to keep the "nun's thing" on. She felt her phone under the garment and slid her hand over it.

Mike's eyes turned her way. "You might set that on airplane mode so it's less likely to be tracked. For a little while at least, we want to remain as unobserved as possible."

He always had the same grin. She didn't trust it.

"Mike, what's the next move?" she asked.

"Good question. It's a basic plan. We're taking a boat out of the Pozzuoli harbor. It's a big boat, to an island off the coast. There's a resort kind of place called Ischia. The Italians won't imagine you going there."

Rennie wondered how this guy can work for the Vatican but refer to "the Italians."

"Mike, what's your relationship with the Vatican. I don't get it. Why can't they fix this thing with me more directly?"

The man next to the driver turned to Mike and spoke Italian. Mike said, *"Grazie."*

"Rennie, we're almost there. I'll explain more on the boat. When the door opens, we must quickly get on board and go below. You'll have a private cabin where you can freshen up at your leisure."

He rose to see out the front window. "Get ready."

Rennie studied him and remembered Angie's advice to trust herself.

Mike, you don't know who you're dealing with.

Rome, Italy
The Vatican

III / 2

Joseph checked his watch and considered when Father Angelotti would arrive from the landing point in the helicopter. His temples pulsed with anger wondering if Scarpia and Busca would be with Angelotti. They were unpredictable factors that need to be dealt with.

A luminous glow danced through the hallways of the administration building as the heels of Joseph's shoes clicked a steady beat on his way to the office of the abbess. He enjoyed his sense of superiority over others. He entered the waiting chamber outside her office but was stunned to encounter Angelotti, Scarpia, and Busca already there.

Slipping into humble Italian, he muttered, "Forgive me, I wasn't aware you were here. May I announce you to the abbess?"

Angelotti twirled around and reached out with both hands to greet Joseph.

"Ah, dear Joseph, her secretary was here and has gone inside."

Joseph grasped the two limp hands offered by the priest and felt unsure what to do with them.

"I'll go to the abbess and see if you can begin soon. You must be exhausted, padre."

He opened the massive door only wide enough to slip into the office of Abbess Serena. She stopped speaking to her secretary when he entered and called to him.

"Just observe, and keep his associates away from me," she directed.

The abbess then told the secretary to bring in the visitors.

As Angelotti, Scarpia, and Busca entered, Joseph noticed that Scarpia held Busca back and whispered to him. Their interaction was so brief, Joseph thought only he may have seen it. He moved toward the door to intercept Busca, but the man was quickly gone.

Abbess Serena greeted Father Angelotti with open arms but offered a stiff-armed handshake when they were close enough. His expressive and clumsy gestures generated open amusement between the two. Sitting at a small, baroque-style guest table, she asked him to summarize the dramatic events of the day.

His narration was full of innocence and surprise, devotion to protect the Holy Church, and confusion on the motives of the police. He had been asked to do this "errand" but felt entrapped in a larger story that he knew nothing about.

"Why did you have the American woman go there?" the Abbess inquired.

Angelotti lost his composure and stuttered. Joseph thought Angelotti should have practiced his excuses for every detail. He apparently didn't for this important one.

As Angelotti struggled with his answer, Scarpia sneezed loudly, stunning all in the room.

The abbess glared at Joseph and flicked her head in the direction of the door.

Joseph finally had orders, and he moved to them with energy. Striding across the room he slid his arm through Scarpia's and walked toward the door.

"My friend, let's leave them alone."

With little resistance, they were gone.

They paced on opposite sides of the entry area like caged animals preparing for a fight. Scarpia's visage seemed thoughtful but concerned. Joseph's confidence grew. He hoped Scarpia would show signs of either fear or anger, the response to fear. He wondered if the man knew the vulnerable positions that Angelotti and his associates had fallen into.

Scarpia stopped, turned away from Joseph, and removed a cell phone from his jacket pocket. His lips could be seen saying a few words. The return of the phone to his pocket yielded a subtle curl of the corners of his lips. Scarpia eased into a sculpted chair covered in tapestry material and appeared to relax.

The heat of Joseph's anger rose again. The stupid incident in Naples was putting events out of control. The abbess was weak and in trouble, and she didn't seem to know it! He cared little for her, but it was time to step in and get direct with this lowlife Scarpia.

The door to the office opened and Angelotti stepped out sideways, awkwardly looking back as he talked with the abbess while trying to hold the door for her as she followed.

"Yes, sorella, these things will be done. I'm fully confident," he said in good humor.

"Let me recap, padre, so there's no misunderstanding. There are two things. The American girl will be brought here with no media attention, and she'll help you arrange in flawless manner the display of the letters of our Lord. After the great opening, you'll have her on a plane back to America. The other item is that you'll repair our relationship with the Italian state and the police. Considering the banking and uglier issues the Holy See has had to deal with in recent years, we don't need more aggravation."

The abbess took his hands in hers and held them firmly.

"The Holy Church is ready to move into a new era. Your work as secretary for the Propagation of the Faith can bring joy to the hearts of new believers and heal this tension we have with the Eastern Churches. Go with God, fratello."

Angelotti was mute and still. His hands drifted down when released from her grip.

"Excuse me, my friends," were her last words before sealing

herself behind the great door.

As Father Angelotti departed in silence, Scarpia began to follow him but Joseph stepped into his path leaving them alone together.

"A moment please," he slurred in rough Italian. "The abbess is too polite. You and your companions need to know the church has only one purpose, and it would be most unfortunate if you strayed from that goal. Do not bring trouble."

Joseph felt stronger with each syllable he sputtered in Scarpia's face. He sucked in a breath of satisfaction. Scarpia never looked into Joseph's eyes. His chin rose as he reached up to straighten his tie. Suddenly, Joseph's body slammed back against the entry door. Scarpia's hands locked onto Joseph's biceps, holding him with relentless pressure. Scarpia's foul breath filled his face as Joseph tried to get past the shock of the assault. His cheek was pressed with the other man's, followed by words whispered in his ear.

"We're on different paths, Father Joseph, but we have the same goal. You might not know this, but I too am a priest. I too, will defend the church."

Joseph tried to turn his face away. He was embarrassed with his weakness and hated the feel of the other man's flesh against his.

Scarpia pressed his cheekbone further into Joseph's.

"My friend, in two days, a certain theologian in the Antiochian Eastern Church in Lebanon will die. The media will learn that it must be a sign of an internal dispute in the Eastern Churches and payment for the death of the Greek. They will believe Rome has nothing to do with either of these. But that person is one of the heretics. This would be a good thing, yes?"

Joseph felt his arms released and their bodies separated. He still looked away.

Scarpia growled, "Thank you for your devoted service and loyalty, my brother."

III / 3

An overcast day made downtown Des Moines, Iowa feel more lifeless than usual. It added to the darkness inside Angie McGrady as she struggled to grasp ideas, determined to help her friend Rennie. They had been through so much together in finding and saving the letters. She ground her teeth as she entered the newspaper building searching for the office of the editor. She had only been here twice before. Passing by the cubicle where Rennie had worked, she slowed for a moment. Empty now, she stared at the clean, gray surfaces and thought of the dynamic color that Rennie brought to this place.

"I've got to help her," she said to herself.

Bud wasn't in his office, so she tried to find a comfortable position in the hardwood chair in front of his desk.

He stomped in, shaking a fist full of paper.

"Doesn't anyone know how to get a story anymore? Angie, what's up?"

He tossed the papers on his desk and dropped into his chair.

"Thanks for seeing me, Bud. I didn't know who to talk to."

"It's okay. Tell me what you know at this point. I'm an old reporter. First, we get the facts, and then we have a story."

"As I said in my message to you, Rennie called me and was in a panic. She said she was in Naples, Italy and in danger. You know she went to Rome to help the Vatican display the letters. I don't know what she's doing in Naples. It's pretty far from Rome. Bud, she's in danger. I've never heard her like that."

"What about contacting the US Consulate in Naples or the

embassy? I don't know what they'd do but they should be able to work the system. I don't know what they did for that college gal that was accused of murder."

"Rennie said she was with a priest, but the police were after her. I don't get it. She said we shouldn't trust anyone, so I should get ideas from you and Matthew. I had a short talk with Matthew and his health isn't good. He has a grandson who might be free to go to Rome to help where he can. Do you know anyone who could help with this? You're in with all the big-wigs in the area."

"Angie, we're in Iowa. Interpol doesn't have an office here. Do you think our farm delegation to Congress has any skills or connections for this? Heck, they cause more foreign-relations problems than fix them. What about that antiquities collector from San Francisco who was chasing the letters?"

"Bud, that guy might have contacts over there, but he's shady. I wouldn't trust him."

"Angie, do this—call Matthew again. He's got archeology friends all over the Near East. He probably knows the religion people, too. Call him, and I'll figure something out here."

"Good, I'll follow up with Matthew. Thanks."

She winked at him as she hurried out of his office.

"Margaret!" he yelled.

The head of a young woman popped up from behind a cubicle wall. "Yeah, Bud. What?"

"There was an Italian reporter in Rome who investigated corruption at the Vatican. He wrote a book, too. Find someone who can get me his contact information and have them see me right away. I need to talk to that guy, the one in Rome! Look it up!"

Angie gripped the steering wheel as she drove through the city. Her speed and energy rose as she moved onto the highway leading out of town to Simpson College. The pastures and fields of tall corn offered her a sense of hope. Maybe it was an insight. Something happened in Naples, and if it was big enough, it would have made the news. She could search for a news item in the Italian media that might relate to Rennie's crisis. The library was her refuge and resource, and she loved the power of information to solve problems. Her light-blue eyes squinted above a broad smile. Looking for relevant facts would be a start and maybe the answer.

A young man with three black studs in each ear greeted Angie as she hurried past the check-out counter at the library. She called to him as she entered the lobby.

"Robert, I need one of the students to do an urgent research project for me. See who's available. Also, contact Dr. Fredericks in the Languages department and see if we have anyone who knows Italian. Okay?"

He looked into the air.

"Well, Joe is free, I think. He could help with the research thing."

"Okay, have Joe come to my office, and please call Dr. Fredericks."

Angie hustled around the end of the counter into her office and went through a stack of paper in her in-box and mail. Her finger slid across her tablet checking her online connections.

Robert stepped into her office. "Miss McGrady, there's a guy on the phone for you. I think he's British. Do you want the call?"

"Put him through."

Angie laid her hand on the phone to snatch it the moment it buzzed. It was fast.

"Hello, angel? Are you there?"

"Yes, Matthew. Thank you for your call. Your timing is as sharp as your wisdom."

"My dear, you honor me without warrant. Do you have a

moment? I thought I'd offer a quick update to our call earlier today."

"Please do. I've not been sure until now what I can do from here."

"I regret I must be brief. My energy seems to be escaping me faster than ever. I spoke again with my grandson, David. He's a dynamic young man with a brilliant mind. He's been working for several years as a research physicist at the Large Hadron Collider in Cern, Switzerland. You know, that's where they smash atomic particles to see what they're made of. David worked for a while in Italy a few years ago at a similar facility. They were testing the speed of light. He speaks Italian and has a few friends there. He said he's on break for a few weeks, so he will go to Rome and see if he can meet with Rennie or help as needed."

"Matthew, that's wonderful. We need someone there to help her. I wish I knew where she was and if she's okay. The lack of information is painful."

"Yes, my dear, and I'm making contact with old friends in the region who could also help. She mentioned in a voice message some things she heard. I've spoken with a colleague at the British Museum and another in the Ancient Documents section of the Topkapi Museum in Istanbul. I believe they will be able to help."

"Thanks for that. I'm going to pursue an idea from here as well. David can call me at any time if he needs anything. My cell phone is the most reliable way."

Matthew coughed and then laughed. "Of course, and I'll try to remember that. I'm not sure if my mind has yet escaped the previous millennium! Very well, angel, I must go now. Stay in touch."

"I will, dear friend, and you take care of yourself. You're not a spry eighty anymore!"

"Ha, that's true. I'm becoming a relic like the ones I've dug up. I should have them put on my gravestone, 'Nothing Valuable

Here,' so no one digs me up and puts me on display! Ha! When you speak with Rennie again, give her my love, and the same to you."

"I will, Matthew. You'll be able to tell her yourself very soon."

The phone went silent. She set it into the holder and dabbed a tissue to her nose. The phone rang again.

Robert stepped into her office. "Miss McGrady, Dr. Fredericks is on the phone."

Angie picked up the handset again, composing herself before speaking. "Hi, Rick. Thanks for calling. Do you have a moment to hear about an urgent research project I need done? I could use your help."

"Of course, Angie, and Robert said you want someone who knows Italian."

"I'd like to have a resource lined up. I need to find news items that happened recently in Naples, Italy. It might involve my friend Rennie. Do you remember her?"

"My goodness, everyone knows her name, and you introduced us at that library event. What can I do? I'll get the help you need."

"She's in Italy and might be in trouble over there. We need background information."

"Great! I'd be delighted to be in the next adventure of Rennie and Angie. Can I get a small part in the movie, too?"

"Rick, this is real life."

"Sorry, of course. I'll get started and await your call."

Angie laid aside the phone and began a focused search of the library's data files for any relevant news sources for Italy.

She yelled, "Robert, get Joe in here!"

III / 4

The grinding sounds of the boat's engine and creaking of the hull echoed through the cabin as Rennie slid the deadbolt from the door lock into a brass clasp on the wall. She waited. The door looked weak. She thought she heard a noise in the passage on the other side. Above, men were walking and talking. Engine and equipment sounds rolled through the boat from all directions. She shook her hands and swung her arms to release tension. Her focus stayed on the door as she backed away.

The air in the room was stale, but with a hint of lemon and maybe bleach. She went to a small, neat bed that was attached to the wall and covered with a dark green blanket. On it were stacked a knitted sweater of mixed blue and white colors, dark grey slacks, and folded socks and panties. A denim jacket lay across a pillow. An empty, black backpack rested on the floor. Once again, she was imprisoned and given something to wear. She snorted defiance and turned back to the door and the lock.

Her thoughts replayed through the swift move from the truck across the ramp onto the boat. She was guided down steep stairs by a man from the van and she glanced back to see Michael speaking with someone on the dock. Thinking about it, Rennie wasn't sure if he actually got on the boat.

She felt trapped in her small cabin. A few feet away, another door was open an inch and a light was on inside. Her muscles loaded for action. She stepped across the gap to the door. Peering through the crack, she saw a sink the size of a mixing bowl. Slipping a finger around the edge of the door, Rennie opened it another six inches. When the hinge squeaked, she slammed the door shut. She closed her eyes and laughed. Her thoughts raced in sarcasm. *Now I'm afraid of a bathroom!*

For the moment, she was alone and felt safe.

Rennie surveyed the facilities and made the most of the opportunity. She removed the nun's habit and threw it into a corner. She found an electric outlet and used an adapter to plug in her phone charger. That brought a satisfied smile to her lips. Shedding her jacket and boots, she pulled her blouse from her pants. Her determination grew. She found the towels and soaps she needed to clean her body. Now and then, she stopped and listened. Once she got going, the room was hers and no longer a prison. She was pleased that the clothes left for her were comfortable and fit. Checking herself in the mirror on the wall, she thought, *Not bad. I could probably get away with being Italian.*

As she removed the grime and dirt from her unexpected adventures of the day, Rennie felt more energized. She ran a comb through her hair and took a deep breath to give her focus. She placed the backpack on the floor then filled it with her clothes from the day. Sitting on the bed, she stretched her long limbs the length of the thin mattress and eased back. Her eyelids fluttered together and closed.

Rennie awoke relaxed, looking at a dull tan ceiling. Her watch showed twenty minutes had gone by. She listened and sat up, wondering what was next. Should she use her phone? Everything was a risk. Yet, each moment was sufficient in itself. This was now, and it was hers.

The events of the day dashed through her thoughts – London, Sister Marjorie, a helicopter, Angelotti, the lieutenant, and now this. Questions filled the gaps. What does it mean and who are these people? How are they connected? She knew Matthew would be the best sounding board. He knows history, the church, places, and people. He's the one who can connect the dots. His age and health wouldn't allow him to travel, but she could call him, and he'll know who can help—

A firm knock on the door stopped her. She waited for a moment before calling out.

"Who is it?"

"Hi, Rennie. Are you okay? It's Michael."

She went to the door and listened.

"Rennie, we'll arrive in a little while. I wondered if you'd like to talk. I can fill you in on a few things."

"Uh, yes. Where?"

"It's up to you. The sea is calm and there's some light, so we can be on deck or in your room. Whatever's comfortable for you."

"Give me a minute?"

Her thoughts raced through the best options. She had little or no control over anything. The first thing to focus on was what she needs to know. Knowledge would give her some power. Besides, she didn't know this guy and the open deck was preferable to the containment of her room.

"Mike, I'll meet you on deck in another minute."

A crescendo of energy let her know she was ready to get the story behind all this, not for the story, but to rid herself of the threats and get back to Rome. If she made another discovery along the way, then that's what reporters do. It was time to work Michael to see what she could learn. Rennie visualized the basic facts she experienced, prioritized them, and applied a few categories – the basic who, what, when, where of story management. Investigative work was her passion but it was also challenging, and often exhausting. She realized long ago she didn't have a mind for conspiracy or other forms of deceit, so applying those traits to figures in a mystery was a challenge if not an overwhelming obstacle.

She took the backpack and slid it under the bed, grabbed the jean jacket, and flipping the jacket over her shoulder, she hit the lock bolt with the edge of her palm and jerked the door open.

Be a reporter, she thought, marching up the ladder toward a dark blue sky.

Stepping from the stairs onto the deck, a crew member walked by and ignored her. She expected more attention. Michael stood near a railing not far away, his hands in his pants pockets. He seemed too calm.

"Hey, Mike," she said as casually as possible.

He turned and strolled to meet her. "I hope you're doing okay. I'm sure this is tough to understand."

"Well, maybe you can put it together for me."

He motioned to a bench near the opening to the stairs. "Would you like to sit or walk around the deck? What feels good to you?"

"I could use the walk, I guess."

They slowly moved along the deck pausing now and then to look at the sea. Rennie scanned the horizon and saw faint lights past the bow.

"Is that where we're going?"

"Yes, that's Ischia. You'll have a more comfortable room there. In the morning, it's back to the mainland and the Vatican, if you want."

Rennie's lips were tense. "If I want?"

"Right, please know I'm here to help you." Michael chuckled. "This is pretty intense for me, too. I've not been involved in anything like this. How about if we set aside how we got here and for now just be a couple of people enjoying a quiet boat ride on a pleasant evening? That would work for me."

Moments of quiet passed as gusts of sea breeze cooled Rennie's face.

"You know Michael, this is nice. So, what do you do when you're not saving damsels in distress?"

"It's normally routine business stuff like coordinating activities, researching projects, and administrative busy-work. Boring usually. How about you? I understand you came to Italy for a big exhibition of the letters you found. What was that discovery like?"

Rennie turned to the rail and drew in a deep breath.

"It all seems so long ago, and my life before that, actually who I was, is almost hard to remember. I know I was hungry to get a big story, uncover corruption, expose bad government or business practices. But the only assignments I could get were trivial local activities like the county fair or where traffic problems were not being solved. I was really frustrated, and frankly, I can't say I had friends. I even avoided family. I was alone and angry."

Her head dropped and her thoughts disappeared as the movement and sounds of the ship and the sea washed through her.

"Let's keep walking," she said.

Michael turned with her and listened.

"So, one day my editor, Bud, called me to his office and said he had a story for me to chase down. It involved a local college professor who went to England for a sabbatical at the British Museum but died in some mysterious way. Wow, I thought. A murder. Finally, a real case."

They approached a bench where Rennie sat down and drifted against the back rest. Michael joined her.

"I met Angie, the librarian and archivist at the college where the professor came from, and I got involved in the facts of the story. The library archives had his belongings, including his diary. I think I was the first to open it since his last entry. It felt intensely personal to me, and it revealed his discovery of the letters. Angie and I had to go there, to England."

"So, you found the letters at the library among his belongings or at the British Museum?"

"No, and I don't know if anyone other than him even knew they existed."

"Rennie, this is fascinating. You're given this case that seems meaningless, you pursue it even though you don't want to, and it ends with perhaps the greatest ancient find of all time. Amazing."

"Yeah, right. But it wasn't just the letters. It turned out that not only did Professor Justus find the letters, he also found new love."

A big smile spread across her face. "He met a woman at the museum and, well let's say, their love became a child. Sadly, the professor never knew she was pregnant because he was killed shortly after their love affair. What's even more incredible is this child became a professor who had a distinguished career in archeology and ancient languages at the British Museum."

Rennie leaned forward and shook her head. The images of people and places, and memories of the volatile emotions she went through to fully uncover the story flashed through her thoughts.

"Rennie, that's quite a journey of discovery, and now you're here to be celebrated at the Vatican. It's a beautiful thing. Maybe, divine."

She spun toward him. "Michael, Let's be straight. What's going on? I faced ugly threats to my life in finding the letters of Jesus. It seems to have started all over again, except this now has me chased by the police. Is the Roman Catholic Church involved in this? Is that why I went to Naples and why you're here?"

She stood and glared at him.

"Rennie, as with any organization, especially really old ones like the church, there are all kinds of interest groups. They're often in conflict."

"So, this priest from Greece got killed because of some in-fighting among Christians?"

"No, we never thought it would go this far."

"Who's 'we'? Aren't you with the Vatican?"

"No, I'm not. But, I'm on your side."

He got up and turned to the sea. "There's a lot of history. It goes back two thousand years. There's never been agreement on anything in the church, and people continue to suffer."

She stepped in front of him and straightened her neck to try to look down at him.

"You're not telling me anything. Let's get past the 'good guys, bad guys, oh gee, people get hurt' overview. What do I have to do with this? Who killed the priest and why? And what's the deal with Father Angelotti?"

Rennie realized she was leaning toward him. His eyes were dilated.

In a whisper he said, "Those questions don't matter. There's always a collision between fact, belief, and doctrine on any issue. Does it matter to you?"

"Haven't you noticed I seem to be on the run?" Her teeth clenched. "And, it mattered to that dead priest on the beach."

"What's important, Rennie?"

"Truth!"

She was startled she shouted the word.

He snorted, "Forget whatever you think is truth. The world is flat. The moon landing never happened. All immigrants are dangerous. Every false idea is a truth for someone. People believe things despite—or at least without—the facts. Reality is what's important. Only a few know it, and they're the ones in danger."

He spun around and walked to the railing.

She went with him and grabbed his jacket. "Michael, you're confusing belief with truth! There is truth! It's the business I'm in and the powers of the world don't like it. It's there, just not easy to find. Reality is what's distorted!"

He glared at her and marched away.

Damp, cold air blew into her face. Her eyes watered. She put on the jacket and saw three crew members appear from the settling darkness to take positions on the other side of the boat. A man at the bow called simple commands in Italian. The horizon was full of lights that grew larger. Rennie stepped near the railing. A large piece of plastic rode the black, gentle waves past the boat. Her mind transformed the debris into the dead priest. Phantom birds landed on the body as splashing waves teased them away.

Mike returned to her. "Does it scare you?"

"What, the water?"

"That which you can't see. You want and deserve answers, but darkness obscures them."

"What you call 'reality' distorts things. Give me answers, Michael, not ancient history."

"There's a group known over time as *Societas*, or *Consortio*, or *Porta*, depending on the language and place."

"Is that the crime organization?"

"No, that's *Camorra*. The fellowships I referred to are definitely not criminals. They can be either the good guys or the bad guys. The doctrine of these fellowships is quite different from the modern Christian faith. It's based on a tradition about writings of women from the early church that runs counter to accepted doctrine. The continuing power struggle between the established church and these groups is what gets people killed."

"What? So, the dead priest was part of this fellowship, or was he on the other side?"

"Rennie, it comes down to simple things—"

A bell clanged twice, somewhere on the boat

"We're almost there. Let's talk when we get to shore. I need to arrange a few things before we dock. You can stay on deck or in your cabin until we're ready to go."

He turned to go but Rennie pulled him back.

"Which side killed the priest? The good guys or the bad guys?" she insisted.

"In *your* terms, the Greek was a good guy. Like you, he looked for evidence of a hidden truth. A player on the other side did this." He turned and hurried across the deck.

The ship's bell rang again. Rennie felt a darkness settling on her world.

Her thoughts raced through what Mike said and what she needed to know. *Some reporter*, she thought. *I learned nothing.*

She returned to her cabin, retrieved the backpack, and checked the room and bath area for her things. She sat on the bed and thought through the conversation.

Putting her face in her hands she whispered, "I just want to go home."

The noise of the engine almost disappeared and was replaced with stuttering gears, shouts of men above, and a *thud* sound against one side of the boat. More calls of men to one another were followed by an empty silence in the hull.

Rennie flattened the palms of her hands on the bed as the engine roared back to life, jamming her body forward as the boat stopped. Quiet filled the cabin until she heard footsteps on the ladder.

"Miss Haran? Time to go, please."

"Okay, I'll be a minute."

Rennie took her phone from her jacket pocket, took it off airplane mode, and checked for a signal. It was good. It sounded various notification tones as her text and email messages and voice mail were updated. She shoved it into her pocket to muffle the sound.

"Miss Haran?"

"Yes! I'm getting my things! I'm coming, thank you."

Adrenaline stoked Rennie's internal fires. She scanned her messages from Angie and Matthew. They said they're concerned, and Matthew says he can send someone, but who's David? She listened to one of Matthew's voice-mail messages. His professorial side was fully engaged. A determined knuckle rapped on the door.

Rennie turned off the phone in the middle of Matthew's message and grabbed the backpack. She pulled open the door, finding a poorly lit hall that made the cold face of a large man in front of her all the more of a shock. Despite that, she flashed a smile.

"Hey there, let's get this party started!"

In two steps she was past him and on the stairs. Three more quick steps had her pacing through the light of lanterns across the deck to where Michael stood. He wore a dark blue windbreaker like the other men.

"Is everything okay, Rennie? The guys were concerned."

"Mike, if you aren't used to waiting for women, you need to get out more."

His pleasant attitude was gone. "The car at the end of the wharf will take us to the hotel."

"Michael, this probably seems odd, but I'm concerned about Father Angelotti. Does he know I won't arrive tonight?"

"Of course. We informed the priest who was driving you."

Michael didn't wait for a response. He walked down the short gangway to the car without looking back.

She felt more alone and vulnerable. She was back in the real world, away from the solitude of the sea, and it was dark. She hurried down the walkway.

Michael waited at the open back door of the vehicle.

"Tomorrow morning, when you're rested, we'll talk again. We can get you to the Vatican or even back to America. You can go to the police or the military if you like. There are other options, too. It's up to you."

"Thanks, I've got a few more questions."

Rennie threw her backpack into the back seat, slid in, and

closed the door.

The old, stone streets were dark and desolate. It was more of a village than a resort as Michael had called it. No shops were open and only a handful of people were seen in the few minutes needed to arrive at a small hotel. Michael shared a few words in fluent Italian with the driver.

Rennie stepped from the car and looked for signs with street names, advertisements, or any reference point. There was nothing.

"Rennie?"

She turned to see Michael on the other side of the car, leaning on the roof with one arm.

"This is where you'll be tonight. I'll be in a house nearby. They have food for you here and you can rest. You'll be okay."

That damned smile was back. She'd like to change that and had a few ideas on how. Instead, she shifted to investigative-reporter mode.

"I thought we might have a chance to talk. I'd like to know about the letters from women you spoke of. Another thing, what's a crosier?"

"A crosier? Why do you ask?"

"It might be the murder weapon."

Mike stared past her into the darkness. "Rennie, you've had a long day. I recommend you don't use your phone. And, please don't leave the building."

He pointed at her. "No sightseeing."

A door opened in the building behind Michael. The silhouette of a man appeared against the light of the entry.

"*Scusi, signora,*" the man said with hesitation. "*Buona sera.*"

Mike took a few steps to greet the man with an embrace. They exchanged a few words, then he walked away and around the corner.

"*Signora?*"

The silhouette man waved to Rennie.

She jammed her arm through the backpack strap, paused, and shook her head as the car drove off, leaving her alone in the empty street. *Into the valley of darkness, here I go.*

The light of a bare bulb on the entry ceiling revealed the man who welcomed her. She followed as he turned and climbed creaking, steep, old stairs in silence. Rennie wondered whether he was badly worn at fifty or reasonably spry at eighty. On the second floor, he struggled with a key to release the lock on an arched door. Rennie studied his weathered and swollen fingers. Old-man stubble was scattered across his chin and cheeks. Long strands of hair emerged from bushy eyebrows.

He jerked on the old brass doorknob as his fingers worked the key in the lock. He seemed surprised and stepped back when he gained entry. His round, old body settled into a hunched-over, motionless pose. The sour, musk odor of his age and frailty were sucked into her senses. An aura of peace surrounded him. She took the key from his fingers when he offered it.

As he shuffled to the stairs, she thanked him. He slowly descended into the world below. His head reappeared. "In the morning, I fix you a meal."

Rennie locked the door the moment she was in the room. She listened and heard nothing—no equipment, no people, no traffic. The quiet felt heavy. Dark blue embroidered drapes hung over a small window. A plump mattress wrapped in white sheets filled a wrought iron bed. A patchwork comforter was folded across a plain chair. In the corner, a white porcelain bathtub with claw feet dared her to try its cold, hard depths. In another corner, a table held a small basket of bread covered by a white towel with a banana and apple nearby.

She moved mindlessly about the room, opening a floral cotton curtain along a wall and discovering a toilet behind the curtain. Three shelves displayed a variety of towels, cleansers, and two rolls of bathroom tissue.

Walking back to the center of the room, she tossed the backpack and her jacket on the bed and settled in for the night. Falling back on the bed, her body melted into the rumpled comfort of the old linens and mattress. Her breathing deepened and her thoughts drifted into ambiguity. Then, her phone started to buzz. She spun around slapping her hands through her jacket to find the phone. Hitting the power button, she flipped her hair and put the phone to her ear. Nothing. Looking at the screen, she realized it was notification of a text message.

"Matthew," she whispered. She needed to talk to him.

Rennie touched the phone number shown in the message and listened. Her body rocked in anticipation.

"Hello, Rennie, is that you?"

Her face warmed with emotion.

"Yes, yes. Matthew."

"I'm worried, my dear girl. I've tried to reach you and spoke with Angie. No one has heard from you. We're very concerned. What is going on? Are you okay?"

Rennie nodded an answer. She struggled to swallow.

"I don't know where I am. It's an island – Ischia, or something. I'm okay. I'm not supposed to make calls, but Matthew, I'm so alone."

"Are you safe? That's the first thing. We'll figure out everything else."

"Yes, I think so. I don't know why they have me, but I don't think they mean me any harm. They said I can return to Rome or whatever."

"What do you mean 'they' have you?"

"It's a long story. I was with Father Angelotti from the Vatican. He had me come to Naples where he was looking into the death of a Greek Orthodox priest. By the way, what's a crosier? That's the murder weapon. The police somehow implicated me with this priest, so I ended up on the run. Another group got me and now has me on this island. I don't know what's going on! This guy who brought me here, his name is Michael. He said there's an ancient feud in the church. It's about writings of women from long ago that had a different view of church doctrine."

"Did he say what group he's with? Did they kill this priest?"

"No, but he said a few names in Greek or Latin or something. One was *Porta* I think. He referred to it as a society or fellowship. Matthew, who are they?"

"I'm not sure. I have a few old friends who are anthropologists that specialize in aspects of sacred history. There's also a fellow at the British Museum who I've worked with on old documents. Rennie, what era are we talking about?"

Her eyes closed. She slumped forward, her head falling into the palm of her hand.

"I don't know. I don't know."

"Rennie, we'll get through this. Whoever this *Michael* is and whatever is going on, it's not about you. I'll work on it and connect again with Angie. For now, get some rest, be careful, and follow your best instincts. You don't have to fix the world. We're called to do what good we can with what we have and give love along the way, nothing more. Don't worry, we'll get answers. I know that always makes you happy."

Her full lips spread into a wide smile.

"You know me so well. Thank you, Matthew."

"Oh, one other thing, since my health doesn't allow me to travel right now. I called my grandson David. He speaks Italian and works in Switzerland. He said he could go to Rome to help if you'd like that. I gave him your number."

"Good, thanks. I'll take anyone right now."

"He's a brilliant young man. When he was a boy we had delightful discussions about theology, and I taught him ancient Greek. We visited a variety of ancient places, like Corinth and

Ephesus. Now he works on an atom smasher, opening the secrets of the universe. He'll be a useful resource."

"Thank you, Matthew. I must hang up now. Let's be in touch tomorrow."

"Rennie, put your sharp wits to work and be aware. Your zeal to find truth is deep and meaningful."

Rennie heard a click on the line. "Hello, Matthew?"

"Yes dear, I'm still here."

"Did you hear that? I'd better hang up. You be safe."

She ended the call.

Rome, Italy
67 CE

III / 5

Dusk drifted upon Roman streets and the howling of angry animals shattered the quiet air. Within a humble house, a woman's eyelashes tickled the dry wood of a window shutter when she peered through a crack into the darkness to see if the noise outside was a threat. Seeing scrawny dogs scavenging for survival in a quiet alley, she released a comforting breath. The dogs dashed away between buildings when a woman with a black scarf over her head hurried around a corner. The observer tensed as the visitor paused at her house, glanced back, and stepped near the door. She gasped when she saw the visitor touch a leather pouch peeking from the edge of an outer gown.

In the house, two other women huddled in quiet conversation on floor cushions. A knock on the heavy wooden door demanded their attention. Flickering candlelight highlighted the fear on their faces. Thecla, mature in age, moved from the window to the door.

Phoebe, young and thin, grasped the arm of Junia sitting next to her. "Who is it? What do we do?"

Wide-eyed but focused, Thecla's lips pressed together in self-imposed silence. Then she whispered, "We must be strong."

The others relied on her for the wisdom and determination to move forward whatever the circumstances. She hesitated at the door. Another knock startled her and made her step back. She leaned forward, grasped the bolt. Steadying herself, she took a deep breath, and jerked it to the side. The door quickly opened revealing the visitor pressed against it the outer side. Together,

Thecla and the new arrival eased the door shut, securing it again against the outside.

Embracing, Thecla ushered the guest into the warm presence of the other two disciples of Jesus. Junia became animated, retrieving a ceramic pitcher of water from a shelf and filling a cup for the guest. The four settled onto cushions in the small room.

"Mary, what news do you have? Is he all right? Will they release him?"

Mary took a sip of water and studied the ripples in the cup. Finally, she looked at the concerned faces of the women. "It's over." She paused and shook her head. "It's over. Our apostle and voice of the Christ, Paul, has been slain."

She took another drink.

Those listening covered their mouths and faces in silent grief.

Mary set the cup down and stood. "It is now our time. We must be strong. I'm old, but I will go on and speak for our Lord. We all must."

Their raised eyes, some with tears, inspired them to stand with Mary Magdalene. Her presence strengthened Thecla's resolve to support their fragile but determined cause.

"Mary, you were with our Lord from the beginning. Then you continued with courage after He was gone. Paul spoke with wisdom, but with him gone, what can we say or do to protect the faith and build the church?"

"Thecla, by providing your home in Rome as a refuge and meeting place for the brothers and sisters here, you keep that light shining. In our own way, we've all helped spread the words Paul has given to us. Timothy, John, Mark, each of you and so many more keep the faith alive in this way. Now our dear apostle has given us one last letter to share with all the church and believers."

Junia gasped. "He did? How? When?"

"Earlier today. He knew this would be the day of his death. He had to write one last letter and needed assistance. As you know, he had become almost helpless in the misery of his situation. With little food and water, and confronted with the reality of imminent death, he continued to preach to the jailers and other prisoners. This morning when I was allowed to see him, he told me that a visitor from heaven came to him with a special message."

Phoebe expressed shock. "Was it the Lord? What did He say? Please!"

Mary looked toward the ceiling, her face filled with peace. "It could have been, and Paul thought so. He was given a new understanding of Jesus." She beckoned the women to join her again on the floor cushions. "Here, let's sit."

As they settled onto the cushions, Junia hurried to bring more water, bread and fruit. "Mary, say nothing until I return," she urged.

Thecla reached out and took Mary's hand. "Sister, how is it you have this access to Paul?"

"I've been blessed with not only the precious gift of faith, but also resources from my father and good business sense. I found safety here and elsewhere by nurturing connections with important people, even women in the Emperor's family. This helps me get special favors like visiting Paul and bringing him extra nourishment and papyrus for his writing."

Thecla placed bowls of food and the water pitcher between them and sat down.

Phoebe shifted on her cushion. "Mary, tell us this new message from our Lord."

"The jailers allowed me to assist Paul from the dungeon to the main floor, which was cleaner and had a bench. They knew he was too weak to escape, and they also trust me. Of course, I pay them well for these services."

Again, Phoebe demanded, "What did the Lord say?"

Mary patted a leather bag at her side. "I have it here in my pouch. Paul had me write some of it and he added in his own words besides the actual message. It's not a long letter, but he believed it more powerful than all that we have received before. It's a simple new understanding of God's will. He wants us to copy it and send it to all the churches. I will take it myself to Corinth and bring copies to the other churches. Then, I will go on to Jerusalem— the people in Israel are filled with fear. We must hurry. They say the area will erupt in violence at any moment." Mary opened the flap on her bag. "Here it is. Paul is a wonderous vessel through which God pours His message into the world."

As she reached inside, every eye watched her delicate fingers as the letter was eased from the pouch.

Junia gasped, "Read it, Mary. Fill us with the voice of God."

III / 6

Early in the evening, a small crowd gathered in the court-yard of the house considered the Church of Corinth. As dusk became night, the intensity of the light from oil lamps and candles seemed to grow as eyes adapted to the darkness. Conversations softened to whispers in the changing gloom and the voices of those assembled shifted from friendly greetings to quietly shared confidences.

Priscilla studied those present and those arriving while motioning servants to distribute food and wine among the guests. Aquila was gone, and she had to care for the new congregations alone. She saw Mary Magdalene at a corner of the patio making her way through the crowd with Thecla close behind. The eyes of those they passed silently tracked the distinguished visitors.

The women embraced in greeting and gave a light kiss to each cheek. Mary's steady gaze and clear voice gave Priscilla courage. "Sister, your home is again filled with love. What you've done here in helping build the church is celebrated in heaven."

"Thank you, Mary. I live as my heart directs me, just as you and Thecla do. We know who creates all this."

"Amen," Thecla responded. "Please tell us about the church here."

Priscilla's thoughts struggled for an answer. She leaned forward and spoke with a gentle manner. "Years of effort have brought much discussion but little understanding. Regardless of what apostle or prophet visits Corinth, confirming and bringing their wisdom, there's endless argument among the members.

This dissension chills the faith of new believers. Questions about the right path became obstacles. There are many here who think the longevity of their connection with our faith and not their maturity in it gives them privileges of leadership."

"I've seen this in many places, sister," Mary responded. "Those who have met and heard from Paul, or Timothy, or Apollos think those experiences have anointed them with power. Their depth of understanding remains shallow as their desire for possessing more power deepens. For them, faith is not as important as control."

A mix of anger and helplessness filled Priscilla. "Mary, what's the news from Ephesus and Philippi? The little we now hear from them has become more and more troubling. Aquila and I worked so hard to build the church. Are the sheep scattering?"

Priscilla turned to observe several men enter the courtyard.

Mary and Thecla followed her gaze into the crowd.

Thecla touched Priscilla's sleeve. "Are they the ones?"

Priscilla squinted to see who the men went to speak with. "Yes, no matter what I've done to nurture them as brothers in faith they separate from us. I know the church struggles everywhere to have common doctrine, but the gaps in understanding must be sealed. Otherwise, there will be no real faith."

Mary's deep voice, seasoned with many years of hard travel and speaking, caught Priscilla's attention. "Sister, to answer your question, similar events continue in each church we see. As churches grow, a few see it as an opportunity to take over and have prestige. Even when Paul was present, people with attitudes instead of wisdom demanded to be heard. When I walked with our Lord, the disciples had endless questions and doubts. Look at how quickly believers become concerned with their own interests despite the call to serve. This will not go away, so we must remain steadfast. Now, I will add to the doubts and the arguments."

Priscilla was stunned. "What do you mean? We know that Paul is gone. Is there something worse?"

"Not worse, and actually better. It's a new letter from Paul. I have it here in my pouch with a copy for you. He explains an understanding of our faith from a fresh new perspective. It may generate new questions and arguments, but as this happens, we must listen to his voice and stay on the right path."

Priscilla didn't need more change but yearned for stability. Her soul and body felt the years of struggle she had endured in her journey to welcome, to lead, and to comfort. She regretted none of it but hoped the community would embrace the simple love that was promised. "What does the letter say? Does it complicate our teachings?"

"Priscilla, it's a change but also a simplification. And, it comes directly from heaven, maybe Jesus. This is what Paul told me. I was with him and supported him as he wrote and dictated the message. I wrote for him his comments and he wrote, in his own hand, the voice of the visitor."

Priscilla snapped a look at the small crowd in the courtyard. "Sisters, we've got to begin. If we don't lead, they will."

Mary and Thecla followed Priscilla to a corner of the courtyard as the assembly watched and whispered. Priscilla lifted the hem of her garment and stepped up on a small porch. Now in her sixties and having endured successes and hardships in several lands, this old tentmaker could speak with soft sincerity but still make an impact. Her modest attire didn't hide the focused determination that kept her on course and true to the teachings she believed in. Her expectations were also not hidden by her patience that quickly gave way to clear speech.

"Friends, welcome! Can everyone hear me?"

She waited for the crowd to pay attention. "We have many guests this evening. If you see someone you don't know, please greet them. We are all family in the eyes of the risen Lord Jesus.

In a few moments, we'll share a meal and speak of what God has done for us."

A man's voice interrupted the flow. "Priscilla, why are you here and not in Ephesus? Who here speaks for Corinth?"

He was taller and older than most of the men. Gray hair flecked his beard.

He asked again, "Who here speaks for Corinth?"

"Gaius, what is your wish?"

Priscilla tried to seize the moment. "You're one of the first in the church here. Paul himself baptized you. I know you, and I love you. I'm your sister. May I speak? Then we all can share our thoughts."

He stared at her. Men next to him leaned in and mumbled.

"Go ahead, speak," he retorted.

Mary Magdalene gave a light tug on Priscilla's sleeve. "Do you want me to mention Paul's new letter?"

"Not yet, let me move this forward."

She raised her hands. "Friends, and Gaius, thank you for being here tonight. We all need to be nourished in faith with fellowship and learning. Our Savior Jesus reached out to the lowest and to the most desperate of all people, even though he was the presence of the one true God, full of glory. He gave his message to special followers for them to spread the word so that peace could fill the hearts of all people. Our dear apostle Paul, who was here and who wrote to us and to other churches, received God's word and guided us all. Yes, as Gaius said, Aquila and I took this message to Ephesus to build the church there. Now, Timothy is there continuing those efforts. I've returned to Corinth to support our church here and will always go where I'm needed."

"Woman, you're not needed here."

All eyes turned to a man next to Gaius. He glared at Priscilla and pushed away another man who tried to speak to him.

"We have no need for you," he continued. "You may go.

Return to Ephesus or wherever you can offer your woman's voice. The men here will now lead."

He stroked his beard and his chest expanded.

A murmur of, "Yes, go," rippled into the crowd.

"Friends," Priscilla called out. "Let's discuss all things in love. Brother, I don't know you. Please tell us your story."

"I am Joseph Bar Simeon of Judea. I met with the disciples Peter and James in Jerusalem and I have learned from them. Like many here, I too am a Jew and a follower of Jesus. I am both, a Jew and a follower! I don't know your teacher Paul, but there are many teachers, and I will believe the ones who were with Jesus. Peter and James are steadfast in the law. Sin fills the world and it's only through discipline and righteousness that we can stand in the presence of God."

More bubbles of agreement gurgled through the crowd. Some patted Joseph Bar Simeon on the back and gave him room to speak again.

"This I know," Joseph said with more emphasis, "those who knew the Messiah are mostly gone and soon all will be. We must be firm now and in the future. Leadership must be strong or all will be forgotten. The law must be resurrected!"

A chant of, "Yes, restore the law," was begun by a young man near Joseph. A few others joined him. Joseph crossed his arms on his chest and nodded with satisfaction.

"Wait," Mary called out.

"Who is this? Another woman?" a man near Joseph shouted.

"Friends, please!" Priscilla pleaded. "Listen to her. This is Mary of Magdala. She walked with the Lord and the disciples. She helped Jesus. She heard His words directly from His mouth. As our brother Joseph Bar Simeon has said, we must listen to those who walked with Jesus and who have been filled with the Spirit."

Priscilla felt the familiar agony of a crowd in rebellion and division. She knew the church in Corinth had long suffered from internal strife. The city was large and prosperous with an independent-thinking populace, full of a constant flow of new ideas. The temple of Aphrodite with its glamour and a thousand young women available for an "offering" was only one of the many opportunities for a self-satisfying lifestyle.

Priscilla turned to Mary, "Please, say something."

Mary looked to heaven for a moment before scanning the crowd. She walked into the throng, steady yet pausing now and then to look people in the eye. She continued until she reached Joseph Bar Simeon and Gaius.

"Brothers, we've not met before, but I'm grateful to meet you now. You are bold, and you speak clearly. Those who follow Jesus need this strength. You can help me understand what we are to do, who we are to be."

With squinting eyes, doubt appeared on Joseph's face. He turned to Gaius who frowned.

"Men," she continued. "are you flesh and blood? Do you breathe and sometimes laugh or even fear?"

Gaius demanded, "Of course, all of us here are the same, except for being men or women. All were born and all will die. Are you any different? Do you claim to be an angel?"

Several in the crowd laughed, but Mary didn't lose eye contact with Gaius. "And Gaius, when Paul was here and when you read his letters, was he here as a man and did he speak as a man?"

"Of course, what else!" Joseph blurted out.

His nose twitched, and he shifted under his cloak.

"So brothers, his words came from him as a man?" she asked.

They didn't answer. The crowd waited.

"I'll ask you for more understanding, so I can learn. When Peter or James or any other disciple, apostle, or teacher speaks to guide us, are they also speaking as men? Are they voicing the authority and wisdom of men?"

"Yes," Joseph said firmly. "They are men with authority. They know truth!"

"Ah, truth! This is good, brothers! Now I'm learning. And, this truth comes from where? From the law? From other men?"

Joseph was about to speak again, but Gaius grabbed his shoulder.

Looking at Mary from an angle, Gaius asked, "What do you say, woman?"

She clasped her hands and turned to the crowd. Those near her backed away. Mary quietly paced in an arc, creating an open space that grew larger with each step.

"What say you?" Gaius demanded.

"Through all the years I was with Jesus, when the twelve and other disciples were with Jesus, we heard His words as those of a man. We hoped He was something else, a prophet or a teacher, but we didn't know until near the end that He spoke from the Spirit of God. We often couldn't understand, but He made us think in terms of how God wanted us to be and never how men wanted us to be."

"God gave the law to men to make us righteous!" Joseph called out and pointed at Mary for emphasis.

"Ah, yes, the law and righteousness. May I tell you a story? One night as we sat on a hillside with Jesus, one of the disciples, it might have been Andrew, asked the Lord whether they would become righteous in following Him. As Jesus always did, He asked questions in return. He asked if a baby was fully righteous or fully sinful and when could the baby become righteous? Then, He asked if someone from far away who was good and gentle and generous but didn't know the law, if they could be righteous. Then before anyone could answer, He asked if the leading Pharisees of the Sanhedrin, with their power and wisdom of the law, were more righteous than all others."

Mary continued her stroll. Questions were whispered among the people. She stopped when she came close to Joseph and Gaius. "Brothers, was Paul righteous? And, more directly, did Paul speak to us with his mouth and through his letters as a man, as a person of flesh? Or, were his words those of the Spirit?"

A man in the thick of the crowd called out, "He spoke the words of God!"

"Amen," another said, and then a woman, and then Priscilla, and soon it rippled around them.

Mary raised her arms high. "Brothers and sisters, if Paul wrote a final letter, just for you, with words he said came directly from heaven, would you want to hear those words? Would you treasure them in your hearts, the word of God?"

The crowd erupted, "Yes."

"Read the letter!"

"Say the words!"

"Or," shouted Mary, "do you want to hear from these men, or any other men who are gathered here? Do you want the words of men?"

"No!" they demanded. "Read the letter from Paul!"

Priscilla and Thecla linked arms. As Mary walked back to the porch where her sisters stood, Gaius leaned toward Joseph. "Let them have this moment. When that woman is gone, we will take over."

Rome, Italy
The Vatican

III / 7

The priest knew it was time to take the next steps. The quiet power and immediacy of a mobile phone connection is a useful means to quietly execute one's will in the world. He placed the call.

"Good evening, my friend. How are things in Istanbul?"

"Ah, there's intense discontent here. Baba, sorry I mean Father. The people want and want and want. Why can't they just live and do what's right? My friend, the times of traditional ways are escaping us. The world is overflowing with nations at war and refugees. What is new in the holy city of Peter?"

"People remain obsessed with self-interest. We must take decisive action. We might be the last defenders of the true apostles. As leaders in governments are taking control from the rabble, it is time for us to stand up for the patriarchs. Two thousand years of patient dialogue has been a disaster for the true way."

"Baba, I think it will be easier than we expected. There's so much violence in the world, the deaths of a priest or a scholar here or there are not noticed. The media ask a few questions for one day, and then they chase the next story."

The priest paced across his office and paused to observe an emergency vehicle drive by on the street below his window.

"Agreed. So, the beginning is now with us. We must move quickly and with full strength. The Greek and the other two were good tests. Their sniveling, intellectual abstractions about the will of God are now empty of life. At the same time, any ancient writings supporting them must be found."

"I agree and must admit Professor Erkan did remarkable research about Paul. The Institute in Izmir gathered an impressive collection of documents and studies because of him."

"But it's fantasy! Yes, you respect a fellow scholar, but he engaged in dangerous, meandering mental games! He distracted believers from the correct doctrine."

"Of course, of course. You know me, Father. I respect the ways of a skilled researcher even though his beliefs are mistaken."

"My friend, it's time to launch the next plan. As soon as the exhibition of the Lord's letters is underway, key people must be removed. Is my back secure?"

"Yes, and Sister Katherine keeps watch. I have Stavros and Ahmed ready if needed."

"And in Turkey? Will things be cleaned up after Najat's work?"

"All is well on that. The Turk takes care of business."

"Good, now we must make plans. We here in Rome are ready."

"Father, we must begin with the leaders of the great deception. This Michael, we must find him, his partners, and those he reports to. His agenda is unclear, so it must be clarified. We can ignore the hypocrites among us for now. The first to go are those in the Fellowship and their associates. I'm hungry for action."

"Here in Italy, there are a few inconsequential obstructions. We've been unable to track down Michael for now. The woman Haran is the best resource. We will give her a little space for the exhibition. Once it's underway, I have someone who will see what they can get from her."

"We'll stay focused on finding the documents, here in Turkey. For you to find the woman Haran, maybe Michael will appear if she's in trouble again. I know where she is, and we have someone on the way there now."

"Good. Maybe we get two in one. Turk, we don't have to make a mess this time."

"I'll remove any outsiders that come near, but we'll keep it clean."

"The media and ROS will be easy to deal with. Politics is the best tool for that. We're well connected. Of course, who can deny a request from the Vatican?"

The men laughed and wished each other well. It felt good to be on the right side of life.

PART FOUR

Island of Ischia, Italy

IV / 1

Rennie jerked aside the drapes to see a new day. The morning sun glistened off the Mediterranean beyond the roof tops. Television antennae and lines of laundry covered the hardscape two floors above the city streets. She scanned the scene for direction. The layout of the town wasn't obvious.

The baritone blast of a ship's horn demanded her attention and refreshed her determination. Rennie glared in frustration at her phone. She couldn't activate it to get a map or the authorities might be tipped off on her location. What if they were on the way? She needed to do something and now.

Wearing her "going to Rome clothes," she reviewed her belongings to make sure she was ready to go. She slipped the backpack over one shoulder and wondered what information she could glean from the old man downstairs. He and Mike seemed close. He might reveal something to this poor, lost American girl before Mike came for her. Confident satisfaction filled her. She leaned her head against the door and released the lock.

Each step down the stairs went with quiet, elegant authority. Only mystery and risk lay ahead, but the morning light and fresh air waving the white curtains in an open window gave innocence to the scene.

The old man was surprised seeing her standing in the entry as he came from the kitchen with a plate of cheese and meat.

"Welcome, Miss Haran. Please have a seat."

He slid a chair away from the table.

Rennie was delighted with the invitation in clear English.

"Thanks, will you join me?" she replied.

There was hope! She surveyed what she could see of the house and the old man as she sat at the table.

His tattered, black suit coat and pants appeared to be the same ones he was wearing the night before. He sat across from her and moved a few thin slices of food onto a small plate for himself. He poured hot coffee into two cups and slid a plate to her then picked up an old dinner knife and began to cut up the meat and cheese.

"I hope you were comfortable. I wasn't expecting a guest and rarely have one." He looked up. She thought he had nice old eyes. "But you are welcome to be here. Please, eat. Oh, I forgot the fruit. I'll get it."

She was surprised with how well he spoke English. He sounded American but without a regional twist. She took her coffee cup and smelled the brew. As she sipped to test it, he returned.

"My name is Raphael, and no, I'm not the artist," he chuckled. "He's a little older and quite dead. Please have some food."

He settled into a chair with a grunt.

"I'm sorry, do you want water or juice? I forget Americans have those for this meal. By the way, Michael left this phone charger for you. He thought you might need it. There's an outlet over there."

Realizing she had left her charger on the ship, she was excited to reconnect to her phone—even if she wasn't supposed to switch it on. Without a thank-you she jerked the phone from her pocket, took the cord and plugged it in the wall. Hope and trust renewed her.

"Raphael, are you an American? Your English is excellent."

"I once was and grew up there until I was eleven. Then, my father moved the family here from the States. He and my mother were from southern Italy. After the war, they decided to return to their roots. He had served on US warships as an engine mechanic, so they moved to this little seaport. He started a business working on ship engines, so here I am."

He poured more coffee into his cup.

Rennie listened for clues as she ate.

"Who is Michael, and what's he to you?"

He nodded and took more sliced meat. "Yes, Michael. He gets around. Always ready for action."

Raphael set his fork down and leaned back. "Michael has a unique awareness of God's call to Him. People can agree or disagree of the merits of his understanding. Do you understand your call?"

"I have my moments. I guess many do. I don't feel alone."

"Would you be alone without God?"

"Well, I have friends and family, but that's different. I'm not sure I understand what you're asking me."

"It's common for people to see themselves as individuals. There's this person and that, this thing and that. There are animals and plants, the sea, the air, outer space. You have friends and a world full of people who aren't your friends, even enemies."

"So, do you consider that truth or reality?"

A smile revealed yellow teeth from under his heavy, grey mustache.

"What if God sees all those things as one thing? We might call it 'creation.'"

Rennie felt growing tension in her shoulders. She didn't need an exploration of theology right now. She needed to get to Rome.

"Miss Haran, I know you think you have more urgent issues to pursue. As you run down what you think is your path to your goal, be aware of the treasures you pass by. Those treasures might be why you're on this path. The opportunity to enjoy each moment and do special things must be recognized and seized.

Would you like something more?" he pointed to her now empty plate.

She studied him.

"I recently met a nun who said something similar," Rennie said. "But for the moment, another saying comes to mind; when you're up to your butt in alligators, it's hard to make plans to drain the swamp. The alligator facing me right now is the death of this priest and what's happened since. Raphael, do you know about him?"

"Ah yes, I heard about Father Anastasios. He was a brilliant and gentle man."

"Michael said something about a conflict in the Church involving women and letters. Were these more letters from Jesus, like the ones I found? Is that what everyone is after?"

"Not at all, but these might be as important. If found, they could change Christian doctrine that's been around since 325 CE. The idea of what might be in this correspondence threatens many people, especially institutions."

Rennie's mind raced through what she knew of Church history.

"I'm sure this is interesting to theologians, but is this why the priest was killed? Who could do that, and why did he have my name in his journal? Where was he killed? Those are good starting points to clear this up."

Rennie realized she had stood up and sat down again.

The old man seemed pleased.

"This boldness might be why you've become involved. Let me clear this away."

He picked up the plates and started toward the kitchen. Rennie grabbed the utensils and cups and followed.

"Who could do something like this? It was so ugly."

He rinsed the cups and placed them on a mat. "Our modern views of life have no depth and are purely self-serving. We've nearly lost awareness of the deeper forces in reality and the intertwined connections of nature and spirit. The darker human instincts will always compete with the universe."

Rennie grew more annoyed.

"Where was he killed? The police lieutenant said the priest was lashed to a door from a hotel. It was in a place called Ventotene, or something like that."

"Ah, Ventotene, of course. Long ago it was known as Pandateria, another small island not far from here. There's a lot of history there. It's not well known."

"Like what?"

"In the early days of the Roman Empire, family members of some Roman emperors were exiled on the island when they adopted forbidden religions such as Judaism and Christianity. All those exiled were women. Some say a ship carrying the apostle Paul stopped there while on the way to Rome."

Rennie was out of breath with tension.

"I'm sorry for all the questions Raphael, but Michael implied that the Roman Catholic Church might be involved with this deadly dispute."

"Like any big institution, they've got their own extremists. An organization is just policies and procedures. Like all centralized religions, there's nothing evil about it. They become machines that feed on the energy of their believers. Those machines become the masters and the believers the slaves. It's the plot line of many science fiction movies, but people don't see it happening around them in real life. Along the way, groups form that have their own agendas to run the machines. Most believers don't see what's going on, many have other priorities, and the rest choose to not get in the way or they feel they can't do anything. So, the groups do their own thing."

"But isn't that wrong? Isn't the Church supposed to have higher standards?"

"Rennie, the people of your country claim to have what you call 'higher standards.' But you have capital punishment when all other advanced nations have ended it. Your so-called 'Bible Belt' region has the lowest living standards in your nation. And your federal government ignored all the immoral behavior causing your country's economic collapse. Do you think those abuses of consumers have ended? At whom do you wish to point fingers?"

He went to an old cupboard door and removed what appeared to be a small flashlight from a shelf.

Placing it in her hand he said, "Miss Haran, until your journey has ended, keep this close at hand. If you are threatened by someone, point it at them and press the button. It will stop them. Never point it at yourself or even at a mirror."

Rennie rolled it in the palm of her hand. It did look like a small flashlight. Eager to get more information, she hurried after him into the dining room, and slipped the device in her jacket pocket.

"Raphael, do you think Michael would take me to Pandateria? I might find something there to solve these mysteries. I don't have any spare time because I need to get to Rome for the exhibition. But, if it was on the way—"

He spun around. Alarm spread across his face.

"Are you all right?" she asked.

He put his fingers to his mouth. "Don't speak. Follow me. Be fast."

He waved her to follow.

As they passed by her backpack and phone, he said, "Take these, now."

Rennie followed orders for a few quick paces until they stopped at an armoire-like bookcase against the wall. He slid his fingers along the back edge and tugged. It was hinged on one side and opened to reveal a dark opening in the wall.

"Go in here. Wait until they're gone."

"Until who's gone? I'm not going in there."

A shock ran through her body when the front door thudded with pounding from the outside.

"Hurry inside, please," Raphael urged. "Stay quiet. Don't open this."

He gave a gentle push to her arm.

Rennie backed into the darkness, resting the palms of her hands on the wood panel as it closed. She eased herself back and came against a wall. Rennie reached into her pocket for the device he gave her and then remembered it wasn't a flashlight. She heard Raphael greet a visitor followed by loud responses in Italian from angry men. The plaster above her head thundered as a man ran up the stairway. More yelling ensued.

She pressed her ear to the panel wanting to open it to see if Raphael was all right. His voice changed from indifferent to pleading.

The sound of a gunshot slammed through every molecule in the house.

Rennie jumped back against the inner wall in horror.

She had to help. Bursting out of her hiding place, she saw a man standing over Raphael sprawled on the floor. The man looked over his shoulder at her with a cold stare. She was riveted in position as he turned toward her, a silver pistol at the end of his relaxed arm.

Rennie felt the small button on the side of the "flashlight." Feeling helpless, she pointed it at the man and squeezed. His body flew through a doorway and across a dark sitting room into a wall. He crumpled to the floor.

Another man ran down the stairs into the entry and appeared confused. He saw his partner in the other room and Raphael on the floor, but he didn't realize Rennie was behind him. He turned and discovered her the moment before he was crushed into a corner of the entry by another silent, invisible blast from the device.

What is this thing?

Rennie's heart pounded in her forehead. Her eyes dropped to see the little piece of metal in her hand, mystified with what happened. She turned to the door needing to escape but her heart called her to go to Raphael.

Kneeling next to him she pleaded, "Raphael, wake up. Please wake up."

The color of his skin became as gray as his beard.

"Raphael, please. Don't die!"

The man in the other room moaned. Rennie glanced to see his limbs stutter in small fits.

Raphael whispered, "Go, you are needed."

She touched his cheek. "God is with you. I'll get help."

She slowly arose, flipped the backpack over her shoulder, and turned to the entry door. Rennie looked back to see a corner of his mouth curl into a smile. She hurried out the door, surveyed the scene, and dashed across the street between slow moving cars in the morning traffic. She stared at the ground to avoid eye contact. At the corner of a building, Rennie darted down another street against the traffic. She paused at a shop that was opening for the day. An old man opened a lock on an iron gate and swung it open. She stood a few steps behind him, and as he opened the door, she followed him in.

Her body was jolted by the yell of a man outside. He hung out a car window and shouted again at another driver. The old man turned toward the street scene but stopped when he saw Rennie.

"*Buon giorno. Che cosa volete?*"

"Oh, hi. Do you speak English? I'm a tourist."

"*Sei un turista?* A tourist? Okay. What you want?" the store-keeper repeated himself as his weathered face opened into a wide smile. "You like chocolate? We have cold pop!"

Rennie's head bobbed *"yes."* She glanced down the street and hurried inside to the back of the store. As she moved down the aisles her hands worked through her coat to find her wallet. A shiver froze her flesh when the hard, slick surface of the "flashlight" slid on her fingers. Raphael. Should she go back? She looked over the shelving to see out the window.

Was she followed?

The storekeeper's activity drifted into stocking items behind a counter overflowing with goods. Rennie approached him, unsure of what she should do.

"Pardon me, *scusi*. Where do I get a ferry boat?"

"Ferry boat, *si*. No problem."

He squinted and rocked his head side to side. The words must have been missing.

"Here, come."

He escorted her out the door and pointed down the street.

"There, you go two roads." His hands and arms punctuated the directions. "This way, two roads. One more that way then this."

He seemed quite satisfied and returned inside.

Rennie backed against the stucco wall of the store. She had no idea where she was and felt exposed. In an instant, her phone was on and the map feature beckoned her. Her hands shook.

From inside, she heard the storekeeper, *"Buon giorno, Stefano! Come stai?"*

Rennie spun around.

A man in the store was gleefully speaking to the old man. They looked out the window at Rennie. The man gestured for her to come inside and offered a friendly grin. He greeted her at the door.

"Hello, miss, I am Luca. My dear old friend Stefano says you wish to go to ferry boats. Is this right? I can take you, only a few minutes here to there."

His heavy eyebrows framed large, dark eyes that glistened. A wide mouth full of white teeth completed the presentation of an irresistible young man.

"Well, I don't know. It's a nice day, and I can walk."

"Please, a beautiful woman on these streets alone is not good. You have another here with you? We take them, too."

"No, thank you. Do you know when they go? The ferries?"

"*Si*, yes, not often, but soon. You must hurry. Come, my car is right there."

The old man nodded in agreement.

It was morning, the streets were coming alive. It seemed safer than being alone on the sidewalk where she was easily seen. Maybe this was the adventure she had hoped for.

"Please," he pleaded, "it's easy for us, an honor for me. I am Luca. You are?"

She tried to suppress a laugh.

"I'm uh, you can call me Susan. Pleased to meet you, Luca."

"*Bravo!*"

Luca shook Stefano's hand with energy, turned to Rennie, and gestured to the street.

"This way, the black one."

IV / 2

The sour expression on Joseph's face was enough to poison the air. He spat German curses with disdain. Hiding behind multiple mobile phones instead of talking face-to-face was cowardly and wrong for real warriors.

"What have you told the others in Turkey? You don't seem to be committed to our cause. These are easy things to do. Our church fathers gave themselves to lions and did all that was needed for our faith and for our Holy God. So, are you with God or with the pretenders?"

"I'm committed. I'll give everything, as you will. These missions are confusing with so many priests telling us what to do. Sometimes, there are conflicting messages. We do our best."

"That's expected. Let me know when it's finished. There should be no hesitation. When do you arrive in Izmir?"

"Tonight. I'll leave within twenty-four hours. He's staying at the Swiss Hotel in Konak, so I'll be on the ferry away from there long before anyone takes notice."

"What's your plan from there?"

"I go to Bostanli and at last, Istanbul. I'll report when I get there."

"Does Najat know what to do?"

"He's prepared. He'll encounter the professor in the evening as he goes through the park. A blow to the head will stun him, and the crucifix in his jugular will drain him of life. It won't take a minute."

"Don't call me when it's done. Get rid of your phone properly."

"I will. What will happen to Najat? Have arrangements been made for him?"

"Of course, we leave no debris."

Joseph hung up and slid his phone across the desk as if it offended him. *Fear makes people weak*, he thought. *This will get them buzzing.*

He felt empowered and needed to share his energy with Sister Katherine. His call to her resulted in no more than leaving a voice-mail message, but it was enough.

Jumping from his chair, he tugged on each cuff of his suit jacket and marched from his office. He waved, almost saluted, to other Vatican workers as they passed in the hallways. He wasn't sure where he was going but he needed action. The idea of eliminating another enemy of the patriarchs was the best adrenalin rush he could have. It didn't bother him that he could only know a few of the many who were involved. They had the same goals and seemed well coordinated by someone.

Joseph made a quick turn at the intersection of two hallways. He realized another priest had matched his pace and was at his side. Joseph turned into a large inset doorway and stopped.

"Father Joseph," the other priest began. "May we share a minute, in private?"

Joseph was startled. "Yes, of course, there's a small library across the hall."

Once inside and alone, Joseph was rigid as the priest eased into a chair across from him at a worktable. He thought he knew most of the local staff, but this young priest was unfamiliar. Dark hair with a styled cut, alert eyes among angled features, and probably interested in forbidden fruit. Joseph figured this kid thinks he's smart.

"Please," the man said, "have a seat. Here's my card."

He waited as Joseph slid out the chair and sat away from the table.

"I'm Father Daniel. I'm secretary for the cardinal of the Congregation of the Oriental Churches. As you can imagine, our office has been quite busy after the death of the priest from the Greek Church. Our congregation has obligations to develop positive relations with the Orthodox churches. Now, the Italian authorities are in touch with us and we're trying to obtain all the information available. We don't want surprises, so we'd appreciate any assistance you and your office could offer."

"Yes, this news has been around, but I know nothing but gossip."

"And what does that gossip say?"

"Well, he drowned and was washed ashore."

"You work closely with Abbess Serena. Is that right? She assists His Eminence, the secretary of state I believe."

"I am at the service of the abbess and His Eminence. That's correct."

"There's no additional information they have shared with you?"

"If they have more knowledge of this, it has not come to my attention. I'm sorry."

Joseph's face felt warm and tight. Small beads of sweat teased at his hairline. He hoped it was not visible. His breathing felt shallow.

Neither man said a word for a few moments.

"Father Joseph, I appreciate this brief visit. I hope I've not delayed you from an important meeting. Of course, this is quite important to the church and confidential."

"Yes, I'm sure. May I leave now?"

"Of course, this was a friendly visit. If you or the abbess need to reach me, just ask for Father Daniel at our main number."

"I will. Are you American?"

"Yes, and I believe Abbess Serena is as well? And yourself?"

"I've always thought of myself as Roman Catholic."

They looked at each other for too many awkward seconds.

Joseph stood and turned to leave but Father Daniel interrupted him.

"Oh, Father Joseph, one more thing. An odd question has come up. I don't understand it."

Joseph's heavy head and dark eyes turned to the young priest.

"What?" he growled.

"As I said, this issue is perplexing, but I must ask."

He tilted his head and presented a puzzled look. "The question is who might have access to a crosier? I understand that the abbess has one in her office, and she uses it for certain ceremonial occasions. Is that correct?"

"I've seen it."

"So, in your role, might you be responsible for this and other belongings of her official office?"

"Responsible is a strong word. I help with her arrangements for official duties."

"Is the crosier in her office now? Do you know when you last saw it?"

Joseph's eyes raced along the walls of books. He struggled with a comfortable response.

"I ... I don't, well, I've not paid attention to that. Why do you ask?"

"It's a foolish question. I'm sorry to bother you with it. Things get said. It's something we need to look into. Oh, one other thing. Has the *Carabinieri*, or ROS, or other Italian investigators been in contact with you?"

"No, not with me."

Joseph stopped breathing as he stared at the young priest.

"Well, if you hear anything that might be helpful, please let me know."

Joseph left the room without attempting a civil departure.

The wooden heels on Joseph's shoes tapped across the hall and clattered down a marble stairway as he escaped the encounter. The lower level was quiet. He paused to let his thoughts settle down. They raced faster.

"Joseph, are you okay? You seem to be shaken."

Abbess Serena stood in front of an elevator a few feet to his left. Joseph knew he couldn't erase the shock on his face.

"Oh, I'm sorry, Abbess, I didn't see you. I'm a bit surprised."

He wondered if he should tell her of the meeting with Father Daniel.

She stepped closer. "What's up Joseph? Something is heavy on your heart. I will listen if you wish to share it."

"No. I mean, it's not about me. I'm concerned about so much and cannot help. Do you have need of me? There are preparations for the exhibit of the letters of our Lord, and I thought I could help in some way."

She studied him. "Something new has happened, Joseph."

He waited.

"A Muslim cleric, an authority on ancient religions, was murdered in Lebanon."

He felt like hurrying away. "That area has so much violence. It's very sad."

"Yes, Joseph, but this doesn't appear to be part of the civil war. He was hung by his hands, his pants were removed, and the killer slashed the arteries in his groin. He died quickly of blood loss."

Joseph noticed her expression was blank, expectant. He felt pressured.

"War generates ugliness. All standards disappear."

"Yes, quite true. You hadn't heard this?"

"Not at all, sister, I'm shocked. Why is this important to us?"

"We don't know if it is. First there was the Greek priest here in Italy, and now we hear of this Muslim cleric in Lebanon. We hope they're not connected. The authorities and media will be snapping at us more than ever."

"About the exhibition sister, is there anything that I can do?"

"Thank you, there is. We need that American woman here immediately. Have you heard anything of her? Any news from Father Angelotti? I need you to speak to him now and get the latest information. Tell him we expect her tonight, without exception. And, Father, she had better be in good health. Understand?"

"Of course, that's our wish."

"One other thing, if there's another death of any servant of God anywhere, this beautiful place will change into something ugly no one has seen before. The church is recovering from much harm committed to it from the inside. Any new problems will have glaring lights on all aspects of the church and open any sewers that might be there."

"Yes, Abbess, we don't want that. This is all too complicated for me. I need your leadership."

A faint smile appeared in the parchment that was her face. "Very well, Joseph."

The elevator doors opened. When they closed, she was gone.

He was disgusted with her use of English, a language from self-obsessed cultures. He needed the guidance of Sister Katherine. He couldn't deal with this anymore.

Returning to his office, Joseph snapped in rough Italian at the bountiful woman doing nothing.

"Find Father Angelotti. He's the secretary for the Propagation of the Faith. I must speak with him immediately."

He marched to his desk and slipped his suit jacket over the chair. His thoughts raced. *Can he or should he reverse the plans in Izmir?*

His cell phone buzzed. It was Sister Katherine.

In his native German, he whispered, "*Schwester*, we have a problem. I need to find a replacement crosier for the abbess."

The Island of Ischia

IV / 3

Rennie relaxed into the car seat as her attention riveted to the sights and sounds of the city. Her new friend Luca eased his car through traffic and spoke of his family and the town with a fresh, joyful spirit. Somehow, she entered a new day. The car was a world far from the dangers of the last day or this morning. A few blocks away, she could see the harbor. Hope lay ahead.

"Luca, you turned down this street, but the harbor is straight ahead."

"*Si*, this is quicker. Up there all the traffic comes together and then we're stopped. This way is—what you call?—shortcut. Quick to the ferry ticket offices and good parking for you. I have some time and am happy to help you get the right tickets. Not many speak good English."

Happiness flashed large on his face.

"You don't have to go in with me. I'll be okay."

"Okay, but sometimes not too clear."

He remained cheerful enough and the ride was not much further. And, despite the talk about his wife and kids, she couldn't help but find him attractive.

"Okay, Miss Susan, around this corner and you will see the building. This is the back of the place, a secret entrance just for you. Inside, we go to the front and you are there, first in line!"

Old warehouses lined the street. Crumbling docks on the shore didn't suggest a functioning seaport. There didn't appear to be a front of the building that could have a street available to it. Luca stopped at a rough door that had no official appearance.

"Luca, this doesn't look like the place. There must be a mistake. This building can't be it."

"I know, it's old. For this area, it serves the purpose. Come, I'll help you to the office."

He jumped out his door and ran to hers, flipping it open with a swooping gesture to the building.

"Luca, I think you should go first to see if it's open. I'll wait here."

Her breathing became shallow and quick. Her mouth was dry.

"Okay, I do that."

He hurried to the warehouse door and jerked at the handle. He tried again. He hammered at the door with the side of his fist. More banging with force brought an old man who peered outside. They exchanged a few words, the man shrugged his shoulders, and opened the door wider.

Rennie turned on her cell phone again and returned it to her coat. It might alert authorities of her presence and location, but it was her only safeguard. Her senses sharpened and the muscles through her neck and shoulders stiffened.

Luca returned more exuberant than ever. "It's good. You can come in now."

Rennie closed her door and rolled the window down. "I'm sorry, I'm not comfortable with this. Can you drive me around to the front where the main entrance is?"

"Sure, sure, but it's too busy there. Here, let me have the boss come out. He will give you confidence. We are okay."

Luca ran to the entrance before she could respond. He jerked it open and entered the darkness.

As a minute ground past her, Rennie noticed the keys were not in the ignition. She looked down the street and saw nothing civilized. A couple of beat-up delivery trucks went by. *This is bad.*

Rennie rolled up her window and found the "flashlight" in

her pants pocket. It might be needed.

The old man who first opened the door came out and waved to her. He didn't appear to be a businessman much less an official of any kind. As he walked to the car, Rennie could see him slide money into his pocket.

"Welcome, welcome. Tickets inside. I show you. Luca will help. Come now."

His teeth were covered with brown stains.

"Does the ferry go to Ventotene? Can you sell tickets for that?"

"Ventotene? I think of that. Wait please."

He straightened from his bent position and gazed into the clouds. "Yes, Ventotene. A good trip for you."

"Can you sell me the tickets and I will wait here? I appreciate your help." Rennie fluttered her eyelids.

He frowned. "I will check and come back. Maybe I have the tickets."

The man returned into the darkness with Luca and came back almost immediately.

"First, I need your passport, and you must sign some papers." His face and voice became cold. "I'm busy." He tossed a dismissive hand into the air.

Holding the device in her hand, Rennie opened the car door and stood tall over the old man. She felt ready for action.

"Let's go and get this done."

Lights went on in the hallway as they entered, and Luca came around a corner.

"Wonderful, *grazie,* Vincenzo."

The old man continued down the hallway as Luca ushered Rennie into what looked like a storage room.

"There that door is where we go to the ticket office. This is the shortcut."

Rennie's heart pounded as she struggled for breath. She

wanted to run to the door. With her first quick step away from Luca, she was stunned in her right temple and stumbled sideways. She grasped her head, unable to hear or see. Another blow hit her in the back. She crashed to the floor, with the "flashlight" device spurting from her hand and sliding to the wall. The point of a shoe hit her in the gut and her mind went blank. The out of focus ceiling and light fixtures drifted over her. In a dim recess of consciousness, she felt her powerless body dragged across the rough floor. A doorway and a dark room engulfed her.

"Now, my baby, we have some fun. You will like me very much."

Luca's blurry face appeared over hers.

Rennie felt hands fumbling at her belt and the waist of her pants. His knee jammed between her knees. Her body jerked around as he pulled at her clothing. He growled in anger.

"Come on, baby. Make it easy for old Luca."

A pounding rhythm of steps bounced through rough wood floors followed by an explosive sound and a moan. The heavy odor of Luca no longer covered her face. She tried to roll to her side and found she was free. More grunts and thuds landed across the room.

In a glance, Rennie could see a man lift and slam Luca onto the floor. Luca's distorted face was covered in glossy red. Rennie rolled further onto her belly and she saw the shoes of two men enter the room and go to the corner where Luca lay.

Above her she heard, "Rennie, can you breathe?"

It was Michael's voice.

"Yes, help me."

"I'm taking you to safety now."

Rennie's body floated up, her head falling onto Michael's shoulder. A moment later, the sun and fresh air hit her face as he carried her out of the warehouse into the side door of an awaiting van. He laid her onto a firm floor buffered with thick cloth. Doors slammed shut and the motor roared into action.

Michael knelt beside her. "You're safe now. Can you drink some water?"

Rennie nodded. "I need water."

She drank as he tilted her head up, the water pouring over her cheeks into her nose. She coughed hard and sneezed.

Michael helped her sit up. "How are you doing? Can you hear? Where do you hurt?"

"I don't know. I ache all over. My head hurts. I'm dizzy."

She opened her eyes. "Michael, how did you find me?"

"We went to Raphael's place and saw what happened. The authorities were there so we couldn't stay. We've been searching for you. It's a small town and you stand out. We can talk later. What do you need?"

"Take me away. Get me out of here."

Her eyes fell shut and her body eased onto the floor.

"Michael, is Raphael okay? Who shot him? why?"

"We're not sure. First, let's go to a safe place and get you well. We'll talk then."

A deep ache pounded in her temple and back. She slid and bounced with every move of the truck. Rennie felt Michael's hand cover her eyes. The darkness and the touch brought calm as her mind slipped into the hazy confusion of her ordeal.

Rennie felt something, or a lack of something. It was the truck. All was quiet and they weren't moving. Her body ached, even her eyes. She sat up and sucked in a breath.

"What?" Michael said as he spun to see her. "What? Are you okay?"

"I don't know. Where are we?"

"We're at a small house in the countryside, a safe distance from town. We'll go inside, refresh ourselves and get ready to move on."

The men in front climbed out of the van, slammed their doors then opened the side door. They helped Rennie as Michael led the way, looking cautiously from one horizon to the other. Inside, they found simple furnishings, a pitcher of water, and fruit on the table. Rennie stumbled for a moment on her own and paused, holding her head. She gave it a shake, blinked, and went straight to food. She poured a glass of water and snatched an apple. A small refrigerator revealed sliced cheese and meat covered with plastic. She ate quickly.

Michael came inside. "This was a good find. When you feel better, we can meet in the living room. I'll fill you in."

"Let's do it. I've become pretty good at meeting men in dark rooms."

"I'm glad you haven't lost your humor. Rennie, that was an awful situation. Bring the food with you."

She fell into an overstuffed chair and set her plate on a stool with the water pitcher on another.

"Okay, I'm all set. Shoot."

Michael stood nearby. "Rennie, what were you doing in the warehouse and with that guy?"

She looked away. "It was a mistake. I was dumb."

"Rennie, I need to know what was going on."

She ate more and drank water.

"Why were you there?"

Michael's voice was less supportive.

"He said I could get a ferry boat ticket to that island, Ventotene or whatever. He said it was easier to go in a back way to the ticket office."

"Okay, keep going. And, you were going there for what reason?"

She glared at him. "Look, Michael, my celebration trip to Rome has been hijacked. I've been jerked around by cops and nearly raped by that bastard because something happened on that island, and I plan to find out what. That priest believed something valuable was on that island and he got killed looking for it. Isn't that the story? Some ancient Roman women were exiled there, and people suspect they left behind documents or letters or something. Isn't that the story here?"

He sat down on an old wooden chair near her. "It's our understanding that Father Anastasios was there for a kind of spiritual retreat. The area has been studied and excavated for over a hundred years. There's nothing to find there."

Rennie sat upright and seemed to grow. "Michael, people don't get killed for going on spiritual retreats. The people who did that thought he was there to find something."

"We don't know why he was killed, but it wasn't because he found or was about to find treasured documents as you did. He's Greek Orthodox, and they place great value on the idea of experiencing the power of God through icons; you know, the bones of a saint or another relic conveying a holy presence. We believe he went to the island because of its religious history with those women you mentioned and the tradition of Paul visiting there. He probably thought that history could inspire him for new discoveries with his research."

She set her plate in her lap and noticed a bulge in her pants pocket. Resting her hand on it she realized it was the device. Her doubts about Michael reappeared. He must have put it there.

"I'm parking your explanation on hold for the moment until more facts are in on the priest and maybe who did it. What's next for us?"

He seemed energized. "Okay, here's the situation. We know one group knows you're here but I'm not sure who they are or what their intentions are. We can't be sure who else might be on the island or watching passages back to Italy. That leaves us only one option."

Rennie stuffed cheese wrapped in meat into her mouth. "So, you're going to have to kill me, huh?"

"What? Of course not."

"Good answer, so what's the plan?"

He shook his head. "The only way to get you back safely without being intercepted is for the Vatican to take you. It's the best option, and they can do whatever they want without interference by authorities. I've been in touch with Father Angelotti's people."

"His people? He has people?"

Except for Rennie's eating, all was quiet for a moment.

Michael glanced out the window. "Let's continue in an hour or so. They'll have a helicopter here then. That's one reason we needed a place in the country. It's large enough and far enough away that it won't attract attention. They'll take you to the Vatican. You'll stay there, and you and they can decide what's next."

"Hmm, I thought they were the bad guys."

"There are bad guys everywhere, even there. Most people just try to do their job and not get in the way."

"So did Luca. What happened to him, anyway?"

"He'll awaken later today in a park that townspeople like to stroll through. Poor Luca though will be naked and smell heavy with liquor. He'll be quite a sensation for years to come."

"Oh, that's good. Nice job. Maybe you have some style after all."

"Rennie, this is work and isn't fun. Let's talk again in an hour. Rest up."

As he left, Rennie put her feet on the chair he had used. Her mind and body ached for rest. Her breathing became soft and the world went away.

Bang!

The front door slammed against the wall as it opened.

Rennie's body stuttered awake as light and sounds flooded her senses.

Michael approached.

"Sorry, the wind caught the door. Were you sleeping?"

"Huh? I guess I dozed off. Where are we?"

"At the farmhouse. The helicopter should be here soon. A landing area has been prepared."

Rennie set aside the dish she discovered was remarkably still on her lap. Tumbling clouds filled her aching head.

Michael gathered some things nearby.

"Before you leave, let's talk. It's important that—"

"Wait, I need to know a few things. Michael, I liked Raphael. Is he dead and why? I asked questions of you before and didn't get answers. Why am I caught up in this?"

"As I said on the ship—"

"Speaking of the ship, you never finished your explanation of this deadly dispute that's going on in the church. Does it involve the letters by the women of the church or Paul or what?"

"In the little time we have, that's a good place to start. Put simply, the letters we have in the Bible from Paul speak of encounters with Jesus, or with spiritual beings of some kind."

Michael slid aside the dish on the table.

"Rennie, there's a tradition that there are more letters. These encounters led to a new understanding of the faith and created intense controversies. Supposedly, he gave this message to women in the early church as well as to the women of royal Roman blood on what was Pandateria Island, where the priest was killed. The specifics of the belief and what supposedly happened are missing from church teachings or commentaries."

"So, this power battle over some religious concept continues today. Did I happen to stumble into it?"

"It does continue, but I don't know if you somehow walked into the scene, or if there's a larger purpose for you in this. Maybe your proven skills in finding ancient biblical documents caught the eyes of some. What's important is that we get you to safety."

"Amen, brother! My trip was devoted to relaxation and fun, not more discoveries, so you can tell that to the bad guys. But what did Raphael have to do with this? Was he involved?"

"No, he's always known of it and had an interest as a peacemaker. It just caught up with him in a bad way."

Michael got up and went near the window.

"Rennie, the helicopter is approaching. When you're with Angelotti's people, or anyone else, don't speak of this. You're innocent of all that's going on. Let people know you want to return to your normal life after the exhibition. If you learn anything significant along the way, let me know. I'll be in touch later, okay?"

"Fine, with me," Rennie said as she rubbed her temples.

She could hear in the distance the thumping sound of helicopter blades pounding the air. It was almost here. Ugly memories of her trip to Naples, only yesterday, tore at her emotions.

IV / 4

A few reporters tapped away on keyboards in remote cubicles, but the newspaper offices were dark. Bud was still in the editor's office. He snatched his mobile phone from the desk and dialed a number.

"Hi, Angie, this is Bud. I got some good background from a guy in Italy. Do you have a moment? Sorry, it's awful late, nearly midnight I guess."

"Not a problem, I've also done some research that might help us."

"Yeah, good, well, this source in Rome says there's a lot of chatter going on about plays being made by people at the Vatican, but no one's sure who's in the game. And there have been killings in Lebanon and in Turkey possibly related to what Rennie fell into. It's not only the Holy See that's involved."

"Bud, what does this have to do with Rennie?"

"Nothing. She's probably collateral damage. The authorities over there seem to be dumb as rocks so they can't separate her from anyone actually in the game. With all the chaos about refugees and terrorists, they'll go after anyone and anything that's not mundane. My source says there is something big underlying all this to cause such a ripple in so many places. He said it's not the usual money, power or sex thing. There's a powerful presence no one sees. Speaking of rocks, do you remember that guy in London by the name of Galila? He's the one who came out of the shadows to try to get the letters."

"That's right! I talked with Matthew. He thought this is

linked together. Like you, he's perplexed with who's involved and on what side. He didn't mention that Galila, but it makes sense. He said no one knows of an institution like a religious or political movement that's been around for a couple thousand years in opposition to the church. But Matthew says he's heard there are secret groups within the church that have always fought for some reason. He's trying to get detailed info from scholars he knows. Bud, Matthew is extremely weak. I'm afraid for him."

"Yeah, I like the old man, too. Angie, it's clear there are competing players in the background and Rennie might be caught in the middle. I'll try to contact that guy Sfumato in San Francisco again and see if he has any ideas."

"Good, and get this, Matthew added there is an old story that there are these documents, if found and revealed, that could undermine the authority of Christian doctrine. The secret groups have been trying to get to them forever. Sfumato is a collector of that kind of stuff. He might know the players. We need to talk to him."

"Why are all these people who claim to be so close to God always killing each other? Have you heard from Rennie? I haven't."

"No, and it's been too long, Bud. I sent her another text and left a message on her phone. What do you recommend?"

"My guy said it's not likely Rennie will have problems with the religious folks, but maybe with law enforcement authorities. Of course, religious zealots don't care about facts. She needs to find safe people to be with. No matter where she is right now, it's not good. He also said he wants to meet her for an interview."

"If I can reach her, I'll let her know. Bud, should I go there?"

"As fast as things are changing, I don't know if you could find her. I hate to say it, but we both know that Rennie can be impetuous. I hope she stays focused on the best things to do. Angie, call me when you hear anything."

"I will Bud, and please stay in touch."

PART FIVE

Rome, Italy
Vatican City

V / 1

Thumping continued to pound through Rennie's head from the heavy beat of helicopter blades on the trip to Rome from Ischia. The Pope must have been using the better version of the aircraft that picked her up from the airport when she first arrived in Italy merely a day ago, as the one she was in had been totally stripped down. It was lucky she found the headphones for her phone to wear for some comfort. Touching down, the quiet of the black sedan offered welcome relief as it journeyed through the rain from the landing spot in Vatican City. But her thoughts focused on what and who might await her.

The car approached what looked like a palace. Looming tall behind it was the classic monument of the Vatican, St. Peter's Basilica.

I guess we're here, she thought.

No one came with an umbrella. There was no diplomatic welcome, only darkness and rain. The driver opened the door and motioned to the building. Fifty feet in the rain, alone. Halfway there she thought of her luggage, and then saw the car drive away.

The door to the building opened, and a priest emerged, inviting her in. He was old and sour. Stepping quickly inside, Rennie shivered and shook her hands and her head. She tried to fluff her hair with a few finger strokes. A young priest nearby was wide-eyed and breathless. When she realized he was there,

Rennie thrust her hand forward to shake his. Reluctantly, he grasped her fingers but quickly let go. The old priest glared disapproval.

She removed her soaked jacket and held it out, unsure of what to do. The young priest's mouth slid open and he continued to stare.

"This is pretty wet. Can I hang this up somewhere?" she asked.

The men didn't respond.

A nun with a gentle smile came through a doorway.

"Miss Haran. I'm here to show you to quarters. You'll be comfortable there. Your luggage is in the room. Let me take that for you."

"Great, thanks. And you are?"

"I'm Sister Angelina. Let me know of any needs you might have. This place isn't set up for overnight guests, but we've done our best until other arrangements can be made. This way please."

Rennie noticed that as the nun spoke, she glanced down at Rennie's blouse and pants.

"Miss Haran, this way please."

As Rennie followed the young woman in black, they passed a large, elegant mirror. Rennie slowed to look at her hair. As she did, she noticed her clothing. The rain had glued the thin, white blouse she wore to her chest and her bra hid less than was expected. Mischievous delight flowed through her. She glanced back at the yin-yang priests in the entrance. The young one looked happy.

Welcome to the real world, boys, she thought.

Halfway down the hallway, the nun marched up marble stairs. The steps were so wide one could almost make two paces on each. On the next floor they passed a few doors, and then entered an unlocked room. A quick survey suggested quiet luxury but not comfort. Ornate gold moldings, fabric wallpaper, and tapestries on the wall were accented with what seemed to be a dormitory-style single bed covered in a burgundy blanket, with a small table nearby holding a large bowl and two towels. At least her luggage was there. "Plain" was apparently a theme for the people but not the church. Her quizzical look at the nun prompted a response.

"This is usually a meeting room. The ladies' facility is out the door, to the left, at the end of the hall turn left, up the stairs, straight a few meters, and you'll see it."

"Well, Sister, I guess we need to plan ahead. Thanks for your help this evening. I'm sure my coming has been confusing for everyone."

"You're most welcome to be here. Could I ask, I mean, it's not my role here, but I have a question."

"Yes."

"I wondered if you touched them. Did you hold them?"

"Who are you talking about?"

"Not who, but the letters. Did you touch them? I've wondered what that must have been like."

"Yes, of course I did. Sister, you don't need to touch them to be touched by them. You'll see."

"Thank you, and please know that you are as safe here as any of the treasures. God bless you."

The nun hurried out and closed the door.

For a minute, Rennie collapsed into a chair and gazed at the textured beige surface of the ceiling. Moments later a sheet of paper slid under the door. Snatching it up, she found a hand-drawn map to the ladies' room and on the other side a schedule of events for the next day. "Meeting with Abbess Serena at 10:15 a.m."

The map to relief was a delight. She wondered if there were showers. First, dry clothes were needed. Rennie dove into her luggage as if she was starving and found a feast in a basket. The wet clothing landed in a pile as she tugged on a sweatshirt and jeans. This was living! This was home and felt safe!

A soft light warmed the long, empty hall. Rennie skipped for a few steps and threw her arms up. She giggled and pulled the folded agenda and map from her back pocket. After a brief review, she was up the stairs.

Two steps from the top, she heard a dull thud echo down the hall. Fear took away her breath. *What was that?* Rennie leaned against the wall and listened. Footsteps were coming in her direction. She needed to see around the corner.

Approaching her, and now just twenty feet away, was one of Father Angelotti's men. It was Busca, the quiet one. He saw her and slowed his pace.

Rennie pulled back around the corner to recover. She'd try to bluff her way as she had so often.

She almost jumped from the stairway.

"Hey, Mr. Busca, isn't it?"

He didn't slow down.

Peering through his eyelashes he said, *"Buona sera,"* and walked past.

As his steps were swallowed in the emptiness of the stairway and halls below, she wondered why he was in this building.

Wait a minute, she thought. *Was he connected to that heavy sound a moment ago, and what was that?*

It was odd, but she would stay centered and not let fears take over. It was time to be refreshed at her original destination, the women's bathroom.

Returning to the stairway, Rennie's memory saw Busca descend into the lower level. *Did he go to her room?* She had no key to lock it. She felt her pocket and realized Raphael's "flashlight" was not with her. Footsteps approached, clicking on the marble steps above her. The black-stocking legs and gown of a nun appeared and then the rest of her body. Another young, attractive woman was carrying a bundle of clothes.

"Miss Haran? Hi, I'm Sister Serena."

Her voice was clear and sounded American.

"Yes, I'm Rennie Haran. Sister Serena, I guess I've become a bit lost. Could you guide me to my room?"

A warm glow lit Serena's face.

"Of course, and I wasn't sure what you had for clothing, so I brought a few things. I'm sorry I had to guess at sizes. If you need anything else, let me know."

A gray fog centered in Rennie's thoughts. She tried to grasp the name *Serena*.

"Oh, are you Abbess Serena who I'm meeting with tomorrow?"

"Yes," the nun chirped. "Thank you for remembering my name. Will that time be good for you? We had to set a schedule. There's so much to do in our preparations for this miraculous exhibition. You must be quite excited."

"Well, considering all that I've dealt with, excited doesn't cover it. Did Father Angelotti tell you about it?"

"I've heard some dreadful things. This has all been a great shock to us, but we're overjoyed you are now with us. Let's discuss more about that tomorrow. For tonight, you must rest. I'll walk you to your room."

Rennie took the bundle and started down the stairs.

"Sister, your accent? You're American?"

"Yes, Illinois. Corn-fed, as they say."

They shared a laugh. Rennie reflected on her background in Iowa and felt for a moment as if she was at home with a friend.

"You know, it's funny how I ended up with all these religion issues dropped in my lap. When I was in college, I considered going to seminary. I wasn't that spiritual, but I had questions about Christianity and God. Our family was not what you might call 'on fire' with faith; just quiet Protestants. My dad is a professor of religious studies at Iowa State, and I think his intellectual approach influenced my questioning attitude, but it also made me decide against seminary. My mom is very accomplishment driven, so she was on committees and led a lot of activities. Her prompting for me to be involved may have made me avoid participating. Now, here I am, personally invited to the Vatican. Crazy, huh? Did you always want to be a nun?"

"Not really. My dad was a small-town lawyer and my mother was a social worker." Serena snickered. "I guess that's why I became a lawyer who tried to solve people's problems. We weren't too involved in the church, but over time I came to see it as a place where people brought their problems. I offered free legal services to the diocese now and then, mostly on issues of diplomacy and negotiations. Ultimately, I felt driven to get directly involved on the inside. So, here I am."

"That's impressive. I'm sure you do a lot of good. So, what is the title 'Abbess?'"

"It's an old position that's rarely used. It was intended for a kind of head mistress of a school or nuns' abbey long ago. Here at the Vatican, old things hang around, if you know what I mean."

Rennie noticed a slight laugh from her companion. Her investigative instincts were engaged.

"In your situation now, what do you supervise as the abbess?"

She was answered with silence and withdrawal.

At the bottom of the stairway Serena nodded to the right.

"I think you're down this way. That's an interesting question. I think not many people really supervise anyone here. In a true Christian sense, we're all free to express God's will as our spiritual gifts allow us. For me, I'm kind of a coordinator. So, I guess one could say I supervise progress and good communications in one department."

As they reached Rennie's door, Serena turned to her.

"Saying that feels good. Thank you for asking."

She seemed authentic, but a knot in Rennie's gut sensed

something else, something hidden.

"I'm glad to meet you, Sister, or should I say 'Abbess?'"

"Rennie, between us, 'sister' is fine."

"Good. I have no idea what's to be done here, so I'll need your help in getting through the next few days. Could someone show me to your office tomorrow morning?"

"Of course, I'll have someone here at 9:30. The grounds are large, and it takes some time to get around. Have a good night."

As the nun glided down the polished marble in the gilded hall, Rennie noticed vague sounds in the distance of doors closing and hard heels on the floor.

Where is Busca? she wondered again, *and who else is in the building?*

Rennie checked the door handle to see if it would lock but it didn't. She slid one of her suitcases against the door thinking it might hinder an intruder or at least make a sound to awaken her. What's next? The device. Have it at hand. Check the phone and charge it up. She took it off airplane mode—they obviously know where she is. Now, she can get back to business.

Finally feeling that she was back in control of her own life for the first time in two days, Rennie got into comfortable clothes for bed and set the alarm on her phone. As she set it down, a call came in from an unknown number.

"Hello," she said with caution.

"Hi, there. Is this Rennie? I'm David Justus. My grandfather Matthew asked me to contact you. I hope this isn't too late."

His youthful tone and British accent were welcome in her ear.

"Oh, no, David. I'm glad to hear from you. How's Matthew? I am really concerned about him."

"Grandfather is not well. We are all concerned. He's tough but he's at peace, and that's a bit troubling. We want him to keep fighting. He's quite eager for me to be of assistance to you."

"Thanks, David. I could use a resource. I'm now at the Vatican. Are you coming to Rome?"

"I took the train from Switzerland today and am here now, in a hotel near Vatican City. Whenever you can meet, I'll be there."

"Great, how about tomorrow, at say noon?"

"Fine. It's been a while since I toured the grounds there. How about St. Peter's? The view of Rome from the top is marvelous, where all the big sculptures are. Let's meet in the middle of the visitor's vantage point at noon. If that doesn't work or if you need directions, call me."

"I'll be there, David. You've made my day. Oh, and David, be safe."

"Nice to talk with you, Rennie. I'll see you tomorrow."

As she set down the phone, the events of the trip flowed through her head like a loud waterfall. She eased onto the bed and thought of the events of the past two days. Her chest tightened, and she wondered what might come next. She slipped off the bed with a gentle twist and found herself on her knees, resting her arms on the mattress. This was not a familiar position. Rennie let her face float down to between her elbows.

Without thought, she murmured into the blanket, "Help me, guide me."

Her breathing became deep and slow.

The Vatican
Rome, Italy

V / 2

Rennie struggled throughout the night to rest and understand. Her thoughts tumbled around the conference-room bedroom with an unlocked door secured only by the weight of a suitcase, Busca roaming the halls, the face of a dead priest on a seashore, and the moaning of old Raphael. She was finally safe but more anxious than when in her room in Ischia. Blinded by all that had occurred, she couldn't determine what day it was, and the so-called bed she was on must have been used to test the endurance of novitiates in a nunnery. Then, there was the location—and the distance—of the women's restroom! Worries erupted about who she might encounter along the way.

She buried herself in the sheets and blanket for security, but the old and sterile scent woven into the cloth caught in her nose. The growing glow of new-morning light in the room forced her into awakening as the windows welcomed each sliver of light. Still safe in bed, her mind launched quickly into itemizing what needed to be done, when, and reviewing her situation. The nun Serena seemed okay, but there's probably more to her story. And, why was Busca in this building?

Rennie sat up and scanned the scattered bags and belongings from last night. She tried to remember what outfits she had brought and whether any were suitable for the meeting with Serena. She heard people's voices in the hallway and noises that suggested a lot of activity in the building. Who are they? Were they talking about her? For the moment, her main priority was to get to the bathroom upstairs before too many people were in the halls.

Rennie jerked on jeans and a dark sweater to accomplish her mission. She grabbed a bag of toiletries and a couple of towels left for her and opened the door just wide enough to see if anyone was nearby. With the way clear, she hurried out the door but found the end of the hall scattered with men in business suits, priests, and nuns. Their surprised looks offered little grace to this lost sheep. The stairs didn't come soon enough! With two steps at a time she got to the top and hurried across to her goal.

On the vanity was a folded paper with *Miss Haran* printed by hand on it.

I hope your evening was comfortable. Please ask for me if you need anything during your stay. We are honored to have you as our guest. Feel free to lock this door for your privacy.

It was signed by Sister Angelina, who welcomed her last night.

"Nice personal touch," Rennie whispered.

She hadn't noticed last night that the restroom had a lock on the door. She snapped it shut. She opened the window and inhaled a fresh breeze. Looking at the blue sky and rooftops in the distance, a little glee finally bubbled inside her and brought a full smile to her lips.

"I'm in Rome," she said aloud.

Rennie moved quickly and happily. Refreshed, she unlocked the door and started back to her room. From across the hall, a priest approached her.

"Miss Haran, I am Father Joseph. I'm an assistant to Abbess Serena. I will accompany you to her office at 9:30, precisely."

"Okay, thanks Father Joseph. I'll see you at that time."

After an uncomfortable pause in which his dead expression offered nothing, she backed away and headed down the stairs. Rennie realized she was listening to know if he followed her.

Back in her room she was focused. It was time for business;

a black suit, heels, and a notebook in her messenger bag. She checked her phone and reviewed the emails and messages. It was too early in the States to respond to any from there. She had an odd feeling that Father Angelotti should have tried to reach her, but nothing. Rennie sat on the bed and thought, *What the heck has been going on? A dead priest, her adrenaline-fueled escapes, and for what?*

A sharp knock on her door brought her into the moment. The time on her phone indicated 9:10 a.m. Father Joseph was early. She shoved aside her suitcase and opened the door to discover another priest.

"Hi, Miss Haran, may I have a moment with you? I'm Father Daniel."

"Hey, sure, why not. What's another priest?" Rennie said as she stepped aside. "Have we met before? I don't mean to be rude, but," she gestured to his black cassock, "you're all beginning to look alike. Did I meet you last night?"

He carefully stepped past her things on the floor.

"I understand the confusion. There are a lot of us here. Of course, this is the Vatican. No, we've not met, and I'll be brief. I'm the secretary for the cardinal of the Congregation of the Oriental Churches."

Rennie crossed her arms and leaned against the door frame.

"So, what do you need, Father Daniel?"

"I understand you are aware of the death of the Greek Orthodox priest a couple of days ago. It created quite some, uh, 'confusion' is probably a useful word, especially in the Middle East. And, you and Father Angelotti apparently walked into a mess trying to help sort things out."

"Father, from my perspective, I innocently flew into this 'mess', as you call it, and it has nothing to do with me ... What's it about, anyway?"

"Frankly Miss Haran, I have no idea, and I've been asked

by our group to see if I can shine some light on it. Our leadership is facing a lot of questions by our congregations, especially with the awful death of the scholar in Izmir and a Muslim cleric in Lebanon."

"I don't know about those. Are they all related?" Rennie thought back to Raphael, sitting next to his dying body feeling utterly useless. She studied this priest as he seemed to struggle with an answer. He's an attractive guy, but he could be another player in this bizarre and deadly game she'd been unwillingly dragged into.

"Father Daniel, I don't have a clue what's going on, but considering what I've been through, I'd sure like to know. If you can help me, you'll be my best friend."

"We are equally in the dark as yourself, Miss Haran. But I'd like to work with you so we both can get answers. For the next day or two, you'll be focused on the events for the display of the letters of our Lord Jesus. People from the British Museum are coordinating all the details. Abbess Serena has a ceremonial role for opening some gatherings. There's one later today at a church nearby. By the way, when you see her this morning, ask about the details of those opening events. Between you and me, I'm curious if she'll carry her crosier."

"Her what? Her crosier?"

Rennie's senses were alerted. *Crosier...* A stream of anxiety flew through her as distant bells rang in her mind, but she couldn't quite place them ...

"Oh, it's like a staff. Few people in our church use it anymore. It's common in the Orthodox churches, though. For an abbess like Serena, which is also an old, traditional title, the crosier is a staff that they sometimes carry for functions and a traditional symbol used in that role. It would convey a kind of authority, like Moses waving his staff to part the Red Sea or bring water from a stone in the desert."

"What does it look like? Is it like a sword?"

"No, it has a long shaft, but the top of the shaft is usually embellished to look like a cross. I guess the top could appear to be the handle of a sword if the bottom was gone. Anyway, I'm curious about how these ceremonies might be done." He laughed. "Maybe I'm a little jealous, too." His eyes narrowed. "Miss Haran, you discovered a profound treasure. We're all grateful."

Suddenly, Rennie remembered the photo of the dead Greek priest and what she was told was a crosier. *Is it connected with the abbess? What is this priest's real interest in this?*

"Miss Haran, I don't want to delay your appointment with Abbess Serena. I'd like to be in touch with you later. If you have any thoughts, let me know. Our people need to understand these murders. Here's my card with my cell phone number."

"Priests have cards? Sorry, this is new to me."

"This is probably a strange land for you. Sometimes, I think it's a little strange, too. Call me when it's convenient. Thanks."

Rennie noticed he paused after opening the door. Another hesitation in taking his first step was followed by a quick pace away from the room. Her hand grabbed her phone. She wasn't sure what to do with it. The time on its face told her nothing.

Joseph saw Sister Katherine as he approached the building along a private path. He appreciated sharing the familiarity of the German language with an associate. It not only tasted good across his tongue and in his throat, the language carried for him a sense of power that bonded well with the self-discipline he and Katherine shared. They were committed to a mission that imbued glory on its goals and reverence for the ultimate power, God.

"Good morning, *Schwester*. It's a beautiful day."

"Yes, it is, *Bruder*."

She gazed into the distance.

"I've heard of more tragic events abroad. They have nothing to do with us, do they?"

He turned in the same direction as she before responding. "Things happen, and I don't know why for the most part."

"Have you been watching the young woman, our visitor?"

"No, she's nothing to us."

"Joseph, she's something to someone. We need to know who that someone is. Maybe we should arrange for them to swallow a stone. Watch her."

He could smell onions and garlic on her breath. It was enticing.

"I will have it done. I've sensed we might be approaching a time of revelations and cleansing. Is this possible?"

Her thin lips stretched wide but a smile didn't appear.

"Keep such thoughts to yourself, *Bruder*, but know that good news is coming soon."

As she drifted away in silence, Joseph renewed his journey to meet Miss Haran.

Hopeful determination replaced the duty in his pace. He jogged up the marble steps and made a military turn into the hallway. Instead of a polite knock on her door, he gave it two sharp raps with his knuckle. It swung open.

"Pardon me, I guess the door was ajar," he said with deep authority.

He didn't appear gracious.

"May we leave for your appointment? The abbess likes to stay on schedule."

Rennie grabbed a few items and approached him.

"Of course, let's go."

On their way out of the building, Joseph attempted polite conversation.

"We have fine weather for the exhibition. Did you have a good night?"

"It was okay. I'm eager to know what the exhibition plans are. Do you have a schedule of events?"

"My apologies, I believe the abbess will provide that. I only assist with things."

"I've met several helpful people, Joseph, and it's nice to know you."

"Thank you, ma'am, I'm a servant of the greater church."

He was quiet for a few steps. He thought about how critical this moment in time is for the church, and how any risks must be eliminated. It was stupid for Father Angelotti to have this woman go to Naples. Angelotti is a coward. He can do nothing alone. This woman must be contained and then be removed as soon as possible.

"And, who is the greater church, Joseph?"

"I only know I have a small role, and that's enough. The leadership is always changing, but God is always there."

"Of course. By the way, there was a young nun who greeted me last night and helped make things comfortable. If I don't see her again, please thank her for me. There was also a priest. I think his name was Daniel, another interesting person. Do you know him?"

Joseph let silence hang in the air between them. His breathing became tight. *This Father Daniel could be trouble.* He sensed a need for action but didn't know what.

"I'm not sure of these people. We have many here with different functions."

He became quiet and more military in his pace.

They walked across the grounds of the Vatican for fifteen minutes before Joseph turned at a crossroads of sidewalks and pointed ahead.

"That's our building."

V / 3

David Justus enjoyed the moment. It was an idyllic setting; Rome, a lovely morning on holiday, overlooking the city with breakfast on the Hotel Scoperta rooftop patio. He leaned back in his chair, closed his eyes, and felt the morning sun on his pale face. A rare moment of simple pleasure away from the abstract and intellectual world of science or business or whatever one's professional calling might be. Peace and blue skies with good food and drink can restore and do wonders for motivation no matter what obstacles may loom ahead.

Soon, he would meet and help as needed, Rennie Haran, a friend of his grandfather. Then he would get some rest, maybe have some fun, and return to work. The Large Hadron Collider in Cern, Switzerland was down for repairs, so the phone call from his grandfather had proven the perfect opportunity to return to Italy.

The Collider is the largest, most powerful "atom smasher" in the world, but except for the excitement of the scientists, it operates in silence. David liked silence; quiet, logical, and complex was how he wanted his world. It was where the finite properties and intense relationships of things remained unseen and yet precisely described with mathematics. Few understood those beautiful equations, but to David it was wider society that he considered to be the real puzzle; arbitrary behaviors beyond knowing or understanding.

But today he wasn't going to think about that.

He lifted his drink and strolled to the barrier at the edge of the roof, thinking of past adventures in Rome with his Italian friends. They were also scientists, and they came to know one another when he was on loan from his projects in Cern to the Italian physics team for the Gran Sasso speed-of-light experiments. He had to smile.

The Italians knew how to party. He liked that and was often surprised with how they could be as analytical and detached as he, yet also celebrate the more passionate aspects of life. He took another sip and squinted at the horizon, processing that question.

David chuckled. His Italian friends wouldn't analyze it. They simply enjoyed life in every way; the work, the food, and the drama of relationships. He raised his glass as a toast to Italy. *La dolce vita.* Loving the food, the beautiful scenery, the cars, and the people was understandable, but drama was not for him, especially when it involved women. It never seemed logical.

He appreciated the contributions of his female colleagues and thought of them as wonderful mysteries. But their perspectives and behavior were so different from his. They understood one another, and that highlighted for him his inability to grasp their nuanced ways. Again, he raised his glass and offered a toast to the wonder of women, then returned to his table.

Sitting in peace on this sunny rooftop in Rome and enjoying a light breakfast, the buzz of subatomic particles and the drama of relationships faded out of his consciousness. Simplicity and quiet comfort permitted a welcome peace in David's mind as he tasted fresh sliced fruit, deli meats, croissants, and coffee.

But that peace was all too sweet as a fearful emptiness grew within him. He thought of how his grandfather, Professor Matthew Justus, had asked for his help and how he was on the next train from Cern to Rome. His grandfather meant so much to him and the sickening reality began to sink in. The old man was seriously ill and possibly dying. And, where was he? In Rome, enjoying coffee and pastries in the sunshine. He had to honor the request from his grandfather to help the American woman rather than return to London. But he couldn't help feeling guilty. Despite the sun's warmth on his face, he would much rather be at home in London, that great city, where he could be with Matthew, surrounded by friends and family.

A year earlier, after Matthew met Rennie and her friend Angie, David learned through his grandfather of the discoveries they had made and how the women had left Iowa and gone to London to inquire about the death of David's great grandfather, Professor Matthias Justus. Matthew hadn't even been born when his father was brutally murdered. Matthew's mother Priscilla never spoke of the astounding discovery of the letters. She didn't know of it, and they could have been lost forever. David's thoughts formed a three-dimensional model of those involved with their relationships and titles as if he was portraying a system of sub-atomic particles and related forces. Then he realized it was all unimportant compared with the well-being of his grandfather.

David sipped his coffee and noticed the varied textures and tones of brown in his cup. Like the swirl of distant galaxies, the relationships of family and friends and events floated back into his mind. But, the condition of his grandfather bubbled bitter concern within him. David wouldn't acknowledge it, but emotions not logic prompted a call to London.

"Hello, yes I'm calling for my grandfather, Matthew ... I'm David, David Justus. I'm concerned about how he's doing, and I'd appreciate speaking with him ... Why can I not speak with him? ... I'm sorry miss, what is your name? ... Miss Strathmore, I'm calling from Rome and I've not heard from my grandfather for more than a day. He's been in touch with me regarding an issue here. You are his nurse? ... Why does he have medical staff in his home? Excuse me, are any of my family members there? ... Miss? ... No, please do not hang up. What is urgent? Miss?"

London seemed to be on another planet. How could she hang

up? The numb ache of fear locked him in its cocoon. The brilliant logic that thrust him forward into new worlds of theoretical physics were overcome by a fierce, emotional threat. This was not familiar territory. Is the health of Matthew, his beloved grandfather at a critical stage? He needed data!

"Excuse me, may I take this chair?"

Without looking up, David motioned his approval.

The man sat down at his table instead of taking the chair.

"Hi David. My name is Michael. I know who you are. I also know your grandfather. He's a brilliant and good man. Long ago, I met him when he tried to get approval from the Turkish government to excavate at the site of ancient Antioch."

"Sorry, who are you? Wait, how do you know my name?"

This intruder violated every framework of David's sense of propriety and logic. He had no experience in dealing with such impertinence. He struggled to grasp how to challenge the stranger. Yet, he says he knows Matthew.

"Michael is the name, and I'm a friend of Rennie Haran. I think you may meet her soon. I understand you're concerned about your grandfather, but would you come with me right now? I'd like to discuss with you some background data you may need when you meet with Miss Haran."

Michael's composure exuded calm and nearly swept away David's fears for Matthew.

"Michael, if you don't mind, I'd like to stay on top of a family matter. I don't need to wander about. If we have something to discuss, let's do it here."

"David, there's nothing for you to do right now except stay on top of this matter with Miss Haran. I'm sorry I must be blunt. It's simply a fact, and I believe you prefer facts."

"Exactly who are you, Michael? What is it you want?" David was getting irritated now.

"I can answer your questions, but not here. This is noisy,

busy. There's a pleasant boulevard, *Viale degli Ammiragli,* close by where we can speak privately. Let's walk there. It's not far and close to the Vatican, so it's easy for you to connect with Rennie when you need to." Michael pushed his chair back as if he would stand. "May we go?"

David stared at his watch as if it would offer advice. "Okay, but I must follow up on the status of my grandfather."

The close quarters in the small elevator shut off conversation, especially for those naturally shy to speak like David. His thoughts remained with his grandfather and the all too disconcerting call he just made.

David followed the bold stranger as he dashed across the street and down the sidewalk for a short distance. The up-down wail of emergency sirens burst through the canyons of buildings and sparked fresh anxieties in David. Tragedy was in the air.

When they stopped, David politely demanded, "Michael, I'm sorry I didn't catch your last name. How is it you know Miss Haran and what's your purpose with me?"

"She and I have been through a couple of tough situations in the recent past. She's a good spirit. Right now, she's under some pressure with the exhibition and background issues. She'll need your help."

"Precisely. That's why I'm here."

Turning onto their target street, Michael slowed his gait to a stroll.

"This is better. David, are you acquainted with Corinth? I believe you and Matthew did some exploring in Greece."

"Yes, but for Corinth, only a brief visit. We spent some time on Mount Parnassus. My grandfather was curious about the oracle at Delphi. That period of history in the few hundred years preceding the Christian era and the few hundred years of the Christian era were of great interest to him. Why do you ask about Corinth?"

"Corinth was the location of one of the earliest churches and work of the apostle Paul. It was quite a place in history, economics, and in religion."

"Of course, it was. What's your point, Michael?"

"I thought that if you and Rennie have a chance to get away, she might appreciate the place. She's never traveled in Europe. Turkey is another place that Americans rarely go to. It's also rich with history and cultures."

David's back stiffened with resolute British propriety.

With clipped and precise formality, he demanded, "I don't know what you are insinuating my relationship with Miss Haran may be, but I can assure you we are not holidaying together. Are you some type of travel agent? I fail to see your point here! My grandfather had a sense of urgency for someone to assist Miss Haran and he asked me to help. I'm not sure of the details, but I believe she was under threat. I don't plan on touring with her. Now if you don't mind, I need to try to reach him again. Excuse me."

David jogged across the street and stood near a tree in the wide, grassy median. He dialed the London number again and asked for information from another useless source at the other end of the line. Family numbers weren't responding. Calls to a few friends went straight to voicemail.

"Ridiculous!" he swore, using one of his worst epithets. He marched back to Michael with teeth clenched.

"Who the hell are you? What's this nonsense about me and Miss Haran? What's your agenda, sir?"

"Sorry, David, I know you prefer thoughtful action. It's tough to not know Matthew's condition. I'm sure we'll find out."

"What! Who the hell? What do you mean 'we'?"

David's phone rang. He walked away holding it firmly to his ear. He stopped and stood quietly for a long time. Tears suddenly flowed from his eyes. He felt no shame. His handkerchief helped contain the effects of unexpected although all too bitterly inevitable grief. Putting the phone in his pocket, his head hung forward.

Composing himself somewhat and turning around, David saw the mysterious man had gone. He began a slow return to where he and Michael had been. It was time to begin the walk to St. Peter's to see Rennie, but suddenly, nothing was important.

Matthew was gone.

Rome, Italy
The Vatican

V / 4

Walking across the grounds of the Vatican, Rennie now celebrated her new freedom. Manicured lawns and precisely sculpted bushes and trees offered a sense of permanence and safety as well as elegance and nurture for her senses. The quiet passing of one or two people on a walkway, with polite acknowledgement from Father Joseph and herself as they walked in silence, was the only noise that disturbed the tranquility of the gardens. As they travelled from a building that resembled a castle to another that appeared to be a palace, Rennie couldn't help wondering whether she was still in the real world, but rather a special place where only peace and goodness can reign.

She barely noticed the cool presence of Father Joseph at her side as they strolled up a granite stairway into a stately administration building. Inside, she paused for a moment, not expecting the oozing of power and wealth and history that covered every surface of the corridor. Rennie gawked at each detail until they arrived at Abbess Serena's office. She marveled at the large entry doors, the rich swirl in the grain of the dark wood, the multiple levels of carved trim, and even the ornate handles. They spoke of the same power, wealth, and history exhibited throughout the building. Joseph appeared to be bored with his duties and this place.

Rennie wondered, *How can he be so devoted to the church and not express some delight entering this grandeur?*

Joseph motioned to a chair.

"Please wait here. I'll see if she's ready."

He opened a door to the inner office enough to peer in, then shut it again with a soft touch.

Rennie rehearsed her plan. For the moment, this was about the exhibition. She considered the key points. Was it safe? What was the schedule and who was doing what? Then, the ugly intrigue of the previous days could be sorted out at the end. Rennie found Serena to be so friendly last night, she thought this meeting should go well and lead to a wonderful exhibition and celebration for the rest of her stay. Questions and answers about the horrors that happened earlier could come later once she better understood this American insider at the Vatican.

A door to the inner office opened and Joseph peered inside. His face hinted he smelled a foul odor. Rennie couldn't see what lingered behind the door until Scarpia exited. He paid no attention to Joseph but nodded at Rennie as he left.

Father Angelotti followed, chatting with the abbess as he departed the office.

"Oh, Miss Haran, I'm delighted to see you." Father Angelotti cried, seeing Rennie waiting outside. "I have much regret for all you went through. Are you well? You look wonderful!" He glanced around seeking confirmation.

"Will you ever forgive me for bringing you into that awful situation? I had no idea."

"I'm here now. That's what's important."

"But, of course. We thank God for that. How contrived our authorities make all things!"

The abbess stepped forward.

"Miss Haran and I have much to discuss. Perhaps you can catch up later."

Rennie was surprised when Angelotti grasped her hands.

"Yes, yes, and I must give you a special tour here. I don't know how to offer my regrets enough."

As he let go, she said, "I appreciate what your men did to get me to safety and bring me here. Please thank Michael for me."

His eyes were blank while a polite smile rested in his face. Too many moments passed for everyone's comfort.

"Yes, but I have no men as you say. There is great devotion among all in the church to do what is good. Please excuse me now. Work awaits, I'm glad you're here."

Rennie wondered if his deceit was obvious to everyone. For now, she had to be all business.

"Father Angelotti, will you attend the program today?"

"I may not, my dear. I must connect with the people from the British Museum who are at the Vatican Library. The finishing touches on the display of the letters must be completed."

Serena turned to Joseph.

"That's all for now. Are all the details ready for the first event?"

"I believe so, Abbess. I'll check."

"Yes, do. Miss Haran, I have a worktable in my office where we can review the exhibition plans. Please join me."

Without further courtesies, she disappeared behind the door leaving the men behind.

Rennie followed in her wake, aware of a new and cold side to this woman with apparent power. Old world, palatial opulence filled the room. *Wow,* flew into Rennie's mind as she experienced the office. *And this is ordinary to them!*

Serena handed Rennie her business card.

Rennie slipped it into her pocket and tried to begin on common ground.

"Thanks, I had no idea people at the Vatican carried business cards. This is my second one today! So, what do I call you? Last night you said, 'Sister Serena', but it seems people here use 'Abbess.'"

"Either is fine. I'm not that much on ceremony, but around

here titles seem to be important. You can call me 'Sister.'"

"It's nice to meet another American, and an American woman. Especially after this 'adventure' you might say."

The abbess didn't flow with Rennie's attempt at an informal approach.

"That was indeed an unfortunate beginning to your trip. At least you're here now."

"So, what's the plan, Sister?"

The abbess almost flinched as Rennie used the word *Sister* in that familiar manner. She turned the attention to her conference table with stacks of files and papers.

Rennie scanned and did a quick study of the schedules and drawings on the worktable, each with formal titles in Italian or possibly Latin. As she did, she noticed that Serena discretely observed her.

Serena pointed at one schedule.

"I've laid these out in chronological order. Starting on this schedule up here, there's an afternoon mass to be held at the Basilica Eudoxiana. It's a church also called San Peitro in Vicoli. This is the building that holds some precious objects of the church such as the tomb of Pope Julius the Second and chains that bound Saint Peter while he was in prison in Jerusalem. It also has the sculpture *Moses* by Michelangelo. It seemed like the perfect intersection of items of faith for the recognition and welcome of the letters of the Lord Jesus."

Rennie felt dizzy and placed one hand over her eyes.

"Sister, do we have time for a quiet moment? I need to sit down. Frankly, this is the first time I've felt safe in days."

"Of course, sit here. Do you need water?"

Holding dark red goblets filled with water, Serena and Rennie settled into tall-back, upholstered chairs. Rennie leaned back and closed her eyes.

"Thank you. I'm sorry."

She took a long drink and set the glass on the marble top of an adjacent table.

"I'll be fine in a minute. I guess I should have eaten this morning."

"Rennie, can I order some food for you? There's no hurry. I can give you the schedules and locations, and you can decide what to attend."

"It's okay, I'd like to see everything now. I'm sure the ceremonies will be impressive. I'd love to see the places and learn the history."

"There are plenty of both. A Protestant friend of mine says she particularly likes the 'smells and bells' versions of our services instead of the contemporary styles."

Serena looked into the distance with a peaceful expression that didn't fit the moment. Rennie took a deep breath.

"Thank you for the water—that was what I needed. I'll get something to eat when we're done. So, what do you wear and do in this first event?"

"The basic garment is a plain white robe although the trim on the sleeves and openings is nicely done. Then, there a couple of vestments laid over it that represent the perspectives of my order and the role of the church as shepherd of the faithful."

"Do you have a particular cross or carry a crosier?"

"The cross is a traditional piece that's been in my congregation for a few hundred years."

"What about the crosier? I think those are cool. They seem to show a lot of authority."

The abbess didn't respond. She went to the worktable and moved some papers around.

"People seem to be devoted to challenging authority now. Symbols like a crosier or even the cross become unimportant."

"Is that a problem?"

Serena glared at Rennie.

"We can't have the chaos that comes with dissent. Some things are absolute."

The dilated pupils of her eyes looked empty and dark.

The presence of unquestioned power was suddenly revealed. Cold dread filled Rennie's chest. She had to escape for a moment. She returned to the table and began making notes of the plans. Quick details of place and schedule tapped a steady beat for events of grand drama and helped separate her from her fears. Nothing had prepared her for this place and these people.

"As I said, Rennie, the church does not have a role for you in this program. Our focus is entirely on God. We also thought it best to not engage in personal publicity for this. The public is here to see the letters. I hope that's acceptable to you."

"Of course, I'm not here for me. Given what's gone on recently, I'll enjoy being out of the picture. Before we end this, do you have any of the vestments, the cross, or the crosier here? I'd love to see them up close. I didn't plan on attending the event at that church."

"It's close to lunch, and I regret I cannot entertain you for that. My schedule calls for me to move on."

Rennie had been around enough politicians and lawyers to note the evasion. More trust slid away.

The abbess motioned to the door and led the way.

"We can discuss further tomorrow if you like."

"Oh, there is one other thought that came to mind. I've heard some names along the way, and I'm not familiar with them. They were in Latin I think. One was something about a group known as the 'Fellowship.' Is that an organization in the Roman Catholic Church?"

The pale skin of her face made the abbess look less than human.

"Miss Haran, Rennie, like you, I'm an American. I'm constantly trying to figure out what's what in this massive organization. Even His Holiness the Pope doesn't know who all the players are. If you learn anything else, please let me know. These are serious times, and I must get ready now."

"There's another thing I'd like to know. Who's behind all this?"

"What 'this' are you referring to?"

"You know, the killings."

"We wish we knew."

"You're well connected. What are your thoughts?"

"I don't know. You're a journalist. What are yours?"

Calm filtered into Rennie and formed a smile. She knew this woman was shrewd and her self-control was well developed to suit the position of authority she had achieved. Rennie could relax knowing she would not be able to fool this woman into disclosing whatever she held secret, but perhaps she could prompt Serena to consider one of Rennie's deepest concerns ...

"I think a little evil becomes powerful in organizations when good people turn the other way."

"Miss Haran, let me know if you have any ideas on whatever concerns you. I'll then see what we can do."

Serena turned away.

The meeting was clearly at an end. Rennie left the office with a desire to understand this woman of subtle but strong contradictions.

The massive door closed with a powerful thud. Rennie glanced back. Authority is often gilded with ornamentation to disguise raw power.

She has position, but does she have the power or wield it for others? It could be a life or death question.

V / 5

The dome of St. Peter's Basilica stands with dignity and grace above all else in the Vatican grounds. Against a pastel-blue sky, it would appear to be a refuge calling the faithful, but as Rennie approached, the structure felt ominous. Meeting with David was an application of time she wasn't sure she wanted. She checked her phone and noticed a new text from Angie. It said:

Stay safe and don't talk to the authorities. Do you want to meet a reporter? One in Rome wants to see you. Deaths in other countries may be related. Trying to connect dots. Can't reach Matthew. Let me know you're ok.

Rennie called Matthew. There was just his voicemail greeting to leave a message. Something seemed wrong.

"Hello, Matthew. It's Rennie. I'm okay. I'm in good hands at the Vatican. The exhibition of the letters is about to begin. Please call me. I have some important questions. Are you all right? I'm concerned about you."

A few steps later, her phone chimed an incoming call.

"Hello, Matthew! I'm so glad you called! Are you okay?"

"Miss Haran, I regret I'm not Matthew. I'm a colleague at the British Museum and calling on his behalf. My name is Alistair Thorsten Snapper. I wish I could give you good news about our dear friend Matthew but I was told things appear to be grim. His family said he's unable to speak with you, so they asked me to call. Do you have a moment? I have some information I can share."

"What do you mean grim?"

"They said his medical support is with him, and he is comfortable. That's all we at the museum know. Do you have a moment?"

"Oh, poor Matthew. Umm, Yes, of course."

"Matthew told me that you had questions regarding the island known as Pandateria. Legend says it has an interesting Roman history that intersects with Christian history and some notable women."

"Yes, Mr. Snapper – or Professor, apologies– thank you but I've heard this. Do you know any more, perhaps, what does it have to do with these recent events?"

"It's not clear, Miss Haran. We're just getting started on this, at the moment. Doctrine wars have always been going on, sometimes behind the scenes. There were the conflicts with the Knights Templar, the horrible acts of the Inquisition, and even the Protestant Reformation. However, Matthew and I discussed your situation and other information you described to him, in complete confidence, of course, and a theory emerges."

Rennie listened carefully. "What's that?"

"One ancient story suggests the apostle Paul had a new revelation regarding Jesus and he shared it with the women who were among the early leaders in the church. It conflicted with his other teachings and what many had come to believe. So, a power struggle on doctrine developed that's been hidden in the church all this time."

"I've heard that too, but why would that involve murder now?"

"I have no idea, ma'am, but that's not an uncommon reason for the endless internal struggles within institutions with absolute status. More information would be needed to conduct this research. We do know there have been commentaries made on the secret groups that have pursued Paul's rumored documents. If those were found, they might give credibility to one belief system or another. Names like the Servants of the Apostles or Shield of the Patriarchs or Porta – also called the Fellowship – were used by various groups. They claimed to know the so-called real reason for the crucifixion and where God supposedly is. The conflicts of their beliefs with the orthodoxy are what makes them dangerous for the establishment. It's a mysterious issue. You don't want to get caught in the middle."

"We're on the same page, Professor, and I might already be in the middle. This guy Michael referred to that name *Porta* and to fellowships. So, they're still around and in this fight?"

"It's possible some of these groups are active. You also mentioned to Matthew something about use of a crosier as a murder weapon. If so, it would give symbolic authority to the act of a church or affiliated group. There are no clear references to past or present acts. Throughout all time, religious groups have used icons in acts of violence to represent divine will. It's a kind of validation of the horror caused by heresy."

Rennie shook her head in disbelief.

"Thank you for your call. This is all really useful. Please keep in touch as you develop an understanding of this. Most of all, could let me know when you get an update on Matthew? I love that man as if he's my own grandfather."

"I will, ma'am. He did tell me how special you were to him as well. He said you are to carry on a great tradition, although I don't know what that means."

Rennie needed a moment to breathe. Pressure suddenly formed in her eyes.

"Ma'am, are you there?"

"Yes, I am. Sorry, I must hurry. Please call when you can. Thanks."

An urgent anxiety propelled Rennie into the basilica to meet David. Matthew's grandson would be safe, like family. He might be helpful and would at least be trusted company. Each stride forward wasn't enough. Her pace quickened. She wanted to run.

In the sanctuary of St. Peter's, the vast interior between the walls and the ceiling poured an unexpected wonder through her. The real world disappeared as holy grandeur filled her senses. Remnants of incense in the cool air hinted at ancient mystery. Massive gold columns swirled high into a royal canopy above the altar. Power absolute was centered here.

Rennie wandered through groups of tourists with open mouths as they gazed. Small chapels and places to kneel in homage called for supplication of the soul to those inclined to humility. But as she walked, ugly tension grew in her. The contrast between the offer of loving grace and the threats of authority and death twisted in her thoughts. She wondered what scheming had gone on here for centuries and what was going on now? The face of the dead Greek priest filled the eyes of her memory. Anger followed.

Where is God in all this power, wealth, and chaos?

She wandered down vast aisles and discovered she was in front of a statue of St. Michael.

"Hey!" a man shouted.

Rennie spun around and backed against the base of the statue. It was a tourist yelling to his kid. Hanging high above him on the wall, a gigantic painting of Jesus with his arms spread wide professed suffering and death. As she studied the painting, a man casually walked by and put a postcard in her hand. In another moment, he was lost in the crowd delivering the cards. On one side was a color photo of blue sky and clouds. On the other was a blank area for an address along with the caption, "God is present and wants you to be."

Frustration boiled inside her. She struggled for control.

I am present, so where are you?

Checking her watch, she realized she had to find a way to the roof to meet David. A nearby priest spoke some English and helped her with directions.

The containment of the elevator and close proximity of tourists felt to Rennie like she was captured again, prompting another desperate need to escape the moment she was released onto the roof and into the broad sunshine of Rome. Rennie flowed with small groups of visitors along walkways between metal railings to the front of the great façade. Aligned before her and looking out over the massive, round plaza far below were the towering statues of the disciples with Jesus in the middle and Peter next to him. She held back. It was too much, too big, too powerful. Carefully moving to the barrier of the roof, cold fear crawled up her lower back as she peered over the edge to the pavement hundreds of feet below. She had to walk it off. Not far away, she saw a tall, slender young man standing alone with his back against the statue of Jesus. A brown sport coat over a blue dress shirt didn't suggest he was a physicist. The glasses helped.

"Are you David?"

"Why yes, I am. And you are Miss Haran?"

"Please, just Rennie. I appreciate your coming. Did your grandfather fill you in on what's been going on?"

He looked away.

"I, ah, know some details."

"A lot has happened since I last spoke to him, so I can fill you in. He said you studied or did research with him? Any insights you might have would be helpful."

"Of course."

"David, I've left messages for Matthew but have heard nothing. Is he okay? When I saw him a couple of days ago, he was not well, so I'm concerned."

He ran his fingers through thick brown hair and bit his lip.

"Miss Haran, I mean, Rennie, I regret I must give you unfortunate news. I've learned that my grandfather is no longer with us. I received this information only a few minutes ago."

"What? Not with us? Did he ... has he passed away? Is that what you're saying?"

"Precisely."

David's face was blank.

"No! He sounded tired the other day, but no. No!"

Her eyes felt wet. They fluttered and lost focus.

"Tell me more."

"He's gone. That's all there is. He was old and not well. Rennie, it's a natural conclusion."

"Conclusion? This isn't a math problem! This isn't physics!"

"Rennie, I don't know what to say. I'm a scientist."

"And, Matthew is your grandfather. He was precious and good. Dear God, I need time. I need time. I'm going downstairs."

David followed her from a distance as she hurried across the terrace to the elevator.

She spun around and waited for him to catch up.

"You don't know what I've been through and what I've seen. Death is ugly. It's more than facts and figures. It's about people and the loss of that miracle of life that throbs within us. I'm done riding a roller coaster with deadly games and being helpless! I'm done with it! I am present, and I will be accounted for."

She stepped closer and said with clenched teeth, "I'm now a player."

He seemed stunned. He blinked as if processing unexpected data.

Rennie's face felt hot. She had to walk away. The elevator door opened, and she bolted in.

On the main floor of the basilica, she found a quiet place away from the heavy stream of tourists. Grief poured through her soul, her face fell into her hands, and she turned to the wall. But, instead of tears, she felt fierce, ruthless, ready to attack. Anger and determination took the place of tragedy. Matthew said she should carry on the tradition, and he handed her the baton. What she wanted was a chainsaw.

Rennie turned and saw David exit the elevator and walk through the basilica with cool detachment among the gawkers of ancient glory. Through the emptiness of her grief and anger, Rennie studied him and wondered if in this place of spiritual passion, he felt any contact with his soul or grief. Her passion conflicted with finding peace in this holy temple, but she couldn't understand his frozen behavior. Matthew died!

Finally, she was ready.

"David, I'm here."

Rennie approached him with arms crossed.

"Ah, there you are. I'm sorry I was so blunt. It was a shock, and it's difficult to absorb from a distance. But understand this, Miss Haran, I have no need for your judgmental attitude."

His upper lip raised into a snarl and his diction became sharper.

"I may express myself differently but do not, do *not* dismiss my affection for my grandfather. You knew him a little, but he was part of my entire life. I don't know why he asked me to help you." He turned and walked away.

Rennie looked into the crowd trying to find order in the chaos.

Finally, she touched his back. "David, can we leave here? We need a break. I was told there's a visitor center and restaurant not far away. I need something to eat."

He looked over his shoulder. "Yes, I can show you the way. I've been there many times with friends and with my ... well, you know, Grandfather. It's this way."

He walked away without looking back.

Like schools of fish in the sea, the crowds parted and formed and swirled as Rennie followed David through the basilica. Stepping into the sunlight at the entrance, David took a deep breath and surveyed the scene.

"If you haven't seen it, the front of this great place is quite impressive from the plaza. I know a good spot."

Rennie couldn't feel the sun or smell the cool breeze. A flood of grief filled her with darkness as she walked into the vast open area and felt its emptiness. Her pain was about to pour from her mouth and eyes.

David pointed, "If we stand over there ..."

She bent over, her hands on her face.

"Oh, God."

Her shoulders shuddered. She crouched as David stood guard over her. He took a handkerchief from a pocket and held it out, but she was oblivious to the gesture. He nodded at those who walked by with concern, amusement, or anger on their faces as they noticed the odd couple.

"Rennie, I don't know what's going on, but Grandfather advised me that I am to do whatever you need. I will do that."

She finally stood, with her back to him. She breathed deeply, then turned to look into his eyes.

"Matthias would have liked that too. Let's go to a quiet place. I have a lot to tell you."

Topkapi Palace
Istanbul, Turkey

V / 6

Aslan Yilmaz, Director of Istanbul's Antiquities and Topkapi Museum Operations, scanned the renovated reception area of his building with pride as he walked toward an unknown visitor. His secretary had passed on the man's business card, but the visitor had given no explanation for this intrusion in his schedule. After all, Yilmaz was the director, and someone else should do initial contacts. No one had met this person!

As the visitor arose from a chair, Aslan addressed the stranger with traditional formality. They conversed in their native Turkish and settled into modern, plush chairs around a small table. It's the only place where Aslan allowed his guests to be. He endured the frequent strain of official visitors who interrupted his duties in the Topkapi Museum and Palace as a necessary but unwelcome part of the job. However, he would not allow them into the "business" areas of the facility, especially the underground archives and storage area. Centuries of plotting and treachery oozed from the building. The ignorant public thought this was a museum, but it would always be a palace of the sultan to him.

"And, I understand you are Umit? Umit Yildirim? I was given your card. It offers only your name and a number. Are you with a business?"

"I'm with our government, Director."

"Would you like tea? It's always prepared for our special guests."

Friendly humility with formality would be a safe approach with this visitor. It pleased important people and he didn't know how important this man might be. Formality was important.

"I appreciate your seeing me, Director. Your time and assistance are invaluable to our nation."

Aslan detected the style of Umit's speech. It was clearly central Anatolia. He may be from Ankara, but he began in a small town. He's a villager.

"You're too generous. I'm here to serve. Forgive me, I'm not clear on the reason for your visit. Who are you with?"

Aslan poured tea into two glass cups on a wooden tray. His thoughts blitzed through a maze of connections of first impressions, suspicions, pending appointments, and strategies. He would play ignorant. Times were difficult with the government, so having no agenda when meeting officials was a safe routine.

"Director, with hundreds of thousands of people crossing into and through Turkey, there are deep security concerns. We've suffered violent incidents. Terrorists can strike at any time anywhere. It's difficult to know who refugees are and who are extremists. Topkapi is a precious jewel to our people and to all of history. Your work to preserve these treasures of Turkish history—of Islam itself—sets it in the sights of dangerous people."

"We understand. We've been sickened by the bombings in Istanbul and Ankara and horrendous destruction of treasures in Afghanistan, Syria, Iraq, and Tunisia. The military has a presence here of course. But, for me and the staff, we do research and offer no trouble. Forgive me, what department are you with?"

"The Interior Ministry, Director. The staff are not a security concern. Topkapi itself is a concern. It's what might be called a 'soft target.' It has little armed presence so terrorists could inflict significant damage and achieve worldwide publicity."

"But they could carry away little from here, and our most beloved items are in secure areas."

"That may be, but they don't want to steal. They want news stories. The media gives them power. Wealth and history mean nothing to them."

"I don't understand. The state has already taken serious steps in security."

"Director, terrorists have anger and an agenda. One must be vigilant and controlled."

"What do we do? We're a museum. We have a steady stream of visitors and people doing research."

"I must interview you and your key people. We need lists of who works here and who has access to the palace grounds. We need information on who people are in contact with. The trails of the terrorists are short, but the linkages can be revealing."

"We'll cooperate, of course. What prompted this?"

"We must stay a step ahead. From the incidents you mentioned, the great treasures of Istanbul could be next."

"What can we do?"

The agent removed a file folder from a briefcase. "Here's a list of what we need from each person, and also a form to complete with all information."

Aslan's eyes scrolled down the paperwork. "This is comprehensive. What staff shall I make this request to?"

"All of them."

"All? We have many classes of personnel: full time, part time, students, guest researchers, executive staff."

"Yes, everyone."

Aslan heard a harder edge in the response. This was a demand and not a request. Aslan often had to deal with bureaucrats from Ankara and Istanbul, representatives from the offices of Cultural Affairs or Tourism and even the Interior Department, but he never before sensed ominous consequences in whatever requests they made. The project expected from this visitor didn't carry any options for discussion.

"Mr. Yildirim, we'll get it done. I'll assign one of our people to it."

"We wish to receive the information by the end of next week."

"Oh, my friend. We have many current projects. Researchers come and go with little coordination. Although our collections are well organized, our people are less so."

Aslan thought a little humor might gain some consideration.

The lifeless expression on the investigator's face didn't change. He didn't move.

"Mister, ah," Aslan looked at the visitor's business card, "Yes, Mr. Yildirim, could we say we'll have this to you in the next month?"

"It's needed next week."

The director shuffled the papers again. He struggled for another argument to delay. "I'll put staff on this immediately. I'll have them contact you as soon as it's ready."

"Who will do this?"

"I'll check with the ancient documents curator. Yusuf is thorough."

"His full name please."

"Yusuf Pashazade Mustafa Bey. He's well-known among those interested in the ancient world."

Umit wrote the name on his notepad. "Thank you, Director. This is a high priority."

"And, now it is for us."

"Goodbye, Director. We appreciate your assistance and cooperation."

"Goodbye, Mr. Yildirim."

The men stood and shook hands with more formality than when they met. The hands of Umit Yildirim were strong and rough. He was not a bureaucrat. It seemed he clicked his heels together as their hands released their grasp.

The government agent grabbed his briefcase, gave a brief

nod to the director, quickly strode to the entry doors, and was gone.

Aslan studied the stranger's departure. He thought he had seen everything, but this fit no category. Now he had to explain this to Yusuf. The man is an archival curator who has chosen a life alone in a vault with old documents and artifacts. The demands of modern society weren't often welcome to Yusuf, and their relationship was purely professional, even distant, so Aslan anticipated difficulty in conveying this assignment and its deadline without conflict and disruption of their valuable work.

Rome, Italy
The Church San Pietro in Vicoli

V / 7

The ceremony to begin the welcome of the letters of Jesus was still nearly an hour away but the chairs were filling with honored guests. In a vestibule in the back, Abbess Serena placed the last adornment on her vestments when Father Daniel entered.

"Pardon me, Abbess. *Dominus vobiscum.* Do you have a moment?"

"Et cum spíritu tuo. Have we met? I do have a moment, but that only."

"I'm Father Daniel. I'm a secretary for the cardinal of the Congregation of the Oriental Churches. Although I've been assigned to researching the ugly matter of the death of our Orthodox brother from Greece, my doctorate was in the study of early writings of the church fathers. So, having the letters of our Lord here is particularly thrilling."

Serena continued her preparations without comment.

"So, Abbess, since your office is handling this exhibition of the letters, I wondered if you would permit me to see them. I won't handle them, of course. I'd simply appreciate being able to spend some quiet time with them, for study, and, of course, in reverence."

She kissed her cross and placed the chain around her neck. A final adjustment to center it finished her preparation. "I have no control over this matter. Our office was one of several that coordinated with the British Museum. All management of access to the letters is in their hands."

"If you could connect me with the right person, I would be grateful."

"Who are you again? Father who?"

"Daniel. I'll leave my card here."

"I'll do what I can, and someone will contact you."

"Can I do anything to help? Is there anything you need?"

"Father, at the moment, a little peace would be fine. This is an important event. *Ad altare Dei.*"

"Indeed, Sister, to the altar of God. This is a perfect crossroads to launch this event, the physical chains of St. Peter introducing Christ the Redeemer. This is a great honor for you to open this historic moment. I don't see your crosier. Isn't that appropriate for this event?"

Her nostrils flared, and her lips formed a tight line. "Father, it seemed appropriate for us to come to God in all humility rather than as persons of authority. Would you agree?"

"I fully agree. Your perspective is precisely what's needed. Thank you, Sister. *Ad maiorem Dei Gloriam.*"

Daniel looked energized, but it contrasted with his sad face. She thought he must be disappointed with not gaining personal access to the letters.

As he left, she whispered, "For the greater glory of God."

Moments after Daniel was gone, the door swung open again, but this time it was Joseph.

"Pardon me, *Abbessa.* Is there anything you need?"

He took a step back as she approached him. Her focus didn't waiver from his eyes.

"Perhaps, you might bring me either my crosier or an excuse why it isn't here."

His eyebrows bobbed up and down. "I cannot explain it."

He looked at his mirror-polished shoes. "I've reviewed our records for events, for access to your office, for all visitors. It's a mystery. I've tried to arrange for an alternative, but access to them is complicated."

"Who is Father Daniel? Do you know him?"

"Ah, there is a Daniel who handles schedules of mass at the basilica, and there's another, I'm not sure if he's still there. Which Daniel do you mean?"

He looked too nervous to be honest.

"This Daniel!" She handed him the business card. "Find out about him. Now, let me prepare."

The tap-a-tap of his hard heels on the old marble floor echoed down the hall until he was gone.

From a dark shadow in the back corner of San Pietro in Vicoli, Father Daniel studied the select attendance gathering for the opening mass. Whether to stay for the ceremony or go to the Vatican Library to possibly get in on the exhibition preparations was a tough decision. Regardless of the background issues, history was being made in both places. He had to stay, at least for the opening minutes.

Among the last to enter and be ushered to a privileged seat was His Eminence the secretary of state.

Of course, Daniel thought, *He would have to be here to represent the Holy See and the Abbess is one of his key associates. That's why she was so intense. Might he be involved?*

Almost too softly to hear, Rimsky-Korsakov's 'Procession of Nobles' began from an invisible place, opened by a single violin instead of horns. The piece proceeded with slow elegance instead of arrogance, a cello hitting accents where the drums would sound. The small crowd was instantly caught up, eyes widened, and souls were immersed in the grandeur of reverent simplicity. Daniel was pleased.

This is what our Holy Father would want.

He studied the abbess as she entered from a side alcove. She glanced for an instant to see where the secretary of state was sitting. Daniel admired her composure. It was almost commanding and contrary to some of what he had learned about her. He was confused with trying to understand her and if she had a role in the intrigue he was assigned to investigate. Some said she had a "servant heart" in all her duties, yet her quiet, brilliant mind and tough exterior left some to suspect there was another, more sinister side. Her career first as a state prosecutor, then quick success in corporate law dealing in international contract negotiations suggested she was ambitious and self-focused. But then, she offered free legal services to the local Roman Catholic diocese, and finally left the "good life" to become a religious sister. Some wondered if there was a dark moment in her past that caused the change, but he couldn't find it. The respect she had earned at the top of the Vatican hierarchy was consistent and deep. Yet, he wondered if she was connected with the deaths and suspicions now troubling the Vatican.

The music drifted to a quiet end as the abbess raised her arms to open the service with a blessing. The audience gave its devoted attention to her, and Father Daniel thought, *she's good.*

As the service eased forward, Daniel left by a side door and hurried to his motor scooter. He secured his helmet and slipped his frock under his legs. The scooter raced into traffic. Drivers gestured and yelled at their windshields as he cut between them, frustrated with this priest who defied obstruction.

He entered the Vatican in a back gate off of Via Leone IV and parked his scooter near the garage next to Belvedere Palace. New security people stood at this entrance to the Apostolic Library, but they hardly looked at his identification when he offered it. He was stunned when they gave him a quick wave and freedom to enter. Then, he stopped. He noticed a man about ten meters from the door, dark complexion, long hair combed back with a greasy flourish, leaning against a car. The man dragged heavily on a cigarette and blew the smoke to the side. He was an ominous presence in that place, in that way.

The call of the letters inside propelled him forward. He hurried down the hallway, his emotions fluttering in his chest. In a few moments, he encountered uncompromising English-speaking guards, not Italian men or priests, and was told there was no entry at this time to the exhibit hall that held his precious goal: the letters of his Lord.

Daniel felt like a child who couldn't open his Christmas gifts. They were there on the other side of the door! A moment of hope arose when the door opened. Father Angelotti slipped from the exhibition hall and past the guards into the hallway. He stopped to greet them, but they weren't interested.

"Father Angelotti, hello," Daniel said with cheer. "Do you remember me? I'm Father Daniel, from the —"

"Yes, yes from the Congregation of the Oriental Churches. We worked on a program some time ago. How is my devoted friend?"

"Very good and thank you for remembering me. I'm quite excited about seeing the letters. You apparently have access. Can you get me into the hall?"

"Oh, my, I know a few people, but I'm just an obedient messenger here."

"You're too modest. I understand you arranged all this."

"I help where I can. I find it's best to facilitate but stay out of the way. The hope, good news, and power that these letters portend is humbling. I stand aside for others to lead."

For the first time in his experience of working with Angelotti, Daniel sensed a scheming trait that he hadn't seen before. "Father Angelotti, I'm like a little chick here looking for a hen to take me under her wing. If you could help in any way, I'd be forever grateful."

Angelotti's head bobbed from side to side. "I will do what I can. Everyone wants to get close to these holy writings."

"I do as well, as an historian in addition to seeing the words written by the hand of God. My dissertation was on the first 100 years of the development of our faith. These letters are a profound part of the missing story."

"They may be, but they stand alone, of course. Do you have a moment now? I'll see what I can do."

Angelotti whispered to the British guard and turned to Daniel. He tickled the air to beckon the priest to his promised land.

Father Daniel entered the hall and scanned the room to find his treasure. Large, bronze kiosks of layered, curved glass stood in offset lines. Purple curtains draped each structure. Security people sat on stools in the five meters of space between each vestibule of holiness.

"I think they've done a marvelous job in presenting them with simple reverence," Angelotti said with a hint of pride.

"Indeed, and when will the curtains be removed?"

"Following the welcome mass that's going on now. Our holy brother, the prefect of the Supreme Tribunal of the Apostolic Signatura and his secretary will open this event."

Angelotti seemed pleased and leaned closer to Daniel. "That gives all the top boys a role in history."

Both chuckled. Angelotti noticed someone far away and excused himself.

Daniel took hesitant steps toward the closest display. The guards expressed no humanity as their eyes studied his movements. He wandered to other displays, hoping to see under the curtains as staff hurried to prepare the area for the honored crowds who would soon arrive. The guards, however, were diligent and escorted him out of the hall.

Daniel intercepted Angelotti as he came through the hall. "Father, if you have one moment, I'd like to ask about another matter."

"Yes, but I must hurry."

"There was an incident outside of Naples. A priest was found on the shore, and you went there."

Angelotti gazed into the distance and crossed his arms. "Ah, that sad event. Yes, I was sent to the scene to report back to those higher, including the offices of the secretary of state. That's all I know."

"Many are talking about it. Has anything been learned? Do we know who did such a terrible thing?"

"It's not in my hands. It's the old story of divine power in the heavens and gruesome dark forces below with humanity caught between them. We see these things daily. It's so sad."

He waved his hand toward the exhibition hall entry. "Thank goodness we're sometimes reminded of the right path. Forgive me, I must take care of a few things. Enjoy the event."

Rome, Italy
The Vatican

VI / 1

The tourist cafeteria and rest area in the Vatican Museum complex was spacious and bright. Open seating was scattered throughout, and rows of stainless-steel serving areas projected out from two walls. Organized sections of sandwiches, hot entrées, candy, desserts, drinks, and ice cream were held in racks and shelves behind glass windows and under hot lamps as appropriate to their needs. With only an occasional glance at an awaiting visitor, disinterested women in white uniforms and hats poked at and stirred food with serving spoons and drifted together for conversation.

"There's a booth." David pointed to a corner area.

Rennie needed to escape this torrent of crises. Death continued to intervene in life. Investigating an environmental spill on a farm in Iowa would be a plum assignment right now. Murder and religious intrigue fell heavy on her soul. She needed something else to fill her mind and replenish her soul. She eased onto the vinyl seat on one side of the booth, eager for a normal moment.

"What do you do, David? Your grandfather was proud of you. He said you were a physicist. You work in Switzerland?"

"Yes, in Cern at the Large Hadron Accelerator. It's the most powerful research tool in the world. I'm privileged to be there. We've been revealing new knowledge of the subatomic world more quickly than any of us can understand."

"I saw something in the news about discovering, at least in

theory, the Higgs boson, if that's the right name."

"Exactly. For those of us doing theoretical research, a confirmation of the Higgs is quite exciting."

"Why? What's the point? Isn't the real world enough for you? What's the point of exploring invisible worlds that exist only on paper and in atom smashers? Excuse me, I need some coffee."

Rennie slid off the booth cushion and maneuvered through tables to the counter. She realized she wasn't ready for polite conversation. Glaring at the packaged food in a display case, she found a suitable victim to devour. Her anger needed to kill it, eat it, and fill herself.

A voice across the case said something like "—help you?"

Rennie realized a server on the other side was speaking to her. "No, *prego*."

She stepped back. Up again, "*Si*, this and this, and coffee."

The server put the items on a tray, handed it to Rennie, and pointed to the check-out station. Back at the booth, Rennie settled into the seat and arranged her food in silence. She sipped her coffee, followed by a moment of intensity as she looked at her food. Finally, she picked up half the sandwich and pointed it at David.

"David, I apologize, and I appreciate your being here. You don't deserve my anger. I'm afraid I've lost some of the centered peace I had until a few days ago. My old self is back, and sometimes it's not too reliable, or pleasant."

She put down the sandwich.

"I need to tell you what I've been through in the last few days. I've been kidnapped twice. I saw the shredded remains of a priest, and the cops suspected me of being involved in the murder. I saw the murder of an old man who was kind to me, and some jerk tried to ... he took me into a dark place, and — oh, God and now, Matthew. He's gone," she noticed she was crushing the sandwich.

"Rennie, I —"
"This is what happens to the next guy that messes with me."
She threw the smashed food onto the plate.
"Excuse me."

David studied her as she walked away, shaking her hand to the side to remove the mess on her fingers. She powered her way through the crowd to a restroom. *Female behavior* registered in his thoughts as if his brain was doing a topic search. He admired but never understood them, and at this point, his purely rational thinking would be quite willing to say "goodbye" to this one. Yet, he had an assignment and she was unique, even attractive. He appreciated women, and he wondered if there was a syllogism that fit their behavior. The problem was that emotion could not be quantified. He also knew emotion was an uncomfortable quality for him. He wanted to understand Rennie and help her. A smirk slipped across his lips as he realized how similar she was to subatomic particles. She captured his attention with energy and mystery.

Hmmm, this could be interesting.

Rennie returned to her place at the table. "I'm sorry, David. It's all been too much."

She glanced around and spoke in a near whisper. "I think there's more to come. I need your help, David."

"I'll do what I can for you. It seems you're safe now, and the exhibition is apparently ready. Feel free to give me the details you think are important. Grandfather said you were a top-notch investigative reporter. I'll trust your instincts."

She checked the area again and then gave him a quick synopsis of people, places, and events. Several times, he redirected her thoughts back to the historical elements of the story.

"What difference does that make, David? We've got to deal

with the people who are alive now."

"Yes, but we have a cause-and-effect process happening. There's something about this that intrigues me. I'd like to research it to learn more."

"A friend of Matthew's at the British Museum— I think his name was Snapper—he was looking into it. You might contact him."

"Yes, that would be old Alistair, a brilliant professor of archaeology. He was on a dig with Grandfather and me long ago. We were near Corinth. Huh, that's interesting. Corinth."

"Now what?"

Calculations and analyses ran through his head. "I don't know."

Rennie's phone buzzed. She checked it and excused herself.

David's thoughts continued to swirl until they landed on the loss of his grandfather. His shoulders sagged and his breathing lost energy. The request from Matthew to help Rennie emerged with clarity, and with it, a sense of determination to get involved as she needed him.

David lifted his long frame from behind the table, adjusted his glasses, and decided to enjoy the savors of the restaurant. Given his academic appearance and build, one might expect a hesitant staccato to his pace but there was balance, almost grace in his step. When co-workers and people he met noticed this, they would ask him if he was an athlete or musician. He enjoyed those questions and responded only with oblique allusions to his profession.

He strolled along the display cases and decided that sweet was what he needed, light and not tart. His selection of a pale, lemon drink and a fluffy pastry from the case were returned to the table with anticipation of delight. His fork, pressed with a light but firm feel between his fingers, was guided through the creamy layers of the dessert. A surgeon might have done as well.

As he swallowed a last sip of the drink to finish his refreshment, the bands across his back tightened.

Corinth?

That guy Michael asked him about Corinth, but the moment flew by without further inquiry. David sat back and wondered if he should ask Rennie about Michael. The thought that she seemed fragile yet explosive cautioned his desire to risk more outbursts.

Rennie dropped onto the seat cushion. "That was good."

"What?"

"I finally had a chance to talk with a friend back in Iowa. They've been very worried. They feel helpless so far away, knowing I was in danger."

"I see. I suppose they're pleased to hear from you."

Rennie's face showed doubt. "Yes, I suppose. They're doing research to see if they can offer insights on what's happened with me."

"Rennie, please know I'll do what I can for you, especially to be sure you're safe."

"Thanks, after the exhibition, I just want to go home. I wish I'd brought my ruby-red slippers. Of course, I'm from Iowa and not Kansas."

"I don't know what that means Rennie, but I like seeing you smile. Would you care to eat now? I'm sure they have some indestructible food."

She laughed and looked at the mangled sandwich.

"I guess I killed that one, huh?"

"Right. Nice work. You provided a good summary earlier but anything more you remember about what happened in the last few days will help. Every insight might be important, so don't skip anything. We're both specialists in research. Together we might find the clues to solve these mysteries."

Rennie's posture rose up. "You've said the magic words, my

friend. Together, we solve this. Okay, stop me as you like, but here are some other thoughts. As I said, I flew to Rome, and from there —"

VI / 2

Deep underground, a cool cellar of polished stone hummed with the sounds of machines that control temperature and humidity. Aslan Yilmaz, director of the magnificent Topkapi Palace complex, searched between the racks of ancient artifacts for his chief archivist, Yusuf. As the ancient documents curator, Yusuf rarely departed from this vault of glory and history. Despite his devotion to his craft and the treasures that surrounded him, he referred to the below-ground archival facility as "the dungeon." He was there for the work and nothing more.

Aslan saw his man and called to him in their native tongue. "There you are, Yusuf. How you find anything in this maze is miraculous. What's on your agenda today?"

"Well, today we're comparing the *tughra* used by Halife Suleiman the First with that of Halife Ibrahim. Usually, there are distinct variances in style from one sultan to another, but these have many similarities. Given the hundred years between them and the history that filled that period, it's odd to find such agreement. There must have been a desired connection by Ibrahim for Suleiman."

"Ha! You have the eye of a hawk for details. May I speak of some administrative matters we must take care of? This has been thrust upon us by Ankara."

"Yes, of course. I'll put these on my work-station. We can sit over there."

They settled into deep blue, overstuffed chairs. The chairs were wide, but the sturdy men filled them. In rougher clothing, they would blend in well with construction workers. Yusuf handed the director a small glass filled with a clear liquid. Dark hair stood out from his hands.

"This will ease your tension and embolden your desires."

They tossed the liquor into their throats.

"Yusuf, an agent from the government met with me yesterday. He said his ministry is concerned with risks of terrorism here at the museum. As you know, there are crazy people with guns attacking the public and destroying priceless treasures of history in Syria, Afghanistan, Tunisia, and Iraq."

"Does he know we have military and other security here?"

"Yes, but it's not enough for him. You know how tense Ankara and the rest of the country has been. It is true the region is coming apart. Now it's in our country."

Yusuf took the glasses and refreshed them.

"What must we do?"

"He wants us to complete a brief dossier on all our staff, including students, visiting scholars, all who work here in any manner. It's outrageous, really. And, he wants it next week."

"We can't do that. We would need the cooperation of each person. We have work to do, serious work."

"That's why I need your help. You have the best skills with details and documentation. I'd like you to lead this project. With your guidance, it would be done quickly, and then we can move on with our real work. Here's a form he needs filled out on all the staff."

Yusuf's eyes flowed over the document. His face tightened and he stood. He took a few steps.

"This is nonsense. Our administration people must have this information immediately available. Why not have them do this? You and I have more important things to do."

Aslan got up and perused the workroom. "This is true. At the same time, I need someone with the proper level of authority to oversee it. Yusuf, I was once an archivist, too. I know the importance of what you do and the time required."

Yusuf continued to study the spreadsheet. "They want cell phone numbers, personal information, travel. I don't get it! You and I visit other institutions on a regular basis. You've been to Rome and Athens, and I was in Izmir. Is the Institute of Religious Studies in Izmir a breeding ground of terrorists? Certainly not!"

Aslan stroked his cheek with a finger. "The death of Professor Erkan at the institute was horrendous. Maybe they noticed that."

Yusuf collapsed into the chair, the information form slipping from his fingers to the floor.

The director was conciliatory. "My friend, you decide how you want to proceed. I'd recommend getting information from the part-time and visiting staff first. As you say, information on the regular staff can be done quickly at the end. Let's go after the difficult targets first. Maybe your intern could help? What's his name?"

"Chetin. Targets? That's an interesting way to put it."

"Yusuf, we sit in the center of treasures, ancient treasures. We might all be targets, of the government, of terrorists, of others."

"Director, I'll do my best, but I must keep my projects moving forward. History doesn't stop. It needs us or the truth becomes lost. Cell phone numbers, unbelievable."

"Well said. Let me know how things go."

VI / 3

The exhibition hall displaying the letters written by Jesus hummed with inadvertent conclaves of the righteous and the studious. Two rows of polished bronze pedestals held convex glass display cases like large eyes gazing back at the observers. A mellifluous chant of tenor voices floated softly from the unseen to cushion the tension of expectations and wonder. Visitors came perilously close to touching their noses against the thick, museum glass that shielded the documents. Guards circulated with smooth, polite precision along the displays to caution the overly eager viewers. Individuals and small groups of allowed-clergy stared and adjusted their glasses, pointing at writings in ancient Aramaic that few could read.

Father Angelotti escorted Rennie into the chamber with David a few steps behind her. She hadn't expected such an entrance. Her palms glistened with sweat and she tugged on her clothes to straighten any likely wrinkles. Quiet came over the buzzing room as the intensity of the moment was displaced with her arrival. Whispers shifted from topics of ancient words on papyrus to the attractive, young woman. A moment later, the murmuring returned to dramatic indulgence of holy discoveries.

"Father Angelotti, I didn't expect this," Rennie said. "No one told me. I'm not prepared."

"It's okay, signora. You have no formal role. They know who you are and what you've done. Some will want to touch your hands because you held the letters."

"Tell them I washed after that. I'd like to see the displays.

Can I do that?"

"Absolutely, and your friend as well. David, is it? Did Miss Haran share with you the story of this profound discovery? It is a very big moment for all of Christendom."

"Yes, my grandfather Dr. Matthew Justus told me the story. He was a part of the story, even before Rennie."

"You must tell me this sometime. Please forgive me, I must speak with the security people."

David interrupted, "Father, I'm familiar with some of the staff at the British Museum. Where might they be?"

"There are many I've worked with. I'll see if they're available. Excuse me."

Rennie walked among the display cases. The documents looked so different. Taking them from that old box and laying them on a table conveyed no dignity or reverence until a realization swept through her. *These are in His hand!* But here, they're distant artifacts, objects to study, and impersonal. Unlike all those attending, sadness crept into her senses.

"Well, Rennie, what do you think? Is this a pinnacle moment for you?"

She forgot that David was there. "No, not at all. In fact, I'd like to leave."

"Leave? Shall I wait? I'd like to review them. Perhaps I can read a few words. It's quite interesting."

"Quite interesting? I guess that's how the researchers think of it. Matthew didn't react that way, though. Oh, dear God. Matthew. He was there, and now he's gone. I've got to step out."

Rennie wove through the crowd. "Excuse me, pardon me," she muttered.

The door was in sight, but someone was following her. She slowed her pace and turned to the side a few steps to see if the person continued to the door. As they did, she looked back to see who it was. A middle-aged man, trim build, nice suit, and shiny shoes, unlikely to be a scholar or a priest with hair that long. Perhaps the British Museum? She pressed on. Her heart fluttered with a dose of anxiety, giving her the energy to charge forward.

In the hallway outside the event, loose gaggles of men and a few nuns jabbered quietly. One lone man with his back to the wall checked his phone. He appeared to be neither British nor priestly. A bit odd though. She walked past. She wondered where the other stranger had gone, and then he was there.

"*Signora* Haran."

An Italian accent was distinct.

"May I speak with you?"

"I'm quite busy. What's this about?"

"Several things, and I respect your time. A few minutes, please. It's a security issue. Could we meet in this side room? It's open and empty."

He motioned to a door a few feet way.

Rennie slid her hand into a pocket to feel the device Raphael had given to her.

The lavish Renaissance effects of the building flowed into the small room. They settled into chairs covered with heavy, drapery-like material, so common wherever she had been.

"*Signora* Haran, I'm with a branch of Italian security services."

"ROS?"

He seemed pleased.

"You know something of ROS?"

"Only the cars and the epaulets."

"Interesting. Let me explain. There were some questions raised about your entry into Italy, and your visit to a crime scene in Naples. From that, concerns arose about who you are beyond your notoriety in the press. Congratulations, and thank you by the way for your magnificent work in finding the letters."

"Thanks, I've heard that. I was in the right place at the right time. It seems in Italy, I've been in the wrong places at the wrong times."

"Well said. How did these things happen?"

"Finding the letters?"

"Italy, events in Italy."

He seemed less pleased.

Her phone buzzed. It was David.

"Excuse me, I must get this."

The man said nothing.

"Hi — Yeah, fine — No, I'm okay — Just across the hall — I'm being interviewed, I guess. I'll be back in a minute — Okay."

She laid the phone in her lap.

"*Signora* Haran, only a moment more. Your help to clarify matters will settle this."

"Fine, regarding getting into the country, people here in Vatican City will have to explain that. One of their priests met me at the airport, took me to the pope's helicopter, and flew me to Naples. I had no idea why. I met Father Angelotti – he's someone you should get to know to help you with your questions."

"We've met with him."

"He arranged all my travels including to Naples."

"There's the matter of your name in the dead priest's diary."

"Yeah, that's another mystery. We discussed that with the cop in Naples. No clue as to how. Is that it?"

"For now, and I'm pleased to share this time with you."

This was too easy. Something else is coming.

"Oh, one other question."

"Of course, there is."

"I'm curious how you got from Naples to Rome."

Her fingers rubbed the coarse cloth on the arm of the chair.

"Once again, I thank the Vatican for that. A helicopter brought me here. Helicopters seem to be popular with them."

Rennie's gut churned as she fought for control of her

thoughts and growing anger. She showed nothing. "Is that all, Officer? What do I call you?"

"We will call you if there are more questions, and there is another one. Are you familiar with something called a 'crosier?' It's used by some church officials."

"Vaguely. I think Abbess Serena is supposed to have one. I don't know who else."

Her phone buzzed. It was David again. She put it to her ear.

"Rennie, where are you? Shall I meet you somewhere? I've met an interesting chap. He's a priest. His name is Daniel. He said he knows you."

"David, I'm in a meeting. I'll be right out. Bye."

"*Signora* Haran, these are not amusing events for us. The world is overflowing with refugees and criminals. We are at risk of violent groups becoming bold and causing great harm. Be careful. You want to be on the right side."

"Officer—or agent or whatever—I've heard about those problems. As you say, I want to stay on the right side. No, wait. I don't want to be on this or that side. I want my life back on no one's side but mine. I want to go home. Can you help with that?"

He shifted his gaze to a tapestry nearby. The intricate colors and weavings of an ancient event revealed powerful human drama.

"As with this work of art, we are all threads in a greater story. Thank you for your time, *Signora* Haran. You may return to the exhibition."

VI / 4

David moved with energetic focus from one displayed letter to the next. The excitement buzzing in the exhibition encouraged his attention to the history of the documents and with the profound innocence and clarity of personal messages from the one called Christ. Analytical complexity was not just easy for him, it was a special delight! Here, stunning information was revealed that connected and challenged ancient traditions, history, scripture, and images of Jesus.

"Father Daniel, look at this. Have you read this?"

"What, which one?"

"Here, right here. Help me. My Aramaic is rusty. It's been a while."

Daniel tried to follow the writing in the area that David pointed to. As he did, one of the security people from the British Museum arrived.

"Gentlemen, not too close please. We have transcriptions available if needed."

"Yes, yes good," David responded. "See, here. This line, am I reading this correctly?"

Father Daniel got as close as allowed. "Hmm, it's a reference to Mary of Magdala. He suggests that Mary's father supports the ministry through her. Is that it? He says her father is grateful for the change in her life from her meeting Jesus. There's a reference to the father as a fish merchant who met Jesus in Sepphoris. Fish merchant? Is that correct? So, that's when and where the healing of Mary occurred?"

"I read it that way, too. I regret not getting involved more in this, especially as my own grandfather was involved. I struggle to imagine his reaction as he first looked at these."

Father Daniel studied the adjacent document. "David, we essentially know this material from the Gospels. There's a little filler here, but not much that's either new or problematic."

"True, but that filler shows background and rationale. It speaks to motivations, and it confirms key information. In my work, particles or energy exist in some state but also relate to other aspects of matter. That creates a system which leads to understanding and prediction, not simply knowledge."

"I'm not following you."

"What if we or I wrote an algorithm that represented key elements of the interests and behaviors of Jesus? It could show what parties He was connected to and the attitudes and motivations coming from those events. If we incorporate in that formula the topics in the letters, we might define an entire system that represented the experiences and thinking of Jesus when the letters were written."

"That might be an interesting project, but I don't see the use of it."

"Daniel, we would know His thinking. Physicists analyze quantum-level behavior by computing probabilities for the behavior of phenomena and then compare that with whatever real findings can be generated. This creates a predictive map of the particle in question. In this case, we can't predict the future behavior of Jesus, but could look back to see a consistent personality portrayed by the theory."

Daniel leaned close to David and whispered, "Some people suggest future actions by Jesus are possible. Your algorithm might be a good idea."

"Daniel, if such a system created a personality map, Jesus as a person would be more fully, deeply known. It's like science learning the mind of God. Applied to other writings in the Bible, we could discern with a measure of scientific reliability what is consistent with His thinking and which are just stories about Him. Has anyone done this? It seems so obvious."

"I don't know. The Jesus Seminar back in the eighties attempted to determine that intuitively. Not many people mention the words *algorithm* and *Bible* in the same context. Miracles and angels and other matters of faith are not subjects for much scientific review."

David leaned back and looked into the distance above the display cases. "Daniel, I just thought of something. My grandfather was a highly-regarded archaeologist and biblical scholar. In my early years of studying physics, he asked me to do some research for him about angels. I've not thought of this for a long time."

"So what? There are plenty of references to angels and other visitors from heaven throughout the Bible and in many other religious traditions."

"Yes, but what Grandfather asked me to do was to write algorithms as I just described, describing the situations, people involved, what happened, and all that. He wanted to see if there was a system or design to better understand this belief of visitors from the divine and see if the actual process of such visitations could be understood."

"The belief in or the behavior of angels?"

"Well, the behaviors if you think of them as real."

"David, messengers of gods have always been considered to be real by people open to mystery. Consider the Egyptians, Persians, Greeks, and others. This is not new. Did you write these formulas? Did they yield anything?"

"The list of references to angels was extensive, but there was a limited number of actual appearances. Focusing on just those provided data for the system."

"What did he do with it?"

"I don't know. I gave him the analysis and described how they seem to operate. At the time, I was busy with theories and discoveries in my own work, so I forgot about it. The results of the analysis suggested, as a comparison concept, our current views in physics of multiple or parallel dimensions. I thought it amusing."

"What's amusing?"

"The idea of angels or divine beings stepping in and out of our dimensions from another."

"David, it might be interesting to do your analysis of the behaviors of Jesus, create the theorem, and see what happens. We now have more material to work with. I'd like—"

Rennie stepped in. "David, can I speak with you? Hi, Father Daniel. You get around. Excuse us, please."

"Rennie," David said with glee. "These letters are wonderful. Is your interview over?"

She didn't look pleased. "Could we talk?"

"Of course. Daniel, I'll be right back."

David polished his glasses as he followed Rennie through the crowd. His thoughts roiled with how to design a system to identify the future behaviors of a person. A program like that must exist for all types of predictive personal analyses! For a moment, he lost her.

"David, over here."

She went through an arched passage into what appeared to be a sitting room. The noise and commotion of the display area was left behind.

"I was just questioned by a guy from Italian security. That's who he said he was with anyway. I'm still followed. I can't shake this thing."

"Rennie, is it you they're after? They probably think you're a piece in a puzzle that will point at the real villains."

"Don't you get it? I don't care what or who they want. I want out of here. The exhibition has begun, and I didn't play a role in this anyway. If I'd been a guy wearing robes, they'd bring me in on a golden carriage."

"If you're really done with this, let's get out of here."

"What's Daniel doing here? How did you meet? I don't trust him."

"He's quite fascinating, a fellow researcher in a sense. We hit upon something in one of the letters. I must look into it. Daniel could be useful to us. He's very knowledgeable about the early Christian era."

"Be careful who you let in. Too much trust is a dangerous thing. Your encounter with Michael today still bothers me. I can't figure out who he is and which side he's on."

"Rennie, from what you told me in the cafeteria about your experience with this Michael, my guess is he's CIA or NSA. But regarding Daniel, I see no risks. By the way, he offered to show us some of the private collection of Vatican documents. These date back to the first century. No one gets to see those. He had access to them when he worked on his PhD. Rennie, let's do this."

"David, I'm playing it safe. I don't want to get caught in some secret archives and have to explain it to the authorities."

"We'll be all right. He has the clearance to go in. He said we can do it tonight when everyone is distracted. You might like the special section they created to hold the letters."

"What? They're not staying here!" Rennie covered her mouth, shocked at the volume of her outburst. "They're not staying here," she continued urgently but somewhat quieter. "They're to be permanently maintained at the British Museum. That was the agreement."

"Maybe it's just for while they're here. There's so much in those archives that we might find. I mentioned to him the story you came across about the apostle Paul and letters from some women in the early church. He's quite excited about that."

"You told him? That wasn't for others to hear."

"Rennie, it's a topic for research."

"No, it's not. People are getting killed over that. Dear God, don't tell anyone what I said."

"I understand, but there are times when risks must be taken for a great discovery. You did that once and here we are. Let's go with him. Think of it as a trip to the library, an incredible library. Rennie, you might discover something wonderful."

"Or, deadly."

Rennie turned and gazed into a window full of evening darkness.

David studied her. He'd begun to see her as mysterious as his physics quandaries. "Rennie? Daniel's a good guy. He can help us, and we might find the answers to all this."

She seemed to awaken. "David, I'm not ready, but maybe Daniel has the key to unlock this mystery. Stay alert. Bad things keep happening around here."

VI / 5

Abbess Serena Magdalene approached the museum exhibition room with attitude. She encountered at least a dozen Vatican officials after the grand opening ceremony, and no one bothered to compliment her on what she considered an exquisite beginning to the exhibition. That event was a tribute to her as much as to this distinguished event, and few seemed to notice.

Although she had changed into her standard attire, the guests in the exhibition hall were wearing their most saintly outfits and acting as if this was their first school dance. They glanced about to see who might be looking at them. It was a celebration of self, and no one was satisfied.

The eyes of the security people from the British Museum were attentive for their own reasons. The threat level was low, but uninvited others appeared to be in the room conferring with ranking clergy.

Serena snapped her fingers to catch the attention of Father Joseph. He hurried close by. "Where is Miss Haran? Where is Angelotti? Aren't they running this part of the program?"

"*Abbessa,* Father Angelotti is in the far corner. I saw Miss Haran leave a few minutes ago. She was with that young man who met her today at the basilica."

"Who is he and where did they go?"

"I asked Sister Angelina to follow them, to make sure they didn't get lost or need anything. Sister Angelina greeted Miss Haran when she first arrived. I thought if they crossed paths,

Sister would be a friendly presence for Miss Haran."

"Okay, I like that. Update me before the evening is over. I want to know where they went and if they meet anyone."

"Absolutely, *Abbessa*. We won't let her, uh, get lost."

Serena bolted into the crowd with energy but style, nodding to those who caught her eye. The sea of robes appeared to part as she swept ahead. Angelotti was her target.

"Good evening, my friend," she whispered from behind him, interrupting his conversation with other priests.

Her presence oozed over him.

His usual feigned look of delight joined his nervous eyes.

"Oh, dear *Abbessa*. What a glory-filled mass you presented today. A humble and reverential opening for this profound event."

"Thank you, Father. I didn't see you there."

"Yes, well, I join all who were there in gratitude for your inspiration and devotion. May I introduce these other dear brothers? Oh, I'm sorry. You must know them."

All nodded at the same moment as if the magical strings holding their heads up were cut.

Serena spoke with commanding yet diplomatic grace. "Would you excuse me, Brothers? I must be rude and bother good Father Angelotti here with business. You know he's the person responsible for bringing the Lord's letters to us."

Hands swiftly crossed their bodies in blessing. Serena's shoulders shifted back to lift her frame into an imperious presence. Angelotti slumped.

He followed her to a quiet spot next to a small table.

"Someone is with the girl Haran. Do we know him? There must not be any more catastrophic escapes." Her crisp enunciation delivered the message.

"Yes, he's a researcher of physics they say. I spoke to Father Daniel after I saw him with them. He told me this. They're somehow connected with the professor from London who first assisted her there. What was his name?"

"I don't care about him. Who is this Father Daniel, anyway? We don't need anyone stirring about."

"My inquiries suggest he's harmless. Of course, he's a lawyer." Angelotti's cheeks seemed to struggle to not smile, so he looked down.

"I was once myself you know. Do you consider that a problem?"

"Your background, *Abbessa,* is most impressive, as is your work for the office of the secretary of state. You have survived, pardon me, *served* there admirably."

Her nostrils flared. "Father, you got Miss Haran here. Now, watch her and anyone around her. They all need to go and quickly. The opening is done. Let me know of any further needs the exhibition may have. I'll be sure our resources are put to your disposal. Please watch that woman."

Their shared bows as they departed conveyed another battle fought to a draw.

Serena drifted into the hallway. The quiet allowed some perspective. Her body relaxed as images of people and hushed words tumbled through her thoughts.

What now? Where is Haran?

Movement far down the hall caught her eye. A man, long shiny hair, sauntered around a corner. Something looked wrong. He didn't fit in.

Where is Joseph?

Rome, Italy
The Vatican Museum

VI / 6

Daniel hurried down the gilded hallways of the Vatican Library with a steady, determined pace. Rennie and David followed a discrete distance from him. The casual innocence of their pace conflicted with their dour expressions and the colorful, turbulent scenes of biblical drama covering the walls and ceiling.

David paused and gestured toward a massive painting. "Isn't this incredible? Each time I visit the museum and other buildings here, my experience is the same. The vivid life in the art and the brilliance of the design of these walls and ceilings seems excessive. Yet, it fits this place."

A white, plastic sign emblazoned with a red arrow stood high on a brass pole and clashed in merciless, modern arrogance with the elegant pastel frescos on the walls. *Sala dei Papiri*, it announced.

"Hey, that looks like papyrus on the wall." Rennie waved a limp hand at the long columns of documents preserved in frames. "That's what the letters from Jesus were written on."

"Right, that's what this room holds. Wait, I've passed through here a dozen times on the way to other places and never paid attention to the documents. I wonder if there are translations of these. We must ask Daniel."

They turned a corner and noticed that Daniel had stopped and was speaking with a young woman.

"What's he doing?" Rennie asked. "This isn't a time for socializing. He's a priest for God's sake."

"True. She's not bad, though."

"Oh, get over it. What do we do? We can't stand here in the hall and look stupid. We shouldn't be here. Oh no, she's coming this way."

As Daniel and the woman approached, he seized the initiative. "Maria, these are my fellow researchers David and Rennie. As I mentioned, they need to join me in the library for a short time. Friends, Maria is the principal art restoration specialist for the Vatican. Her current project is evaluating the oldest Bibles in the library to establish priorities for their care. They're richly emblazoned with fine art."

Young and animated with light brown hair held back with a clip at each temple, Maria's eyes sparkled with welcome.

"Daniel tells me you need to join him. I can open the access, but I must leave soon." A firm nod added authority.

David extended his hand. "Maria, I'm delighted to meet you, and we appreciate this courtesy. Any time allowed is most useful."

Daniel waved Rennie forward, clearly eager to share his special sanctuary of discovery.

As the group headed toward modern glass doors etched with the keys of St. Peter, David engaged the woman in conversation. "Although I've been here many times, I just noticed the papyri in the last hall. Are there translations of those available?"

"Probably so, but at least forty percent of our collections have not been studied."

"So, there might be something of great significance hanging in public view, yet unknown. Amazing! Maria, if you could email to me whatever translations of the papyri that you have and are convenient, I'd be grateful. It would help our research. Here's my card."

Maria studied his card, laughed, and ran a hand across her head to smooth her hair. "I'll see what I can find. Thank you, uh, Professore Justus. I'm sorry I was not prepared to meet people and have no card with me."

Above the glass doors the words *Bibliotheca Apostolica Vaticana* announced the entrance to the private library of the pope. Before reaching them, Maria and Daniel turned to a plain wooden door on a side wall.

"You may enter here. I will wait. I must lock the door after you enter." The words seemed to roll and dance along Maria's Italian accent.

A shot of caution ran through Rennie. She waited until the others entered the private access. She took a deep breath and followed.

Why did this Maria stay behind to lock the door?

A cavernous, dark room with a barely visible ceiling at least fifty feet above them swallowed the little group. Rennie felt the books, maps, parchment and art watching them. Two rows of dark wooden reading desks with antique lamps quietly sat empty along each wall with a wide center aisle, interrupted at three points by large cabinets with dozens of small drawers.

Daniel led the group down a softly lit passage to a metal stairway. The hard, dull ringing of shoes on the steps echoed as a muted alarm to persons unseen. The handrail was a cool, unfriendly assist in climbing to the second and then third levels. In tense silence, they followed Father Daniel along the walkway. Rennie glanced far below to the silhouettes of the study tables against a white marble floor.

"Here we are," Daniel said with satisfaction.

"The oldest documents are up here, out of the way. The book at the end of the aisle offers some reference to where we can look first for information on your concerns. Frankly, I'm assigned to look into the matter of the Greek priest and hadn't thought of looking here until meeting you."

"Father Daniel," Rennie asked, "could we get some light in here? I thought this might be more elegant, I don't know, 'Vatican' or something. It seems so industrial."

"Well, you're not in the main library. That's a flight down from the floor we came in on and then over. We're in what some describe as the 'hidden archives' because it's more like an attic for the main facility. Few people come up here or even know about it. I love the place."

A deep quiet filled the air except for the delicate crackle from his turning of pages in the library reference book.

"Okay, this is a good place to start." Daniel pressed a finger on a notation. "Let's go."

David leaned in to read the labels on cardboard binders standing in precise order on the shelves. "What's in these?"

"When people hear of the secret archives they think it's intended to be hidden, but the word 'secret' is really intended to mean private. This is the pope's private library, and while one might think of it as a collection of all things Christian, the focus is on documentation of the Holy See and Papal authority. Much of it is the diplomatic history of the Vatican. There's even a school here to train researchers on Vatican diplomacy. Okay, check this out."

Father Daniel slid a wooden panel out from beneath a middle shelf and placed there a box of documents.

"These are copies of orders of the Secretariat of State in the 1500s. Over in what they call 'the Bunker,' the parchments documenting the trial of Galileo Galilei, gold seals and all, are preserved for rare viewing by researchers."

"But those aren't old," Rennie interjected. "I mean, we need to find materials a thousand years before that."

"Exactly. We have a copy of one of Paul's letters on papyrus that was transcribed from the original at some time in the second century. It came out of Egypt. Much of the best evidence of early Jewish and Christian scripture comes from there. The bishop of Alexandria and other religious leaders in that area did a great job preserving the earliest writings."

"The letters from Jesus that I found were discovered in Egypt and brought to England. They were on papyrus, too."

David seemed eager to be on the path of a fresh discovery. "Father Daniel, does the library have an identifier resource for the origin of documents? A database, so could we do a search for papyri found in Egypt? Also, since the early church became strong in Greece and Turkey, documents with those tags could be valuable too."

"I like it. Over here. It's not fast but we've got a system we can check to do that."

Rennie, walking near Father Daniel, said, "You'll be my best friend if you can find anything related to what might be behind all this."

He grinned, looking too handsome for a priest.

Rennie was surprised and a bit embarrassed feeling a sudden interest in this happy American man in priest clothing.

David broke the spell. "Friends, could we continue?"

They hurried to a computer in a dark corner. Rennie paused and peered down tall rows of shelving packed with ancient lives, ideas, and mysteries. Shrouds of darkness filled the distant end of each aisle.

"Hey, did you hear that?" Rennie asked as she grasped from her pocket the device Raphael gave to her.

Daniel sat at the computer desk and punched a button to launch the system. He looked back.

"What? Maria said we're the only ones here, and she's waiting outside the entrance door. Maybe it's her. There are other access points, but they're rarely used."

Rennie returned to the main aisle and surveyed the deep, black emptiness of the library with all her senses on alert. Was that another noise or her imagination? The muffled, excited jabber of Daniel and David annoyed her.

212

"I've got a flash drive with me," David offered.

"Can we download whatever is in the Egypt, Greece, and Turkey folders so we can look at them later with more diligence?"

"Good, almost there."

Screens on the monitor quickly changed as Father Daniel searched the files. "Here's a folder. Let's get whatever we can. It's not like we're taking actual documents. These are only the digital scans and one might offer a lead."

Attempting a hushed voice from a distance, Rennie asked, "See if you can also find anything related to Pandateria or Ventotene. Paul might have been there."

She backed away from the central aisle. The open drop from their third-floor level to the hard surfaces at the bottom gave a hollow, empty, and reverberating tone to every sound. It chilled the bottom of her spine.

"Come on, guys, finish this up. I want out of here."

They stopped and swiveled in response to a soft bump sound in the darkness. Something was there.

David tapped Daniel. "Let's go."

Another closer noise caused Rennie to point her device in that direction. "Who's there?" she shouted.

Her voice bounced around the cavern.

David spun around. "My gosh, Rennie. I almost peed. Don't do that."

She was ready. Her fist was tight on the device.

"Okay, done. I think you might have some useful information in this." Daniel removed the flash drive from the port.

"Here, you two go that way, turn left and go down a stairway two levels then out the door you see there. That puts you out on a terrace. You can go around the corner back to the exhibition. People will think you were out for fresh air. I'll close this down and lock up with Maria. Hurry."

Rennie took a step in the direction of the noise. She listened.

"Come on, let's go."

David nodded in the other direction. "This way."

She waited, rigid, ready.

"Rennie, now," he said softly.

She looked at Father Daniel as the program shut down. "Are you okay?"

"Yeah, good. I used to be up here alone a lot. I'll see you down there. Go."

David was already down the aisle at the corner.

"Be safe, Father Daniel," she ordered and laid a hand on his shoulder.

He flashed another smile that warmed Rennie's senses.

A few quick, quiet steps later, she and David disappeared around the corner. Her hand grabbed the railing at the first step. She stopped.

"David, we've got to stay. Something's wrong here."

"He'll be fine. Noises happen. I'm a quantum-level physicist. Believe me, odd things happen."

A few moments later Rennie felt a fresh, evening breeze on her face as she left the building. She thought the grand buildings around them appeared to be growing up into the evening sky. But she had to look back. Questions and fears charged through her thoughts, as she considered Father Daniel alone in the building. Light poured from windows in the adjacent reception building, appearing to gain intensity and creating sharp contrasts of light and dark as the sky went to night.

"David, wait. Was that a shout? Should we go back? Let's wait here for Father Daniel."

"He said he would go out the way we came in."

A few lone souls silently crossed the grounds in the distance from different directions.

Rennie stopped and glanced behind her. She strained to see into shadows. "Who said that?"

"What? Rennie are you speaking to me?"

"Someone said something. They were over there, but I don't see anyone. Didn't you hear it?"

"No, I didn't. Are you sure? You seem tense."

"A voice, a man's voice said, 'Start over.' It was clear, like right behind me."

Rennie started toward shrubs nearby. "Where are they? I heard it."

David gently grasped her arm, turned her, and warmly embraced her.

"Please hear me. No one came close. We're alone. Rennie, you've mentioned you used to be affected by situations rather than manage them. This is a good time to manage this and move forward. Let's go back inside, please. They might be looking for you at the exhibition."

"I know, I know. You're right, but I heard it, David. It's not my imagination. What does it mean, 'Start over?'"

She pulled away from him and took a few steps onto the lawn. No one was nearby. Rennie listened. Was the spirit of this ancient place speaking to her?

David slid his hand into hers. He stepped in front of her and gently touched her cheek. "Rennie, I don't know what that might mean, but we must go inside. Please. Father Daniel's probably in the hall already. Rennie, you're a very special woman."

She closed her eyes and leaned against him, resting her cheek against his. Their bodies warmed as they quietly held one another.

PART SEVEN

Rome, Italy
The Vatican Museum

VII / 1

Sister Angelina arrived at the intersection of two hallways as she looked for Rennie. She liked the American and wanted to know her better. The fact she had discovered a magnificent artifact of the Christian faith but maintained a humble attitude was a profound contrast to those who had done nothing of importance for humanity yet presume they deserve the highest respect. Angelina believed that Rennie's destiny called for more wonderous things, and if she, a simple nun could help, she would be there.

No one could be found in the corridors of the Vatican Museum. All was quiet. She shrugged, thinking there was a misunderstanding and wondering if she should return to the event and report to Father Joseph. It seemed late, and she was missing the fun and history of this great moment. She decided to go to the right but sensed someone was down the corridor in the other direction.

Maria and the nun saw each other and offered friendly greetings in Italian.

"Hello, I'm Sister Angelina. I am looking for a Miss Haran, the American woman. Have you seen her?"

"There was a woman here earlier with Father Daniel and another man, David. Daniel said they were researchers. They needed access to the library. I let them in."

"Oh, good. I was worried I'd lost her. Where did they go?"

"I'm not supposed to allow unauthorized people to enter. But I've got to leave. You can come in with me and we'll find them."

Maria unlocked the side door and propped it open with a hinged bracket at the bottom.

"It's dark in here," Angelina whispered.

"I'll get the lights."

Click, click, click sounded as Maria flipped the switches. The women closed their eyes to adjust to the instant glare.

Maria pointed ahead, "We'll go this way, to the central study area. It's open to all the collections. We should be able to see them from there."

Angelina followed Maria down a short corridor to a curved reception desk. They paused and gazed around the quiet, massive emptiness of the building. The central hall was surrounded by tall dark shelving filled with erect sentinel folders of the written past.

"Father Daniel, are you here?" Maria called out. "Father Daniel? Wait, that's odd. There were no lights on. Let's go over there. Father Daniel!"

Angelina stopped in the middle of the study area as Maria turned toward the tall racks of documents at one side.

Reaching the end of a row of tables, Maria turned and jumped back slamming into the end of a shelving unit. She appeared to be frozen in horror.

"What, Maria?" Sister Angelina called out. "What is it?"

Maria covered her face with her hands and shrieked at the ceiling. "No!"

Angelina raced to her side.

On the cold marble floor, the body of a man in priest's garb lay face down, a burgundy splash of blood scattered from where the face hit the surface.

Maria opened the fingers of her hands and looked down. "Oh, dear God."

Sister Angelina knelt beside the body and made the sign of the cross over it and on herself. She looked up at Maria.

"Who is this? What happened here?" Pain spread through her face.

Maria's eyes blinked in shock.

Angelina rose and escorted the distraught woman through the chamber of death and past the tables to the door they first entered. As they arrived, Father Joseph appeared.

"What's the problem?"

The women couldn't respond. They were lifeless, stunned.

"What happened?" he demanded.

Angelina pointed into the library.

"A priest, in there, he's dead."

She saw the gray eyes of Father Joseph. "It's horrible."

"Say nothing. I'll handle this. Go to a restroom and calm yourselves. Go nowhere and speak to no one until you see me again. Go that way."

The women huddled together as they stumbled to the door. They looked back in disbelief.

Sister Angelina watched Joseph dash down the central aisle and scan between the rows of tables. He stopped and looked back at her when he saw the heap of black cloth on the floor. He marched toward the victim, studied the situation, then looked up the levels of racks above him.

She was startled when a guard pushed past her and called in Italian from the entry door, "Who's there?"

Joseph snarled, "I'll be right there. Do not come in."

The guard motioned for Angelina and Maria to step back. Maria asked why he was there and he said the library door was supposed to be shut at that time and an alarm had sounded. He demanded they explain the open door but got no answers from the two women. Joseph arrived and informed him that a private Vatican matter was being handled.

"Show me," the guard ordered.

"You may not enter here," Joseph responded with a firm, deep voice.

The guard glared at him but stepped back. He peered past the priest into the great library. He raised his chin, threw his shoulders back, and marched into the hallway away from the library. There, he put the cuff of his sleeve to his mouth, whispered, and stood at attention.

"What have you done?" he demanded of the guard. "I said there is a private matter that will be handled by the Holy See."

"I'm doing my job," was all the man would offer as he crossed his arms and stepped in front of the door.

Joseph snarled, "We shall see about your job."

He charged into the corridor, but he slowed when Father Angelotti appeared, his robes flowing as his pace gained speed.

"What's going on?" Angelotti inquired. "Some of the security team in the exhibition hall gathered and are coming this way. Tell me now."

Sister Angelina and Maria recoiled in fear.

Joseph's mouth opened but said nothing.

"What?" Angelotti demanded.

"A priest has died, in the private library. He was found by this nun, Sister Angelina. A guard came to the door, but I didn't let him enter. The door is now locked."

Angelotti pressed his fingertips to his temples and closed his eyes.

"I must tell the abbess. Oh, Holy God, guide us."

Rennie and David found their way around the museum to what appeared to be a possible back entrance. David led the way and spoke with a security man at the door to confirm it was the exhibition hall.

"David, what's that? What's happening?" Rennie pointed at a series of windows in the building. People were running down a hallway.

The security man's radio erupted in rapid conversation. He pressed it to his ear, spun and opened the door, and dashed inside. David caught the door before it closed.

With cautious steps, they made their way inside toward the exhibition hall. Gaggles of guests appeared to be leaving. Worried looks and suspicious glances charged the air.

Rennie grabbed David's arm and stopped.

"Wait, something's going on and it doesn't look good. Ask someone."

David interrupted two passing priests and asked in Italian if the exhibition was still open. He listened, nodded, and thanked them.

He turned to Rennie. His eyes flicked around as he struggled to keep up with his thoughts.

"What, David?"

"We've got to go. We must leave the Vatican. Now. Now!"

"Tell me what they said!"

"He said there was an accident. Someone was injured. Rennie, it was in the library."

"Oh God, it's Daniel."

"I don't know what, but we've got to get out of here until this is sorted out. You can stay the night at my hotel. No one here knows me."

"We've got to go to my room first. There are things I need."

"Rennie, we don't have time. You're right, something bad is going on. We must leave, now."

VII / 2

Yusuf slid his finger across the glass holding the certificate for Distinguished Achievement in Religious Artifacts he received from the Association of Catholic Diocesan Archivists. They thought it was a profound break with tradition to award it to someone outside the church, especially someone in Istanbul.

"Not so unusual, my friends," he whispered to the award.

His name in gold and red script, *Yusuf Pashazade Mustafa*, coasted through his thoughts. Turning, he gave a nonchalant wave to a young man entering the archives' restoration room. They spoke in Turkish.

"Chetin, thank you for finally coming to work. The night life of an intern must be exhausting."

The thin, twenty-something man looked awkward and uncertain. He was more like Harry Potter than the rugged stereotype many have of Turkish men.

"Not at all, sir. I mean, I wouldn't know really. I was working last night and am replacing the manuscript I reviewed."

The answer stimulated in Yusuf his deep disdain for obedient, selfless commitment to an organization. His devotion was to the artifacts not any system. Years of inadequate funding enhanced his frustration of being unable to properly care for the treasures he served. Seclusion and sarcasm had become the trademarks of his recent work.

"Well then, you can start on a new project. This one has supreme national importance!" Yusuf thrust a finger into the air.

"Very good, sir. Whatever you wish. I'll be honored."

The chief archivist had no time for pandering. The work was important, not the people.

"Enough. You are far too capable to do this project, as we all are but, our priorities are now dictated by barbarism. Here is a list of data that is needed for all the people on this list of staff. It's required for some security matter that has landed on Topkapi."

"That's interesting. Is there a particular format they require?"

Yusuf considered the fresh face of the intern. Chetin's eyes, obscured behind thick lenses in his glasses, stared across the information sheet as if discovering an ancient treasure.

Yusuf had already tired of the conversation. The task was unwelcome, so he resented dwelling on the details.

"I imagine they want a spreadsheet, in digital form. Use whatever is most common for such data. You can set it up by name with status such as full-time or whatever."

"Of course, and they can search and sort the data by whatever criteria they like."

"Yes, yes, don't bore me with your technical insights. Just get the information and finish the project. They want it next week, I think. Check with Personnel on any needs. They know of this."

"Is there a security concern within the staff?"

Now, Yusuf was annoyed. "No, it — well, I don't know why this is required. The state made the request and we're responding. They're afraid that terrorists will seize Topkapi and cause a disaster."

Chetin settled back in his chair. "We know the horrors they caused at Palmyra. They have no respect for the ancient world or the current one."

"True. I don't know what would interest them here. Topkapi was a harem of all things, and the artifacts are mostly of historic interest to the people of Turkey."

Chetin sat up, looking alert. "Sir, there is also the collection of Emperor Constantine. It's rarely considered or even researched. And, I'm not sure if we've scratched the surface on knowing what we have. There may be more in the storage area."

Yusuf began to pace. He thought of how little has been examined due to a lack of funding for staff and facilities. The thought of treasures waiting for him within this place maintained his excitement for the work, and the Constantine files always beckoned his interests.

"Yes, it's unlikely terrorists know of it since almost no one does. We might have Christian artifacts the Vatican isn't aware of. Ha!"

He looked sideways at Chetin and gauged the response.

"I didn't know that, sir."

"And, you shall never remember it. Confidentiality is the centerpiece of our art. We manage what needs to be preserved for the ages. Sadly, the vast majority of it is still in storage and hasn't been reviewed for the catalogue. If too many people know of this, the treasure is at risk."

Chetin arose from his work chair and began to follow Yusuf. "Sir, I've seen the archival assistants bringing something from storage to shelves each week. What are they bringing? How do they choose?"

"It's mostly random. You say you didn't know of these things. But you've worked in those records."

"Yes, but I wasn't aware of how few know of the collection. The conversion to Christianity of Emperor Constantine should be of great importance to Christians. We have the records."

"Yes, but we don't know what's in them. Altogether, the major archaeological museums have tens or hundreds of thousands, even millions of artifacts that remain unknown, untouched."

"My professor at the Institute of Religious Studies in Izmir —"

Yusuf studied the young man. The recent murder of Chetin's

mentor, Professor Erkan, struck everyone in the professional community. The intern became pale.

Yusuf was not comfortable with sensitivity to the emotions of others. In this case, he had to try.

"Chetin, your professor, Ahmet Erkan was a fine man with a brilliant mind. I'm sorry what happened to him. Terrorists strike anywhere, even on a college campus in Izmir. The crucifix in his throat was quite bizarre. Chetin, please take care of this busy-work for me." Yusuf referred back to the paperwork needed by the security people. Discussing it aroused his anger. *It's a detestable project, invasive.* But seeing his intern's face, he softened a little. "I find that being down here helps to put aside the world out there. Perhaps, it will help you for now."

"Yes, sir. By the way, Professor Erkan had great respect for your work. That's one reason I'm here. He said he wanted to come here to pursue his research. Perhaps, I could carry on some of that when there's time? His particular interest in the writings of the Christian apostle Paul and the later councils such as at Nicaea might be included somewhere in our collections."

Yusuf blurted, "No, that's not possible!" He caught himself. "I mean, there's so much to do, so much backlogged work. Taking on extra projects is not feasible."

"My apologies. I'll get to work on this spreadsheet. Since I'm here, sir, may I have your information for each of the categories? That will help me create some structure for the data."

"Not now, start with your own information. Come to me last. In fact, I'll personally include my data and that of our director when all else is complete. That is the director's plan. Now, move ahead."

Yusuf drifted into the stacks of ancient boxes, folders of preserved documents, and unique pieces of history. His technical mind was hungry for the something special he secretly yearned to find. There were shocking discoveries hidden away, he knew it. He must find them and do so before anyone else.

VII / 3

David, my phone is buzzing. It's Bud, my editor back in the States. I've got to get this."

"Wait, Rennie. Your signal — Hurry, we must keep moving."

"Hi, Bud. I have to be quick. What's up? No, I'm okay, and I'm with Matthew's grandson, David. He's good company. Meet a reporter, here? No way, especially not right now. We're in a hurry to leave. Something's happened, and possibly another murder. Yes, at the Vatican. You contacted Sfumato in San Francisco? *Why?* Does he know these groups that Michael mentioned? David and a priest friend Daniel downloaded some of the Vatican's ancient records onto a flash drive. We've not checked the data yet. Bud, I'm sorry, we've got to run. Thanks for helping. Please thank Angie, too. Bye."

David stepped into the shadows next to a tree. "Rennie, is that the building you're in?"

"Yes, I'm on the second floor about the middle. Let's go in that side door. Wait, is someone over there?"

A figure cloaked in forms of darkness began to hurry toward them. In brief moments when caught in the light it appeared to be a nun. As she drew near, Rennie could see it was Sister Angelina. Rennie stepped into view.

"Sister, I'm so glad I found you. Do you know of the accident at the library? What happened?"

Angelina buried her face in her hands then crossed herself. "It was Father Daniel. A terrible accident."

Rennie turned and clutched David's arm. "Oh, no, no," she pressed her face into his shoulder. "I feared it was him."

Angelina took a few quick breaths. "Signora Haran, there is something wondrous about you. I don't know what it is, but I will help you. Terrible things are happening, but I know there's a heavenly plan that includes you. You must leave the Holy See and do so now."

"Sister, David here also said we should leave until this horror is resolved. Could you help us?"

"Yes, I'm yours."

"I'd like to not be in a public place right now. I need you to go to my room and grab whatever you can get to put in my backpack. Bring whatever you think you would want if you had to leave quickly. We'll stay out of the way until we see you. Make whatever excuses you must but please bring it quickly."

The young nun spun around and ran up the walkway, her robes flapping along the way. Rennie and David moved deeper into a clump of shrubbery with a few trees. David put his arm around her. A heavy shroud of fear enveloped them.

"Rennie, I don't know what she's thinking, but it confirms my instincts. We're going to my hotel for the night and sort out what's next. I don't know what that is, but we'll know tomorrow."

"Bud said there's a journalist here in Rome who's revealed some of the Vatican's secrets. He wants to talk to me."

"Is that the direction this should go? Do you even know what you'd say? Rennie, first we need to get out of here. Maybe we should go to Switzerland to my research center. It's safe, and from there you can return to the States, meet with journalists, or whatever you want. Okay?"

"How do we do that? People are searching for us. Look!"

She pointed into the darkness. They knelt down and watched several men run down a path fifty meters away and stop. They gestured in different directions and separated. One of them jogged toward the administration building near the hiding place of Rennie and David. A sound near one man, as if from a small speaker or phone, chattered something. He stopped and put the device to his ear. He turned, looked at the basilica, and ran toward it. His elbow jerked in the air as he tried to hold the phone near his head.

"They want us," Rennie whispered. "How will we get out of here? There's a huge wall around the place."

"We might get a cab at an interior street, although that has many risks. If we walk to the gates, I'm sure the guards have been notified. I wonder if that woman in the library, Maria, could help us. I hope she's all right."

"There were quite a few civilians at the event. Could they all have left already?"

"Rennie, we can't go back to that building. Security people will be crawling all over it."

"Maybe we could hide here. It's the last thing they'd expect. Sister Angelina could get us to a safe place."

"Here she comes."

The trio crouched behind the shrubs.

"Okay Signora Haran, here's your backpack and I have another small bag with more things. I hope what I put in it is sufficient. You can always purchase what else you need."

"Sister, Miss Haran and I wondered if there's a place on the premises where we could hide until morning. Their search for us might have been called off by that time."

"Hmm, it's an interesting idea. Of course, you'll be out in full light in the morning. When I was in collecting your things, I had an idea. I was interrupted by a man who didn't seem to fit in. He's gone now."

"Who was this man?"

"I don't know. He came in as I was leaving. He asked if I'd seen you. I asked him who he was. He said 'security.' I replied that anyone in this building must have credentials and I needed to see them. He told me he would ask the questions. When I asked again, he hurried out the door on the other side of the building."

"Thank you, Angelina, for all your help. What did this man look like?"

"He was dark and had long shiny hair. He spoke with an odd accent. I hear and recognize many but this one was different. I don't think he was part of the exhibition."

"Okay, Rennie, we need to get out of here tonight. Sister, what do you suggest?"

Her face seemed to light up with excitement. "Very few people know there's a hidden passage out of the Holy See. It's in the great wall that runs from us to Castle Sant'Angelo. A few popes actually had to use it over the last thousand years or so."

David began to stand up until Rennie pushed down on his thigh. "That's amazing, Sister. I thought I knew so much about this place already. It's in the wall? Rennie, my hotel is only a couple of blocks from the Castle."

Rennie whispered, "How do we get into it, the passage? And, can we get through it? After 500 years or so, it might have fallen apart inside."

"Actually, the Vatican had it renovated maybe a dozen years ago. I got the idea for you to use it when I was in the admin building, so I found the keys to the gate. Then, that guy interrupted me."

David leaned in, "Do you think he knew what you were doing?"

"No. We can access the passage at the wall over there. We must cross some open area but there are plenty of trees we can move through on the way. Also, Signora Haran, I brought you what might be a useful disguise, for at least tonight."

The nun unfolded a handful of cloth revealing a tight, black hat and a larger piece of material.

"This is a cape and there's another item here, a skirt. I'm

sorry I don't know your size, so I grabbed what was close."

Rennie laughed. "Sister, it's okay. I've done this before, and recently."

"At least in the dark it will change your appearance enough so people won't give you a second thought. And David, your surprise is a priest's collar."

Angelina suppressed a giggle. "Again, just in case."

David removed his tie and struggled with the collar.

"Okay, let's do this."

VII - 4

Father Joseph swung open the tall door to Abbess Serena Magdalena's inner office. She steamed past him without comment. She wrenched off an outer robe, threw it across the room, and went to her desk.

Father Angelotti cautiously stepped in and stood to the side. He glanced back to see if Joseph had followed. He was alone for now.

Serena shoved a few papers around.

"Where's his business card? He gave me his business card!"

She glared at Angelotti. "Who was he? Who did he work for? I've asked these questions before and I've been told nothing!"

"He was secretary for the cardinal of the Congregation of the Oriental Churches. They're located in the Palazzo dei Convertendi."

"Ah, in the Palazzo — Are you suggesting I stop by and pay a social visit? We're going to get slammed with a hundred questions in the next few hours and we have no answers to anything! What can you offer? This situation is critical."

"*Abbessa*, this is indeed tragic. At this point, all we can do is be sympathetic and let those who inquire know we're devastated. We're looking into this and intend to find the answers."

"He was a secretary, not some priest with a to-do list given by an administrator. He had influence. He knew things and knew people. And! What did he know about recent events that even we don't know? He was smart and skilled. Someone was blunt about how they felt about him."

"*Abbessa*, we can't answer any of that right now. But, one line of inquiry that could be helpful is to find out why he was here and what he wanted. Those questions could best be explored between the office of His Eminence, the secretary of state and that of the Cardinal Prefect of the Congregation."

"How convenient, Father. That would then be my responsibility. I'm asking the questions and now I'm to answer them. We know the Congregation of the Oriental Churches has authority over the churches of the Oriental Rite in the Middle East, North Africa, and of course Greece and Cyprus. Guess what! This is also where we've had some unexplained recent deaths. We have no understanding of those issues and now we have this one, here in our midst. Something is going on. It's like a cancer metastasizing in front of us. And, it happens on this glorious day of the exhibition of the letters."

"Speaking of the letters, do we know where Signora Haran is? I hope she's safe."

"Thank you for another question instead of answers. I recall that you and Joseph were going to attend to her. Joseph!"

The abbess called before turning her attention to the priest before her. "Father Angelotti, you were going to further investigate the incident in Naples. What did you learn?"

"I made a few inquiries. My resources are very limited, and it was just a couple of days ago. However, someone from ROS contacted me, probably because I went to the scene and the Carabinieri met with me."

"And, the results?"

"He didn't seem to have much interest in us, the church. I think they're consumed with immigrant and refugee issues. His questions suggested that the sad event had some connection with those groups. I helped as I could. I think it ended there."

Joseph made a timid entrance. He peered at Angelotti. "*Si, Abbessa.*"

"Father, we're re-grouping tonight to see how to proceed with this latest disaster. What information do you have about Father Daniel or the cleric deaths that recently occurred?"

"*Abbessa*, this all began only days ago, and we've all been busy with the exhibition. There's nothing new I can report. Father Daniel asked me a few questions, but he offered no information. I know nothing about him or his work."

"When did he talk to you? You told me earlier today you didn't know him? Did he ask anything that suggested his concerns?"

"No, he thought your office might have useful information, so I thought he would contact you directly."

"That's it? Nothing more?"

"Well, he did inquire about your crosier. I don't know why."

Father Angelotti glared at Joseph. "*Abbessa*, may we talk privately?"

After Joseph closed the great door, Angelotti approached the abbess's desk.

"*Abbessa*, this matter of your crosier has come up before. The agent from ROS contacted me with some questions about the death in Naples and the one in Izmir. He offered little information, but he also asked about your crosier. My impression is the murder weapon in the Naples case might have been the top of a crosier staff."

"Why have I not heard of this before?"

"It became known in the last day. We've all been focused on the exhibition of the letters. Signora Haran has been another distraction."

"So, where is she right now?"

"I assume—"

"It appears you don't know. Is there nothing I can learn so I can inform His Eminence, the secretary of state that we're not all ignorant bureaucrats? Would you like to join me when I meet with him?"

"*Abbessa*, you alone are supremely gifted to deal with this. I'll find Signora Haran and let you know everything that's relevant. This is a sad moment for us all. I'm so sorry."

A determined pace took him out the door.

Her fingertips pressed hard into the desktop.

Rome, Italy
The Grounds of the Vatican

VII / 5

Rennie felt like grabbing Sister Angelina's belt as they dashed through the shadows toward the Vatican wall.

"Sister, slow down."

On the other side of the wall, the busy traffic of Rome shouted down the stillness of the holy preserve they occupied. The air carried hints of exhaust gas and risk, but hope was over there.

Angelina slowed. "We're almost there. Is David close by?"

The nun glanced back to see him ducking, stumbling, and looking from side to side. His height wasn't helping his athletic ability for running in a crouch.

Modern double doors served as the entrance to the "secret passage." A black awning above the doors suggested a casual venue for eating instead of an historical site. Sister Angelina struggled with the keys for what seemed like too much time as Rennie and David stood exposed in the light.

"There," Angelina grunted as she pushed the door in. "Hurry now, close the door and I'll turn on the lights."

In an instant, a warm glow flashed down the long hall. Rennie stepped behind the young nun as if to hide.

"Okay, Signora Haran, this is easy. Go in that direction until you can go no further. There will be doors like these at the end. No key is needed to open them from the inside. Along the way, you'll see other doors on the side walls for storage and other uses. It would be wise to turn off the lights at the other end. Any questions?"

"What do we say if we meet someone along the way?"

"That would be unusual at this hour. If it happened, don't say anything. Just nod, look down, and keep going. David, you could be authoritative. Men who act like they have positions of power are never questioned here."

Rennie's voice was full of tension, "Sister, this is happening fast. I'm not sure what I should do next."

"Rennie," David said with a deeper voice than what she'd heard before. "We'll figure it out. Let's first get out of here and then check our options."

"Our options? We might be in the same place physically at the moment, but you and I are in very different places, David."

Sister Angelina laid her hand on Rennie's shoulder. "One option I recommend is to go back. Consider where you were before you came to Italy. What was your vision? What did you do? That was your real life."

"You mean, start over? Someone said that."

"Perhaps, but we all become dazzled by things and by events that lead us astray. Find or return to the path that the real you is called to walk. That's where your strength, your peace, and your truth are."

"Truth, there's that again. Sister, for a few days now, truth doesn't seem to exist. I used to believe I could find it in each situation. Now, all I find are dead people."

"Ladies, I believe we need to get moving. Sister, how far is it to the castle?"

"You'll be there in less than ten minutes. As you exit the doors, if you see any of the Swiss guards or other security people, wave and keep going. You'll turn to the left and another left to reach the street."

Angelina whispered, "Signora Haran, Rennie, in the morning, get in touch with your quiet center, pray for guidance, and set aside all your fears. Don't listen or speak, just wait. Let go of judgment and feel what your inner drive directs you to do."

"You remind me of a dear friend back home. She's a librarian, and her name is Angie. This can't be a coincidence."

Rennie embraced the nun. "Thanks."

"Peace be with you Rennie, and be peace."

David, already turning, offered Angelina a wave and a polite nod mid-step. "Let's go, Rennie."

The echo of their footsteps in the tunnel of stone seemed loud until the crash of the entry doors behind them shook their senses. They spun around. Angelina was gone, and now they were on their own. Fresh steps down the hall quickened to match their heartbeats. Who initiated it wasn't clear but for a short distance they held hands. It was okay, and okay to let go.

Angelina had told them there would be doors for storage areas and other needs along the way, but each one caused them to slow and wonder if it was an exit. The near success of their escape heightened their anxieties. Soon, they were jogging and even smiling, dashing to a finish line. Racing each other. The exit doors awaited them ahead.

Rennie stopped, grabbed David's lapels, and pulled his face close to hers. "I need to, uh, your priest's collar is crooked. Here."

She tugged at it. "There, it's ready. Now, how do I look?"

His face relaxed into a personal look she hadn't seen before.

"Divine, in a nun-sense, of course," he responded. "Yes, 'get thee to a nunnery'!"

For a long, comfortable moment, they said nothing. Then, David suggested they get out of there.

At the doors, Rennie did a quick examination of the door area. "David, do we just push through the doors and walk away or what? If we meet someone, the less said the better."

"I agree. I think the street will be to the right of where we leave this tunnel. However, if we exit into the castle, we must find the nearest exit, maybe to the left as Angelina said, and get out of there without appearing suspicious. Remember, you're a nun.

Cross yourself or something and smile sweetly if we're stopped."

"I think acting friendly is good. Wave and keep moving as if we do this all the time. Here we go."

Firm, steady pressure on the doors released them into a dimly lit lobby occupied only by a few benches and two tapestries on opposite walls. There was no obvious exit in the paneled walls.

Rennie stayed at the door and held it open as David entered the room. He quickly paced along the wall searching for an exit.

"David, I'm waiting here in case you can't find the door."

He didn't respond. David squinted at the wall as he slowly turned. "There it is," he said pointing at one panel. "See, a sliver of space under those two panels. Now, how do they open?"

Rennie glanced back into the tunnel. Did she hear something? Where's that device? Her breathing felt tight. "Hurry," she whispered.

Men's voices sounded down the tunnel as a hollow echo. Angry words were thrown at each other in a distant place that came closer with each comment.

"David, they're coming. We've got to get out."

"I can do this. If I can find the spot where —"

Rennie turned away to see into the tunnel. A beam of light danced along the floor. Off to the side, in a recess of where the tunnel met the lobby wall, she noticed something reflect the light. It looked like a door handle.

"David, I found something. Come here." Her hand jerked in a quick wave. "This might be our door out."

He scratched his head. "I'm sure there's a door here in the lobby. Why they hid the mechanism is quite odd."

"Come here," she hissed.

The voices down the tunnel were now clear, but they became quiet and one whispered, "Shhhh."

Rennie gave the door she was holding a slight push open, took a few quick steps, and grabbed David's coat sleeve. She pulled it and ran back to the door before it closed.

"Now," she mouthed and shook her fist. "Get over here."

He drifted over and took the door handle as she sprinted a few steps into a dark corner to try the other door. A look of shock hit David's face as the approaching noise of the men grew louder. He let the door to the lobby softly close and hurried to her side as she turned the handle to the door in the wall. A delicate click opened the mystery door and released them to fresh hope in the dark of night. David dashed out as she eased the exit door shut just as the search team passed by.

"Here, follow me," David ordered.

Crouching, they stumbled along the outside wall on ground heaving with a rolling contour and rugged soil. They could smell the river at the bottom of the embankment.

"There's a street," he whispered. "We're almost there."

"Who's there?" A guard yelled in Italian. He was between them and the street.

David looked into Rennie's face. "Go with me on this. We're lovers."

David stood up from his bent position and lifted Rennie by the arm. He waved to the guard and responded in Italian. "A man and a beautiful woman enjoying a quiet moment by the river. You understand."

He turned to Rennie and kissed her with passion. After a moment of shock, her lips became wet and full as she joined in the hunger, pressing her body against his, enjoying the liberation of her desire. He pulled back but she pressed ahead, her heart pounding as she held him.

"Rennie, Rennie," he said.

She stopped and eased back. David turned to the sentry and said in Italian, "We'll go now. Good night."

Rennie was numb and confused. David grasped her hand and led her past the guard. A hundred meters down the street, they realized they wore the clothes of a priest and a nun. Quiet laughter brought a warm embrace, linked arms, and fresh steps.

In a few minutes, they were around the corner, in the real city of Rome and on the way to the Hotel Scoperta, safe at last.

PART EIGHT

Rome, Italy
Vatican City

VIII / 1

Angelotti and his associates gathered in an unused office in a dormant section of a distant office building within Vatican City. Seclusion is easy to find in vacated facilities. Dull lighting and dank air set a heavy presence but affirmed the detached nature of the meeting. Without an agenda, each man was quiet and guarded. There was no preparation, no announced main topic of the many that needed to be discussed. Each wondered who would take the lead to move on to meaningful action. The lack of a table or desk made it easy to select a chair without defining one's position.

Paolo Scarpia held up the day's issue of the *L'Osservatore Romano*, the Vatican newspaper. In Italian, he spoke with concise precision, as was his way with all things.

"'Praise and wonder with the exhibition,' nothing else. The same with the *Corriere della Sera*. It's Milan, but their connections are better than *Il Messagero* here in Rome or *Il Mattino* in Naples. No other news that concerns us. Busca, what have you heard?"

Francesco Busca attempted to get comfortable in his chair. It was easier to direct him than get useful input. A shrug and down-turned smile from his bulldog face were his typical responses.

"Also, nothing else. Nothing from Naples or elsewhere. Security resources are also quiet. They're dealing with 400,000 refugees on our shores. Our issues are of no importance to them."

He flicked his hand to the side as if he was finished. Then, with a hint of anger in his voice, he surprised everyone and continued.

"Regarding the woman, the grounds were searched, guards were questioned at exit points. We checked the passageway to the Castle. No evidence of a departure was found. Some of her things seem to be missing. No one knows anything. We have people doing a more thorough search of the grounds now that it is day. The man who was with her must have helped her, so we're trying to locate him. We'll find them."

He shot a determined glare at the others.

Father Angelotti listened, eyes closed. In the Vatican circles, it was often said that Vesuvius would blow again before Angelotti lost his temper. Grace, diplomacy, and peace were themes of his presence. He removed a white handkerchief from his pocket and applied it to each temple. His free hand calmly stroked through the thin hair above one ear. He stood and breathed deeply as if he was going to sing an aria. A deep, solid vocal force came from him that no one had ever heard before. His face twisted into rage.

"Newspapers! Conversations! You're helpless and worthless!"

His voice deepened into a growl. "We expect this of Vatican security, but you? Who are you? What have you done with the two soldiers that look like you and work with me? Two thousand years of stability are coming apart and no one knows what's going on! It's time for answers. It's time to take care of this cancer!"

Scarpia's instincts were conflicted between launching a fight and obeying authority. He always responded to an attack. His eyes darted as he struggled for a response. "There's also the question of the death in the library. Who will pursue it? How will this be addressed?"

Angelotti eased into his chair and leaned forward.

"Exactly, my friend. These questions are part of the problem and possibly the act that will expose the players. The denouement may have arrived."

Busca blinked in confusion as he awaited orders. He didn't need an oration.

"There was a man present last night that no one has identified. He seemed to have full access and used it. Sister Angelina encountered him and couldn't identify his accent. It was maybe Serbian, Bulgarian or Turk. Don't we know Turks?"

Tense silence filled the room. Busca stumbled forward. "It seems we should discuss this incident about Father Daniel. How can we help make it go away?"

Scarpia and Angelotti appeared frozen.

Busca pressed ahead. "I mean, that happened here, not in Naples or Turkey or somewhere. People are asking if it's related to this woman from America. Some say she was with him. Was he involved with her?"

"My friend," Scarpia said, "as I asked a moment ago, what do we do with that matter? It's not likely the American woman did this thing. People like her only ask questions. They do nothing else. Some are concerned about her, but it's for political reasons, nothing important."

Angelotti was up again. "Don't underestimate the significance of politics and how much trouble it can cause."

He wandered the small conference room, cleaning his eyeglasses. "So, how do we use this trouble?"

"What?" Busca said. "Use trouble? I thought we're to keep order."

Scarpia's phone buzzed in his pocket. He ignored it until it buzzed again.

"Do you need to get that?" Angelotti fitted his glasses on his nose. "Hmm?"

Scarpia studied the number of the caller and returned the phone to his pocket. "It's nothing."

Busca stood up and slid his chair away. "Do you want me to step into this Father Daniel situation? I can see who might be investigating and what is known. I have a contact with the prosecutor's office."

"Francesco, thank you, but it's not needed straightaway. This only happened last night."

Angelotti continued his stroll around the room, his hands clasped behind his back. "No, but how can we find out why this Father Daniel was there? What was he—or they—trying to find? What? How can we learn this? Knowing that will point us in the right direction."

"What if he was just showing them around?" Busca looked more awkward than ever.

"That wouldn't cause him to be killed."

Scarpia appeared thoughtful, stroking his chin. "Or, was it unrelated? The investigators might be interested. A jealous lover? A death like this is too dramatic for anyone to connect it with what he might have been doing in the library."

"Yes, and crude."

Angelotti paused in his journey. "Crude. And, what does it mean? This could not be by someone here, on holy ground. Or, could it?"

Angelotti stared at a wall and gently raised a hand, with his index finger in fluid motion as if timed with a music score. His thoughts flowed with the rhythm.

"What was the message?" he breathed into the melody. "And, who composed it?"

Turning with a serene appearance, Angelotti spoke clearly. "Here's what we must do. Francesco, my friend, you let your sources in security know that there are rumors regarding possible romantic intrigue between Father Daniel and others, and this might be a cause of his tragic death. Say that the Vatican is looking into all possibilities, but given the sensitive nature of it, the investigation will be confidential."

Busca was again surprised. "How do we know that? This is new information."

"But our friend here, Paolo has said it."

Father Angelotti seemed pleased. "Now, Paolo, our areas of concern with the Churches of the East are not affected by this local matter. They are unlikely to hear of it or think of it further. We must begin a fresh and positive campaign to affirm and expand the devotion our churches show to the faith and to our Holy Father. Yes, that is how we proceed. Even our politicians will appreciate that."

Scarpia appeared interested. "Where do we begin? Greece? Lebanon? Turkey?"

Angelotti mused, "What gives us the most traction forward? Wouldn't there be trouble in Turkey, given that state's shift to a conservative Islamic view?"

Angelotti was now energized. He quickly took a seat next to Scarpia.

"Maybe we should split up," Busca added. "We each could visit communities in different countries and pursue the effort with real impact."

This seemed to surprise the other two men.

"I mean, if that's our mission. I want to help." Busca tossed a limp hand into the air.

"I must say I like it." Scarpia finally came alive. "We'll need a consistent message and coordinate our timing. The theme can be simple, like traditional teachings with new blood."

"No, no," Angelotti interrupted. "No mention of blood. How about something like, what has always been will always be, in bold new ways."

"Genius!" Busca blurted out. "Can I go to Turkey? I've always wanted to see Istanbul."

"Very good, my friend, and you, Paolo, go to Greece. That

will require your skillful diplomacy considering the events outside of Naples."

A deep pool of intense quiet filled the room. Opportunity
and unknown risk lay ahead, but they had power and now, new
direction.

VIII / 2

Rennie awakened to the feel of a soft bed and sheets as her senses welcomed her to a new day. She felt safe and rested, and having David with her gave a sense of bliss. She could feel the weight of his body lying next to her. Savoring that awareness, she lifted the sheet over her face.

His voice asked, "Are you hiding?"

"Do you want to find me?"

"Most definitely. Hmm, where do I begin?"

"Wait, first tell me who you are."

She laughed.

"Woman, you are incorrigible!"

Rennie slowly moved the sheet down from her face so she could see him. "Good morning. I assume it's morning?"

"Yes, but still early. You can sleep in if you like."

"David, why are you wearing your glasses? Have you been up?"

She leaned up on an elbow to fully see him. A hint of disappointment arose in her as she realized he wore a fresh top and workout pants. He even had socks on his feet.

"Yes, and I'm glad I didn't wake you. It was very early. You needed the rest. The moment I awakened I thought about the flash drive and wondered what might be on it."

He sat up, his legs hanging off the side of the bed.

Bright lights went on in her head. Rennie tipped up with some awkwardness and newly found modesty, holding the sheet against her.

"What? What did you find? Is there anything we can use?"

"Very possibly, but I think we must first decide where we go from here and how we get there. Switzerland is the best option. I think it's best you do not go directly to the States. Rail is the quickest to Switzerland but most easily checked by authorities. A car is more flexible but takes much longer and it's expensive. Air is out of the question. Hmm. But I do have friends at a lab in northern Italy. A few days of rest at Lake Como would be nice. Milan would be fun too."

"Hello, Earth to David. Did you solve this small matter of being chased by guards and possibly being wanted for murder? Can we just stay here for a while?"

David got up and stretched. He turned to look at his laptop on the small desk by a window.

Rennie used the moment to slide off the bed and jerk the sheet with her. She pulled it around herself and marched into the bathroom, grabbing items of clothing on the way.

When she reappeared, her rested, bathed, and refreshed presence projected new determination. She stood over David as he worked on his laptop.

"David, I've been thinking. I don't want to run. That's not me. Last night, that voice said, 'start over.' I don't think it means return to Iowa to my little life before I found the letters. I need to figure this out, what's going on."

"So, a phantom whisper in the night determines your fate. Really? Simple logic tells us —"

"David, simple logic has little play in what's been going on."

"Precisely, and that's why inserting that vital ingredient into the mix would be most valuable. Rennie, we're in uncharted territory where beasts roam. We must remove ourselves to a position where your research can be done in safety."

Exasperated, Rennie tried a different tack. "I'm hungry. Let's get food. Then, we or I can plan what comes next for me. I need to eat."

"Very well, I shall go out and get it. You stay here."

He grabbed a shirt from his bag and pulled it over his head, stepped into a pair of shoes, and stuck his wallet and some money in his pockets. "Is there anything in particular you'd like?"

His attitude felt cool to Rennie. She didn't look up. "The usual, whatever that is. Maybe a pastry, coffee of course, juice if available."

She could be all business, too.

As the door clicked shut, Rennie checked her phone for email and other messages, then took David's notepad from beside his laptop and began to jot notes and simple diagrams. Her eyes closed as her intuitive powers grasped insights on what had happened over the last few days. Sights, sounds, and faces flowed out of darkness across her inner vision. She flipped a page of the notepad and wrote again. An occasional upturn of a corner of her mouth suggested understanding. Notes and arrows filled spaces on the pages. New energy filled her. But the facts as they were laid out didn't offer a sense of direction for her.

She gazed into the distance, not at anything but just looked. She was always quick with questions and now struggled for one. This situation with David filled her awareness and she didn't understand it or even have a good question. They have a strong connection. She can feel it.

The men she had known in Iowa were predictable. Some were quite smart or attractive and a couple were both. They had a blithe approach to life that seemed refreshing and an effective counterbalance to her serious attitude. Pickup trucks felt carefree. Throw a cooler and beach chairs in the back and head for the woods or the river. There were the dummies of course, and some of those were hot. More Apollo and less Plato. One guy had a flannel shirt that was missing a couple of buttons. A big smile came to her face.

So, what's this thing with David? He's brilliant and so British. She mouthed the words "so British." He has a kind of old-world wisdom that seeps out with unsuspecting force. Maybe it's the danger, being in the crucible together, bonded in battle. She wasn't sure if she wanted him like the guys in Iowa, although she did appreciate him. Maybe that was more important.

The notepad demanded her attention. How are Angelotti and his partners connected with people here? And, who came after Raphael, and who the heck is Michael? Rennie hates it when there's no transparency. Power hides behind a curtain like a manipulative coward. Her anger returned.

Rennie opened the files on the laptop. She would reveal what's behind this dark veil. There had to be something in all these files that would guide her.

David returned with two plastic bags and placed them on the bed.

"I not only purchased coffee and things for this morning but also food to take along. We need assured supplies for this journey."

He noticed her focused work. "So, what's up?"

"I'm trying to sort things out. A lot has happened in a few days, a lot of players. I'm at no risk here. This isn't about me. It's about bigger issues and the people committed to them."

"Exactly. Brilliant. This isn't about you. You're free to go, and you should."

"No, the point is I want to get to the bottom of what's going on. I'm safe to do that."

"Was Father Daniel involved or was he a safe bystander as you think you are? How many journalists and doctors in war zones are not involved in the conflict but die anyway? I see them as heroes for bringing out the truths the world needs to know, but many do not come home. Rennie, I respect your drive, this profound and meaningful curiosity you have. That's also part of me. But I don't want to see you condemned by your innocence in pursuing this story."

"David, it's not just that. This is a journey, my destiny. It's what I'm supposed to do."

"Rubbish. Your destiny is the result of your decisions or your failure to decide. Rennie, people end up in financial or moral ruin by their choices. They don't choose to have disasters. Your decision to remove yourself to safety is wise. It's a tactical step, a controlled retreat, shall we say."

"Isn't that what they expect? That I'll run away?"

"So, what? They're probably not even thinking about you. But if you insert yourself into their games you can become collateral damage — no intended harm but dead anyway."

"David, you don't understand. You're filled with cold logic. Where's your passion?"

David glared at her and turned away. He picked up the trousers he had worn yesterday and threw them at his bag. The pants grazed the bag and landed in a corner. He hurried to them and smashed them into the bag.

Rennie held her breath and slid her chair a few inches away. Confusion and fear filled her.

He pointed at her. "Passion! Passion kills people! You've lived your little life in some small town and think emotions are something to ride around on for thrills or discovery of new places. Your escape from a routine life is found in passion, but it's a deadly human emotion. It killed my great grandfather Matthias. It's going on here now, and you think it's a plaything that won't hurt you. People die from it and others die inside but go on living. You don't know how my grandfather was wounded in his heart when you came to London and resurrected the story of his father. The memories had been buried for half a century. You brought the pain back to life!"

Rennie gasped. Moisture filled her nose and eyes.

"That's right," he continued with added energy. "He would never say it, but I could see it. I knew him and loved him. He grew up without his father. Your discovery of the letters filled his last year of life with pride but also countless questions. Grandfather was in comfortable retirement, bliss. And then you came along. He loved you Rennie, in part because you were full of life and brought Matthias back to life for him. You also refreshed his father's death."

She shuddered. "No, no," slipped from her lips.

"So, where does this end, Rennie? Who's next? You? Me? Then, who picks up the pieces? Who lives, wounded inside? Answer me!"

"I don't know. I don't know. Please stop."

She buried her face in her hands and turned away.

David marched to the door and slammed it as he left.

Rennie struggled for breath. She stared at his bag as if answers would arise from it. She stood and sat again, weak and shaking. Doubts flew through her thoughts about what she knew, about herself, about David, about Matthew. Had she been so totally wrong about everything important to her?

She got up again and went to the window. She held herself as she watched the people in the street and wondered what in life was real. Was the confidence and clarity and peace she felt after finding the letters real?

Rennie needed to get out of the room, but she didn't know where to go. She felt trapped and afraid. She paced back and forth, grabbed the room key, and hurried into the hallway. As the door closed, she felt as if she was again on the run, chased by unknown threats. She looked up and down the dark stairway. A noise above her pushed her to dash down the stairs to the entry door. She stepped outside into a noisy world of strangers. Her frantic energy drove her down the sidewalk, across the street between cars, and then back again, confused and searching.

As she approached the entrance to the hotel, a man grabbed her arm jerking her against him.

"Rennie, stop."

Her eyes met David's. "Rennie, I'm sorry. I was wrong, terribly wrong. I'm sorry."

Clouds of confusion swirled through her mind. Helpless, she pressed into his body, desperate and wanting. They held each other.

"Rennie, please forgive me," he softly said in her ear. "I'm afraid, too, and still grieving the loss of my grandfather. I can't take any more death. I want you and want you to live."

They said nothing for a long minute. People passed by gawking at them.

He looked into her eyes. "I'm sorry. Let's go back to the room. May we do that?"

She couldn't answer except for turning toward the hotel and keeping an arm tightly around him.

They walked in silence into the hotel and up to the room.

"Uh," he said. "I guess I left without a key. Did you bring it?"

She nodded and opened the door, throwing the key on the bed as they found places in the room.

"David, you said a lot. I don't know what it all means. I'm in shock. You've turned my world upside down."

He sat down, bent over, shaking his head. "I don't know what to say, or even what I said. It poured out of me, out of control from some mindless place. Maybe that was passion."

She wanted to understand and care. He was clearly hurting and fragile. At that moment she knew they shared the same pain and fear. She had buried it and pressed on but his was near the surface under the control of his prodigious logical mind. She went to him and laid a hand on his shoulder.

"David, I had no idea. I wish I knew. What you said wounded me to the core. It might be truth, but it hurts. It's too much to take in. I might never be able to process it.”

He wrapped his arms around her legs, laying his head against her belly. She ran her fingers through his hair.

“Come on, get up and hold me.”

They stood quietly for a long time, occasionally giving a light kiss to the cheek of the other. Soon, hesitant smiles and relaxed breathing came to them. They turned away from each other, searching for mindless things to do.

As minutes drifted by, Rennie’s thoughts rolled through images of her first meeting with Matthew and the historic events that followed. It was so exciting for her, and she savored the changes it brought to her life. She realized she never considered what it did to Matthew’s life. She loved the old man. She wouldn’t dream of hurting him. But David saw it and felt it.

She looked at him. This was not some cold scientist. She held back tears. “David, could we talk? Just for a moment?”

He gave her a sideways, reluctant look.

“It’s okay. We don’t have to. I just want you to know that what you said hurt, but it was something I needed to know. And, I want to learn from it.”

“Rennie, please give it a rest for now. Let’s eat, rest, consider the options, and make a plan.”

David brought her a cup of coffee and a pastry on a napkin. “I’m still sorry. I never want to hurt you. I want you safe and happy.”

“That’s what I want too, for us.”

They embraced and kissed softly, then more.

She giggled. “You know, we’d better stop this passion stuff. It’s dangerous.”

A wide smile revealed his teeth. “Well, that’s logical. We seem to have changed roles.”

“David, what is it about us?”

“Rennie, men shiver when women ask them to define the

relationship. I'm already quite nervous."

"Ha," she laughed, and slapped his shoulder. "We'll discuss this later. You'll have to decide if passion has a role in your life."

"What do you say we consider passion for the moment and allow inspiration to suggest what's next?"

"You are such a man. What happened to that serious research physicist I once knew?"

She winked and turned away.

Rennie propped up pillows on the bed and settled in with the coffee and pastry he had given her. She paid little attention to what she was eating as her mind shifted into journalist-mode. Who's behind the intrigue? Where can she get the information she needs?

She studied David as he sank into a chair, drank his coffee and relaxed, gazing out the window. She realized she knew little about him. They knew little about each other. She wondered if her priority should be to work on that rather than the mysteries surrounding what she's been going through.

David set his coffee cup aside, took clothes from his bag and went into the bathroom. As the shower sounded, Rennie sorted through the food bags. The routine was helpful in freeing her mind to stay in project-mode.

When he emerged, she was pacing the floor. Four steps, turn, and back. Her plan was ready.

"Okay, here's what I want to do," Rennie said. "We need to review the materials we saved on that flash drive. If I can find anything on there that relates to the issues I've learned in the last few days, I'm pursuing the story. If the documents are inconsequential, I'm willing to discuss letting this all go, for now. But I need and expect your dedicated effort to do a proper search."

David laid his towel on the bed and tossed his foam coffee cup into a trash basket. He was quiet for a few moments.

"Well, let's get at it. You have a proper researcher with you to do a proper search. Please note that my quick review of the files revealed a vast number of documents and in several languages. I recommend we employ the efforts of Professor Snapper or others at the British Museum to help us. Their availability is questionable, especially right now. So, let's devote a good hour or so to identifying what may be immediately useful and defer the remainder until later."

Rennie jumped up and grabbed his arms. "Good, good. Thank you. Let's get at it."

David placed his laptop case on the bed with the computer on it. He ran a power cord to a different outlet as Rennie pulled two chairs into position facing the impromptu workstation. She laid out a notepad and flipped open a new page while David found the flash drive. She checked her phone again and set it aside.

He booted up the system and inserted the memory stick as she sat ready, pen in hand. David clicked on the new drive and a series of folders were revealed.

"The first thing is to see if there's any order to what's saved here. Are they topical or chronological or what?"

They were well matched for observational speed and decision-making. He opened a file and searched, then closed it to open another in rapid fire manner. She would say, "Go back," or, "Not this one," or "Find this word." They blazed through massive volumes of data. After an hour and a half, they agreed to take a break.

Rennie needed the break for perspective and deeper thought. She took her empty coffee cup into the bathroom and rinsed it out, filled it with water, drank it, filled it again, and returned to her chair. She pushed the chair back a little and rested her feet on the bed.

"David, what do you do when you're not discovering what the universe is made of?"

"Well, I like the people I work with. We understand each

other. So, it's nice to get together at someone's home or a restaurant and talk about anything but physics. Philosophy seems to be a popular topic, and we play idea games. Einstein did that. Nonsense can be fun. What do you do when you're not saving the world?"

She snorted a laugh. "Lately, I've been kidnapped, followed, threatened, interrogated, you know, the usual girl stuff." She closed her eyes. "But my intent isn't to 'save the world' as you say. A story is a story. My hope is that exposing the issue will bring a little good, teach a lesson. I'm bored with the obvious." In a mocking voice she announced, "And down at the county fair, we have the hog show at four p.m. with a pie eating contest at six!"

"And, the non-work activities?"

"I don't know. I like to go out with my friend Angie. She dumped her almost-fiancé so now we go out and tease the boys."

A full, happy smile swept across her face and made her eyes glisten. "This letters thing changed a lot and demanded our attention away from the natural course of things, I guess. There hasn't been much personal life for me since then."

"So, what will you do for fun, other than tease the boys, when you return to Illinois?"

"Iowa. I don't know. I'd like to do a road trip, get in my car and drive to Colorado or Oregon or anywhere. I feel I've lost track of myself, my center. I once had it. I felt a kind of peace, and no matter what was going on I knew what I should do. The 'should' wasn't imposed from the outside. It's a natural drive, the right thing."

They drifted away into silent, far places. Rennie thought about her parents and how they had changed after her discovery. They had fewer expectations of her and were more open to her ideas and personal boundaries. Her parents even seemed to act warmer to each other, less independent. She imagined relationships all over the world becoming more personal and less functional. Rennie wondered if a radical discovery might be an outcome of the situation she was now going through. If so, would it be for healing or cause harm?

After a few minutes, David suggested they get some fresh air. He mentioned a patio on the roof that would offer privacy and escape. Rennie eagerly agreed. Without a word, they journeyed to the roof and entered the bright and noisy world of a Roman day.

With eager steps, Rennie crossed the polished tile, past iron tables and chairs with bright seat cushions to the short fence at the edge. Her fingers brushed through the leaves of plants growing in colorful pastel ceramic pots intermittently placed to soften the view of the barrier at the edge. The words *finally in Rome* drifted into her mind and triggered a desire for indulgence. The sun felt good. This was what she wanted. This. She hurried to where David stood.

"Hey, let's go to a piazza. Let's go to a piazza and get pizza. HA!"

She pulled at his sleeve. "Come on. I need this. We deserve it! Let's have fun."

She threw her arms around him and pulled her body against his.

"Temptress! That would be fun, indeed. But, let's think about this."

"What's your body thinking, smart guy? What were you thinking last night when you kissed me on the riverbank?" He didn't respond so she let him go.

"David, do you ever do anything without thinking it through? I know logic isn't the only rail you can ride on. Come on. Life is bigger than that. What do you feel like doing right now? Get in touch with what it would feel like to sit at a table out there where life is thriving, watching people go by with a glass of wine in your hand, speaking to people without your guard up. That's the life I want."

"Rennie, I understand. It may surprise you, but my Italian friends and I have done that, at times with considerable enthusiasm. I also know we must be cautious right now, not impulsive. Much has gone on that we don't understand. I want you safe."

"Oh yeah, safe."

She turned and gazed across the skyline. She could feel the throbbing pulse of Rome. She wondered what he meant by partying with his Italian friends. She felt left out.

"One can be safe without living, David. Life demands change and risk. It is growth and testing. Life shouldn't be too controlled. I've heard that things deteriorate more quickly if they just sit. If they're put to work, they thrive. David, I want to thrive."

"Let me see if the hotel restaurant will sell us some food that puts us at risk yet keeps us alive. I'll check with them and be back in a few. After that, we decide if we're going to work or party."

"David, we can make the work a party."

As he turned to leave, Rennie slapped his rear end. His mock look of surprise was betrayed by a wink.

VIII / 3

Which phone to use had become a troubling question for the conspirators. Was the last one returned or disposed of? Is it safe to make calls on different days with the same device? Is anyone listening or is this worry a waste of energy? The way the phone was purchased, it can't be connected to anyone so it's probably safe to use again. It's time for action, so forget risks and go with it.

"Hello, is this still a good time?"

"Yes, but we'll have to be brief. I understand there was a new development there."

"It was unexpected so a bit confusing. Did this come from you or is it freelance?"

"Not from here. If not by your people, then we must look into it."

"It's too recent to know. I've not made full inquiries yet. We have heroes among us like any devoted group. They might have acted on their own initiative. This priest was a potential problem."

"I understand, but we must stay focused on the real problem and not get carried away."

"How are things in Istanbul? You had mentioned that the security people were gathering information. Is that process complete?"

"No. What we submit to them will probably be incomplete when it happens. The remaining information will be delayed of course and might not have accurate data. They're a bureaucracy, too. It won't surprise them. Missing and incorrect data must not be obvious or have any clear method to it. What about the woman, Haran? Is she contained?"

"With the disturbance and activities last night, we lost track of her. She's not in any of the places we thought. Inquiries were made but nothing has been uncovered. There are questions about whether any follow-up is needed."

"If the woman returns to America, forget her. She'll be gone. But if she remains, she must be removed. We are at a critical time to preserve the real church. Find her, watch her, and observe if anyone comes to her aid. If it's someone from Societas, we can get them at the same time. For now, we will begin with the first targets on our list. The pulpits must be cleared of revisionists."

"I don't have the current list. Where does it begin and who does what?"

"The first ones are Kenya and Morocco in Africa; Nicaragua and Argentina in South America; in the US, California, Minnesota, Oregon, and Massachusetts; in Canada it's Ontario; and then Switzerland. Of course, there are also two in Italy. Wait, there's another one in Greece. I'll be in touch with our German friends for the European targets except for Italy. Those are yours. We have a few people in the other continents for that work."

"Is the directive still to proceed quickly but not simultaneously? It was my understanding these would be spread out over a week or so."

"Exactly, beginning in one week. All in one day would be a delight but would be much too visible. The idea is to be effective, not dramatic. That fool Galila and his desire for the dramatic hampered his work."

"Yes, but we tend to spill a lot of blood. I think we should be quick and less artful. The termination of Father Daniel is a good example."

"I agree, and we'll act accordingly. We don't want publicity.

The explanations to the press are all approved and ready for spreading as this develops. Social media is a wonderful gift for this purpose. At least in this way, technology is finally supporting our agenda instead of degrading it. The world will think Muslim extremists are to blame."

"I need to go. Send me your next phone number through our channels and I'll respond with mine. God be with you."

"And with you."

Satisfying thoughts emerged from the call. This is good. This is it. How satisfying to finally get here. Over the next two weeks, the throats of the fellowships will be slashed, and the body will become disorganized and confused. The orderly bureaucrats won't know what's going on and power will be consolidated.

Stepping into the midday sunshine, a light, dry heating of the flesh felt almost sensual. A friendly wave surprised those who passed by. *Let them continue in their ignorance. They're just sand in our mortar.* A breeze refreshed the senses as his pace became fueled with determination.

Let it begin.

VIII / 4

The hotel stairway was narrow with dim light and an odor that said it was clean but old. An occasional window offered welcome. Rennie and David took awkward, hesitant steps down. The conversation was more teasing than sharing.

"David, you promised only one more hour on the computer and we can go out, right?" Rennie felt silly and enjoyed it. "David, the clock is ticking!"

The hotel was quiet, allowing Rennie to feel safe. A few paces down the hallway brought them home to their special retreat. David opened the door and motioned for Rennie to enter first.

"Agreed. At midday like this, the streets will be full of people, so we'll not stand out to anyone searching for us. The only thing is, you will have to be shorter and less, shall we say, noticeable."

"It's okay. You can say 'hot' or 'beautiful.'"

A ripple of laughter began in him that he couldn't contain. He took her in his arms. "Rennie, you can't be less of either. For now, just be shorter."

"You'll have to be less British."

A moment of searching in each other's eyes was followed with a quick kiss. David relaxed his arms, but she pulled him against her.

"So, Mr. Scientist, do you have an interest in combustible energy?"

"Indeed, and we have all the ingredients."

A heavy truck rolled by and downshifted, causing the exhaust to backfire. They jerked apart.

David turned to the window. "Rennie, I need to think." He took a few steps to his overnight case. "They lay Grandfather to rest in a few days. I'd like to return to London for that. I don't have a firm date, so I need to contact the house."

"I understand. I'm sorry. My heart breaks for the loss of Matthew. I'd like to be there with you, yet here we are. He would know what to do. With all we've been through, the sadness of his death has been buried by other things. Let's get back at this and make plans. You might call that guy from the British Museum who contacted me. Matthew asked him to research the topics I ran into. Let me look up his number."

"Be careful. Don't take your phone off airplane mode. We must remain cautious."

"Oops, well, I already did it a couple of times. Here's the contact name and number. You Brits have such funny names. *Alistair Thorsten Snapper* and here's his number. You call him, and I'll start reviewing the data files again."

David gazed at the idyllic street scene below and made the call. His crisp accent became even sharper as he spoke to others in London. He was so polite. There was a moment when he cleared his throat and put a handkerchief to his mouth. Rennie studied him. He was much deeper than he would allow others to see.

Rennie shifted her focus to reviewing the folders and files on the flash drive. They had developed a search system that had gone well but produced nothing of interest or use. All the documents they could read or interpret, thanks mainly to David's language skills and language software, were about the popes, what they decreed, who they appointed, where they went, and even the gifts received and given. When she heard David say, "Ventotene," she spun around.

"Hey, that's where that Greek priest had been when he was killed, or maybe before that. What's your guy saying?"

"Ah yes, Prof. Snapper, would you hold a moment? Thank

you. Rennie, what did you say?"

"Ventotene is where the Greek priest was before he was killed. What's up with that? You said the name."

"The professor is informing me that they spread their research among several colleagues. One noted that Ventotene is the island known by the Romans as Pandateria. It was a place of exile for Roman nobility."

"He told me that the other day. He said there were women on the island who were like daughters of emperors and they'd been exiled there because they became Christian. This isn't new to me."

"Let me speak with him further, please."

Rennie glared at the laptop screen. What can she find that will help? Her fingers and eyes moved quickly across the translated titles. She searched folders for the word "Pandateria."

Wait, what's this? Heretics and their writings. Synoptic gospels are mentioned. Condemnation of references to Mary of Magdala and her followers? Ask David about Mary of Magdala. Is that Mary Magdalene?

"David, be sure to ask him about those fellowships or whatever Michael called them."

"Rennie, please let me do this. I need to listen."

She continued with renewed intensity. It felt as natural as the innocent freedom she enjoyed on the roof minutes ago. Her drive and focus were back!

"Thank you, sir. I'm most grateful for this information and all the work you and others have put in on this project so quickly and with such diligence. I'll relate this to Miss Haran. Please call if you find other information. And, thank you also for your thoughtfulness regarding my grandfather. I hope to attend if all works well here — Very good, sir. Goodbye."

"What did he say?"

"Let me catch my breath."

"What?" Her fingertips rested on the keyboard.

"First off, the burial will be private and in three days. The next day there will be a memorial service. If possible, I'd like you to join me there."

"I'd like that too. What else?"

"Let me think how to put it all together for simplicity and chronology."

"Thank you, Professor."

"Let's see, regarding Pandateria, emperors and Roman nobility exiled women there to either get rid of them or as a kind of 'time out' for bad behavior. This began before the Christian era as early as Caesar Augustus. It continued well past the first century. During World War II, the island was used as a camp for prisoners of war."

"That's a little later than what interests me right now."

"Agreed. So, let's jump back to Mary of Magdala or Mary Magdalene as she's commonly known. Coinciding with the reference to her in one of the letters from Jesus, Mr. Snapper's researchers include a fellow who's an expert on the synoptic gospels, the Gnostics, and writings and stories deemed heretical after the first century. Of course, they've also reviewed the letters you found."

"Yes?" Rennie stepped up close to him, apparently too near for his comfort.

David backed off. "Ah, let me gather my thoughts."

He paced for a moment then continued, "Well it seems there are stories that are referenced in other materials that after Jesus was gone, Mary became a fervent missionary of His message. She distinguished the new church from the Jews saying they were peace loving and had no animosity toward the Romans. She took over her father's successful business as a merchant, and that gave her legitimacy with the Romans."

"That seems reasonable, but I don't see why any of that disregarded history would play into what's going on now."

"In Rome, she made converts to the new faith and many were women. For example, Priscilla—who is mentioned by Paul and others—and her husband were in Rome and then went to Corinth and Ephesus, and ultimately Syria to help Paul establish new congregations."

"That's interesting. Raphael and maybe Michael too said this issue in the church dealt with women in the early church and letters between them. I can see how the women would try to encourage each other with correspondence. But, what's the big deal?"

"Well, women such as Julia Livilla, the wife of Nero, and other women of Roman nobility were banished to Pandateria for being followers of an unacceptable religion. That suggests there was a small colony on that island and in Rome of exiled women who followed this new faith, and this could be related to the Greek priest who got murdered on said island."

"David, I don't think this old business of converted women got the priest killed, and Michael said some think he was there on a spiritual retreat."

"It's not clear at this time. One other thing Rennie, Professor Snapper said two of the scholars of this specialty area include— or included—Father Anastasios who you witnessed on the beach outside of Naples, and Professor Erkan, a visiting scholar to the Turkish Institute of Religious Studies in Izmir. Professor Erkan was murdered recently. They probably knew each other and may have coordinated their research."

"So, what bizarre levels of misogynistic hatred does it take to murder people and cause a major schism in a religion because a number of leading converts were women? As I said, it doesn't make sense."

"I don't know, Rennie. Lesser things cause murderous results and even war. Maybe that's not the issue. But it fits with what you heard. It's disappointing."

Rennie went to the window and looked down at people on the street.

David continued, "All that means nothing to them, ordinary people. Power plays are so meaningless. There's got to be something else. It's not just men keeping women in their place."

"What are you thinking?"

"There's an idea in that correspondence between the women of the early church that we're missing. That's what this is all about. The initiatives and bravery by these women were annoying to men but there was some big factor that threatened to take away the men's power."

"David, what's the real power that church leaders had or have?"

"Well, for one thing, they make the rules. Break the rules and you get punished. And, as they say, the real golden rule is those with the gold make the rules. So, wealth and rules, that's power."

"Yes, but why do they get to make the rules? From where does that power come?"

"I guess from might. If you're stronger, bigger, and you have traditions of superiority on your side, you're in charge."

"True, but the church was a new institution with no traditions for leadership. In fact, the initial themes were supposedly love and generosity and humility."

"Yes, Rennie, but all of those people lived at a time when male domination was a feature of all cultures. And, they also spoke for God or for Jesus."

David began to arrange his belongings to pack them.

"Oh, my God."

"Well, Rennie, if you want to make a statement of faith, fine."

"No, I mean, it just hit me. The men speak for God. They always have. Women don't have that privilege. It's the men who know the will of God and they make rules accordingly. After all, God is a man, *isn't he*? At least that's what was said. That's what this is about. There must be a statement in the correspondence between the women and maybe with Paul that changes this basis for power. If women can speak to or for God, that upsets everything!"

David looked thoughtful. "I don't recall where but somewhere in scripture, Paul says women are not supposed to be leaders or teachers or even speak."

"David, that's offensive to all women and doesn't fit with any teachings of Jesus."

He remained focused and continued to pack.

"Rennie, if a power struggle between men and women is the issue, and it's gone on forever, let's get out of here and go to London. You, as a woman, most definitely should not get into the midst of such a dispute. You'll be at great risk. This is not one of your mysteries you solve so well. It's a game as obvious and old as relationships themselves. Let's go please."

"When I was in St. Peter's, a man handed out postcards and on one side it said, 'God is present and wants you to be.' Doesn't that mean I should be involved in this?"

"Grandfather told me to pursue happiness being who I am with the gifts I have. That tells me we must go to England. After that, you decide what comes next. You can take your time changing what's been created over two millennia."

"Maybe you're right."

"I am, and I'll check train schedules right now."

"Wait, David, let me continue to search a little longer. We're not in a hurry now and you're in the midst of packing."

"Of course, it's your nature."

A flicker of joy ran through her. She liked their connection and sharing a mission.

"If I flutter my eyelashes, will you get me another coffee?"

"Oh, please," he laughed. "Yes, I'll get the coffee."

Istanbul, Turkey
Topkapi Museum

VIII / 5

Aslan Yilmaz, the director of Istanbul's Antiquities and Topkapi Museum Operations, enjoyed his morning walks through the palace grounds. The simple, refined landscaping accented each building regardless of their architectural designs. He loved the appearance of the main museum with its classical Greek entry in the middle of a traditional European façade. It was one of many buildings in the complex but this one felt permanent, powerful, and wise.

Across the garden and accented by the vast Gülhane Park as a backdrop, the Tiled Kiosk Museum sat like a delicate cake among boxes of gifts. Built six centuries ago, it contained Istanbul's Museum of Modern Islamic Art. For an instant, a chilling fear ran through Aslan's thoughts. Islamic art and anything modern would be high on a list of targets for terrorists. Maybe it's not the antiquities collection they would hit. He must discuss this with the government agent when they next spoke.

His secretary, Belgin, hardly noticed him as he entered the office and greeted her. She was disciplined, focused, and always in motion. Messages in order of importance were lined up on his desk. The classic Turkish sensibility of structure and unchanging duty permeated the workrooms. Ignoring the computer monitor, this could have been a 1950's government office. He was fine with that. Life was changing too quickly. Roles and rituals were being washed away like sandcastles in a heavy tide of technology and globalization. At least he had the ancient and unchanging world in his hands. No one had the power to revise it, and if they tried, he would stand in opposition.

He called out in Turkish, "Belgin, please get Yusuf on the line for me."

As he waited, he wondered why there had been no contact from the government agent. That foolish data task must be disposed of so real work can proceed. He knew Yusuf would take care of it. His phone buzzed.

"Yes, Yusuf, thank you for calling. How are things? I see. Can you come to my office? I have a few matters to review, projects and plans. Thank you."

Human resources issues, building maintenance decisions, required meeting agendas, documents to sign, procedure changes, and ideas for new archival techniques stood in thick file folders on one end of his desk. He managed a daily march through them with regretful diligence. If he wasn't so dedicated, Belgin would have heard heavy sighs pouring from his office when he opened each folder. The art of his signature embellished the last form as Yusuf arrived.

"*Aslan bey,* how are you? Whenever I come to your office, I see stacks of paper. This is why I want to stay at my level in the dungeon and not be in the executive class." Yusuf laughed a generous guffaw.

"Go ahead and taunt me with your free spirit. Someday, I'll be gone and they'll come for you to fill this chair. You'll accept the duty and be more useful than I am."

"If this is prophecy, Aslan, I shall rend my garments now and succumb! For me it is enough to be a simple curator."

Aslan removed from a desk drawer a small bottle of *raki* and two glasses.

"Let us savor this ancient discovery as we deal with modern nuisances."

"I assume you want an update on the staff documentation project? I have Chetin on this, and he is doing well. We should be done when our agent friend returns."

Aslan couldn't contain his pleasure as he sipped from the glass. "Will it be complete and accurate?"

"People's information changes and at other times they don't provide the correct data. It can always be fixed and any missing items added later."

"He's probably pursuing more vital and immediate demands. We shall see. Tell me about Chetin."

Yusuf set his empty glass on the desk and relaxed.

"He's quite thorough, and his research interests are strong. This shows in his work on the personnel spreadsheet. He will become a good archivist if he doesn't become a scholar."

Aslan laughed, "Interesting, so his greater drive is for intellectual discovery and not preservation? What are his interests?"

Yusuf didn't notice but Aslan's focus had shifted.

"Chetin studied under and assisted Professor Erkan at the Turkish Institute of Religious Studies in Izmir. Erkan is the one that recently died, an ugly ending to a prominent career. Chetin has at times asked if he could do similar research in our assets. I've put him off. There are other things to do."

"Hmm, you are devoted to being efficient Yusuf, *bey*. If there are moments when this boy wants to see what he can find, I have no problems with that. It might encourage his career. We need people like him."

"I agree, but we don't want any damage to be done."

"Of course, and yet his fresh eyes might come upon a document that would be a significant find. Yusuf, *bey*, if it's something unique, be sure to advise him to pass the information only to you and me. We don't want to make any claims that might be false."

Yusuf sat up with a thoughtful look on his face. He pulled at his jacket lapels to straighten his coat.

"Excellent point. I'll make this clear to him. No findings go beyond me and I will inform you."

"Please share with me again what Professor Erkan studied

and what our boy Chetin wishes to pursue."

"Director, their special interest was in the development of the original Christian communities here in Anatolia. In the first century, early followers traveled around to create additional followers in local groups. Records of these events are scattered about and Erkan and a few others attempted to locate or gather them. That Greek priest who died in Italy was, I believe, an associate of Professor Erkan."

"Yusuf, *bey*, you and I deal with what many consider dusty topics, and this sounds like another. Even I'd be interested in seeing any manuscripts from that era. I always enjoy observing the ink on the document and thinking of the hand and the times that placed it there."

Aslan leaned back into his executive chair and stared at the ceiling.

"Director, our archives have many of the materials from the early Christian movement, particularly notes from the meetings they held in Nicaea and other cities here in in Anatolia. There may also be letters sent between the people who participated. Very little has been reviewed, but it's of little importance."

"Sometimes trouble is caused by things of no importance. Let's keep the museum out of trouble. Chetin can do his research when he has the time but, as we agree, the findings remain with us. Few may appreciate what we do. We are here to protect the front lines of history, to keep the truth secure."

Yusuf's composure relaxed.

"I like that my friend. If the bottle is not empty, we should toast that thought."

As they enjoyed the liqueur, Aslan reflected on Yusuf's work and career. He realized he had little awareness of the man who was within the professional. Maintaining respectful distance had always been the theme of their relationship. The distant personal space was acceptable, especially given the natural isolation, particularly of the mind. It was a familiar and inchoate factor as they came to know each other.

"My friend, tell me a little about yourself I do not know."

"You honor me with the idea I'm more than what you see. But my work is the only interesting component in my life. The rest is nothing but our timeless traditions shared by millions plus a humbled perception of life."

Aslan admired the simplicity and clever diplomacy in the response.

"Yusuf, you and I, we believe our profession has reverence for traditions as we do with other ancient artifacts. At the same time, we encounter discoveries that reshape our understandings of the past. How can we remain open to this refreshment of our knowledge and our awareness?"

"I don't know, Aslan. Revisionist history seems less like revelation and more like capitulation to me. Perhaps, I'm not creative enough, but finding such things carries a bitter taste. I guess I'm too intent on securing the past instead of blowing it up like these terrorist groups are doing. Well, I must return to the dungeon. It's home for us reclusive human relics."

A weak smile from Yusuf signaled his readiness to leave, although he waited for permission.

"Of course, Yusuf *bey*, and the prison of mine is an enclosure of file folders!"

A limp shake of the hands authorized the ending of the meeting. Aslan wasn't sure what he'd learned, but a breath of assurance offered refreshment. At least the personnel spreadsheet would be done. They didn't need interference right now.

VIII / 6

Rennie studied the digitized ancient texts on the flash drive. She imagined the characters wearing biblical attire as she'd seen in countless images, movies, and Christmas pageants. But the texts were filled with new names, with only a few familiar ones jumping out. People in Corinth and Ephesus, Athens and Philippi, and Rome, of course. She thought Mary of Magdala must have had black hair, but she saw Joanna with dark brown, maybe like her own. As she encountered the name of Priscilla, she thought of Matthias, who fell in love with his Priscilla in London so long ago, and their son Matthew. Rennie wondered if Matthew ever connected this Priscilla of Corinth with his own mother.

Her excitement grew as this small cache of documents revealed hints of key moments in formative Christianity. They came from innocuous files of papal declarations, canonization of saints, and references to the earliest bishops.

This is good stuff! she thought. *Really good stuff!*

Wanting to share what she found, Rennie was eager for David to return with coffee and lunch.

The doorknob rattled. Rennie lifted the laptop and carried it with her to open the door. Her eyes wouldn't leave the screen.

As she unlocked the door she said, "Did you forget your key?"

Without looking, she returned to the bed where her work was scattered among notebook paper.

"Miss Haran, I'm so pleased to find you."

She slammed down the laptop screen as she spun to see who

she had let in.

"Father Joseph? What are you doing here?"

"I'm sorry to startle you. We needed to urgently find you. Our contacts at ROS were kind enough to let us know they'd discovered phone and internet traffic from you and your companion. It led to this location. A little help from the proprietor was an added gift."

"What? Why, I mean why urgently? What's the problem?"

"Miss Haran, your proximity to these crimes and your disappearance caused alarm with authorities. We were concerned for you."

Something was wrong here. Rennie's gut spoke to her. She studied the priest. He's lying, and he's searching.

"What do you want, Father Joseph? I'd like to help, but I'm confused."

"My hope was to find you and acquaint you with the situation. Where is your companion?"

"I don't know. He went to get food."

Rennie stood strong.

"Help me understand this, Joseph. What's behind these crimes? There are rumors there's a conflict within the church, and that it's from the earliest days. Is that it?"

"There always have been conflicts in the church and all institutions. There are many weak people in such places. They go along with nonsense to serve themselves."

"Is this about women in the church and their rights?"

"What a strange thought. The faith has always had strong women. Yet, we all know our places."

She relaxed her expression and posture to calm him.

"Father Joseph, can women speak with God or even for him?"

"Nonsense! Those who think anyone can commune with the divine commit apostasy and self-righteousness! It's a cancer and must never be considered. Sin fills humanity, and the legends that ignore it in favor of the silliness of love distract good people from obedience to church and doctrine."

The door, only half shut, bumped open and David entered carrying bags of food and a container of coffee.

"Oh, hello."

His face wrinkled with confusion.

"David, this is Father Joseph from the Vatican. He says he came to help us."

"Help with what?"

Veins on Father Joseph's thick neck seemed to grow and harden.

"So, you're the companion? Where are you from? How did you get involved?"

Rennie and David glanced at each other, taken aback by Joseph's not exactly welcoming greeting.

"David is an old friend of the family, Joseph. David, would you like to put those things down over here?"

Rennie cleared the tops of two small side tables as David made his way past Joseph.

Rennie pressed forward, "Say, Joseph, David has a wonderful coincidence with a biblical figure. His great grandmother's name is Priscilla — just like the one in the New Testament. In fact, one of the gems of history that Father Daniel spoke of was that it was Priscilla who saved some of Paul's letters and those of her sisters in Christ. Isn't that wonderful?"

Father Joseph's eyes seemed to bulge forward.

"No, this is not wonderful. This is exactly the kind of diversion from faith I spoke of. The followers of this myth diminish the glory of heaven and degrade the church!"

Rennie acknowledged David's perplexed look with a nod. She was on the trail, and it felt good to be back.

She cooed, "Father Joseph, you know Father Angelotti? He diverted me to Naples and then all this confusion began. I'm not part of any of this and I'd like to go home and leave whatever the issues are with the Vatican or other appropriate authorities."

"Enough! You know more than you pretend. We've been informed your friend here travels to many places including Greece, Turkey, and Egypt. That is suspicious."

The rising strain of his voice caused Rennie to step back, putting the bed between her and the intruder.

"So, what do you want us to do, Father?"

"Nothing can be done at this point. You've said things that tell me you know more than you let on and can be a threat to our cause."

His hand slid into a side pocket of his jacket.

Danger flared through her senses. She sidestepped once more toward the small table where a few of her things were scattered.

"Father Joseph, we know nothing about all this. With all the sad things I've seen in just a few days, I want to go home and leave this behind. I have no other agenda. The exhibition has begun so I'm not needed. Is that okay with you?"

Joseph snarled, "We know you are an investigator and a journalist — we've learned you both are risks. We can't have risks, especially at this critical time in our plans. In another week, the blasphemers will be gone, and our true church will stand refreshed and strong. Come here to me!"

Rennie didn't move but she was focused and prepared to act. This man didn't know how capable she can be, and she was ready to show him.

Joseph began slow steps toward her as he removed from his pocket a knife that unfolded into a large, gleaming blade.

"Joseph," she demanded. "What happens in a week? Are people going to die?"

"We think *extinguished* is a better term."

In the instant between two moments, Rennie snatched the

device that Raphael gave to her from the table. She pointed it at Joseph.

"I want you to leave now!"

He took another step toward her.

"Oh, Miss Haran, are you going to shine your flashlight in my eyes? Ha!"

With sudden ferocity and deadly silence, his body slammed against the wall behind him. He collapsed onto the floor. Blood drizzled from his ears and nose.

David was frozen in place, his mouth open, staring at the man on the floor.

Rennie touched his arm.

"Hey, we've got to get out of here, and put your phone in airplane mode. They're on to you. We need to pack up and leave."

"What about —? What happened here?" David asked, staring at the lump of a priest on the floor. "What's that weapon?"

"I don't know. We can't know everything."

Rennie grabbed her things and jammed them into her backpack. She hurried into the bathroom to get her personal items. As she returned, David jerked her arm and pulled her close.

"What happened here? What is that thing? Is he dead?"

"I don't know. I've never checked. We've got to go."

She jerked her arm away and continued her preparations.

"What do you mean you've never checked? How many times have you used it?"

"Listen," she said, pointing a toothbrush at him. "I don't know what's going on here, but he was about to carve us up. He said the authorities are after us, trying to connect us with these murders and who knows what else." Rennie shook her finger in his face. "Somebody has set us up as targets to draw attention away from them. If we sit here and wait, we'll be in an Italian jail cell for the next few years until this is resolved. I've got other things to do and I imagine you do as well. So, get going. We need to disappear and do it now!"

David glared at the body on the floor.

"Did he say that people were going to die in the next week?"

"Exactly, does that give you a sense of urgency? Get a move on!"

Her jaw muscles locked her teeth together. Hurried minutes flew by and it was time to go. She pushed past David and grasped the door handle.

"Ready?" she asked.

"Yes, ready. Wait, do we need to —?" he pointed at the man on the floor.

"There's nothing to do here. Let's go."

At the lobby, he laid the heavy brass room key on the counter and removed a credit card from his wallet.

"Can you pay with cash?" Rennie whispered and turned away.

"Yes, but — oh right."

He counted the bills and thanked the clerk in Italian.

From the front window, Rennie scanned the street and all she could see. She didn't know what she was looking for, but she knew that's what they did in the movies.

When he reached her in the hotel entry, she said, "We can't take a train. We've got to go a different way. Do they rent cars here? Maybe we could drive to a nearby city and catch a train there. The risks are less."

"I like it. Let's walk and talk, not here."

PART NINE

Rome, Italy

IX - 1

David and Rennie strolled down a narrow side street trying to act like common tourists. Their spirits were wounded by graffiti scattered across the walls that impugned the romance and history of the Eternal City with crude, graphic strokes. A haphazard turn found them in an alley with little foot traffic and only an occasional bicycle or motor bike.

David's hand reached out and brushed hers.

"We could go to Perugia. It's on the way to Florence – nice scenery and in the right direction for Switzerland. There's a train station there."

"I don't know. I'm struggling with what to do. When we left the library, someone said I should start over. I don't know what that means."

He stopped. "What does it mean? Maybe nothing or maybe get the hell back to your home. Rennie, we discussed this. There are real dangers. We met one face to face back there."

He pointed toward the hotel.

"This is not your fight Rennie, yet somebody seems to want you in it."

"I know it's not my fight. But I've come to understand this differently. This isn't about joining one side or another. It's about me doing what I feel I must do. That's how I operate, David. It's not about outcomes; it's about action. I've been swimming in ambiguity for days, and I don't know what's right or wrong for whoever is involved in these issues. I only know what's right for me."

"So, what precisely is that?"

"I don't know, *precisely*. We obviously have to leave Rome, and I think we should go to Greece. It seems like Corinth is the place to start, but I don't know why. Matthew said you've been there. What do you think?"

He fell back against the wall and closed his eyes.

A fresh kind of confidence filled Rennie with new determination.

"David, you don't have to come with me. I can do this. You don't have to come."

She wanted to reach out and touch him.

"Really, David, just help me get the car and tell me where to go. David?"

A deep sigh flowed from him as he looked up at Rennie.

"Okay, we'll do this together. I'll help you go wherever you need to go."

A small car with a whining engine slowly turned into the alley and worked its way around people and trash cans until it stopped. No one got out.

Out of the corner of his eye, David studied the situation.

"Let's get a car."

He looped his arm through hers and turned with a brisk step.

As they walked to the end of the road, Rennie asked, "Are you sure?"

"I am about you and a few other things. Everything else, no."

The words *thank you* arose in her thoughts. She squeezed his arm against her body.

Turning onto a busier street, Rennie released her arm from his and ran her hand through her hair. She shifted her backpack and straightened her blouse. David moved his bag from one hand to the other, placing it between them.

"There," he pointed. "There's an agency across the street."

A blue sign above a window indicated *CarRoma*.

Excitement propelled Rennie forward as she dashed with David through heavy traffic. This was no longer a business trip. It was a quest.

The car agency offered a cool, modern feel with gray fabric chairs on chrome frames. Posters of Italian tourist sites were hung on light gray walls with white wooden trim. A young man at a desk behind the counter studied a computer monitor. As David and Rennie approached the counter, a petite young woman came from a back room.

"Hello, you are English?" she asked.

"Well, *si*, I am," David replied. He continued, "We need a car for a couple of days and would like to leave it in ..." —He turned to Rennie— "are we going to Greece?"

She nodded.

"Well, I guess, Miss, um, ..."— he noticed her name tag— "ah, Alessia, yes we'll need a car to drive to Brindisi. Can we leave it there?"

Her brown eyes above a straight nose and dazzling white teeth expressed an attractive and professional presence for their needs.

"Of course, I also have an agency there. We have six in Italy. I'm glad you found us."

"This is your agency?"

"Yes, it's a modest but growing business. Hospitality has always been my interest. We also have tour and lodging resources if you like. When do you want the car and what type of car do you need?"

In a few minutes, the decisions were made, and it was time for identification and payment. Alessia documented David's passport information and his international driver's license. She reviewed the charges and fees and asked which credit card he'd like to use.

Rennie remembered being off the grid was prudent and they

should avoid credit card transactions. She touched David's arm and made a subtle shake of her head.

David responded to Alessia, "We'd like to pay cash. Is that acceptable?"

"We can accept cash for the fees, but we also require the credit card for security."

"I see, yes, I can provide that. May I ask a favor? I'd appreciate it if you would not run a transaction with the card at this time and only when needed when we deliver the car."

He tried to be charming.

"We want to minimize transactions."

"Of course. A romantic Italian getaway should not have limitations. We can do this as you say. Angelo will have the car out front in a few minutes."

Rennie flushed with jealousy as Alessia and David finished the transaction, so she left the counter and attempted to relax in a chair. Moments later, David joined her and suggested they wait outside. She noticed him glance back at Alessia by the counter, furthering her anxieties.

Stepping outside with David, Rennie attempted an Italian accent and said, "Yes, a romantic holiday with your girlfriend. How nice. Maybe I could join you!"

His face wrinkled into a perplexed stare.

She continued in character, "Oh, and I would be happy to show you around. I have so many businesses you know. We can go to my hotel or my restaurant."

"My gosh, Rennie. What's with you? She's a delightful, successful businesswoman. She was helpful to us. You should applaud her. Good Lord."

He gave her a playful punch in the shoulder.

Her eyes closed to slits and she snarled until she laughed. Then, she lost her breath when she noticed a man across the street. He was alone behind a car, doing nothing. He looked familiar.

As David opened a city map, Rennie slapped it down.

"David, do you see that guy over there?"

She nodded in the direction of the character.

"Who, what guy?"

"There, him. He's walking away. I saw him at the reception last night. He's different, not Italian or — I don't know."

"What about him?"

"He has this manner, like he's there but doesn't want to be seen."

"Hi guys," a voice surprised them from behind. "I'm glad to see you."

Michael stood two feet away with the same, odd quiet presence that annoyed Rennie.

"What are you, how did you —?" Rennie couldn't voice a thought. She hoped David would help.

Michael continued, "I'm glad to see you outside the walls. Are you leaving Rome? It's a good idea. Are you going to Switzerland? That would be logical."

Hot energy flew through Rennie. "It's none of your damned business what we're doing. I don't know how you found us, but I don't like it. Get out of here."

Michael ignored her. "Say, David, my knowledge of physics is extremely limited but since you're here. I wonder if I could ask a question?"

"About physics? We're expecting our car."

Rennie glared at him. "David, we need to go."

Michael continued, "Well, I have questions about the surface of the universe and the concept of dimensions. They say quantum mechanics behaves differently to large scale systems and then there's dark matter and dark energy operating beyond our ability to discover or understand them."

"So, what's your point?"

"Well, does the surface of the universe and possibly the dark features of space have what we call 'depth' within them, and might that depth exist in dimensions we're unaware of?"

"There are many theories on these issues. Loop quantum gravity is quite appealing as an expression of the texture of space time. Multi-dimension systems are open for discussion. The relationship between that and — wait. You are an unwelcome element in our universe."

"Of course, sorry. Humanity is unaware of so much. There are many dimensions to all things. People consider ancient rumors of all kinds suggesting there's documentation to be found, and people create chaos trying to find it. Both of you are successful in finding things. You probably understand."

Rennie turned in front of David and nearly pushed him toward the street. "I've had enough. Let's go."

"Rennie," Michael firmly said. "Innocence can be cute. It can also be a grave concern. Consider recent events and who's been there to help you. There are things to do."

"We don't need help and we have things to do. Leave!"

"David, I understand Rennie. She's a rational thinker from the Western tradition. If there's a problem, then there's a solution. For her, that's reality; problems and solutions. Get a story and solve the story."

Rennie shook her fist. "You don't know me! David, where's the damned car?"

"Wait," David said. "Michael, what's your idea of help?"

"I recommend you send a text to your laboratory in Cern and tell them you're on the way there. If any authorities are paying attention to your communications, you'll be less bothered with interference wherever you really intend to go."

"Michael, you may now leave."

"David, you and your grandfather, I'm so sorry for your loss. He was a great man. You were with him when he did research at the Temple of Apollo in Greece? Do you know why he was interested in the story of the Oracle of Delphi?"

"No, but Grandfather's interest in the ancient world knew few bounds."

"Well, the Temple of Apollo is not far from Corinth, which is a key site in the ministry of the apostle Paul. Also, one of the people Paul mentions in his first letter to the Corinthians is his friend Apollos. He's also mentioned in the Book of Acts. Are you aware there are scholars who consider the reference to a person named Apollos is actually a reference to the old Temple of Apollo?"

"What? That doesn't make sense. The Oracle was hundreds of years earlier. Why would Paul refer to an old Greek building as a friend—and a friend with a different name at that?"

"Which is exactly what the critics say. And, how could Aquila and Priscilla be friends with an old temple, as stated in Paul's letter? But, given the dangers for Christians at that time maybe they needed to disguise special places with names of people. It must have held special meaning for them. If you go there, keep it in mind."

Rennie intervened. "That's enough. I'm done here, and with both of you. You can play Bible trivia or science games or whatever. I'm done." She turned toward the rental office.

Michael responded, "Rennie, I'm sorry. I only want to help. You and David do what you want. David, consider sending the text message to Cern. And, consider Corinth. Bye."

He strolled away and dashed across the street. A moment later, he disappeared around a corner.

"That was bizarre." Rennie shook her head. "Bizarre."

A red Fiat 500L arrived and the driver handed the keys to David as Rennie threw her bag into the back and settled into the passenger seat. She jerked open the street map they were given and realized she had no idea where they were. She crushed the map in her hands.

"That Michael. And you. Put a few things into perspective please!"

Grabbing her phone to check its map application, she stopped. "Why are they watching us?" she asked the phone without opening it. She took a deep breath and another.

David studied the car's controls and took the crumpled map. He unfolded it to see where they were and charted a course out of the city.

The car became quiet, and an hour and a half later, they escaped the bounds of Rome and its fearful entanglements. The Italian countryside welcomed them with new landscapes and hopes.

David glanced at Rennie.

"You're right."

"About what?"

He shifted gears as the highway became clear.

"Maybe, I was a bit distracted."

"No, you and Michael were way out of line."

"No, not Michael. That Alessia, she's the first attractive Italian woman I've met. All the others were nuns."

Rennie tried to stop a grin from pulling across her lips. She slapped his shoulder.

"So, you feel safe talking about her? Give me the map and show me where we are before I harm you."

Rome, Italy
The Vatican

IX / 2

Abbess Serena laid the telephone handset into its gilded cradle. It felt good. The secretary of state's office in the Vatican was afflicted with so many issues and media stories that the deaths of a couple of priests were no longer of any interest.

I'm so safe, she thought. *Bulletproof.* Her body relaxed into smug confidence. Now, she could dispense a little of her own authority without questions from those above.

She took a notepad from her desk drawer and sketched a few ideas in a pattern on the page. Added to the page were the names of priests, officials, visitors, and members of the church hierarchy important to her. She thought of possible outcomes and what she would like to see. It was a tasty game, and she was eager for dessert to be served. An image of Rennie came to her. *Miss Haran, and her friend;* she added them to the page.

Joseph wasn't responding to her calls and requests. Despite his Teutonic rigidity, she had worked him like a jealous wife. This absence though didn't fit him, and she wasn't pleased. Serena figured Sister Katherine knew something. When she learned of Katherine's contacts with Joseph, she sensed there was a story behind them, and it was probably interesting, maybe important.

Serena's summons to Sister Katherine was a fitting combination of innocence, ambiguity, and intrigue. Playing dumb had become so easy. It was as elegant and comfortable as the tapestry on her chair. As soon as the good sister arrived, she would begin the deposition and see where it leads. It would be fun and maybe useful.

Serena's secretary called her to announce that Sister Katherine was waiting.

"I'll be a moment," was her curt response.

The abbess removed a thick file from a cabinet and placed it on her desk. She called her secretary and said Katherine could enter.

"Good day, Sister."

The abbess acknowledged the guest as if saying the words made it a welcome.

"Please, have a seat there."

Katherine smoothed her garment and avoided eye contact. The ruddy flesh of her face was smooth despite its age and it sagged to fullness at her jaw with a parallel fold below that against a short, stout neck.

Serena studied the small text of a document in the file on her desk. Without raising her chin, she offered a little curtesy.

"I appreciate your coming in today."

"You asked me to come."

Again, no eye contact.

"There aren't many people with your notable level of service. You've worked in the households of two popes."

Katherine nodded.

"Sister, you have demonstrated the devotion and trust our community values. I admire that and the remarkable privileges you've had in earning the confidence of these great men."

"Except, for the current one. He has his own team as they say. I keep busy with other things."

"Yes, and given the important relationships you developed over all these years, I imagine you can stay in touch with each important matter."

"I'm a small person within this great community of God."

Serena closed the file and turned a few degrees away from Sister Katherine. Although it appeared she was thinking, she was counting backward from the number ten. She stroked her cheek when she got to the number four.

Katherine asked, "What do you require of me?"

"I could use your help to fill in gaps in our information. By the way, do you happen to know where Father Joseph is? I've tried to reach him but didn't hear back."

"No, I don't — I wouldn't know."

Katherine pursed her lips but remained immobile.

"It's my impression you know each other and at times have contact."

"No more than any other persons who have served here for many years."

Katherine stared directly at the abbess. "If there's nothing specific you need, I'll go now."

"Well, I have here, in this thick and well-documented briefing, a good deal of research that's been done and been done well. It's amazing."

Serena again looked into the distance. A tense stillness filled the space between the players.

Serena continued, "You've probably heard of the tragic incident with Father Daniel."

The old nun responded, "They say he fell from a balcony. It must have been dark."

"They also say he wasn't alone, and this probably wasn't an accident."

The nun removed a white handkerchief from a pocket in her garment and placed it between her hands.

"What do you need from me that relates to my work?"

"I'm not clear on the nature of your work, Sister. I thought of Father Daniel because the information in this briefing is based on his research and conversations with others. As you know, the papacy and the Roman curiae have devoted sincere efforts to clarify, shall we say, all the policies, programs, and activities in and leading from the Vatican. The tragic matter of sexual abuse triggered reviews of many topics."

"Abbess, everyone has been diligent on those efforts whether directly involved or just concerned."

"Yes, Sister Katherine, this is true. Serious other matters have recently arisen. Father Daniel was asked to investigate one of these. And, as you may know, Father Angelotti was tasked with helping on another sad death in Naples. Daniel was researching that and trying to see how it connected with other things."

"What other things?"

"Daniel was considering those when we lost him. There are others, of course, who have followed up on his research."

"I'm not clear on why I'm here, Abbess. Do you simply need a sounding board? I served the previous two popes in that way. Leaders need that service. If I can help you in that way, please tell me what you know."

"Ah, Sister, you are so wise. Thank you for that. It's good to know I can share with you and learn from you."

Katherine's composure warmed, and a slight upturn at the corners of her lips tried to form.

"Do you have a few extra minutes?"

The old woman responded, "Of course, I'm in your service."

Serena suddenly stood, apparently surprising Katherine.

"Good. The research that I reviewed thus far suggests there are quiet matters occurring outside of church programs that could have significant negative consequences for the Vatican. Further, it seems you and Joseph might be aware of these issues. What can you tell me?"

Without hesitation and in a stronger voice than earlier, Sister Katherine quickly replied, "I know of nothing about this."

"Sister, this is not an accusation. Forgive me if I misstated. I'm simply reporting the research."

"It's far from correct."

Sister Katherine again smoothed her garment and stiffened her back.

"So it may be, but there is information suggesting your contacts with Father Joseph were not incidental. By the way, are you aware that Daniel and Joseph had met and discussed these questions? Your name came up."

"I don't know why."

Katherine's hands clenched one another.

"There are also telephone records. It's amazing how much data is now available due to digital communications."

Katherine gripped the armrests as though she was about to stand.

"*Abbessa* Serena, tell me clearly what you want to know."

The request shifted into the tone of a demand or even an order. Serena turned away from her guest. She rested her palm on the file folder and gave it a pat. She was onto something hot. Her old litigation skills were feeling good.

"For the moment, a couple of things. A couple of things."

She turned down her nose at Sister Katherine. "The first is again, where is Father Joseph?"

"Again, I do not know. May I leave now? This has become very different from any meeting I've had in this blessed place. Perhaps in America meetings are conducted in this manner."

The abbess turned away and crossed her arms.

"I have collaborated directly with His Eminence the secretary of state and he's been in touch with others. These issues are considered important."

"You mean the current location of Father Joseph? That would be a surprise."

"Not in itself but related to other matters."

"Maybe you should ask that young American woman, Miss Haran. It seems there's been much tragedy since she arrived."

"I have spoken with her."

"When?"

Serena's telephone rang. She put the receiver to her ear and nodded. "Thank you."

"The Holy Father will be here soon. I'll need to step outside to see him. I should not be long."

"What! Here? He's coming here?"

The abbess had been playing games, but with an unexpected and unprecedented visit from His Holiness the pope she didn't know what to do. She didn't expect to open what might be a massive vein of trouble. She was suddenly on a hot trail but at this moment, she was afraid of moving forward. What creature was in the shadows? And, why was the pope coming to her office?

"As I said, Sister Katherine, we're dealing with significant issues. Are you ready to discuss what you know before he arrives?"

Serena was startled as Katherine erupted from her chair.

"Yes, there are big things that need to happen and will!" She blinked and looked past the abbess. "I'm sorry, I don't know what I'm saying. I'm confused. I don't know what's happening."

"What big things? Sister, what big things?"

Serena's mind was racing, and fear flushed through her. "I can help you."

"It all happens soon, and it can't be stopped. Joseph went to find the woman Haran. He should have been back by now."

Cold, dry dread lined Serena's open mouth. Evil was in the works.

A crisp knock on her door hit the women like rifle shots.

Serena could not breathe. She drifted toward the door feeling her life could end soon. As she reached for the door handle, it turned, and the pope stepped into her office. The warmth of his smile overwhelmed her. She felt like dropping to her knees.

In Italian, he said, "Forgive me for interrupting your day, *Abbessa*. I wanted to thank you for the good you are doing."

He noticed Sister Katherine and asked, "Who is this dear

soul?" He reached out to Katherine.

Serena was lost. Should she mention what was happening? There was no research. The file on her desk was a prop, unrelated. This was spinning into chaos.

Serena leaped into action. "Your Holiness, this is Sister Katherine. She and I were just discussing recent matters of vital concern —"

"You can't stop them!" Katherine shouted. She was shaking. "It's happening. It's begun. The church must be cleansed of heresy!"

His hands drifted to his sides and the warmth gave way to focus.

"The Greek priest, Father Daniel, and others. They were little steps to the final goal." Sister Katherine was shivering with intensity.

Two priests who accompanied the pope whispered and approached Serena. Anger exploded within her.

"Enough," she demanded.

She marched past the pope toward Katherine.

"It's time. Tell us what you know. Everything."

Katherine fell to her knees with her hands clasped and head bowed.

"I don't know much. I'm a little person. There are many involved, but each knows only a few."

She raised her face to the stunned group. Tears streamed down her cheeks.

Serena knelt in front of Katherine.

"Sister, this is the time to share all you know. He is here to listen. We need your help for the good of the church."

A snarl slid across Katherine's lips.

"The good of the church? The good was gone long ago! Now, it must be gutted of the foul desecration of false doctrine. You will see!"

The pope spoke, "Sisters, I would like to sit, and I will listen. Will you sit with me?"

Katherine lumbered to a standing position. "I will stand, as I will stand for this cleansing of heresy. Death is coming."

Serena bolted up. "Tell us. What is about to happen and who is doing this? The true authority of the church is here before you!"

Katherine spit back, "The army of God is rising up to cleanse the world of corrupt teaching. Greed and self-adulation fill this place, overlooking the cancer. The Almighty God, and all that is divine listens to and speaks to no mortal other than the high priest. No one else is worthy of such contact, now and always. All doctrine that accepts human ears and eyes witnessing the divine is desecration of truth. No one speaks directly to God!"

Katherine took a breath and reloaded, "The church has allowed followers to pollute their thinking. Humanity cannot experience the presence of holiness! God and the community of heaven is beyond all things and not among us."

The word, "Enough," slowly growled from deep within the pope. "I have heard enough. You will tell us what is needed now, but first you will renounce any allegiance you feel for this evil insurrection that has consumed your soul. You will ask for forgiveness for your deviant beliefs. You will provide to the abbess all information that is needed."

"*NO!*" Katherine was terrified but firm. "No, our cause is right and necessary. It is in obedience to the one true God who is beyond all humanity."

In a clear, firm voice, Serena stated with certainty hammering out each syllable, "Katherine, let me explain the situation to you. What happens right now is not about the church. It's about your immortal soul. You have presented violations of the gravest kinds, heresy and schism. We all know what they are. We also know the consequences: eternal damnation."

The pope looked into Serena's eyes and nodded.

She concluded her case, "Your Holiness, it is with trembling sadness that I must acknowledge to you the witnessing of these violations of the code of canon law. They were said without regret and with full knowledge of the consequences. No civil proceeding is necessary when they occur in your presence. The only action now is for you to write the order of excommunication."

Katherine's eyes darted from person to person, pleading for understanding. Her lips were bit shut of all sound but for a whisper of groaning through her nostrils.

The pope reached out to her, "Daughter, tell me now that you give up all this evil intrigue and join us in serving God. Please tell me."

Her head swiveled from side to side in refusal.

"Give me paper and pen," he said to Serena. He followed the abbess to her desk.

As the point of the pen touched the paper Katherine cried out, "No, don't do this to me. I will tell you all!"

She fell to her knees and forward onto the floor. She sobbed and pounded the floor with her fist.

"I will tell you! Forgive me!"

Des Moines, Iowa
A local restaurant

IX / 3

Bud and Angie tried to ignore the clatter of dishes and interruptions of the server. No, they didn't want anything else right now. Yes, the food was good. They said it repeatedly. The server obviously wanted them to leave so new customers could take the table. But they were compelled to stay until they found an idea to help Rennie. They shared their fears for Rennie and were frustrated with a lack of communications. Except for one text message—*okay, don't worry*—she had gone dark again.

Bud slouched in his chair, stirring his coffee. The idea of retirement had been working through his system. He was tired. Going dark seemed like a good idea for him, too. His career had been about reporting the news. It had to be timely, decent, and objective. It wasn't risky. One had to have a good sense of prose and story structure, and a distinctive style helped. But now, it was infused with politics, the newspaper's "brand," special interests, and personal threats. Maybe getting Rennie home was his last assignment.

"So, Angie, did your friend, the language professor, come up with any leads?"

Angie seemed anxious and eager for ideas. "He's been following Italian media and found there was another priest who died in an accident at the Vatican, but it was back-page news. Nothing big. He and the students searched all the news and data sources but couldn't find Rennie's name anywhere. What about your reporter source in Rome? Anything there?"

"He wants to know where she is so he can interview her. He

wants a scoop, the inside story. I also tried to contact that guy Sfumato in San Francisco. Sfumato tried damned hard to get the letters from her when she found them. I think he respected her tenacity, so I thought he might want to help. His people said he was concerned about her. They want to be informed if we learn where she is and any other news."

This was all going to work out okay, Bud thought.

"Bud, this Sfumato guy. Do we know anything about him? It seemed he had a lot of foreign contacts. What's his business, and the source of his money?"

The old reporter sat up. He felt cold, serious, focused.

"I don't know. Once the letters thing was over, we all went on with our lives. He started the whole thing and then disappeared. We don't know anything about him."

He looked out the window. *What kind of newsman am I?*

"Bud, can you check that out, get background?"

"Hey, and who's becoming a reporter? Have you been reading crime novels at the library?"

"You know, Bud, librarians are outstanding research specialists. A person doesn't have to be a storyteller to get information for a compelling argument."

Fresh passion for his craft blossomed within him for the first time in years. The challenges of dealing with the new management at the paper who cared more about the bottom line than the concerns of the readers and the loss of his wife had sapped him of his drive and, for a while, his will.

"Angie, I'll get someone on it. He knows more than they're telling us. One of my guys has worked on organized crime issues. He knows how to dig out what's hidden."

It felt good to be on a case again. A sly sense of hungry energy arose as he thought about celebrating this moment with a fat cheeseburger and a beer. Then he realized he had just eaten, and also noticed Angie. She looked overwhelmed and exhausted.

"Bud, what else can we do? I thought about going to Italy, but I have no clue where she might be. What I really want to do is go to London for Matthew's memorial service. Losing him hurts so much. He was gentle and wise and had a great spirit of adventure. What a loving man. He'd be turning over every rock to find Rennie."

Bud's loose tie drifted onto his greasy plate as he leaned forward. He wouldn't care even if he saw it.

"You mentioned London. There was another guy over there who was obsessed with this whole letters thing. Rennie said he had a reputation for killing people by jamming rocks down their throats. Could he be involved? Has that come up?"

"No. You're right. We've got to check that out. That guy Sfumato knew about him. Can you put your reporter on that too? There might be a connection."

"Right, let's get out of here. We've got work to do. Angie, I'll go to San Francisco if I have to and interview Sfumato. You put in another call to Rennie. She might respond."

Angie got up to leave. Confident and determined again, she paused to give Bud a light kiss on his cheek. He liked it but shrugged it off as she left. He threw a bunch of bills on the table and wove through the crowd to the front door. He felt like he was back on his high-school football team. Fullback. He hit the front door with a shoulder like he was going through tacklers. An end zone awaited him.

IX / 4

"David, let's take a break when we get to the next place where we can stop. I need coffee and something to eat."

"Good. We also need to sort out what we're doing. Us scientists need plans."

Rennie's laptop was open, and she scrolled through pages of the Vatican files at a steady pace.

"I've been reviewing more documents, and as we found, most of what I can read is pope stuff—appointing bishops, making decrees and all that. Luckily, they put translations with most documents, probably those that have been examined. Many of the older documents, and probably more interesting ones are in the original languages. Are you still any good with those?"

"I can do a little magic with them once in a while. The vocabulary goes too quickly if you don't use it. I found the Aramaic came back nicely when reading the letters at the exhibition. My old Greek isn't bad."

Rennie slapped her laptop shut. She watched the sun setting at the horizon as her thoughts drifted into the past.

"David, the exhibition seems like a long time ago. What happened to Father Daniel, and why was he helping us? Do you think he had something going on in the background? People don't get killed for no reason."

"I don't know. It's terribly sad. I've wondered if helping us prompted what happened. Yet, what we did was innocent, even bland. We didn't take anything. No one could have even known what we were doing."

"It must have been something else. Someone felt threatened."

"Rennie, consider who showed up today at our hotel. Father Joseph didn't bring a fruit basket. Somebody is focused on you and what you're doing. And, one other thing, what the hell was that thing that you pointed at him? My God! Where did you get it? How does that work? I can't get it out of my head!"

"I don't know or really care. It's helped a couple of times. An old guy named Raphael gave it to me. I told you about him."

Staring out the window at the scenery rushing past, Rennie sighed hopefulness. "David, maybe I need to go home as you suggested. People are dying all around me." She studied David. "I don't want you to die, too."

"Well, thanks. That's one thing we can agree on. Up ahead, there's a small town. Let's find a restaurant. My eyes need a rest."

"Did you send a message to your colleagues in Switzerland like Michael suggested? It was a good idea even if it came from him."

"Yes, when I stopped to smooth out that map you smashed together. Wow, you were hot!"

"I assume you don't mean that in a positive way."

"Rennie, there are times when that occurs to me. But, you do a fine job to regularly change that opinion. Look there, there's a place for us to rest."

Rennie got out of the car the moment it stopped. She threw the door shut and stomped across the parking lot alone to the front door of the restaurant. Puffs of dust floated behind each strike of her heels.

David entered the restaurant, closed the door, and greeted in Italian a stout man wearing an apron. The man demonstrated effusive delight in their coming to his empty restaurant and presented David with two menus. He motioned to a table where Rennie was already seated.

With practiced propriety, David sat down, set the menus to the side, and placed a napkin on his lap.

Without looking at him, Rennie asked, "Have you ever been to the US?"

"As a young person, I visited the East Coast a couple of times, once with my parents and once with Grandfather. When I was in college, a few mates and I went to the West—Denver, Phoenix, Las Vegas, and Southern California."

Rennie turned toward him but avoided eye contact.

"That must have been interesting. So, did what happened in Vegas stay there?"

"Other than impressions, there wasn't anything dramatic. We saw a couple of the big acts and I became fascinated with magic. One magician was simply marvelous. My lasting memories regard the mountains and the ocean out west. Oh, and the Grand Canyon. How magnificent. It puts human achievement into a rather puny category. It was a rather soul-inspiring moment."

"Well, David, that's the first spiritual thing I've heard from you."

He studied the menu, adjusted his glasses, and didn't respond.

Rennie broke the silence. "Did you ever do anything with magic?"

He set aside the menu. "Yes, I bought a magic kit at a local store and practiced some of the tricks as we traveled and when I returned to England. The questions of illusion and what is happening found a connection for me with the world of quantum physics."

"So, can you do some tricks for me? Do you use coins or cards or what?"

"Maybe another time. One must have a playful attitude to do tricks and that mood escapes me right now."

Rennie turned away again. "I don't like magic anyway. It's deceptive and secretive. I prefer to know what's going on. People should put their cards on the table."

"Yes, but if you know how a trick happens, there's no surprise, no delight. If people put their cards on the table, as you say, and there's no mystery, then the game is nothing more than moving cards around."

David ran a finger down the menu and suggested a few things. He motioned to the man who greeted them and seemed to enjoy ordering in Italian with artistic intonations. The air remained still as they waited for their food. The proprietor brought some life to the weary hour with his occasional, energetic presence.

As they ate, an aching sense of guilt drifted into Rennie's thoughts.

He doesn't have to be with me. He's helping. I'm not being kind.

"David, I'm going through hell and I don't know why. I'm sorry some of this has fallen on you. Thanks for being patient."

"It's okay. These events are too opaque, and that's unsettling. The world I work in is also obscure, but it's not malicious. People do quite a good job of mucking up the world. The people in charge are as unstable and unpredictable as any sub-atomic particle at moments of instantaneity."

"What? What's this 'instantaneity' thing?"

"It's that moment when a particle or even system of particles becomes an entirely different bit of existence or changes at the same moment and without explanation as something far away. A related issue is 'nonlocality.' The change occurs beyond the rules of the macro system we all understand. There's no known cause and effect. As I said, it's like the unstable behavior of people with power, except whole societies experience the consequences and not just some particle."

"Well, Einstein, I'm not sure how that helps us here."

"Rennie, I'm not Einstein. I'm not even in his area of study. Einstein made his mark in macro-systems with the theories of special relativity and general relativity, which are operations of the big universe. He didn't like nonlocality and those theories. My work and that of my colleagues, is focused on the micro-dimension, the smallest bits of energy and mass."

"David, what you're saying is another obscure language, like Aramaic, and it doesn't offer anything meaningful to me."

"You mean like those letters you found? They were written in Aramaic. Are they not meaningful?"

Rennie swirled her coffee and studied its patterns and textures. She pushed aside a dish and fell back against her chair. She finally broke the silence.

"The letters – no, those were beyond profound. They speak of the divine, another world."

"Another universe you might say. Hmm, perhaps one in a multi-verse. Interesting."

Rennie was suddenly alert again.

"What do you mean?"

"Well, in my work, a key question is whether we are in just one of a multi-verse of parallel realities. We're accustomed to our four-dimensional universe we call space/time but, we can also demonstrate as many as nine or eleven dimensions.

"This is just you playing with magic. David, don't you recognize that's all invention?"

"Rennie, the deceiving invention is the idea that the only existence is what you can experience. Humanity is incredibly limited in what it can sense or even think. Animals and insects are massively more connected with their surroundings than humans in hearing, smelling, seeing, and other senses. Researchers in math and physics try to describe aspects of alternative universal systems we cannot sense but know exist."

"So, can you see into these other dimensions?"

"We cannot. We use unique forms of mathematics to describe

them. There's a kind of veil that blocks our view. One of the unspoken dreams is that the next quantum-level discovery will yield a glimpse of how we can answer that question."

"I wish we could pull aside the dark veil that keeps us from seeing what's behind these killings."

"Rennie, too often I see human behavior as unexplainable as much of the quantum world. At least particles and forces don't have nefarious motivations as people do. Yet, we're supposedly created in God's image. Really?"

"Okay, so is God in another dimension? And if so, does some veil block us from seeing the divine?

"Can the divine come from another dimension into our world? You mean like angels? At the exhibition, Daniel and I spoke briefly about angels and their appearances in the Bible. Now I'm the one tired of questions. We're not far from Brindisi. We need to get there tonight. Maybe there's something in your data file that will help us see into the darkness of this situation we're in once we're there."

"David, there's too much in there for me or us to review, and most of it is in other languages. I also don't know what I'm trying to find."

"You're all we've got Rennie."

She sat up straight. Her hands flew up and brushed her hair back. Her body was tense.

"No, wait. I'm not alone in doing this. Angie could help me. If I could get this data file to her, she could multiply the research efforts."

"Your friend in Iowa?"

"Exactly, she's the chief librarian at a college and a master archivist or whatever they're called. She has other resources at the college. And, she can send the files to Professor Snapper in London."

Rennie stood up and stared out the window.

"How do we get this to her?"

"Well, it's digital. If we weren't so paranoid about being online, you could email it to her."

"David, that's it! Maybe there's one of those internet cafés in town. Would this restaurant have an internet connection? Can you ask the owner here?"

"Sure, I'll ask but—"

"Please, ask him."

Rennie found the flash drive in her pocket as she watched David discuss with the old Italian their needs. Her mind raced through what she'd say to Angie.

No locations. Find references to Paul and women in the early Church. The fellowship, or what was it?

David returned. "Okay, they have a computer and it's tied to the net. They use it for credit cards and advertising. He said it's in the back and he'll help us login. Rennie —"

"I know. I won't say where we are or where we're going. The files have to be sent in several messages because of the size. I don't know how much of it will go. Heck, we won't know if it even gets there."

David's voice picked up some energy. "For the subject line, I was thinking of using 'Matthew's Memorial Service.' What do you think? One other thing, the internet site access is probably in Italian. I should do this."

"I don't care. Let's go. I'll tell you what to say to her."

Within minutes, David was online and created a new email account. With Rennie's help he submitted Angie's email address, and together, they quickly sent four messages with uploaded data. When he logged off, they stared at the screen.

Rennie reached down and removed the flash drive from the computer. As David stood up, they faced each other. She leaned in and wrapped her arms firmly around him, laying her cheek on his shoulder.

"Thanks," she whispered.

PART TEN

Rome, Italy
The Vatican
St. Peter's Basilica

X / 1

Father Angelotti walked alone through St. Peter's Basilica. His head turned up to observe the arches holding the endless expanse of granite ceiling. His gaze stopped there. He hesitated to consider the massive yet ornate structure that covered everything within. *It's too close to God.*

Late in the evening, after the tourists and the cleaning staff were gone, was when he had the vast temple to himself. With well-worn practice, he was moved to pray in one of the small alcoves allowing for humble prayers of intercession by the saints instead of in ceremonial homage at the dramatic, central altar area.

Angelotti didn't pray to saints. He opened his soul to God but would never in prayer address the Supreme Deity directly. He felt unworthy, and his body slumped into a more appropriate posture the closer he got to a chosen place of prayer for the evening. He believed only the pope could speak to God. This is how it was for the ancient Hebrews and the Jews. The high priest entered the holy of holies once a year and communed with the Almighty. The other, lesser priests never dared to be so arrogant.

A quiet, inner spirit led him to a secluded recess. He knelt at the railing and considered the sculpture portraying a saint. He didn't care who it was. The occasional, distant and hollow noises of equipment or persons echoed through the cavernous building as muffled background effects. It was just worldly clutter trying to distract him from his duty. The pained appearance on the face of the sculpture came into focus. Angelotti pondered it.

If I could feel, I know I'd be hurting, too.

A deep sigh filled only half of his lungs. They felt tight. Another sigh. A bit more air came in that time. His head dropped, and he clasped his hands.

It's not easy to be a servant of the Almighty.

The image of a life-size crucifix opened into his thoughts. It zoomed close to the face of Jesus. Angelotti's eyes pinched shut. He couldn't look there. The scene in his mind turned to show observers standing around the cross. One person was on the ground, prostrate toward the horror, arms outstretched with palms up.

There I am.

With this image, his soul could step through the curtain into the holy of holies. Total humility is required. The blood from the cross gave him courage. His shoulders sank, and his hands opened as if holding a cup.

"Holy divine," he whispered. "I am not worthy to be in your presence. Forgive my arrogance and lack of wisdom. Forgive this intrusion by my filthy soul."

His head fell forward. He gazed into the darkness of his closed eyes.

Help me. Help me know what to do.

After many minutes, peace blossomed within him as flickering candles teased his eyes to open. A hint of incense sharpened his senses. A deep, natural breath filled him. Forgiveness was his. Now, he could await the word of the Spirit. His whole being came to rest.

Then, unexpected sounds of someone kneeling nearby awakened him. He risked a glance to the side, revealing a figure in white about eight feet away, head bowed, and hands clasped in prayer. Angelotti swiveled to see if anyone else was there. No one.

He dropped his gaze but couldn't close his eyes or pray.

We are not to wear white. Who is this?

A sudden shiver surprised him.

Is this a visitor from heaven?

He was afraid to behold again this visitor or even breathe.

What happened to all the noise? The world is silent!

Angelotti realized his hands were crushing one another. He released them and placed them on the rail.

I'll push myself up then leave.

"Brother, did you get your answer?" asked the figure in white. His Italian was not the native tongue.

Angelotti felt panic. He had to respond. He turned despite stiff muscles in his neck fighting each degree of rotation. There kneeling, his partner in prayer, the relaxed and gently smiling supreme pontiff of the universal church, the bishop of Rome, the vicar of Jesus Christ, the sovereign of the state of Vatican City and primate of Italy.

Father Angelotti's mouth hung slightly open. He stared. As the pope stood, Angelotti didn't know if he should stand or stay on his knees. He had never been in the presence of the leader of his church.

He's smaller than I thought.

The Holy Father offered his hands as if willing to help the priest up. "Brother, will you walk with me? Sometimes I can't be on my knees too much after a long day."

Angelotti took the hands and rose to his feet. There, he could see into the eyes of the one he believed was God's representative on Earth.

The pope slid his arm around that of the stunned priest's and turned him to begin a stroll along the marble floor.

"Was your conversation with God complete? I would be distressed if it were not."

"Holy Father, my prayers are never complete. They continue in my thoughts, even in my sleep."

The pope nodded. "It sounds as though you might not give God a chance to speak back to you."

He laughed with a soft puff of breath, "I'm sorry *padre*. I meant no offense."

"No, not at all. You always speak with wisdom, and it's true. I could listen more. For someone as low as I, the Almighty must have nothing to say. I think if I keep talking, there could be a moment of silence in heaven when my small voice will be heard."

The little man in white spoke with sharp diction.

"The challenges we see across the world and throughout all of time would suggest that holy ears and eyes have been absent from our condition. Is that your thought?"

The priest wondered what the pope wanted to hear. What would be the right answer for this man who is powerful on Earth and a heartbeat away from the divine.

"You would know best," was all he could think of.

"And your thoughts?" the pontiff again asked.

They shared a few steps and then Angelotti spoke.

"I fear there may be times when God is so offended by us that he turns away. This is as written in the Old Testament when he removes his hand of protection from Israel and they suffer all forms of horror. I hope it isn't so now, but what can explain these times?"

The pope gave a slight squeeze to Angelotti's arm. "Do you think our conditions are worse now than at other times?"

"It grieves me to say yes. We are supposed to know all things in this age. We have the capability to do significant good, but we do harm on a scale never seen."

"And with technology, *padre*, we're able to see it more quickly and easily. Each calamity that comes to my attention affects my heart as if it were an obstruction in my veins."

"Oh, Holy Father, I wish I could help you."

"And, what would you do, good Brother?"

Angelotti felt empowered in the moment. "I would, as Shakespeare's Hamlet says, 'take arms against a sea of troubles and by opposing end them.'"

The pope slowed his pace and drew a heavy sigh. Angelotti's back chilled and tightened with sudden panic as his fears seemed to fill the vast temple. *How could I speak of violence?*

The pope asked, "And, which enemy of God shall we strike down first? Maybe, we should start within this holy community. They say there's much to do here. What do you think?"

Angelotti's ribs sank into his chest. *What's happening?*

The pope again took the priest's arm and continued their walk.

"Forgive me. The late hour makes me crude. Perhaps, I also hear too much from men and too little from God. That must be why I am restored when I'm among the outcasts of the world. If their goodness prevails in the midst of so much pain, then God must be present. My heart is touched by them."

Angelotti's legs became weak and his knees began to fail. He pulled his arm from the sling of the pope's arm and sank to the floor. His consciousness tumbled with fear and confusion. He was awake and aware but helpless.

The vicar of Jesus Christ gathered up his own garment and sat with the fallen priest.

"Shall I call for medical help? What can I do for you?"

"Holy Father, I'm so sorry, for all of it. I will be all right. I just want to obey and do what is right and good. I don't know what I'm saying."

"What do you need, Father Angelotti?"

The priest leaned away from the pontiff with an added worry. He didn't realize that the pope knew who he was.

"Can you stand, Brother Angelotti? Shall I call for assistance?"

"No, please, Holy Father. I've been too much trouble already. I'll be fine. I'm blessed beyond measure to have shared this time with you. My thoughts and my heart are overflowing with renewal."

The pope rested his hand on Angelotti's back.

"You need rest, my friend, and when you are ready, consider your choices according to the way of Jesus, not the way of men. I hope when we meet again, all that we do is filled with grace and love."

They helped each other up, smoothed their cassocks, and embraced. Nothing was said as they went separate ways.

One frightening thought filled Angelotti's mind.

How does he know me?

Istanbul, Turkey
Topkapi Palace

X / 2

On warm summer days, Director Aslan Yilmaz enjoyed visiting the secure area of the ancient artifacts department deep below Topkapi Palace. It was cool and dry, a perfect escape from heat as well as from telephones and computers.

Finding Chief Curator Yusuf was sometimes a challenge. He didn't exactly hide from people, but he could become entrenched in a remote location of the archives for long periods as he examined a document or other treasure.

Aslan searched several aisles of tall racks until he met Chetin, the intern. Their conversation in Turkish was polite but restrained by differences of rank.

"Ah, you must be Chetin. We haven't met. I'm Aslan Yilmaz, director of the palace and museum complex. I was looking for Yusuf. Is he available?"

"I'm pleased to meet you, sir. But, I'm sorry he's not here. He went to the administration department to obtain information on several visiting research people for the spreadsheet we are completing. You can probably find him there."

"I see. I might wait for him here. The administration people can become tedious on detail and entrap you."

Aslan tried to offer some humor, but the intern was careful to maintain the formal relationship.

"So, Chetin, what are you working on?"

With apparent delight, the young man pushed up the glasses on his nose. He seemed to vibrate with energy.

"Curator Mustafa *Bey* said you had given approval for me

to do extra research when I had some open time. I was eager to follow up on work done by my mentor, Professor Ahmet Erkan of the Turkish Institute of Religious Studies."

"Yes, he was a true scholar. We were shocked with his recent death. It must have been one of the terrorists who got into our country. A real loss to our practice."

Chetin sighed. "Agreed. He was a guiding light for me in conducting intuitive research on the ancient world."

"So, what research interests you?"

"Development of the early Christian church remains open to new understanding. Professor Erkan believed that we here in Turkey must have more records than previously disclosed. Records of the assembly of Christian bishops in Nicaea, here in Turkey, in 325 CE and the later meetings in Constantinople are few compared with the history made. He was interested in the way issues of theology were addressed and in a particular tradition or legend that the apostle Paul had a new revelation about Jesus late in his ministry. Some say it was controversial and was spread by women who were early leaders of the church. Professor Erkan thought the marginal issues of faith and politics are often crushed by dominant players but should be explored. He was confident there are additional documents of the proceedings and those would be in our archives."

"That's interesting, Chetin, but it is not an area of my expertise. Why did this subject of Christianity interest Erkan?"

The intern adjusted his glasses again. "I think, and this is speculation, the development of a major religion here in this small region caught his eye. The first prominent Christian churches were in this area. It's only about forty miles from Corinth to Athens and maybe two hundred miles across the sea from Thessalonica to Izmir, near where Ephesus was. Our capital Ankara is near where the church of the Galatians was located. The decisions of the meetings here created the Christian doctrines that have endured for two thousand years! He and Father Anastasios were delighted with this happening here in our area."

"So, Erkan wanted to come here to Topkapi?"

"Yes. He thought Topkapi was a natural repository for those documents since this was the seat of power for Emperor Constantine. Professor Erkan thought that as a scholar of ancient Greek and as a non-Christian, he could offer objective support finding key documents that would lead to a conclusion of controversial issues and resolve conflicts."

Aslan motioned to a table and chairs for them to sit.

"What controversies do you speak of?"

"Professor Erkan understood there was a kind of war in Christianity that has been waging unnoticed since the beginning of the faith. It's a conflict of doctrines, one hidden and one authorized."

"Hmm," Aslan mused, "We Muslims have similar problems with different sects of our faith."

"Yes, and Professor Erkan thought much of the conflicts could be resolved with understanding their origins. In Christianity, one was a belief circulated from the beginning, and by their apostle Paul that God, or heaven, wasn't in a far-off place or time. The divine is present here and now. We just can't experience it due to our human limitations. Our attachment to worldly things is the problem. But that was set aside with the idea we couldn't experience the divine until death if we reached heaven."

Aslan listened carefully.

"So, Chetin, it seems like a reasonable goal to resolve such conflicts with research."

"Many of the leaders of the faith were opposed because, according to Professor Erkan and Father Anastasios, the leadership had more power over the faithful if they believed they had to wait until after death to be with God."

"This doesn't surprise me, Chetin. Is Father Anastasios the priest who was found in Italy not long ago? I read an impressive paper by him years ago. Did he work with Professor Erkan?"

Chetin stammered, "Yes, well, no. I mean, he was interested in what was controversial for the church. It had to do with why Jesus died. I'm not sure of the details of this argument. As a Christian priest, he saw this as a supreme question for the church."

"Very interesting. And there is insufficient evidence of these ideas in the documents that are known to have survived these meetings? Erkan thought others existed?"

"Precisely! He was about to come here to Topkapi to seek approval for more research. The Second Ecumenical Council was here, and other meetings followed, so where else would the records be? But, only limited notes of proceedings have been available."

Aslan was pleased with young Chetin's effervescence. The intern did a quick glance of nearby racks as if the lost treasure might be in sight.

"So Chetin, you think documents may be here and you may be close to finding something special?"

"Yes. If I can find the records of Emperor Constantine regarding these meetings, we should find key documents. That was the dream of Professor Erkan and of Father Anastasios. Legends say that early leaders in the church who were women petitioned the council meetings to present evidence to support their doctrine about the death of Jesus."

"A request from women? I don't know that much about formative Christianity. Our religion, Islam, is better defined in history."

Almost panting, Chetin continued, "Quite true, Director. Evidence shows the earliest years of Christianity had much involvement by women as leaders in the church, but at some point, near the second century, that vanished. No reasons for the dramatic change is mentioned in existing literature. It's an unusual shift considering how important they were at the beginning."

"Chetin, power ebbs and flows in societies. Women have

rarely held positions of authority for long. I like this project. Please do me a favor and don't bother Yusuf with news of any discoveries. He has some important issues to deal with right now, and I don't want him distracted. Agreed? But you can continue your research. Please inform me, and me alone, of any progress."

"I will, sir. I wish Professor Erkan and Father Anastasios were alive to know of this. It would be triumphant news for them."

Aslan stroked his chin. *Two distinguished researchers of the same subject murdered in different places at about the same time.*

"Chetin, do you believe these documents you wish to find are in our archives?"

"I'm confident they're here, and I'm eager to find the surrounding documents that will lead us to them. The world knows of the results of these crucial meetings and some of the discussions, but the so-called minority reports of dissension are absent. Professor Erkan believed finding more about the proceedings might include those other views and raise new perspectives on all thought in the church at that time."

Aslan was intrigued that these possible and long-sought treasures might be in the archives. *Here in my museum.* A discovery like this will give Topkapi significance and mean recognition for him. He relaxed with a comfortable smile and knew it was time to push ahead with energy.

"Chetin, as I said, this new project is to be known only to you and me. Do not bother my good friend Yusuf. I'll meet with him and you at the right time. Until then, move forward and see what you can find. Here's my card. Contact me directly and with discretion if you need anything or find something. Isolate anything you find so we have ready access to it. Let me know where."

The intern stood and shoved his glasses back on his nose. He jammed forward his hand to thank the director. "I will, sir. Professor Erkan and Father Anastasios would have been pleased with your support."

On the Road to Brindisi, Italy

X / 3

The lights of Brindisi appeared in the distance. David was ready to stop driving but he noticed minutes earlier that Rennie had finally relaxed and slipped into restful bliss. Although he was weary of the road trip and all the unknowns, he wished her sleep could continue. She'd been through too much. He would drive as long as possible before she came to.

There was something else. He wouldn't mention it. She didn't need more to trouble her. They were being followed. It was a car. He noticed it shortly after they had left the restaurant. It kept its distance, and during the day it was obvious. The car kept a steady pace behind them, the same gap between them no matter whether David sped up or slowed down. The insolent darkness of people wouldn't let them go, and with the sun down, real darkness would now prevail. He hoped he was wrong. Maybe the other driver had no interest in them. But the bigger story was ominous.

Did Grandfather know how serious this was when he sent me out here? I'm just a physicist.

David needed to know where they now were, but the map they got from the rental car agency was for the nation. There was no detail for cities except for Rome and Naples. He wished he could open a map on his phone, however, they were too close to being out of Italy to risk it.

Signs along the highway became numerous with advertising, indications of surrounding towns, and distances to intersecting roads. As with many cities in Italy, there was no sprawling suburban introduction to the urban center. Rural lands became a city. The only transition was heavy traffic. But that was good.

Now, maybe I can lose that car.

A quick decision arose. A road sign indicated a key highway was coming up. Going one way took him to the airport. The harbor was in the opposite direction. Flying to Greece would be quick. A ferry would take all night. Security would be intense at the airports here and in Greece. The choice was immediately ahead.

Instinct drove him to take the safe option. It was logical. A quick, hard right turn and they were on the way around the city to the harbor. He looked at Rennie. The turn shifted her a little, but she remained deep in sleep.

He checked the rearview mirrors. It was difficult to know whether that car was still following them in all the traffic. Now, the logical thing to do was maneuver between the cars and trucks and speed ahead. Even if someone was tracking them, he might slip away, get to the ferry, and be out of the country before anyone could take action against them.

For the moment, David became a driver, and he liked it. Downshift and acceleration, slight brake pressure, and then into the next lane. He was surprised at how good it felt. Over the years, he had come to think that pleasure was opposed to logic, which meant it should be avoided. Simplicity was good and teasing one's emotions made things too complicated. It got in the way of progress. Maybe, he was wrong.

From the far-left lane, he saw a sign flash by on the right side of the road. The harbor road was the next turn to the right. He had to get over there, now. A glance back showed an opening. The little Fiat jumped forward and angled right. One more lane change was needed. Another glance back and again an opening appeared. As he made his move, the old, over-loaded truck ahead of him slowed down and moved to the right. David hit his brakes and was greeted with horns blaring behind him.

Rennie jumped forward and grabbed the dash. "What's that? What happened?"

"Sorry, some idiot ahead of us hit his brakes."

She rubbed her face and ran her fingers through her hair.

"Are we close?"

"We're getting there. The harbor road is right here. Then we're close."

"Do you know where we're going?"

Rennie picked the map off his lap. After a quick look, she dropped it to the floor.

"No help there. Wait, where's the car agency office? We've got to return this car."

David checked his mirrors again for the car that might be a threat. They seemed to be running free.

"David, should we stop and ask for directions or make a call or something? How about that café?"

"Let's go a little further. I'd like to be further away from that main road."

Rennie removed the folder of rental paperwork from a side pocket. She sorted through the papers, pausing to study them more closely.

"Can we get a light on in here? This small print isn't easy to read, especially the Italian."

She gave David a mocking smile.

"What are you looking for?"

"An address for their place in Brindisi. I see one here for a couple places in Rome, or *Roma!*

She tossed her hand in the air for dramatic effect.

David glanced over.

"It might be in bold letters at the end somewhere, or maybe there's an insert with all their locations."

"Ah-ha! The intrepid reporter finds the missing data. It's on a street called Via Enrico Fermi. Can we find that?"

"Rennie! You've got to be kidding me."

"What? That's what it says."

"Yes, but it's an incredible coincidence. Enrico Fermi was one of the most significant physicists in history."

"Oh, dear God. Here we go again with another science lesson."

"No, Rennie, not only does that fit me, but it also happens to be the road we're on. It's wonderful. Keep an eye out for a sign. If we don't see one in a few minutes, I'll stop and ask for directions. Oh wait, this is becoming an industrial area. We must have passed it."

David turned the car around using a wide place in the road. As he accelerated forward Rennie yelled, "There," and pointed to the right.

A softly lit neon sign indicated *CarRoma*. David turned into the parking lot and stopped in front of the office.

"David, this would be a good time to ask them about the ferry schedule, tickets, and all that. We could also use a ride to the ferry loading dock. I don't want to be on the street in this part of town."

"Good. Do you want to come in? Maybe they have coffee or water or something."

"I don't know. Maybe, I'll wait here."

David exited the car and was about to close his door when Rennie jumped out of her side of the car. She held up the packet of rental information.

"You'll probably need this."

Inside, David greeted a clerk at the desk in Italian as Rennie laid the papers on the counter. He whispered to Rennie that she could sit in a chair and he would ask for something to drink. As she moved toward a seat, David noticed out the window that a car entered the parking lot and turned into a spot distant from the office. Its lights went out. It might be the car he thought was following them.

A man behind the counter greeted him. "*Signor*. Mister."

"Yes, oh sorry," David spun to see the clerk.

"No problem. I think I get your attention in English better."

The fellow appeared to enjoy flexing his language skills and commanding the situation.

As they worked out the billing and payment, David mentioned their concerns regarding the ferry.

"*Si*, not a problem, my friend. We handle all these things. If you like a hotel for this evening, we can do that too."

"Brilliant, I mean excellent. Thank you. If we can catch the next ferry this evening, that will be fine. Oh, and we'll need a ride to the ferry."

"Good fortune falls upon you and your lady. In a few minutes, I close the office. Then, I take you to the ship in the car you brought. *Prego*, let us finish these things now. And, I bring you and the lady bottles of water."

The minutes needed for paperwork dragged on as David attempted an occasional peek toward the parking lot. He wondered if he should tell Rennie. For now, it was best to let her relax.

A few signatures and then the payment was completed. David sighed a moment of stress off his shoulders. He shared another pleasantry with the clerk and heard Rennie's chair slide with a squeak. She got up and went to the front window. New fears rushed through David's mind when a light appeared in the mystery car and he thought he heard a door close.

"Rennie, would you come here, please?"

She rolled her head around as if to loosen her neck as she walked to him.

"Sure, how are we doing?"

"Good. He's going to close the office now and then take us to the ship. We'll use the car we came in."

"Okay, I'll wait in the car. Would you bring another couple bottles of water?"

"Wait, Rennie. It's best to stay here for now. It might be a while."

He saw she was exhausted and uncomfortable as she wandered away. He wished he could let go and relax, even a little. He looked out the window again.

"Okay, *signor* and *signora*, now I will turn out the lights and we'll go." The clerk seemed happy to end the day and do so a little early.

David dropped the car keys on the glass counter causing a clatter. Then, he heard the door. Rennie was going out.

"*Signor*," David yelled, "we'll be at the car!"

David shouted as he hurried to follow her, "Rennie, wait up. Let me go with you."

As he reached her, he put his arm around her waist and slowed down her pace.

"We're almost out of here," he said in her ear.

She leaned in against him.

"We're almost out of here," he said again, with tenderness.

He let her go so he could open the driver's door but realized that she stopped in front of the car and turned to the mystery car in the lot. She took a few steps toward it, paused, and then more.

"Rennie, let's get in the car. We need to go."

She pointed. "That person in the car. Over there. Is he sleeping?"

"I don't see anything. Come on. Get in, now."

She ignored him and walked further toward the suspicious car.

"He's leaning against the steering wheel. Something's wrong."

She hurried closer then stopped. Her hands jerked up to cover her mouth.

David dashed around the car to her. A man in a dark suit was slumped forward. His eyes were open and fixed. What appeared to be a line of blood was running from a corner of his mouth.

David grabbed Rennie's arm.

"Let's go. We must leave here, now."

She pulled free and hurried to the stranger's driver's door. David followed, trying to grab her and imploring her to come with him, and leave.

Rennie stopped at the door and gazed at the man. A quick pull on the door handle and the body fell out to the pavement. The thud of the head hitting concrete and the arms flinging in clumsy, limp moves to sudden stillness froze them in place. The handle of a large knife stood erect from his chest.

"Oh, my God!" she shrieked.

She backed away, casting a desperate look at David, falling into his arms, her cheek tight against his.

"David, what's going on? Who is that?"

X / 4

A steady flow of people, mostly young people, streamed through the corridors of the newspaper office, papers in hand and worried looks on their faces. They regarded the news business as a serious endeavor with possibly, hopefully, meaningful impacts on their readers. Yes, their names would be on the bylines and their reporting was the basis of the news, but the underlying focus of the work was to deliver to the reader something important to their senses. As Bud would say, "It's not your name but your story the people need."

Bud stared at the newspaper on his desk. He circled words and underlined portions of sentences with a green highlighter pen. He closed his eyes and shook his head.

What's happened to good news writing?

His mobile phone rang, demanding attention. He didn't respond. It rang again. He glared at it lying on a side table. As it began to sound again, he snatched it up.

"Yeah, this is Bud."

"This is Angie, do you have a minute? I've got some good stuff."

Bud ran his fingers through what was left of his hair. He grabbed a pen and sat back. "Go ahead."

"I talked with Professor Snapper of the British Museum. He and others are reviewing the materials that Rennie sent to us and I sent to him. He said most of it was unremarkable, as he put it, but a few things were what he called 'treasures.' They were excited and wondered how they could have been kept secret all these centuries."

"Well, duh! Did you tell him Rennie got them from the pope's secret library?' Bud chuckled to himself. "Sorry, what did he say?"

"They haven't gone through all of it yet, so they brought in some extra talent you might say, to translate and understand the importance of the documents. There's a lot of material there."

Bud got out a fresh tablet and prepared to make notes.

"Yeah, it was good she sent the files to us. There's no way she or that guy David could have looked through it. So, what so-called treasures were uncovered?"

"They say there's evidence by references in some documents that the apostle Paul not only wrote more letters than we know, but there were people who wrote letters to each other saying what he told them. I don't know what you in the news business call it, but it backs up some significant stories."

"Corroboration."

"What?"

"Angie, when a reporter gets a piece of information and then finds other information that verifies or validates the first information, it's called 'corroboration.' The follow-up information helps make the first item more factual."

"Okay, good. Well, that's what we got from Rennie, not the actual documents but apparently references to them. Prof. Snapper said the significance isn't obvious at first. What's meaningful is when you weave the pieces together and place that fabric against the material that is Christian doctrine. There's quite a contrast."

Bud laid down his pen. "Now, I'm listening. Give me the pieces first, and then lay down the new perspective."

"Do you have time for this? I know this is a busy time of the day for you."

"Geeze, Angie, will you just tell me? I'll decide on my priorities."

The palm of his hand banged his forehead.

"I'm sorry, Angie. This is the most important thing I could do this week— hell, this year."

"As we know, there are accounts of angels meeting people in the Bible and in other religious documents. And, then there's the event of Jesus appearing to Saul or Paul when Saul was going to Damascus."

She paused but Bud said nothing.

"So," she continued, "Mr. Snapper said they found a few documents in the data files that reported people writing about Paul being visited by a heavenly visitor who told him how we should regard Jesus in a new way."

"So, what's the point?"

"They haven't found direct source material yet. They have references in some documents that these women wrote to each other. I guess there were a lot of women in early leadership roles and they stayed in touch for mutual support. The Vatican documents are highly critical—to the point of condemning—the beliefs of these women. Professor Snapper said he and Matthew were in touch long ago with an archivist in Istanbul by the name of Yusuf who was researching this topic. Snapper and Matthew wanted to go to Istanbul to meet with him."

Bud dropped his head forward and wagged it.

"Angie, I didn't get that much detailed theology in Holy Queen of Peace Parochial School. But what you're telling me sounds like what we already know. Angels visited people in the Bible. Okay, and some women talked about it. Fine. What's new? What's so earth-shaking —or heaven and earth-shaking?"

"Bud, it's fresh for me too. Professor Snapper said this correspondence among the women suggests a position by the apostle Paul that was considered heresy. Imagine that. Paul, heresy! THAT would be earth-shaking. He had basically defined Christian beliefs in all his letters we've known of for years, and these new letters might rebut his own teachings. Snapper said this archivist in Istanbul was searching for documents relating to this conflict."

"Let's step back. So, Rennie said there were a couple of groups fighting some holy battle, and she's caught in the middle. Is that it? A disagreement about religious doctrine is still going on after two thousand years. I'll bet God is real happy with that."

"Yeah, that among many things. The professor said they have scraps of information, and people are speculating how they tie together. They're working on translating and understanding other documents. One of the researchers at the British Museum who's working with him found another item of interest. It's a letter from a bishop, I think to another bishop. The timing he said was around the second century."

"So, was this about the angel and Paul stuff?"

"No, it had to do with the role of women in the church. One bishop said there were complaints that women should be banned from leadership positions. It might be about this accusation of heresy on doctrine."

"Well, Angie, now we know how long this battle involving a glass ceiling has been going on."

Bud expected a response. None came.

"Say, Angie, I asked one of my reporters here to check into this Sfumato guy more deeply. He's come up with some interesting things. His primary business deals with ancient Christian artifacts and not with old stuff from other cultures or places. He apparently negotiates sales of precious things among wealthy Christians that museums don't know about. If he can get his hands on something special, he makes a killing, so to speak. That's why he wanted the letters from Jesus that Rennie found."

"That also explains how he had inside information on where the letters might be and who was involved. He must have a lot of contacts around the world. Did your reporter find anything new as to whether Sfumato might know about the situation Rennie is in?"

"Not yet. If anyone can find out, it's this reporter. Richard is as bright and inquisitive as you can get. He's almost as good as Rennie. She's got that demanding side, you know. Have you heard anything new from her? Heck, I'd like to just know she's okay."

"Me too, Bud. I'll let you know if I hear something."

"Angie, one other thought. You might ask this guy Snapper and your professor friends at the college if they could find anything in the data or in other material that would suggest where Rennie might go or needs to go next. In fact, I'll text you Richard's number and you can connect him directly with your other resources."

"Good idea. Our religion professor said something about the significance of Corinth for Paul. But that's in Greece. I wish she'd come home, and we could all work on this, whatever it is."

"Me too, kiddo." Bud heard himself say it. *Kiddo.*

I'm getting soft, he thought and scratched his head.

"Bud, there's one other thing I've not mentioned. Professor Snapper is very concerned about Rennie. We need to find her, get info to her, and find Sfumato. I've got to go. Let me know of any new developments and I'll be in touch with you."

"Sounds good. Bye."

Bud slid his phone across the newspaper and tilted back in his chair. With most cases that unveil complex information, his thoughts would race through the data to see how connections could be made. He'd explore where the mistakes were and where the facts led. With this one, his mind was blank. Then, an image of Rennie appeared in his mind.

And, why is she so important to all this? I'm tired. I've got to retire.

Adriatic Sea
On a Ferry from Brindisi to Greece

X / 5

The constant grinding, hesitating vibration of the ship's engine and mechanical systems gave little hope that the old vessel could get out of the harbor much less across the sea to Greece. A sickening mix of anger and fear coated with disgust churned within Rennie. She sat alone, gazing through a smudged window at the harbor of Brindisi drifting away from the ship. She was sailing into darkness on what felt like a disastrous voyage that people will read about in the morning headlines.

The general seating area of the ferry was filthy and smelled of too many cultures and lifestyles dumped and never removed. She hoped David could find a cabin for them, something reasonably clean, safe, and quiet would be wonderful.

The past two hours had been filled with horrors. David had pushed her into the back seat of the Fiat and quickly drove the car to a space near the office door, further from the murder scene. He said he didn't want the rental car guy to see it. For a moment, the rental agency clerk saw the other car, but David interceded with questions about how to board the ferry. It was enough to distract the agent. On the way to the harbor, Rennie pretended to sleep in the back seat, lying flat, trying to stop her thoughts from seeing another death scene and endless questions of who and how and why.

Ignoring the ship and the smell, she thought, *Maybe we're safe now.*

David didn't appear to be pleased as he returned from his mission. He paused before sitting and studied the black plastic seating surface. His nose wrinkled with an inquisitive but sickened look.

"Please, David, sit."

He eased himself down.

"It's going to be a long ride. At least we're out of Italy."

"Yeah," she replied, "and what a special trip it was. Wining and dining and first-class accommodations for the woman who discovered letters written by Jesus Christ. Whoopee! She made history! Personally invited to the capital of holy Christendom."

David set his elbows on his thighs and rested his face in his hands.

The lights of the harbor seemed to get brighter but not further away. Rennie's reflection in the window stared back at her. Everything had been so terribly different after she was diverted to Naples.

"David, can we get a cabin?"

"They said they would work on that. They're busy putting out to sea first. We were lucky to get a ship that's only half occupied. Cabins should be available."

"Okay, so how long does it take to get there? Where are we going again? God, I feel completely helpless, not to mention clueless."

"We're going to the Greek city of Patras. It's like a provincial capital. We'll be there in the morning. Patras is where my grandfather and I went after we visited Delphi and Corinth. Oh, no. I've lost track of time and when his memorial service is."

"David, I'm sorry. I'm sorry about involving you in this."

"I'll check on getting us a cabin."

He stood, shook his head, and staggered away.

Rennie hugged her backpack and rested her cheek on the top. Her eyes eased shut but then opened. She looked around, checking for possible threats. Nothing appeared ominous. She allowed exhaustion to overtake her. The sea and sounds were now smooth. The comforting, rhythmic hum of the engines offered a steady reference point for the senses. Sleep came easily.

She awoke in a private cabin with a confused sense of peace. Her fingers slid across the cold vinyl of the seating surface she slept on. Her thoughts grasped for understanding. Then, *murder* hit her brain. She lurched up. The vision of a black handle on a steel dagger sticking out of a man's chest burst into view. She turned to see David on the other couch. He was the picture of serenity.

Rennie grabbed one of the water bottles that David purchased for them last night. A variety of questionable snacks sat on a shelf nearby. The water filled her cells with life as it slid down her throat. The bottle was nearly half gone before she stopped.

She allowed her body to lie back down. Her dreams had been filled with hours of streaming images and questions that spanned years. The themes of fear and an intense need to know had drained her. A few deep breaths brought calm. At least her body was more rested and alive than last night.

David turned over. Rennie looked to see if he was awake and hoped he was. Her thoughts again raced through the issues they had faced. Sympathy softened her. *He's been trying so hard.*

Early-morning light filtered in through coarse curtains on a tiny window and landed in a blur on the door to their cabin. The dull churning of engine noise somewhere far below reminded her of the escape from Naples to that island.

Michael. Who the heck is he? And, poor Rafael.

She closed her eyes and tried a deep, cleansing breath. Too many feelings were struggling for supremacy. Again, she tried a breath. And, again. Now it was working.

Let it all go. We're okay now.

Another hour of physical rest was interrupted when the

ship's horn sounded. A low bass note held for a few seconds. Rennie and David turned at the same moment to see each other.

"What's that?" Rennie asked.

He rubbed his face. "I don't know. Probably routine."

David shook his hands and stood. He twisted at the hips, flexed his shoulders, and lifted his knees. "Maybe we should go for a walk around the deck. The sea air will be refreshing."

He continued contorting and unlocking his worn body.

"David, I'd like to say something."

"Uh-oh."

"No, wait. I wish all this could have been different. I feel so guilty. I'm sorry this has been so awful. Without you, I don't know what would have happened. Later this morning, I need to sort things out and what's going to happen next. David, you saw that guy with the knife in his chest. We've got to decide what we're doing."

He studied the floor and scratched at his scalp with both hands.

"It's been hard for both of us. Let's first figure out how to clean up and get a fresh start. Then, we'll talk."

Rennie stood. Her sadness weighed on her soul.

This is my fault. How did I get to this point?

Their shared time now felt strained as they stumbled and shifted in the small cabin. Polite voices of, "Sorry," and, "You go ahead," broke awkward silences. Finally, it was time to explore the ship and see a new day.

The open air greeted them with new life. Waves, a light wind, and a sliver of land on the distant horizon declared *Welcome to tomorrow!* Rennie didn't hear it. She was still numb. She hugged herself for warmth as renewed steps across the deck felt like a modest sense of progress. Or, it could be escape. Moving was good. She felt more confident. A well-disguised whimper of relief or happiness slipped out. Her pace picked up from tentative to marching. She let her arms swing freely and then with strength. As she turned, she noticed David standing near the bow, a solitary figure.

She paused at a distance and studied him.

Rennie made a sharp left, and with brisk steps, headed down the deck toward the ship's stern. She could now see how the ship was worn, nearly worn out. The white paint of the cabin-wall exteriors was cracked and chipped. The blue trim around the windows and doors had faded into a weak pastel. The other passengers reflected the ship's condition. A class of mostly older, poorer people, a few unlucky tourists, tradespeople, and truck and van drivers, rough-looking and easily cast as villains in a B-movie.

Strolling along one exterior passageway, she saw a man alone, forearms resting on the railing. He was different, out of place. Just before she reached him, he turned to her, their eyes meeting. Despite a quick smile from him, Rennie sensed danger. She turned and moved at a quicker pace. Another turn to the other side of the ship, and she'd be back at the bow.

Along the way, a nagging feeling drifted in her senses. She had seen this man before but couldn't place where or when.

David was ahead, crossing the ship. He walked erect, looking at the sea, deliberate, arms hanging but easily drifting forward and back.

She hurried forward. "David."

He didn't respond.

"Hey, David."

Still, no response.

As she reached him, she could see wires hanging down from small earphones. He stopped, appearing startled, but only modestly so. That was his nature in all things.

"Hey, I called you. I didn't know you were listening to something. Music?"

He gave the wires a slight pull and rolled them into a tight circle around a couple of fingers.

"Yes, it was a nice break. Did you need something?"

He looked away.

"Yeah, I'm feeling better, stronger."

She stepped close to him.

"How are you doing?"

"Also, better. Have you thought about things?"

They continued toward the side of the ship. She tucked one arm under his and glanced back.

Rennie responded, "Nothing specific, but that will come. Do you think we can check our phones or laptops yet?"

"Yes, I'm sure that will be fine. But no, wait. Let me think."

David became quiet again. His eyes darted back and forth as if following an intense game of tennis. Only their steps and the waves could be heard.

"Sorry, Rennie, I might be wrong on that. I too would love to catch up on my email and so on, but it might be best for us to get through passport control in Patras first. The number one priority is being unburdened in Greece."

"Right, I see what you mean. I guess if anyone is trying to find us, they could have us picked up when we reach land."

His arm was stiff, not grasping hers.

"Besides, I'm sure we're not far away. We can wait, rest, and chat about what we might do next. How's that?"

"Can we use our credit cards? I owe you about a million dollars by now, and we could start with food. I'll buy. Do they have anything other than the snacks you got last night?"

He didn't answer right away. They continued their walk.

"Yes, I saw a counter where they sell food. They're not open yet. I checked a little while ago."

Rennie looked back again. They were alone.

"So, David, can we return to the cabin and rest and talk? I'd feel more comfortable."

"Of course, and we need to review our belongings. Mine are a jumble. I think we're more tired than we know."

As they made a last turn to enter the door for the cabin corridor, Rennie glanced behind them. Not seeing anyone spurred her anxieties and prompted a quicker pace to their door.

She hurried into the room.

"Please lock it, David."

"Of course."

"No, it's not for routine precautions. I saw someone. He seemed suspicious. I think I know him from somewhere, but I don't remember where."

"Who? What guy?"

"When I walked around the ship, there was a guy leaning on the railing. When I walked by, he gave me a strange look. He seemed nice, but I don't think he's friendly. I don't know. I felt threatened."

David sat on his couch and fell back. He closed his eyes.

"You know, if we do an empirical review of this, we find an attractive young woman, a tourist by appearance, alone on a ship. And a man, maybe Greek or Italian gives her a look. She feels threatened. Rennie, all this seems perfectly logical without raising another conspiracy theory."

She stared at him and dropped on her couch.

"Or, considering there's been a trail of death following me for some reason, my suspicions might be valid."

He finally made steady eye contact with her.

"True. There's logic in that, also."

"And David, if someone wanted to do something to me or us, where better than on a ship in international waters with no one even knowing we're here? There's logic in that, also."

David rose, slid his hands into his pockets, and peered out the small window. The light wasn't bright, but he squinted.

"The potential for danger is there, Rennie. I agree. You're also correct about our vulnerable status on the ship. I hadn't considered that. It's good information."

"You mean data?"

She felt defensive and knew it, and she knew the old Rennie was fighting for control. She had to resist, but that meant being patient and caring. This seemed like another survival moment.

"What are your thoughts? What's a good course of action?"

"David, I'd like to stay in the cabin while you get us some food and find out how much longer it will be before we get to port. Then, just before we get there, say twenty minutes before, we get online and see where things are at. I've been thinking, Angie might have come up with something useful for us."

"So, you think twenty minutes will not be enough time for any authorities to track us down and notify the Greeks?"

"Precisely."

"Okay, I agree. Now, in case I see some guy lurking in the vicinity, how do I recognize him?"

Rennie jumped up and hugged him.

"Thank you. Maybe you saw him before, too. He's kind of dark or olive-skinned, as they say. His hair is black and long."

"Hmm, not familiar, except for most of the men on this ship. How tall? Thin, heavy, muscular?"

"Medium height, no taller than us, and also medium build. For food, anything goes, except weird food like raw fish tacos or lamb kidneys or whatever. Tourist food will be fine."

David tilted forward so their noses nearly touched.

"Really, you don't like raw fish tacos?"

Rennie leaned back, unsure if he was joking.

A quick lift of his eyebrows suggested he was.

"David, leave now!"

She pointed to the door, restraining a laugh.

X / 6

Where's Father Angelotti?" Abbess Serena yelled out the door of her office to her new secretary. "Did you reach him?"

She shoved papers around on her desk, bunched some together, stacked them, and then slammed them down.

"Where the —?"

She listened. *Is she there?*

"Mimi!" *Who names a girl Mimi?*

A young woman timidly stepped halfway around the door frame.

"*Si*, yes, *Abbessa*. I tried several times his phones, at his office and mobile."

Serena placed her hands on her hips and tilted her gaze at the ceiling. She attempted a pleasant response as she turned to the secretary and motioned her to come in.

"So, is there no one in his office? He's the secretary for the Propagation of the Faith. Is that the one you called? Does no one report to him or he report to others?"

Mimi cautiously entered the office.

"I'm trying to locate someone, *Abbessa*. I find no one yet."

"What about those two sidekicks of his? What are their names? Scarpia and something."

"Sidekicks? I'm sorry, *Abbessa*, I don't know this."

"Okay, all right. Sorry, Mimi, let me know if you hear anything. You can return to your desk."

Serena attempted a gracious nod as the secretary left. She

wandered over to her conference table and leaned onto it, fists on the surface. Picking a pen from a notepad, Serena continued a slow journey around her office. Her mind worked through new permutations of what was going on within the Vatican. Sister Katherine's limited information suggested a deathly cabal that had to be found immediately. The pope affirmed his full support for whatever Serena considered necessary.

What's their agenda? Who else is involved?

She felt she was in the crosshairs of a weapon to be fired. Joseph had access to her office. Angelotti wasn't connected to her but they had worked closely together on some projects. Father Daniel was too inquisitive of her operations. And now, two of three are dead and one is missing. She froze, staring at the thick drapery material hanging in front of her.

Is it His Eminence, the secretary of state? Is he a target? Or, was I?

Serena moved quickly, pacing across the office, tapping her hand with the pen. She stopped in front of a picture of her installation as abbess. Her youth surprised many. There she was in the robe, holding the crosier.

The crosier! Where did it go?

Her steps hurried, turning her in circles. The pen slapped harder on her palm. Only a day ago, she requested a meeting with the cardinal prefect of the Apostolic Signatura to brief him on the events of the deaths. But he didn't seem interested and perhaps annoyed. That office is filled with lawyers. As one herself, she believed the Vatican court should be informed. Now, there were new concerns, Sister Katherine and the Holy Father. Things were happening too fast and all around her.

She went to her door and told Mimi to contact the cardinal prefect's office for an appointment to see him.

"Let them know I have important new information. It's urgent. And, try to reach Father Angelotti again. Thanks, Mimi."

The abbess returned to her conference table and collapsed into a chair. She pulled a notepad off a stack of files and began to write names and topics in an array as she had done before. This time, she added lines between characters and the topics. She added Katherine and the pope, she and put a large *X* over each of the names of Daniel and Joseph.

What were they doing?

She thought of the police notifying her they found Joseph in a car in front of a hotel.

"Pardon me, *Abbessa*."

Serena was startled into the present.

"Yes, what do you need, Mimi?"

"The office of the Apostolic Signatura has a few minutes available right now. But they said you must hurry there. The cardinal will soon leave for a meeting. I've not reached the cardinal secretary of state."

"Excellent. Thank you. Please take messages while I'm gone, but don't tell anyone where I've gone. Okay?"

"*Si*, yes, *Abbessa*."

Serena did a quick review of the paperwork and files and wondered what she should take and would need. She always wanted to be prepared to answer and ask everything relevant to an issue.

Nothing, she thought. *Just a clean pad and pen.*

When she reached her door, Serena looked back and wondered if the room should be locked. Security was vital until more was known. But she hurried on. The cardinal was waiting. Her attitude was set. *Act like an obedient abbess.*

Moving quickly down the halls and up the stairs without appearing frantic and disheveled wasn't easy. Serena greeted people warmly as she went by. She knew that surprised those who knew her.

Arriving at the office of the Supreme Tribunal of the Apostolic Signatura, the abbess knew it was time to lawyer up. She had to be at her best. As the supreme court of the Roman Catholic Church, this office was the highest judicial authority for the church, except for the pope himself.

The office was small but ornate, with a reception area, conference room, and three offices. Serena wondered what the primary location was like in the Palazzo della Cancelleria.

Serena introduced herself to the reception clerk and took a seat. She suppressed a nervous giggle. She felt like she had been called to the principal's office and remembered one of those moments from her childhood. It was pleasant and satisfying.

Her thoughts regarding this sudden and meaningful threat to the church flushed into her mind, focusing on a principle concern and accented with critical bullet points. She would provide enough to make them worry. *And,* she reminded herself, *ask them how I should proceed.*

The secretary of the Tribunal, Archbishop Tommaso Barberini, stepped from an office, but he paused and leaned inside for an extra moment with the cardinal. The archbishop closed the door and welcomed the abbess. His manner expressed polite diplomacy while his eyes suggested a shrewd player.

"*Buona giornata, Abbessa.* Oh, forgive me. I forget you are American. Good day to you."

"Archbishop Barberini, thank you. I'm grateful for your time. My Italian and Latin are workable, but I lack the beauty of the natural tongue. I appreciate this opportunity of a few moments with you and the cardinal."

"Sister, I'm sure it must be important. We have appreciated our previous work with you, and your reputation working for His Eminence on significant issues precedes you."

"You are too gracious, Father. And please, if the cardinal wishes for additional information, you're most welcome to follow up with me."

A slight squint hit his eyes, and an awkward silence fell between them.

"*Abbessa*, I'm dedicated to service and goodness. Whatever follow-up is needed, I will apply my best efforts."

"*Grazie molto, padre*." Serena struggled to come back from a possible subtle error in diplomacy.

The cardinal rescued the situation by coming out of his office.

"Ah, *Abbessa* Serena, welcome, welcome. Let's meet here in the conference room. I regret I only have a minute."

He went in without approaching her.

Archbishop Barberini motioned for her to go first. As Serena went forward, she recognized that these men knew the power in their hands, and it was important to them —one of the hot buttons she would keep in mind.

The cardinal was already sitting. He stroked his chin and motioned to a chair.

She sat as directed and thanked him. A tilt of his head was his response.

Serena felt good. *Back in court.*

Opening arguments were her specialty as a lawyer. She knew she must lay out the case in the most convincing yet succinct way. Give them a taste for more and don't bore them.

"I met yesterday with His Holiness, the pope. He made an impromptu visit to my office that was a precious surprise as well as profoundly good timing. The possible cause of recent tragic events had just been revealed. I've worked directly with him on two other occasions, and those provided an excellent base for our discussion."

The cardinal and the archbishop listened, and she noticed twitches on their faces as she began with this startling news followed by her key points. She supported her concerns with several quick arguments. Then, she concluded with a bit of drama.

"I'm convinced there's a play for power going on behind the

scenes. The pope considers this a grave matter for the church. We must find who is involved and stop potential harm to all we hold dear."

That set them back in their chairs. The cardinal stared at an opposite wall.

After a long breath, he said, "*Abbessa, ti dobbiamo.* I am in your debt. Does His Eminence the secretary of state know of this?"

"I've briefed him in the past, but he's not been available for this last incident. It may be His Holiness has spoken to him. I'm aware that your good work is as our highest court and not as investigator or prosecutor. My coming to you has been out of my deep respect for you and for the court. Your influence is highly regarded."

The cardinal expressed nothing in his face or hands. Then, he looked at his watch.

"I must leave. If something new arises, please inform my dear friend Tommaso here, and he will advise me."

They all stood and moved to the door. The cardinal used two hands to hold and gently shake the abbess's hand. He said nothing and then left.

The archbishop accompanied her to the entry.

She turned to him.

"You've seen so much in the proceedings of the court, Secretary. You know the church and you know people. What guidance do you have for me?"

"Sister, I recommend you pray and stay away from trouble. Heresy is an evil, and we must always be vigilant. God's will must prevail."

The darkness in his statement caught her by surprise.

A weak, "*Grazie,*" was all she could offer in return.

The journey back to her office felt like walking in space. There was no up or down, no left or right. Nothing but an ominous emptiness.

PART ELEVEN

Istanbul, Turkey
Topkapi Museum

XI / 1

Several floors below the palace grounds and museum of Topkapi, the archives facility provided a sense of timeless peace and security. With no one around, Chetin could take a few minutes to explore areas beyond the normal scope of his work. His pale and frail body fit well with the delicacy of the ancient materials he touched. He felt safe in this environment.

The collections were well organized and even predictable. He wandered further this day than ever before. Something caught his eye. There was a grouping of items, none of which appeared remarkable. Yet, the young intern's flesh quivered with excitement. He had not been in this section before. It was where items from storage were first placed for review by an archival transfer technician.

On one shelf, a thick leather folder stood alone among larger pieces. The standard practice for precious documents was to preserve them between plates of archival glass and place them in special boxes. This folder showed plates held together in a leather binder. It was odd. He removed the folder and laid it on a shelf for closer observation. It was easy to open, and the plates were unattached to the binding. Chetin felt shaky and looked at his hands.

He took one of the plates out of the binder. The light was not good, the glass plates he held that preserved the document were not clear, and he struggled now and then with old Greek. But there was enough in the text of this document to spur him forward. His mind wandered as he grasped for a proper translation.

If only Professor Erkan were here.

Chetin whispered the translated words aloud as his mentor had taught him. "— with praise and gratitude to Emperor Constantine, God's chosen one — honors to Bishop Eusebius — in consideration of the requests by members of the ancient Churches of Corinth and Ephesus — a statement of belief to be offered to the general convocation in Nicaea — as revealed by our brother the apostle."

Were they speaking of the new revelation of the apostle Paul?

Chetin looked up. He could hardly breathe. Might this group of artifacts contain what everyone had looked for and some had died for?

He returned his attention to the document, fragile and cracked but held together by the archival glass.

A noise sounded in the distance. It was near the entry to the Topkapi archival vault. Panic caught him by surprise. He had to set aside the find to be easily found again yet hidden.

Where?

He heard his name called. It was Yusuf!

Panic shot through his mind. *What should I do?*

He swiveled around and slid the artifact between larger items.

"Chetin!" Yusuf sounded angry.

The young man had to reveal himself and explain why he was in this area of the collection. He shook his hands to relieve tension as he hurried into a different part of the stored treasures and walked to the end of the row of shelving. As he went, he pulled from the shelf a folder at random and held it to his chest. Suddenly, Yusuf turned the corner almost colliding with the intern.

"Ah, Chetin. Here you are. Why are you in section Gamma? What's that you have?"

Chetin lifted it to see what he was carrying and replied,

"This? It's, uh, some reference material to jewelry designs of the seventeenth century."

His mind raced for an explanation that was expected to be demanded.

"Jewelry design? Why are you reviewing this?"

"Well, it's awkward."

He struggled for time and a good reason.

Yusuf held his ground, in silence.

"It's awkward because, I saw a girl. She works in a jewelry shop. I thought if I went in, and if we spoke, I could mention something about working at Topkapi. I could say that I know something about jewelry designs."

"Of the seventeenth century?"

Yusuf cocked his head.

"Yes, I thought I needed to know something special. People are impressed with Ottoman history, at least the grandeur."

"Please return it to the proper location when you're finished. Jewelry designs!"

Yusuf wandered away, scratching his head.

A puff of breath popped through Chetin's lips. *That was close.*

As he returned to his work area, Chetin laid the impromptu folder on his desk and eyed Yusuf with discretion. He didn't feel safe.

"So, Yusuf, you must know where everything is here. Did you also design the structure of the collections? It all flows so well. I like the use of Greek letters to designate sections and then also shelves."

Yusuf tapped his fingers together and squinted as if trying to see an answer.

"The basic layout is routine, but within it there are innovations when we come upon new finds. As with most museums such as ours, there are far more items here than we have catalogued, much less examined. It's a priority to first safeguard them, and then we identify and record. Finally, we examine."

"It must be a good feeling that you have done so much to preserve the histories of many cultures."

"I'm not sure what feels good about it. Terrorists are destroying vast amounts of antiquities at random and the world shrugs its collective shoulders. The world, or most of the world, has become obsessed with the moment, the now. History is only valued by a small and lonely community. Many have their own collections and keep them private. This place is an oddity."

Chetin struggled with this insight into Yusuf's thoughts. He was eager to bring a hopeful mood to the conversation.

"Yusuf, I'm sure that someday, when you become director here, the world will see a reawakening of the grandeur of Topkapi's rich history and priceless archives."

He forced a happy attitude to encourage one from Yusuf.

Instead, he got a scowl, in fact, an angry scowl.

"What makes you think of this?" Yusuf demanded.

He threw a pencil onto his worktable and stormed away.

Chetin called out, "Yusuf, I'm so sorry. I'm —"

The chief of the archives marched to the heavy entry door, flung it open, and was gone without another word.

Chetin's mind was blank. He felt numb. He blinked, as if it might awaken his understanding. This man Yusuf was notable in the field, an authority. But his words sounded like a rejection of the art of—and even the worth of—his profession! He looked again at the door expecting Yusuf to return. Nothing happened.

Chetin eased himself from his chair and shuffled to the coffee pot across the room. He lifted a cup and turned his sights back to his desk where he had placed the folder containing reference material on Ottoman jewelry design. He shook his head and enjoyed a moment of humor. *Jewelry designs! Really?* Laughter bubbled within him, but he suppressed it.

He hurried to his desk, thinking of Yusuf's reaction to the excuse he had invented. Then, he stopped, remembering the more precious piece of history he had found. Chetin grabbed the folder of jewelry nonsense from his desk and returned to section Gamma of the archives where he had pulled it for a momentary rescue.

His eyes searched. *Was it shelf Theta? Yes, here.*

Chetin found the correct space on the shelf and replaced the packet with care, even appreciation. Excitement grew within him. He pushed up his glasses. Treasure awaited him in section Epsilon! He stopped at the end of the row and listened. He knew he must not be caught again. The quiet confirmed he was free to go. With laser focus on the shelf where he hid his discovery, he quickly found the shelf and the secret stash. He slid the folder from its place and opened it. Removing the plate of interest, he scanned it with care. He wondered, *what else is in this?*

Doubts flowed through his senses. He glimpsed items that were next to his treasure but stopped. *Should I take it to my desk? Should I tell Yusuf?*

Chetin began to return the folder to the shelf but pulled back. He felt cold. He couldn't move. He held it in mid-air. His mind was blank, struggling with decision. The snap of the latch of the entry door sounded and jolted Chetin into action. Separating two of the artifact containers on the shelf, he shoved the one in his hand between them. He hurried to the other end of the row, turned the corner and escaped into another section.

"Yusuf, hello! Are you here?"

It was the voice of Aslan, the director.

"Hello, Director," Chetin responded as he stepped into the open. "I regret Yusuf isn't here. He left a few minutes ago."

"Oh, that's odd. We were to meet here. By the way, I hope I didn't trouble you with our conversation."

"Not at all, sir. I'm pleased with your encouragement. I'm

eager to pursue more research. In fact, I found something of great interest. But, if Yusuf is due to arrive, perhaps I should not mention it."

Aslan's eyebrows pressed together. His chin lifted apparently to follow his thoughts.

"Well, tell me what you know."

The intern learned quickly that his best prospects for survival were based on staying away from people with authority but always obeying their requests with prompt, quality service. This command from Aslan made Chetin feel as if his job was at risk. His superior was gone, and he was asked to reveal a new discovery in the archives.

His mentor in Izmir thirsted for the letters he firmly believed existed but never saw and, now, Chetin might actually be in a position to find and reveal them. His thoughts raced around his mind like the motorcycle races he enjoyed watching, but he sensed those races were much less dangerous than the situation he was now in.

Chetin responded to Aslan's request with tepid understatement. "It's quite interesting, Director. I happened upon a section—Epsilon shelf Delta—and I noticed various artifacts. These are from the earliest times but not in the oldest part of the archives. They might have recently been brought in from storage. The nature of them might be insignificant but it will take a long time to determine that."

"You said it was of great interest. What did you find?"

Aslan's tone was all business.

"Well, there are portfolios of documents and several boxes. The boxes look as if they were never opened. I selected one portfolio and looked at a plate holding a papyrus sheet. It mentions the Emperor Constantine, but I only did a quick review, and, of course, I'm not particularly qualified in this area."

Chetin furtively glanced around then couldn't resist saying,

"I also saw the name 'Eusebius.'"

Aslan nodded but showed no enthusiasm. He pursed his lips.

"Director, should I tell Yusuf or allow these items to proceed according to usual processes? I don't know what to do, and your advice and consultation with Yusuf will be helpful."

He studied every twitch of Aslan's face for an answer. None came.

Aslan strolled over to the stacks of ancient discoveries, hands clasped behind him, and gazed down one passageway. Chetin waited.

Behind the men, twenty feet away, a click and a cracking sound announced the entry door again slowly opening. Chetin and Aslan swiveled to observe Yusuf enter.

Chetin's eyes grew large with a mixture of fear and surprise. He pushed his glasses higher up on his nose and wanted to hurry to his worktable.

"Ah, my friend," Aslan roared as he approached Yusuf. "I must be early for our meeting."

"Not at all, Director. I apologize for being late. I had an unexpected call to make, and the wireless connection is impossible in this bunker of a place."

Chetin held back, watched, and waited. He couldn't stop licking his lips and swallowing as his body wanted to dry out and shut down. If only he could hurry back into the storage area and hide.

Yusuf gave him what seemed to be a suspicious look.

"What's the problem? Are you waiting for something? Do you have nothing to do?"

"Oh, no, sir. Sorry, I mean yes, I have much to do."

Head down, Chetin hurried to his worktable.

Aslan rested his hand on Yusuf's shoulder and walked him toward the work area.

"By the way, did Chetin share with you his new find in the

stacks? I didn't hear any detail, but he appeared to be excited."

"You mean the jewelry design folder? Frankly, it teased no interest in me."

Aslan shifted his focus to Chetin. "So, young man, is this the hot news of the day? Jewelry design? Is that it?"

Chetin felt trapped. His mind went blank. His shoulders sagged, weighing him down. He had no breath.

"Come on, don't be shy. Is there something else?"

Aslan spoke with a gentle, and upbeat lilt to his voice, but his eyes were all business.

"Director, and Yusuf, yes there is. I came upon it by accident. When returning the folder on jewelry design, one area caught my eye. This was while you were gone, Yusuf. I was going to ask you about it. You also, Director, you might have ideas or knowledge of this."

The experts waited passively while the intern paused. Chetin needed more air, and time.

Finally, he said, "May I show it to you?" He jumped up, feeling panic, and hurried into the stacks.

"Ha, Yusuf! Your intern is running to his treasure. It must be amazing! Let's see what it is."

Chetin pulled out the folder with the glass-enclosed document. He felt grateful for Aslan's unexpected action. The men arrived and Chetin greeted them with renewed energy. He held up the plate.

"Here, this is it. I noticed what appear to be the names of Emperor Constantine and that of Bishop Eusebius in it. It needs study if not already done. This is not my area of expertise."

Yusuf stepped up and took the plate in his hands. He squinted at the text and shifted the distance as if trying for better focus.

"Let's take this to a worktable."

Yusuf removed his glasses from a pocket and placed them on his face without taking his gaze from the papyrus. Aslan slipped behind him and bent over to view the document.

The intern waited, hoping someone would offer a thought or even a question. He felt he had escaped a disaster for now and might be able to escape while his superiors examined the document. If it was what he hoped it might be, they were the best people to do the initial review, and they might even credit him with the find.

Yusuf continued his examination of the document then looked up at the director.

"This is indeed interesting. Aslan, do you remember in our records that the patriarch of Constantinople had taken a precious document from our archives and sent it to England?"

"Yes, what was that? Seventeenth century, I think. The Christians in England were going to publish their first Bible. Right?"

"That's it. Their king had authorized it. The patriarch here sent the document from the first century to include in their Bible."

Aslan rested his hand on Yusuf's shoulder.

"Wasn't there also a professor from England who contacted you about some Christian writings?"

"Yes, he was interested in Greek antiquities. Delphi, I recall."

"But, Yusuf, I thought it related to Christian matters?"

The chief of the archives was silent. He continued to study the discovered plate.

Hope evolved into fear within Chetin as neither man spoke. He suspected there was conflict or undefined intrigue playing out between them. Too much time was going by without a response from Yusuf. This behavior is definitely not acceptable in Turkish hierarchies and completely unknown in its academic circles.

At last, Yusuf responded. "This new find will require additional study. Thank you, Chetin."

Yusuf tapped his fingertips together and closed his eyes. "Yes, Director, I was briefly in touch with a professor from England. It was about a legend regarding their Christian apostle Paul. The professor thought an undiscovered letter from this apostle might be in our archives. I helped him as I could. But I found nothing. It was a typical search for something relating to a legend."

Aslan snorted, "Of course. So, what do you suppose this new document is?"

A happy feeling filled Chetin as he awaited the words of his boss. Maybe it was a step forward to the goal of his mentor shared by Chetin.

Finally, Yusuf's voice came out strong. "This is excellent. Fourth century but it refers to much earlier works. We must study it and look further. Director, I will lead this effort."

Chetin drew in a deep breath and blew it out with satisfaction.

Patras, Greece

XI / 2

The ship and its passengers survived the routine overnight journey and approached the wharf as the sun reflected off the city buildings, so white they looked luminous. Despite the time remaining to dock the ship and prepare for release of everyone on board, people filled every cubic foot of open space within sixty feet of the exit doors. David placed his hand on Rennie's back as they approached the passageway to go onto the ship's deck.

"Let me give you a couple of tips for international travel. First, don't look at anyone in a suspicious way. That might be difficult especially for you. If you do that, they will regard you with suspicion."

She felt tired and ready to be on land. Receiving orders wasn't welcome. Under that though, Rennie sensed a playful feeling waiting to emerge. The horrors of Italy were gone. She was ready for something better. That could be in Greece.

David continued, "Secondly, don't expect people to queue for anything, especially the further you go to the eastern part of the Mediterranean. People fight to be first and disregard the concept of a line. When we approach the ramp to leave the ship, hang onto me. The crowd will be fierce and pushing to get off. There's going to be nothing polite about it. Okay?"

"Whatever you say."

Rennie shoved her arm through the other belt of her backpack. She was ready to get onto land.

They stepped into the open air to see the ship in a smooth approach to the wharf. The sky was a delicate blue with traces of feathery clouds. Rennie walked to the bow away from the crowd and surveyed the scene from right to left.

"Now, this is what I'm talking about."

David joined her.

"What were you talking about?"

"It's an expression. Kind of a happy thing."

"Rennie, I think it's good we didn't check our phones this morning."

"Right, I agree. I'm sure there are tons of messages, and we wouldn't have time to review them anyway."

"For now, I suggest we stay back until most of the crowd has disembarked, and then join in with the remainder. We don't want to leave last and stand out for anyone who's watching."

"Okay with me, Captain."

She turned to him and tapped his shoulder.

"Let's do this. I'm ready."

David remained serious.

"I'm glad we agreed on a basic plan of action this morning. Find a hotel close by, get some food, rest, check our communications, and then go to Delphi as soon as we can arrange transportation there and back."

"You're the man with the plan, David."

He shook his head.

"Is that another of your canned comments from some trendy source?"

"Sorry, I'm ready to move on. We can't know the basis of that horrible murder in the parking lot last night. The Vatican and the exhibition seem like they were in another century. And, I don't remember why we came here. Maybe, this is what we need. I'm starting over. Everything doesn't have to have a purpose, I guess."

"Or, the purpose will reveal itself."

"Whoa, step back! Check out who's suddenly all spiritual!"

"You are replete with odd comments this morning, Miss Haran. Here we go. Let's move toward the rear of the crowd but be careful."

He stopped after a few steps and scanned her.

"Take off your backpack and reverse it on you. Put it on your front. If it's behind you, someone will open it and take what they can. You won't be able to stop them."

Rennie saw the wisdom and did what he said. Her jaw was set, and she felt a chilling of her fun spirit. It was okay. For now, they were on a mission.

The crowd surged forward to the exit as if the undertow of the tide swept them off a beach. The gates at the end of the ramp remained shut as dock workers engaged in arguments and threw their hands in the air. People began to yell in multiple languages as bodies crushed together.

"Rennie, now we go."

David took her hand and pulled her into the sea of stinking humanity. Despite the heavier stature of other passengers, the height of David and Rennie appeared to intimidate those they encountered. An initial objection by people led to openings as people looked over and then up at them. David gave each a polite but authoritative nod.

When the gates opened, the masses oozed forward and then accelerated to a quick pace.

David turned to Rennie as they hurried on, "Stay up. Don't fall."

On the harbor platform, the crowd spread out but then congealed as it approached the harbor terminal. Signs in English and Greek directed traffic to passport control stations.

Waiting in a line formed by barriers, David and Rennie tried to appear nonchalant and share a conversation as they considered the security and control environment.

Rennie whispered in his ear, "A piece of cake."

She observed the crowd and saw in a distant line the man who concerned her on the ship. Then, the world stopped. The noise and crowd disappeared.

She whispered to David, "He's over there. The guy I saw on the ship."

David followed her gaze.

"Rennie, everyone looks the same."

She turned her back to the direction of her concerns.

"Three lines over, halfway to the front. Black suitcoat."

"Okay, I think I see him. I'll try to remember his appearance, but he's not distinct."

David put his face against her hair.

"Rennie, the man had to get off the boat. He's not following you or us. I think we're safe."

They didn't move as individuals but flowed with the crowd. As they neared the passport control checkpoint, she faced forward, not wanting to see where the stranger was.

David went first, and Rennie watched the process.

When it was her turn, she gave the agent her passport, leaned forward and said, "Hi, I'm an American. I'm happy to be in your beautiful country."

She continued her bright smile until the agent returned the passport, without a greeting.

She grabbed David's shirtsleeve and they hurried to an exit. After a little fumbling of language arts with a taxi driver, David directed him to a hotel suggested by the driver.

For a few minutes, they could relax again. The little port city presented itself quickly as they slowly cruised along the coastal highway. With a fresh, warm breeze blowing in the window and tossing her hair, Rennie studied their new surroundings. It occurred to her this wasn't the port of Naples in so many ways. No dead men on the beach awaited her. Someone she trusted was with her. A thoughtful someone.

Rennie eased out of the taxi as David paid the driver. She stretched her legs and took a few steps toward the hotel. She stopped as a moment of joy filled her.

This is what normal is like!

"David, let's go!" she demanded.

He responded with a toothy smile and wide eyes she hadn't seen before.

The lobby attempted a rustic appearance, but *well-worn* or even *shabby* more appropriately fit the place. A small lobby with a stale odor, interrupted by an intruding sea breeze and a slow-turning ceiling fan, suggested a welcome to anyone with cash and minimum expectations.

The reception desk was stuck in an alcove on a side wall, but no one was present. In fact, there appeared to be no one in the building. It only took a minute to walk around the main floor. David called out, "Hello." They waited. He did it again. After another minute, Rennie suggested they leave. "I don't like this. Something's wrong here."

From a back room, a woman shouted, *"Kalimera!"*

Youthful and slender, a blonde woman with a warm tan drifted down the hall. A delicate linen dress rested softly on firm breasts as a full skirt flowed around athletic thighs. Her seductive smile hinted fun, unspoken thoughts.

"You Americans? Swedish? Good morning! Welcome! You need a room? You on vacation or maybe celebrating wedding?"

"Yes, but no," David replied. "It's a vacation. Perhaps, only one night but maybe two."

"Ah, you're British! Welcome to Greece."

"Do you have a room with two beds? My sister and I prefer that."

David smirked at Rennie.

"I don't know, my friend. Maybe you must have two rooms. I will look."

David followed up, "Also, miss, do the rooms have the bath in the room?"

"You call me Sofia. I see what we have."

The woman flipped her hair over a shoulder and beckoned David to her side. She casually brushed her shoulder against his and her hand against his arm as she turned a few wrinkled pages of a notebook with handwritten notes in Greek.

Rennie studied every subtle gesture of the Greek female free spirit moving into her territory. *And, once again David is acting like he doesn't notice.*

"There," David stepped back and noted a place with a pointed finger, "does that say 'available?'"

"Aha! You speak Greek! Maybe?"

"I remember a few letters and words here and there."

Her enthusiasm didn't vary. "So, you going to Delphi? Corinth? I can arrange a car. No problem."

She accented her enthusiasm with raised eyebrows and a seductive smile.

Rennie and David lost their cover of serious inquiry and began to chuckle. Rennie's humor felt more sarcastic than light-hearted.

David responded, "Thank you, Sofia. First, we need to get settled."

"Okay! I have a nice room for you. Bath inside. I move another bed in if you need. Easy to do but maybe you can help me. Follow me."

David and Sofia discussed the price and shook hands.

"You got bags? Where your bags?"

"We have what we need here. We're traveling light."

Sofia led the way up a stairway of creaking boards on a path of cleared dust from each step. As the clerk's swinging hemline rose above them, Rennie glanced back at David. He feigned an innocent look.

Down a short, dark hallway of cracked plaster, Sofia opened a room with roof-slanted ceilings and a surprisingly light and spacious layout. It flowed around three sides at the end of the building and offered two windows formed by gables.

"I like it," Rennie whispered as David walked by in inspection mode. She checked the bath facilities and tested the faucets for running water. She gave David a thumbs-up.

"Okay, Sofia. We're good. I'll talk with you later about transportation needs. Also, you can bring the extra bed anytime."

Sofia's face slipped into a scowl.

"Sister, huh? Okay, Mister David. Bed on the way."

Once she was out the door, Rennie stepped close to David.

"You are so transparent. First the hot, car rental agent and now Miss Aphrodite. They want you and you know it, brother David."

"Rennie, they're doing their jobs."

"I know what they'd like to be doing."

"Ha! And, what about you, sister?"

He slowly embraced her.

"What about you?"

Rennie tilted her head and closed her eyes.

She whispered, "What do you want Mister David?"

A hard knock on the door broke the moment.

Rennie pulled away and tossed her backpack on the bed as David opened the door. He helped Sofia slide a bed from the room across the hall and position it near the other bed. Rennie studied David as he thanked Sofia for her help. The women exchanged a look.

Sofia pouted at David.

"If you need anything, I'll be downstairs."

He walked her to the door, mentioned they would discuss with her arrangements for a car later in the day and promptly closed the door.

"Well, okay," he exhaled. "We're here."

"So David, do you want to go downstairs and she what else she has?

"Sorry, what's that?"

"She said she's downstairs if you need anything."

Rennie looked away.

"David, I'm sorry."

She felt a rush of confusing emotions.

"I guess, well I'm a little sensitive about these interactions you have with these women. I know it's harmless and your intentions are good. Maybe I'm just feeling vulnerable."

He remained quiet.

"And, you referred to me as your sister. Really?"

"Rennie, I'm sorry. I only want to help. But, I'm skilled at bungling, especially with women. Please know I treasure what has happened between us. I want nothing to harm that."

They wrapped their arms around each other.

She could feel his nose nestle into her hair and his cheek press against hers. It felt right, and it was enough. Almost. She leaned back and let go.

"David, why the extra bed?"

"I don't know. It just felt proper, and the private side of me is familiar. Emotional intensity is not. Rennie, we've been through so much so quickly. I'm struggling with all this, too."

"Do you want your own room? It's okay, really."

"Definitely not. Things are changing fast, but in the right direction."

The words warmed her. She felt a small surge of energy.

"Okay, good. Let's get busy. We need to catch up."

They sorted through their things and set aside their laptops. Rennie moved her bag to a chair across the room and took out her phone.

She waved it at David.

"Shall I see what's waiting?"

The mood was instantly serious.

"It's time."

David turned on his phone and turned off the airplane mode function.

Repeated beeps and sounds chattered through the room as both studied their phone screens.

"Oh, my God. I've got seventy-four messages," Rennie said in a weary tone. "And, twenty-three voice-mail messages."

She dropped onto the bed. David eased into a chair without shifting his gaze from his phone. Minutes went by as expressions of questions, concerns, and a few pleased looks alternated on their faces.

David got out of the chair and went to the bath where he washed his face. He returned to the room wiping his hands on a small towel.

"I had fewer messages than you. Several from Professor Snapper. We need to talk when you can."

She studied him and shook her head.

"It will take a while to digest all this. It's a crazy amount of material. I even got a message from that Abbess Serena at the Vatican. I don't get it. Did any of yours say something about Istanbul? Istanbul? Really?"

"Rennie, if it will help, I'll review your messages with you to identify key words and establish priorities. That's the key in dealing with big data."

David zipped open his bag and retrieved a notepad and pen. He reviewed his messages again and began to sketch a grid with captions designating column headings. He scratched through a couple and changed the captions. A series of horizontal lines created a table for data to analyze. He then duplicated the table on another sheet.

Rennie set aside her phone and fell back on the bed. A swirl of paint on the ceiling gave her a point of focus. For several minutes, she said nothing. Anger made her nose twitch. Finally, she sat up and pulled off her boots. In a few long steps, she arrived at her bag and pulled out a pair of shorts. Rennie opened her slacks and pushed them to the floor. She turned to David.

"Brother, you can look the other way. I need to get comfortable. Reviewing this information will take a while."

David turned his amused face to the opposite direction.

When ready, she pulled a chair near to his.

"Okay, let's get down to business. How do we do this? What's with the grid or table you drew?"

She noticed he had slid off his shoes and his socks.

"By the way, you don't have pretty feet. So, what's first on your list?"

He started to chuckle, and that grew into a laugh.

"Here we are, running from the authorities I presume, and possibly villains. For some reason, we appear to be the only guests in a hotel during peak tourist season, and we have clues suggesting conspiracies involving biblical figures. Oh *and*, you have a comment about my feet!"

Rennie didn't laugh.

"Are you done?"

David took a deep breath and explained the layout of the grid. He suggested they mutually review his messages first, since there were fewer than hers. Then, they would see what she received and decide on the key issues. She agreed.

David read aloud each message, and they followed it with a brief comment on its value relative to their situation and what they knew. He skipped past the condolences and updates regarding the memorial service for his grandfather, Matthew. These brought a sad, thoughtful setting to the pair.

Rennie placed her hand on David's and said, "I'm sorry. I'm so sorry."

David reviewed his chart.

"Based on what I received and have noted, Professor Snapper offers us several documents. These focus on references to correspondence of women of the church during the time of the apostle Paul. Their letters, which were apparently never found, suggested something that raised quite a row with other church leaders. The issue apparently challenged the message of the crucifixion. Two of the churches mentioned were Corinth and Ephesus, which we know were distinctive relative to Paul's missions."

Rennie responded, "Paul questioned the crucifixion? Paul?"

"It's unclear, and I doubt that could be the topic. Perhaps it was the women. We need more information."

"Maybe that's why they disappeared from scripture. That would have been heretical."

"So, according to Professor Snapper, someone in Istanbul by the name of Yusuf, had been in touch with my grandfather years ago about this question. He's apparently involved in some manner with the ancient collections at Topkapi. Grandfather had then forwarded a note to Professor Snapper that this Yusuf may have found a reference to a letter that the apostle Paul had given to someone, a disciple in Rome that was to be passed on to the churches. That's quite interesting. However, when Grandfather later tried to get access to examine it, knowledge of the document seemed to disappear."

Rennie added, "Your grandfather. That man is—was—wonderful and brilliant. He would've made a terrific investigative journalist."

"In a way, he was. The characters in his stories were just very old."

"David, I think he passed them on to us."

"Rennie, there's another item of interest here. Professor Snapper says that letter from Paul and correspondence of these women was aggregated in Corinth. But he says there are traditions suggesting all of this was taken to Delphi for safekeeping due to what might have been threats against the women and what they were saying."

Rennie stood and stretched and began a slow walk around the room.

"Do we need to go to this place Delphi? Would we even find anything after all these centuries?" She continued her stroll, looking blankly at the floor, the walls, and whatever passed through her view.

"Something occurs to me, Rennie. Do you remember I mentioned to you that Grandfather invited me along when he went to Delphi on a limited dig? Could that have been part of this story? And then, there's this comment about him being in touch with the fellow at Topkapi. I think he was on this case."

"So, do we go to Delphi or to Istanbul? Is that where this Topkapi place is? What would Matthew tell us?"

David scanned additional messages.

"Good question, and I think he answered it! Here, Professor Snapper notes that Grandfather included with his note to the professor a brief file of other observations. In one, he says there's a cone-shaped monument at Delphi near the ancient treasury building. Grandfather observed on this monument an inscription that says—wait let me find it here—yes, it says 'a purse is more valuable than a king's treasury.'"

"Well, I can agree with that."

She continued pacing the room.

"David, let's file that one away and decide what we'll do and where. First, are we going to pursue this? Why is this our issue?"

"Well, I wonder if it's related to those deaths you've encountered. That priest on the beach, for example. You said that fellow Michael spoke to you about a deadly conflict raging in the church since its beginnings. And, dear God, he commented to me about how we should go to Corinth. There's your connection!"

Rennie felt a crescendo of insight she had to ride. She pointed at David.

"But, it's not Corinth, and I don't think it's Delphi. This place in Istanbul is our next destination. And, we find that guy, Yusuf."

"It sounds like you've already decided."

She didn't respond. Her thoughts were scrambling to put together pieces she knew were only little parts of the story. Important but little. Each investigation was like that. She knew she could solve it. She needed more time and information.

She put her hands on her hips.

"David, the truth is there. Do you want to find it? Isn't that what you do? A bit of the universe is in hiding so you hunt it down."

He squinted. "I guess so. Yes, you're right, and I realize now this was a mission that Grandfather began long ago. He would only undertake those projects that were of genuine significance. This must be one."

Rennie sat next to David and rested her hand on his thigh.

"Then, let's go over all this information in a detailed way. We're both good at that. It's time to take charge of our destiny. We are here for a purpose, and I think we'll find it in Istanbul."

Des Moines, Iowa
Offices of the *Des Moines Record*

XI / 3

Angie hurried through the newsroom toward Bud's office. She didn't notice the office staff and journalists along the way. The reflective, peaceful Angie was gone. An intense, fierce Angie had arrived. She grabbed the doorframe and spun into the office with a flourish. In one hand was a folder bursting with paper tagged with colored notes.

She sat in front of his desk without comment and dropped the folder on a half-opened newspaper. Bud looked up over his glasses.

"Bud, what do you mean this guy Sfumato might be in Europe?"

"Hi, Angie."

"Can we confirm that? Is he there because of Rennie being there? Bud, we've got to know."

"Hi, Angie."

"When did you become Mr. Nice Guy? Hi, Bud. Now, let's get with it. We've still not heard from her, and I got more information from Professor Snapper. I'll forward it to her as I did the other things he sent to me."

"Angie, maybe it's a coincidence. Sfumato probably travels the world doing his ancient document sales and purchase deals. But I admit, it raises concerns. My investigator Richard threw some bait his way. He contacted Sfumato's office and said Rennie was in touch with us. He told them she found 'it' and more. They immediately responded with questions. In the past, they didn't respond to inquiries."

"That's good, I like it. So, how do we know he's in Europe?"

Bud pulled a notepad from under a few strewn pages of paperwork.

"Let's see, oh yeah. Richard said they responded that Sfumato was traveling and in a different time zone, so patience was needed for responses. Richard asked how many hours the difference was he so could plan accordingly, and they said it was ten from San Francisco, at the moment. That puts him in Europe or maybe Africa, but Europe is likely. However, they said he's in a place with good cell service, which I think nails it as Europe."

Angie relaxed to sort through the issues and ideas.

"So, the bait was the idea that Rennie found an ambiguous thing that Sfumato knows about, and he thinks we know what it is. He's all hot about getting what we know. So, maybe he's going to wherever he thinks she would be."

Angie sat up and grabbed the edge of the desk with both hands, staring into the distance behind him. Her chest constricted on her breathing.

"Wait!"

Bud looked startled.

"What?"

"He will go where he thinks she is to get this thing, whatever it is. If Rennie's there, she could be in danger. She's alone, Bud, and in a foreign country. She was safe here, but even here they were on her heels. Bud, he's on the dark side and I'm confident he deals with evil people. The vast amount of money we think he plays with buys him whatever he needs, whatever he wants."

Bud's eyes closed to slits. He stared at his anxious visitor and rested his chin on plump, clasped hands.

"You're probably right. If this is a big discovery, like the last one, he won't allow a repeat of the disappointment. He'll get what he wants, no matter what. His greed will drive the agenda."

Angie flipped open the file folder.

"Let me review with you the new information that Professor Snapper sent. One of his researchers found in the Vatican data files something of real interest."

Bud shifted forward.

"Does this up the ante?"

A flash of anger flew through Angie.

"The professor said one document in the file was translated as a condemnation of the assertions of women who attended the Council of Nicaea. The researcher figured this document was written by one of the first bishops of Rome. The document from the bishop rejects an amnesty that the Emperor Constantine gave to a group called the Arians and to a growing movement called—the translation was unclear he said—but it was either the 'Door' or '*Porta.*' Another name he said is '*Societas.*' This bishop in Rome considered beliefs of this group to be heresy. However, the commentary from him applauds and supports the 'Servants of the Apostles,' whoever they are. They were referred to as 'defenders of true understanding.' These are probably the original groups in conflict."

Bud got up and paced behind his desk. He folded his arms. Angie studied him and waited. He paced again.

"Angie, review with me what you see as the key elements being pursued here."

"Okay, we have ..." her voice trailed off. "So, these women promoted a new revelation of Paul that got passed around for a few hundred years. The leaders of the church, all men, were upset because they were in control and kept the old order. But the brave women who carried on the fight wanted the matter addressed at the Council in Nicaea."

"Then, what was the big uproar three hundred years after this revelation by Paul?"

"Bud, there was no defined doctrine for Christians up to then. There were a lot of different sects believing different things.

This council meeting was held to finally set the structure of the religion because Emperor Constantine became a Christian."

"Ah-ha! So, once the powers that be endorsed the faith, people were scrambling for authority and the power that went with it! But, those two competing groups continued their war?"

She fell back in her chair, exhausted.

"You could say that."

Bud jammed an index finger toward her. "*And*, any beliefs that weren't in line with those powers that be, they were out of luck, condemned."

"That's how it works, Bud. Orthodox is what those in power say it is. Everything else is heresy."

He jumped into his chair. A new energy appeared.

"I'm beginning to understand this ... And Sfumato believes there are documents that are the centerpiece of the whole controversy?"

Angie again took on a fierce, focused look.

"Bud, these weren't just a bunch of women. Professor Snapper said his team found references to the sister of the Emperor Caligula, to Mary Magdalene, and many others. They were the first to spread the news of what Paul revealed."

Bud got up from his chair and paced across his office. He looked back at Angie but said nothing. He resumed his journey, gesturing as he went. He returned to the desk and leaned on his fists.

"Okay, what are the missing pieces of the puzzle? What documents? Once Rennie has a chance to review what you and the professor sent to her, she'll figure it out and know where to find them. When she does, Sfumato might be there, and this time he'll do whatever it takes to get them."

"Bud, we need to get in touch with Rennie right now! We've got to warn her."

"Right. I wonder if Sfumato is somehow using her to find the original documents. If he gets his hands on them, he'll sell them for hundreds of millions."

Angie stood tall and organized her paperwork. Her teeth were set. She stared at Bud yet said nothing.

He shrugged.

"What?"

She tapped her finger on the file.

"This time, greed and power don't win."

XI / 4

The hunt for historical treasure filled Yusuf with a surge of nervous energy. Long ago, he gave up on the idea of a tepid career offering a routine life with marginal living. For decades, his hands had held and his eyes had surveyed the treasures of ancient people with none of the wealth rubbing off on him. Administrative duties constantly kept him on the sidelines, frustrating his ambitions, but the inadvertent discovery by Chetin and the young man's enthusiasm lit a fire for hope and action. Success in finding the mysterious documents on Christianity would determine his future. In the past, he became angry with frustrated efforts to find documents and other artifacts that legend suggested were awaiting him. "Only in Topkapi," researchers would say. And, the fingers pointed at him to find them.

He thought of the indifference of the director.

Aslan has become a bureaucrat.

The hated idea of living as a cog in a big system transformed his attitude to be a warrior for action. These legends would be exposed and done away with by Yusuf Pashazade Mustafa, chief curator of the Topkapi collections. Then, he will move on. A new and superior life awaited him.

I'm no bureaucrat, charged through his thoughts.

"Chetin!" he yelled.

Yusuf muscled his way out of his chair like a prize fighter getting up from the stool in his corner.

"Chetin!"

The intern hurried down a passageway in dim light.

"Yes, sir. I'm here."

When they met, Yusuf was blunt.

"Show me all you've touched related to the Constantine items."

Chetin appeared agitated.

"Immediately, sir. Oh, and I found something else. I believe it's related to what I showed to you and the director."

"Good, where?"

The men hurried to where Chetin had noted the discovery of the plate.

Chetin pointed to a thin folder standing upright next to the leather packet that held the other find.

"Here, sir. This is the one. I briefly looked at it, but it seems relevant."

Yusuf snatched a paper tag from the shelf and gave it to Chetin.

"This is where these items came from in the secure receiving area out back. Bring whatever you find that looks as if it relates to these artifacts. Understood?"

"Absolutely."

The young man didn't wait for clarification or other instruction. He dashed away, sliding as he turned the corner around the shelving racks.

Removing a pair of cotton gloves from his suit pocket, Yusuf slipped them on and took as many of the target items as he could safely carry. He placed them on an empty worktable and charged back to the prize shelf. With two more trips, he had it all laid out. He spun around and glared in the direction of the storage vault.

Where's the boy?

He set aside boxes and other large items and then the folders holding the glass plates. The application of the glass on documents was a preliminary step to avoid accidental or further deterioration until permanent efforts could be done. Six plates were in the larger folder and four and three in two others. The relics spread over the entire work surface. Another would be needed.

Yusuf scanned their area. All other tables had items for examination.

We must not mix them, he thought.

Chetin arrived carrying a box with a folder on top of it.

"Be careful with that! If it falls, precious history could be destroyed."

Yusuf was surprised with his own outburst. He took pride in being in control of his actions. Chetin stared at him with wide eyes.

"Sorry. Chetin, is there an open table in the storage room? We need extra space."

"Uh, I think so."

He didn't move.

"Very well, take those items and place them there. Be sure it's clean. Wipe it down well. We shall have two locations for examining this inventory. It's time."

Chetin glanced at the clock. "It's time for what?"

Yusuf was deep in thought, scanning the relics and processing the order and methods he would use to begin this final journey. His plans and schedule had been filled for months with detailed strategies on other vital issues. Somehow, this keystone item, finding the original documents, got lost in other dynamics. In his peripheral vision, he saw Chetin standing with the box and folder.

"Why are you standing there? Go!"

As the young man hurried away, Yusuf followed. He felt power in his limbs as he stormed into the storage area.

When everything was laid out, and they double-checked the nearby storage racks for related items, Yusuf gave Chetin detailed instructions on how to sort, make a preliminary inventory, label, and then conduct an initial evaluation of all the items. The storage room materials appeared to be secondary to those in the primary archival room.

With a final clarification of their plans, Yusuf returned to his worktable and what might be the answer to his destiny. Rarely seen, a strong smile bared his teeth.

An hour later, Yusuf noticed Chetin silently approaching his area. Without looking up from his examination of a document, the chief archivist said, "Yes?"

"Perhaps, I'm moving too slowly. The items are displayed for inspection and I'm halfway through the preliminary inventory. I wondered if you would like to review what is there."

"I can't leave this right now. We're lucky such great care was given to the emperor's records."

"Yes, sir. Have you been able to review the plate mentioning Eusebius?"

"Yes. It appears to be an agenda for the Council of Nicaea. In addition, there's mention of letters from women in the ancient churches and a letter from the apostle Paul. Most interesting."

Chetin gasped, "That's the Holy Grail! Are the letters there?"

Yusuf grunted.

"No. There are many records of that Council. Attendance lists, notes and records of hundreds of attendees. None of it included or referred to these letters. Why is that?"

Chetin stared at the plate.

"This is true. One thing I now notice in this document. Down here, it says something about how the bishop—and I assume they mean Eusebius—wishes to present his comments about the letter from Paul and the testimony of his sisters from Corinth. Hmm, 'his sisters,' interesting. If this is Eusebius of Nicomedia, his voice would have been commanding."

Yusuf sat back and listened. His thoughts blazed through each key word for reference information and what other resources in the archives related to that.

Chetin cleared his throat.

"Yusuf, sir, for someone with this level of importance to request that the Council hear from these women, it must have been significant and controversial. Professor Erkan believed they carried forward the new revelation of the apostle Paul. Traditions say that the message had been fought since Paul's time hundreds of years before the Council. We might be close to finding it."

The focused intensity of Yusuf blocked everything from his senses. His trained vision picked through the faded and broken text of ancient Greek.

Chetin waited.

"Sir, shall I return to the other work area?"

"I don't need your help here. There's much to do. See what you can find. I must step outside for a short while. You continue your work."

Yusuf stood over his worktable and surveyed what was where. He often did this to gain a deeper insight when he was away from his work. He believed his intuition would make the connections of ideas and images to prompt new discoveries. Then, with confident steps, he passed millennia of historic treasures and departed the archives. He knew he would find the long-sought documents and they would no longer be a mystery. He would settle the conflict forever. Waiting for the elevator door to open, Yusuf thought of his only meeting with Professor Erkan and the Greek priest. They were insistent their research led to Topkapi and they wanted access to the collection. He believed them, but he would neither acknowledge that nor allow access to anyone on this matter. Then, those annoying professors from England confirmed the impression the documents were in his facility.

He decided to take the stairs instead of the elevator. A quick run up a couple of flights to apply some of his contained energy felt good. He went through the secure, double entry doors into a waiting area and looked around. No one was present, so he made a phone call. It didn't go through. Frustration exploded within him.

What was that new number?

Patras, Greece

XI / 5

A knock at their door interrupted Rennie's repacking of her bag. She heard water running behind the closed bathroom door. "David!"

"Yes, what?" came a garbled response.

She went to the door and leaned against it.

"Someone's at the door."

"I know, and I think it's you."

She laughed. She liked how his dry humor fit the rest of his low-key demeanor.

"No, the front door. Someone knocked."

"It's probably Sofia. She was going to bring us food."

Rennie was eager to eat and went for the door. She turned the corner and noticed next to her jeans the device that had saved her more than once. She paused, then waved it off.

Rennie said, "Hi, Sofia" as she opened the door, but it wasn't her.

Facing her, just two feet away, was the man she saw on the ship. Neither said a word.

He leaned forward.

"You are Miss Haran, I believe. May I speak to you?"

Rennie couldn't take her eyes from his.

She yelled, "David!"

They didn't move. She wanted to slam the door, but she knew, if he wanted in there was no stopping him.

"David!"

In a deep, soft voice, the stranger said, "If you would like to close the door, I will wait here."

She gently shut the door, never taking her eyes from his. Rennie backed away.

David came out of the bathroom.

"Where's the food? What's up, you look intense?"

"David, that guy I saw on the ship, the one I was suspicious of, he's outside the door."

He tossed aside the towel he was holding as she retrieved her device. David pulled on a t-shirt and led the way to the door, with Rennie close behind. They looked at each other as he reached for the doorknob.

Sudden and fearsome intensity arose in David's face. His eyes grew large and his arms and shoulders flexed. She stepped back and set her thumb on the button of the device.

When the door opened, the stranger was in the same position as before; a slight smile on his lips, and his head tilted a little forward as if ready to move ahead.

David shouted, "What do you want?"

The man responded, "May I have a moment with you and Miss Haran? I bring you no problems."

"I asked what the hell do you want?"

"As I said, sir, I'm not here for any trouble."

David glanced at Rennie, then slammed the door.

Rennie wrapped her arms around him.

"David, please. He knows my name. Let's find out what he has to say."

His facial muscles were twitching. He turned back to look at the door, then said, "I've had enough. This must stop."

"Let's hear him out."

"No, Rennie. You won't be threatened again. This ends now."

Another knock on the door prompted David to grab the handle and fling the door open so hard it hit the wall.

"Again, who are you and what do you want?"

"You may call me Demir. The name is Umit Yildirim, but

Demir is, what you call, a nickname. I will not be long and will stand here if you wish. I'm a security official for the Republic of Turkey. I know you've had problems and I want to provide information to help."

Rennie and David looked at each other then said, "Come in." The three circled as if in a slow dance to the center of the room.

Demir continued, "As I said, I'm with the Turkish security services. You may know, there are serious problems across this region with terrorists and refugees. My work has entered new areas, with untested but dangerous problems. We do not know who is who, and some nations, such as Greece, do not have the capacity to evaluate all who pass through."

Rennie demanded, "So, what does that have to do with us, and how do you know my name?"

"These are good questions, Miss Haran, and I would expect them from you. You stand at the crossroads of suspicious trails that I have been following through Istanbul. I don't understand how you are connected, but this is a fact. You must go to safety."

A surge of fear stole Rennie's breath. For a moment, she felt a sudden bond with this man. She was right all along about feeling like a target.

"Okay, Demir, let's talk. You've got my attention."

"I don't know where to begin," he started to say when Rennie interrupted.

"Just so you know," she said with emphasis, "I don't know what's going on here, but I damn well intend to find out."

He laughed a little. "This is good. I like that."

"Well, I don't like what's happened to me. What have you got, Inspector, or whatever you are?"

"Very well, I will be blunt and prompt. I don't know if those are the correct words ... What I mean is, before you arrived in Italy, our services have been intercepting phone calls between Istanbul, Rome, and other cities. This has been part of our standard surveillance practices for terrorists and criminals, but the calls caught our attention. The Americans also noticed suspicious activity and contacted us."

David and Rennie stared at each other. He mouthed the word, "Istanbul."

"So, what about me?" Rennie demanded.

"There have been some deaths—murders, we should say. One was a Greek priest in Italy, another was in our city of Izmir. There have been others. Rome appeared to be a key place related to these events. I went there and attended a function there."

"So, I did see you at the exhibition." Rennie turned to David. "That's where I saw him. It was only for a second. But it was him."

"Yes, Miss Haran. I was there, but not for any interest in you. We had suspicions that something could happen there."

David answered, "And, it did. Another priest, someone who helped us, he was killed."

"I heard of a death, but it was handled by the Vatican with discretion. My interest was elsewhere. Someone I followed to Rome from Turkey was also there. His name is Najat, and he is a killer."

Rennie felt weak and sank to the bed. She covered her eyes with a hand. Fear robbed her of strength and will.

"Why is death always so close?" she mumbled.

David stood next to her and placed a hand on her shoulder. She tried to take a few breaths, but they were shallow. She felt David's hand press on her.

"So, Demir," David asked, "what do we do about this guy Najat?"

"My friend, there's nothing to do now. Najat is eliminated. I followed him from Rome to Brindisi, and he followed you. He was in the rental-car agency parking lot when you were inside. I'm certain you were his target. It's good I arrived first."

Rennie gasped. Her mind exploded. *That was who was in the car, murdered!*

Demir saw her response and added, "Yes, I did it."

Her large eyes glared at Demir and anger slipped across her lips. Death had come close, again.

David sat down next to her.

He whispered, "It's okay. We're safe now."

She tried to shake her head, but a flood of emotion was churning within her. Finally, she turned to David. Her eyes filled with tears, one slipping down her cheek.

"David, I've been this close to death too much. I hate it. My family always wanted me to settle down, but no. I'm never satisfied. I have to find the truth behind every story and there's always another story. I sacrifice myself, and for what? Truth? There is none!"

Her hands covered her face.

Their visitor stepped a few paces away.

David handed Rennie his handkerchief.

"You always have these!" She blew her nose. "Sorry, David."

He put an arm around her as she took a few deep breaths.

"David, I'm pissed and I'm going to do something about it. I'm going to find the people causing this carnage."

"Rennie, what's the best thing to do?"

She looked into his eyes for a long moment.

"Thanks, you're right."

"Mr. Demir," David said with stiff formality, "what do we do now? Are we subject to other threats?"

"It would be best if the two of you left this area and returned to America or other parts of Europe. I do not know what is behind these evil offenses and how they relate to you. Being far away would allow us time to learn what we need and maybe end it."

"I'm in agreement with that. What do you say, Rennie? Let's go to London, or would you prefer the States? We'll be safe, and we can figure this out."

She stared at the floor. Her thoughts tumbled with images, words, and pulses of emotion. She shook her head to make it stop or get clarity. David caressed her back. Then, it came to her. She stood up and wiped her nose again.

"In the last few days, I've been told the opportunity to do something important must be recognized and seized. I'm going to finish this. I've been sucked or pushed into this and people are being killed. It must stop. Gentlemen, we're going to Istanbul. Demir, will you help us? I don't know why, but I trust you."

He looked stunned and didn't respond.

David did and with emphasis, saying, "Rennie, you heard what he said. Those calls involved Istanbul. We must not go there. I insist we be logical about this."

She placed a hand on his shoulder.

"Honey, you've become kind of bossy, and I like it. But Istanbul is exactly where we must go. You can't start over until you finish what you're doing. I'm going to start over, David, but this must end first. When you get lost in an investigation, you look for the beginning. That dead Greek priest was not the beginning. This started in Turkey two thousand years ago. I'm going to Istanbul to find the start of all this. What's the motivation causing this continuing horror? I trust you, and I even trust Demir. More importantly, I trust me."

Demir appeared to be confused.

"This is a brave thing to do but I don't know if it's the best—"
She turned to him.

"Bravery is taking action despite fear. Passion is acting without fear. I'm not brave on this issue, I've become passionate, but not irrational. So, will you take us to Turkey? There's a reason for your being here and we need you."

He scratched his beard.

Rennie persisted, "Gentlemen, what's the best way for us to

get to Istanbul? We're ready for travel, so let's go. I'm on a mission."

It was clear neither of the men were ready to respond.

David asked, "Demir, you know the area. If we go, what do we do? Drive? Sail? Fly?"

"Conditions in Turkey are tense—no, intense is a better description. You will need me to get you in the country and to your destination. Where do you plan to go when you arrive?"

Rennie responded with eager energy, "We'll go to a museum by the name of Topkapi. Do you know it?"

His mouth dropped open. He stood mute. Finally, he nodded.

"Yes, I'm familiar with the place. We can go there."

She put out a fist to give him a fist bump. He hesitated but responded.

"Rennie?" David asked.

"Finish packing, brother." She winked at him.

Within an hour, they gathered in a local restaurant, ate well, and discussed their plans. As they got into the car Demir rented, Rennie was determined. She had a team, a destination, and a mission.

"Demir, how long is this trip? When do we arrive in Istanbul?"

"Miss Haran, as we discussed, the drive from here to near Athens is less than the wait at the airport there. Our flight would arrive in late afternoon at Ataturk, the airport in Istanbul. Security at the airport in Athens will be some concern but less since we're leaving the country, especially after lunchtime when the security people get sleepy. In Istanbul, my connections there will assist our entry. But, as we discussed, you must get your e-visas online.

"Okay, I'm on it. David, give me your passport."

"One other thought I need to provide," Demir added. "From

Athens, you can also fly to London or even America. That option still awaits you."

Rennie knew what she needed to do and required no time to consider alternatives. An end was coming, and maybe a new beginning.

"Thanks, Demir. Let's get this done."

This wasn't for finding someone's truth, it was for her.

PART TWELVE

Istanbul, Turkey
The Archives of Topkapi Museum

XII / 1

The storage vault holding artifacts awaiting review at the Topkapi archives is a rough place—more of a warehouse than a bank vault. Chetin had once visited Cairo for a conference at the Egyptian Museum and the Topkapi storage facility reminded him of that one, with its random placement of precious items with no distinction of their significance, poorly organized records, and minimal identification of the location of inventory.

He leaned into the back of the bare wooden chair at the worktable that he now dominated. The air pressed a dry chill into his flesh, and he knew the poor lighting would cause him further vision problems. But he ignored all these superficial elements of his work. They were the costs of holding history in his hands, and a history that people hundreds if not thousands of years ago held in theirs. This was the land crossed by crusaders and consumed by sultans. What was theirs was now a gift to a young man from a small village in Turkey.

The pleasant satisfaction drifting through Chetin's senses was blown away when his eyes happened to see a name and a few words on a plate lying at the side of his table. This too, was from the Constantine artifacts. He leaned toward it for a better look. Like the other document they found, this one mentioned the place Nicaea in the present tense. The words were of one who attended but was not a delegate. He drew the plate closer to him.

Athanasius of Alexandria was not a familiar name to Chetin. This person submitted a statement to the Council that a movement of women of the early church and their followers had over time created a false doctrine. He said their denial that Jesus died as a sacrifice for sin must be extinguished as heresy.

At first, Chetin wondered what the implications of this "false doctrine" would be and why it would be considered heresy. Those thoughts lasted only seconds before he realized this was the first definitive statement of the controversy. There were suspicions of a serious conflict, but here it was, defined.

Chetin leaped to his feet. He stared down at the document. *Is that what it says?*

He needed to be clear on the translation. He couldn't run to Yusuf making a wonderous claim and then find it had no credibility or substance. The ancient Greek words slowly ran through his eyes and analysis.

"Yes," he whispered.

He realized that this was it. Together with the document mentioning the agenda for the meeting, *this* document states the issue to be presented to the Council! Now, he could tell Yusuf of his discovery. He lifted it as if it was his one and only love letter. Before he could go find his boss, Yusuf came through the doorway as a powerful, angry presence. His eyes wide open, eyebrows high, in a flushed, dark face.

Chetin waited for the boss to speak first. Something was very wrong.

"Let me remind you, Chetin, of the importance of what we're doing. Everything here is rubbish compared to what we're looking for. That means if you find anything related to our goal, you must isolate it."

Yusuf's eyes looked dead, yet he appeared to be driven by an inner demon.

The intern fell into fearful silence.

Yusuf shouted, "Do you understand what I said?"

"Of course, yes. Isolate."

Yusuf seemed to have difficulty breathing. He scanned Chetin's worktable in a second, and then turned around, as if looking for a blatant outcropping of relevant artifacts. He twisted back to face Chetin.

"I'm finding nothing but bureaucratic garbage in the materials at my table. It must be here, somewhere!"

He looked down again at the items on Chetin's table.

"All of this will show nothing, as it should! The deceivers will be finally proven to be liars!"

Chetin's mind was stunned. *What?*

Finally, he had to ask for some understanding.

"Sir, what deceivers do you speak of?"

Yusuf leaned over the table and whispered, "The liars who quietly undermine the fundamental doctrines. Chetin, consider this. If we were to actually find what I believe could be here, a real statement from the apostle that reverses what he said about the death of the Christ, the Christian faith would be shattered. If it exists, we must find it."

Chetin knew his eyes expressed complete surprise and doubt. He tried to relax. He struggled for a breath as Yusuf glanced around the vault.

Yusuf spun around again, pointing at the racks of items in storage.

"Look," he said. "Old things of no consequence. Junk weighed down by bureaucracy. If we don't find it, you can put me on one of the shelves. After all my devoted work, I'll be an artifact gathering dust."

The chief of the archives turned away and exited the vault, slamming the door as he left. Chetin's mind searched for understanding. He continued to look at the door through which his boss left. Yusuf, the one he respected, had become a mad man.

Chetin swiveled into his chair and, putting a hand on the wooden arm, he eased himself back into the seat.

What happened there? What did that mean?

Minutes went by, then he heard the entry door to the archives open and slam shut. The sound of the door opening again prompted Chetin to hurry from the storage area to greet Yusuf. But, it wasn't him. The director, Aslan, entered the main room with an expression of bewilderment. Shaking his head, he approached Chetin.

With hesitation in his words, he asked, "What happened to Yusuf? Did you have an argument? Did he receive terrible news?"

"I don't know, sir. I was at my worktable in the storage area, and he came in. He was in a rage."

Chetin looked at the floor, searching for an explanation.

"He spoke of needing to find a document with a statement from the apostle Paul. But then, in almost the same breath, he said if it exists it could support the deceivers. The deceivers? I don't understand."

"Did he find something that set him off? Or, did you find it?" Aslan was quiet and seemed detached.

"I think he might be frustrated with *not* finding what he wanted. I just discovered an important document relating to this search, but I didn't have time to tell him because of his fury. Also, Director, I became afraid of speaking of it. I don't know what he would have done."

"Chetin, it was a wise choice to let him vent. Let's go to your worktable and talk."

The men made their way into the storage area at Chetin's work space. Chetin showed Aslan the plate he had found.

"Here, sir, this document has text that specifically refers to the essence of the controversy that was to be addressed at Nicaea. It also refers to an emissary to the Council who was not a delegate but condemns the 'heresy' as he calls it. It has to do with the death of Jesus. This is probably a critical issue for their doctrine, but I don't know these matters of theology."

Aslan set the plate on the table and put on his reading glasses. He leaned over and studied the text. Nervous energy filled Chetin. He paced around the area, looking back to see what the director was doing. At last, Aslan removed his glasses and set them on the plate.

"What do you think, Director? Is it important or relevant?"

"I attended graduate university in America, and people there have expressions of many kinds. One is, where there is smoke there is probably a fire. I think that's how it goes. In this case, there is a lot of smoke. Now, we know there is a fire."

The men heard the entry door open in the main archives room. Chetin felt panic.

Aslan said, "I will deal with this. Take the plate and put it in a place nearby where only you can find it. I need to know what's going on with Yusuf. Do it now, please."

Chetin took the artifact and did a quick scan of nearby racks. He slid the plate behind a large container as Aslan departed the storage vault. Chetin paused, wondering if he should follow. He decided it would be best if he waited to know what might develop.

In the distance, he could hear Aslan warmly and loudly greet Yusuf. The sound of their voices seemed agreeable and temperate, so Chetin decided to wander in. When the men saw him, Yusuf called to him.

"Chetin, please come here."

The young man stopped short, hesitant to come close.

"Please, Chetin, come here. I told the director here I had a bad moment, and I must apologize to you both."

He tried a more casual stance, but it looked strained.

Chetin was filled with doubts but he knew he had to go forward. Aslan motioned to come with a friendly wave. When he was next to them, Aslan offered thoughtful comments to both.

Yusuf responded, "Director, and Chetin, I don't know what hole I fell into, but I'm out again." They all attempted laughter. "If we can forget that, I'm sure there's important work to do. Chetin, I will not intrude on your space again. Aslan suggested we will get more done if you remain with your work in the storage area and I take care of my many duties in the archives."

He confirmed the idea with steady nodding of his heavy head.

Chetin felt his body relax and his natural optimism return.

"It's okay with me if—"

Aslan interrupted him. "Let's work with Yusuf's approach for a while. It's easier to concentrate that way, and then we don't make mistakes. Yusuf is the best in this business because he is thorough."

Yusuf responded with modesty. "Director, you are kind and generous. Oh, I need to inform you we will have visitors tomorrow. At times, I've received inquiries from people who wish to visit our archival facility. By coincidence, we talked about how England had requested a particular document from our collections. On some occasions we consider the review and even the loan of items from our collection."

Aslan's eyes closed part way and he looked down his long nose at his chief of the archives.

"And, who are these people?"

"They are from the Vatican. As you know, the pope has an extensive library, and the holdings in their archives rival most major museums. I don't anticipate they'll be here for even a day. Maybe they have an item we would like to examine or even borrow."

Aslan had a sour look.

"So, Yusuf, what's the purpose of this visit?"

Chetin noticed a resurgent intensity grow in Yusuf's posture and face.

"My impression is they might be interested in exchanging resources in the future. I learned they had an exhibition of what are apparently letters written by Jesus. This occurred in cooperation with the British Museum. They might wish to do a similar event with Topkapi, but first would like to visit the archives."

"Hmm, I had not known of this. Such requests will typically come through the director's office."

"Yes, and my apologies. This has arisen from routine correspondence as I have with many across the globe. Oh, and there's another person who wished to visit, an American. They say he's familiar with many private collections and has an interest in possible mutual review of archival systems."

Aslan became quiet. He rubbed his chin.

The passing time became awkward for Chetin.

"Pardon me – if you don't need me, I'll return to the storage room."

Yusuf motioned for him to go, but Chetin waited.

Finally, Aslan responded, "If you think this is prudent, then this will be a most welcome visit, Yusuf. As director, I have to think through too many details of schedules, security, diplomacy, and all that. Let me know who will be here and when. I look forward to greeting them. That includes the American."

With that settled, and with a sense of peace in the facility, Chetin hurried back to his area. He was eager for history to be revealed in his hands.

XII / 2

Two and a half hours in the car from Patras to the Athens airport went more quickly than Rennie expected. She had hoped to spend some time in Corinth, but as events were developing, it wasn't possible. Urgency demanded moving on. At least Istanbul should be interesting.

"Say, Demir," Rennie said. "You mentioned you've been with the government in different positions for over twenty years. Was it always in what you call 'security,' or did you do other things?"

"I was in the military for a time and went from there to a federal position. That took me to the agency I'm now with. There have been a few changes, but the same purposes."

Rennie wondered how far she could go with her questioning. Family might be a safe topic.

"So, Demir, are you from Istanbul? I've always wanted to visit there."

A long, quiet moment suggested more insights in this mystery man might not happen.

"I have an apartment there, but my travels make it more of a place for me to visit."

"Oh, that's interesting. What about family? My parents are still working, and I have a brother who lives pretty far away. I think of family now as including my closest friends."

"Friends are important." He paused, and for the first time, Rennie sensed he wanted to open up. "It's difficult in this business. Being away and not being able to say much."

"I understand that. Until a year or so ago, I was pretty

detached from everyone. I had tried to make a couple relationships work, but they were just work, nothing really evolved from
them. In thinking back though, I realized I was pretty closed off,
even angry for some reason—or maybe for no reason. Then this
discovery came along, and I began to understand that friendship
and even love are not risks. They're opportunities to more fully
live life in a joyful way. There's no guarantee of happiness in
friendship or love, but the giving of those things can be an end in
itself. Sorry, Demir, I've slipped into babbling mode."

Rennie's body sagged against the seat back. She wanted to
learn about the man who was in control of her destiny, and here
she was spouting about love. She could see his eyes in the rearview mirror observe her. The moment was lost.

"Duty," he said in a low voice. "We Turks have a strong sense
of duty. Personal needs are not considered a high priority. But, as
you say, we are also human."

Rennie again saw his eyes in the mirror. Was this an
opening?

"I agree, Demir. It's a difficult balance. So, do you have kids?"

"I had a son. When he was old enough, he joined the military."

A current of optimism flushed through Rennie.

"So, he was following in your footsteps?"

"I apologize, I do not know what this expression means. He
was assigned to a unit in far eastern Turkey. There has always
been much trouble there with terrorists. He was killed in a
bombing."

"Oh no, Demir. I'm very sorry. I apologize for bringing this
up."

"This is no problem, Rennie. It is a hard fact of life." His
hands flexed his grip on the steering wheel.

"I'm still sorry, though. That can be hard on a marriage, too."

"Yes, his mother was very unhappy. She is now gone. So, I

have my work, which I feel is very important to our nation."

David turned to Demir.

"From our experience, your work is important to us as well."

A nod of acknowledgment was all that was offered.

Rennie tried to sound upbeat. "I agree, and I'm sure Turkey is safer with you."

Miles of scenery passed by the car. Rennie thought a different topic might clear the air.

"Demir, I've been through a lot of difficulties over the last few days. Have your assignments often put you in dangerous situations?"

"Danger is always to be avoided. When it happens, it is quick. One must be alert, and one must be responsive. This is like the military. One always does the simple things, which can be done through obedience and practice. If one waits to act, if one considers options, they will not survive."

David glanced at Rennie and lifted his eyebrows.

"That's interesting," she responded, "and, it's something I need to remember. Too often, I've been suddenly challenged with something and my thoughts jump around until I finally acted, usually badly. Now, I try to draw on a calmer and wiser place for knowing what to do. Demir, it sounds like you feel comfortable working in a system."

"Yes, Miss Haran. Each person finds their place. Mine is, as you say, in a system. When I know and do my role, and everyone knows and does theirs, the system has credibility and trust. Where there is ambiguity and people can do what they want, only trouble occurs. No trust, then confusion, anger, they all happen. Firm action must put things in order so we have peace."

David pointed to the road ahead. "Venizelos. Is that the airport?"

"Yes, we are close."

Demir's voice returned to flat, matter of fact.

"It's good. We are ahead of schedule. We can relax at the airport. But, as I mentioned, remain not so obvious. Miss Haran, if you have a hat, it would be good. Your hair attracts attention."

"Well, thanks, Demir."

"I did not mean this as a compliment. It's to get through security without notice. Security is my business. Please follow my actions when we get there. We are business travelers, not having fun, just business. We are prompt and uncomplicated. If they ask a question, you give them a simple answer. No long answers. Okay?"

A surge of anxiety ran through Rennie. Her voice broke as she started to respond.

"Yes, uh, yes that's good. We'll follow your lead."

The car was quiet until they reached the car drop off point at the airport. Rennie found a rubber band and pushed her hair into a ponytail. She and David then mimicked each action Demir did, and with no emotion. They continued in unobtrusive business mode to the counter of Aegean Airlines for the tickets Rennie reserved online.

With tickets in hand, they went to a waiting area near the security checkpoint and Demir briefed them on what to put out for inspection as they passed through the screening system. The discussion enhanced the tensions tumbling with growing ferocity within Rennie. She wanted no contact with the police. They were still a threat to her. She closed her eyes, blank, and unable to proceed.

David whispered, "Rennie, are you all right? It's time to go."

She couldn't move. Her knees felt as if they might fail her.

"I don't know if I can do this," she responded. "I don't want to be arrested."

Demir stepped near. "Miss Haran, I know this place, and I know their practices. You can rely on me. You are safe and can do this."

She allowed her eyes to open.

"Rennie," he said in a gentle tone. "You spoke about friends in the car. Think of me that way."

"Okay, let's go."

Demir took over.

"Attitude is most important here. Be respectful, innocent, and modest. Show you are not concerned. I will go last to make sure you both get through. When we are on the other side, do not wait or make conversation. Take your things and go. We will meet at the first coffee shop on the right side of the concourse. Do not look up. There are cameras everywhere. Stay quiet and low-key. The two of you can associate but I will be alone unless needed. On the other side, I will disappear for a time, so don't look for me."

David went first, unloaded items of electronics, change, his jacket, and other forbidden items into a plastic tub and put it on the conveyor belt. He walked through the electronic gate without a problem. Rennie was next. She did the same, putting her things in a tub and sending it through the machine. Then, she stepped up to the screening site. She took a deep breath.

A security agent stepped forward with an angry look on his face. He held up his hand directing her to stop. She sucked in a breath of near panic. On the other side, David motioned to her and said, "Jacket."

"Oh, of course, sorry." she said to the agent.

She tried to look silly and laughed as she removed her coat and put it in a tub that Demir quickly provided. With that, she stepped into and through the gate without a problem.

On the other side, David and Rennie gathered their belongings and walked away without putting them on or away. They didn't look back for Demir.

Rennie gasped, "Oh, dear God."

David put his arm around her.

"You're doing great. I'm proud of you."

She turned enough to see him and mouthed a thank you.

An hour later, they were relaxed and refreshed, but Demir didn't appear at the coffee shop. As the time for boarding approached, their worry led to serious doubts about what to do next.

"David, if he doesn't show up, should we still go? He's our ticket to get in."

"Let's wait a few minutes. We have assigned seats."

Each added moment challenged Rennie's assumptions, determination, and confidence.

At last, her hand slipped down and grasped David's.

"Let's go."

Holding hands, they walked to the gate and boarded the plane. Once seated, they waited and wondered what might happen at the airport in Istanbul. Announcements began in several languages. Rennie took a magazine from the seat pocket and perused it to avoid eye contact. She buckled her seat belt as the flight attendants walked down the aisles. She couldn't see Demir and the last of the passengers had already boarded the flight.

Above her, she heard the word, "Okay?"

It was Demir looking down at her. He was in the seat ahead of her.

All Rennie could do was offer a weak smile and nod of her head. She fell back against the seat. A deep sigh filled her and escaped.

Just over an hour later, announcements chattered through the cabin announcing their arrival in Istanbul. For Rennie, this was it. The endgame was about to begin. There was nowhere to go after this except home.

On the way down the concourse to passport control, Demir met them. He was in a jovial mood.

Rennie was suspicious.

"We were worried. We didn't see you at the coffee shop and thought you missed the flight."

They continued to walk without comment.

Finally, he responded, "Rennie, I'm reliable in my duties. For you to know, back in Greece, I was in touch with my people here at Ataturk airport. All has been arranged. When we get to screening, you wait for me. I will take care of the final matters. Give to me your passports and phones, please."

"Why do you need those? Don't the security agents require the passport?"

"Please, it's arranged. You will be okay."

They provided what he asked for, but Rennie's anxiety level grew again. This didn't sound like proper procedure for a guy who only goes by the rules. She put her arm through David's and held his hand as they continued ahead.

The concourse opened to a large, sterile area filled with passengers waiting to enter Turkey. Serious, uniformed agents and soldiers armed with automatic rifles solemnly stood around the facility. Announcements in varied languages bounced off hard surfaces of the room. A vast number of people from diverse cultures pressed together. The air was thick with tension, as if chaos could erupt at any moment.

Demir stopped them. "Wait here but watch me. When I wave to you, go to the entry point at the far right. Understood?"

"Yes, but—" Rennie began to say.

"Understood?"

Rennie and David said, "Yes," at the same time. Demir then walked strong and erect through the crowd straight to a cubicle in the middle of the line of entry gates. He greeted several uniformed men and showed them the passports. Immediately, they seemed to be joking and slapping each other's back. No one looked at the passports. Finally, Demir shook hands with several of the agents and walked past the control point and to the gate on the far right. He waved and motioned to Rennie and David.

"Here we go," she said.

As they arrived at the passport control line, a security agent approached and directed them to the front of the line. They paused for a moment but followed the order as other passengers gave them sour looks. At the entry booth, Demir stepped up and handed their passports to the agent. He stamped them, and gave them back to Demir, motioning Rennie and David to continue on. Pleasantly surprised and curious, they did exactly that.

Greeting Demir, Rennie said, "Wow, you are the man. You've got what we in America call pull."

He surprised them with a moment of humble happiness.

Clearing their few belongings through customs was as easy as passport control, and soon they were at the curb, entering a taxi.

Demir spoke to the driver and then said, "There are many hotels near Topkapi, due to the many tourists. I recommend one that is modestly priced, but close to the museum and comfortable. When we arrive, I'll assist you in checking in. Then, we must discuss your plans for a few minutes. As you might expect, we do not need more trouble in Turkey. My job, as you may know, is to stop trouble."

Rennie readily agreed.

"We're here to ask questions, get information, and then we'll be happy to leave. That's my job. Get information, solve mysteries. David and I have no need for danger, I'm delighted to say."

"Good, then we can move ahead."

Demir appeared to shift into business mode again.

When they arrived at the hotel, Rennie and David were delighted with the modern, clean look and feel of the place. Rennie finally felt she was on the trip she had imagined. It just happened to be in Istanbul instead of Rome.

After checking in, they moved to a seating area to talk. Still standing, Demir provided instructions.

"It is nearly 6:30. You get comfortable in your room, and then we'll meet here again at 8:00 p.m. I will take you to a place for dinner where you can explain to me your situation. Agreed?"

"Absolutely," Rennie responded. "Right, David?"

"Agreed. We'll meet you here at 8:00 p.m. And, Demir, thank you."

Rennie added, "You've not only made this passage smooth. I'll never forget that you saved my life. Thank you."

She wanted to hug him, hesitated, then put out her hand to shake his.

"This is not necessary, Miss Haran. It's what I do."

He paused, then shook her hand.

"One other thing, Demir. Please call me Rennie."

He laughed. "We shall see, Miss Haran."

The Archives of Topkapi Museum
Istanbul, Turkey

XII / 3

Chetin strained to look up to see if additional light was available. Then, an idea came to mind that spurred his desires to press on. He could use the light app on his phone to brighten whatever he needed to examine. He figured the light was not too intense to cause damage but enough for better clarity.

As with the other documents, the name of Eusebius appeared in the current artifact he was assessing but not as a secondary mention: he was the author of the document, and it is directed to the Emperor Constantine. Chetin sat back and mused about the overall setting to determine if the letter would logically exist. Using the archive's research tools, he found that Eusebius of Nicomedia, a distinguished bishop of the early church, the person who gave the opening statements to the council meetings at Nicaea, and a cousin of the emperor, would be in a position to submit correspondence to the emperor. From his studies, he knew that Constantine, as a recently converted Christian, would have relied on Eusebius for guidance and results. He would have received such letter, and he would have preserved it. Enthused with his thinking, Chetin pressed forward.

He took out a notepad and wrote key elements of what was in the document; it's a letter; written by Eusebius to the emperor; and, it's about a potentially controversial topic. Eusebius wanted to brief the emperor with the point of the issue and offer background information. As he wrote his notes, Chetin whispered, "Yes, yes," confirming the validity of the text relative to history and practices.

Chetin made more notes. Eusebius urges consideration of the petition from the women bringing an original letter from Paul and from women of the early churches of Rome and Corinth. The letters will testify to the last evidence known of divine instruction. Eusebius says that throughout all of time and holy scripture "visitors from heaven have come into our world." He says this shows that "the presence of God is here and now, just beyond our knowing." He says to Constantine, whose conversion experience was from a "vision," that angels come into our world to give instruction to special people and we must be open to new revelations.

Chetin sat up and thought through this line of thinking. As a Muslim, he was familiar with Christianity in general but didn't see significance in the text beyond its historical quality. It occurred to him to plug in his phone so the light will remain strong. As he did, he thought of how he should use his phone camera to also capture pictures of these precious documents. Then, he could review them when he was away from Topkapi. As he shot the image, he realized that if this document was lost or destroyed, at least the world would have his photos. He took three more, including a selfie with the document.

A happy intensity rolled through Chetin the more he realized the possible historical significance of what laid before him. That was amplified when he considered this was the dream of his mentor Professor Erkan. His review of this ancient find wasn't a clerical task. It was a historic duty! The document was to be treated with reverence, almost holy respect. As his eyes scrolled across the text again, the power of what it contained shifted from objectivity to a sense of the divine. In parallel with the significance of what the testimony of the women would be, here it is stated that the basis of their argument is written evidence from the apostle Paul. Chetin blinked in shock.

The crack and creak sounds of the entry door to the archives snapped Chetin into the present moment.

Is Yusuf leaving?

Chetin covered and set aside his discovery and listened. Aslan's commanding but friendly voice called out to Yusuf. The voices sounded like a routine conversation, but he couldn't hear exactly what was said. After a brief wait, Chetin went with caution into the main room.

"Ah, Chetin!" the director warmly greeted the intern. "How is your work going? Better? Any new discoveries?"

"Well, sir," Chetin wasn't sure how to respond. "I don't have the expertise to say. All the objects here are treasure to me."

"And to us, young man. That's a good attitude. Don't you think, Yusuf?"

They waited for a response. Yusuf's facial muscles seemed to pulse as his eyebrows lifted and fell.

Aslan didn't hesitate further.

"Men, what do you say we close up for the evening. You've put in some serious work today and for many days. These artifacts will be here when we return. It's time for a break."

Yusuf's chest puffed up and his eyes grew large.

"No, sir. I must stay at this. What is desired is either here or it doesn't exist."

Aslan's expression went blank, but then his eyes narrowed, and his nostrils flared.

"My friend and colleague, we have another day tomorrow."

Yusuf stood up. "And, tomorrow we have visitors arriving and I sense they have expectations."

Aslan's voice softened into a cautious tone. "Another visitor we didn't expect will also be here. You recall the government agent who brought to us the ridiculous request for information? He is coming tomorrow."

Chetin felt fear as Yusuf softly growled.

Aslan continued, "He called an hour ago and said there's

missing information in the spreadsheet. His agency needs it to be complete, he's returned to Istanbul so he's coming in."

"This is outrageous. When?"

Aslan leaned forward, staring at Yusuf. "I don't understand why this is upsetting. It's just bureaucracy, Yusuf."

"Whatever you say, Director. It's bureaucracy all right. If you will excuse me, I will take a break. I need to know if it's night or day."

Without a polite goodbye, Yusuf was gone.

Aslan turned and gazed at the entry door.

Chetin didn't know what to say or do.

"Sir, I think I'll go back to my worktable for a minute. It might be best if I set things in order and leave."

"That's fine, Chetin. I don't understand all this tension and these sudden arrangements. I've noticed things for several weeks about Yusuf that have concerned me. We all go through a challenging time now and then. This, however, this has too much energy in it."

"Sir, it seems to be about this search, a specific set of documents he is determined to find or prove they don't exist. I don't understand. And, there's this new pressure about the visitors coming. He is very tense. But we often have visitors here so —"

"Yes, and visitors are cleared through me. This group wasn't. It's not protocol."

Aslan's eyes were intense.

"Forgive me, Director. With all this distraction, I must tell you that I have come upon another document that I believe could be significant. Would you like to see it?"

"Yes, of course. I trust your judgment. Show it to me."

Chetin led the way to his table in the storage area and passed to Aslan the plate holding his new find. Using his notepad, he explained the key points of value in the find as well as background information.

Aslan rested his hand on Chetin's shoulder. "Young man, you may become famous with this. Your instincts are correct. This establishes a new marker in history. There is more here than we can understand at this time. Make your appropriate notes and set it aside in whatever safe place you preserved the other document."

"And, sir, should I inform Yusuf of this?"

Aslan closed his eyes and sighed. Silent moments passed by. "No, our colleague doesn't need a new find like this to possibly upset him further. Let's allow some time for things to cool and then reveal these as new discoveries. He need not know we waited."

"Good, sir. I'll take care of it."

"Document this well, Chetin. And, keep looking. You have found what might be a continuous vein of gold. There are significant works to be found."

Aslan displayed to Chetin perhaps the director's first and greatest smile seen by the intern. Chetin wished Professor Erkan could be there with them. He too, would be delighted.

PART THIRTEEN

Istanbul, Turkey
A comfortable hotel

XIII / 1

Rennie strolled to the front window of the hotel and felt the warmth of the morning sun on her face and body. Sipping Turkish coffee from a white, porcelain cup with a fresh croissant on a plate, she observed people walking by, getting on with their ordinary day, and vehicles competing for place and opportunity. Peace and comfort were finally hers.

A bellhop hurried by with a bag and paused to adjust his grip and balance the load.

"Excuse me," she said. "Do you speak English?"

"Yes, yes, madam."

"I'm sorry to interrupt, but what is that across the street? Is it a prison?"

He seemed amused as he fumbled with the bags. "No, madam, that is Topkapi Sarayi, the sultan's palace and now museum."

Rennie returned to the windows to study the dark granite walls fifty feet high, like those surrounding a castle. Interrupted at regular intervals by square-topped towers, they spoke of grandeur, authority, and absolute power.

David came next to her and viewed the scene. He put his arm around her waist. "Wow, what's that?"

"Oh, that's Topkapi," she laughed. "See, I know a few things."

"I have no doubt. When was Demir going to pick us up?"

"At dinner last night, he said he'd be here about 9 a.m. You know, that was a nice time. He wasn't so, I don't know, so aloof."

"You mean cold?"

"Yeah, that too. I thought he'd want specific information about this quest we're on. It didn't appear to interest him."

"He might have us figured out already. We're no threat. When you step back from it, we don't seem to know what we're doing. Our travels are more a case of leaving-from than going-to some place."

Rennie didn't respond. She was finally enjoying the moment and didn't want to think for a while. The coffee was potent, the croissant light, and the day a delicacy.

"David, I don't know what's next here, but if it's just meeting a few people, getting some information, and then becoming tourists, I'm in. We'll explore Istanbul and go home. I'm already forgetting Italy, but I'd like to return someday, as an unknown tourist. I know I'd enjoy it."

"I like the plan. When you return to Italy, will you let me know?"

"Maybe."

He shook his head and laughed.

"Miss Haran, you are something. Irrepressible might apply. Incorrigible might also."

"Ha! Oh, there's Demir coming up the street. Do we need to bring anything? I have a couple of pens and a notebook. Is that enough?"

"Rennie, I've a feeling if we need something, he can provide it. Goodness, that man is connected."

"Yes, but you don't want to get too close to power, and he has it."

They greeted Demir near the entry. He had little to say and seemed to be back in a tightly disciplined mode.

Rennie was eager to keep things simple and portray confidence in what they needed. "Good morning. So, is that Topkapi?"

"Yes. We're only a few minutes from the entry to the grounds.

My car is around the corner. Shall we go?"

Demir turned and exited the hotel with them following.

In the car on the way to the palace grounds, Demir briefly commented on the dinner the night before. Then he referred to part of the conversation.

"You said something about a person at Topkapi by the name of Yusuf. What was that again?"

Rennie responded from the back seat, "Yes, he was mentioned in some instructions about contacts he had with professors we know at the British Museum. One is David's grandfather. I don't know when it was, but they say Yusuf was reluctant to cooperate with him. We thought if we could find Yusuf, we could establish the beginning of a relationship and over time learn what David's grandfather was looking for."

Demir stared straight into traffic and without expression.

"And, your grandfather's name?"

David responded. "His name was Matthew Justus. He was a professor of social anthropology and archaeology and was connected with the British Museum. He died just days ago. Rennie met him when she went to London a year ago or so. She was investigating a situation that involved my grandfather's father."

Demir continued in a flat tone. "Your grandfather died recently? What was the cause of his death?"

"I don't know. I was here or rather in Italy when it happened. But, he was quite old, nearly ninety. It happened quickly."

Demir looked sideways at David, expressionless.

Rennie remembered she hadn't checked her email last night, so she took out her phone. With a light spirit, she felt flattered she had received so many messages, and then one stood out. It was from Angie, and the subject was *Danger: Sfumato.*

She looked out the side window. Angie doesn't know she's in Istanbul. She tried to process why Sfumato would be a danger to her.

And here?

Rennie opened the message and read it twice. It sounded logical, but she remembered how Sfumato had protected her from that crazy guy Galila, in London. She never felt threatened by him. She thought, *he's creepy and arrogant, but dangerous?* Rennie read Angie's messages and the wealth of details that came from them. She and David had agreed not to tell anyone where they were, but now she had to tell Angie.

"David, when we stop, could we talk?"

Rennie noticed Demir's eyes in the rearview mirror looking at her.

"It's about a friend of mine, back in Iowa. I told you about Angie. When we have a chance, of course."

"Sure, yeah. She's the librarian, right?"

"Yes, the cute one. You'd like her. She's kind of a scientist, too."

He chuckled and glanced at Demir who seemed disinterested.

Demir turned across traffic and into a driveway. "Up here is the gate for entry. I'll speak to the guard and then we go to the administration building."

Rennie put her phone down.

"Say, Demir, do you know where their museum is?"

"Yes, they have a very large facility extending through many buildings. From what you've told me, I assume you wish to speak to people in the Archives department."

"Exactly, thank you. If they have a particular building, that's where we should go. They might know where this fellow Yusuf is."

"Miss Haran, I believe we will find him."

In a few minutes, Demir parked in a staff parking lot next to a building near the center of the complex. Rennie wanted to mention the staff requirement but sat back. She wasn't going to question him.

Rennie and David exited the car and surveyed the area. She noticed that Demir had become less expressive and more focused as if this was his mission and not theirs. She put her arm through David's as they followed Demir down a sidewalk. He gave her arm a slight squeeze as he looked at the sights. Rennie tugged back and tried to get his attention.

Finally, she said, "We've got to talk."

She highlighted her warning with a squint and a nod. He looked perplexed.

Entering the grand lobby of marble, granite, and opulent furnishings, Demir marched straight to a reception desk. As he did, Rennie stayed back near the entry and pulled David around.

"Angie sent me a message. There's a guy I ran into when I found the letters. His name is Charles Sfumato. He's a wealthy guy, and he deals in antiquities, mostly stolen. He tried to get to the letters ahead of me. Angie said he's probably on the hunt for the same thing or things we're after. She said she and Bud agree that Sfumato won't lose this time. No matter what. David, no matter what."

"Is he dangerous?"

"He could be if he doesn't get what he wants, and if what he wants is valuable enough."

David looked down and scratched at his sideburn. "What does this guy look like?"

Demir stepped up from behind. "Your contact, Yusuf, he's here today. Someone will come meet us and take us to him."

"Great, Demir, you're invaluable. Thank you." Rennie tried to be cheerful despite her new concerns. "I hope you will come to the US sometime so I can show you around"

Demir's answer was a modest tilt of his head. Then, he went to the reception desk again and looked through pages of their logbook. The clerk had a surprised look on her face but stepped away. Rennie observed him and tried to understand why he was helping them.

David grasped her arm. "So, could this Sfumato guy know we're here?"

"If we're looking for the same thing, and it's here, he might show up."

"Rennie, we need to keep Demir close to us. He's our life preserver right now."

"Agreed. I don't know if I should tell him about this. He seems jittery right now."

"Yeah, there are underlying agendas that we don't know about with him."

She studied the man across the great hall. "That's the nature of his work, endless unknowns. He's a complex person but out of necessity. I think he's a good guy."

A middle-aged man with a distinguished step came down a stairway and waved to Demir. They shook hands upon meeting and Demir motioned toward Rennie and David.

"Hey, David, it looks like he already found our man."

They walked toward one another, and Rennie noticed that Demir's expression remained serious and the other man was reserved. Before they met, Demir stopped and spoke quickly to the man with gestures that looked commanding.

Rennie felt intimidated.

They know each other.

Coming together Rennie reached out to shake hands.

"Hello, are you Yusuf?"

Demir responded, "Miss Haran, this is Aslan Yilmaz, director of Istanbul's Antiquities and Topkapi Museum Operations. He has an employee by the name of Yusuf. We think he's the man you wish to speak with."

"Well, sir, I'm pleased to meet you. Demir has been a wonderful asset to us. Meeting you is a great honor."

Aslan shook her hand but turned to Demir. "Demir?"

An awkward quiet hung in the air. Demir said, "Miss Haran, and David, Mr. Yilmaz also knows me by another name, a formal name. You refer to me by, what you call, a nickname."

"Oh, Mr. Yilmaz, I apologize."

Aslan diplomatically calmed the moment.

"Not at all, Miss Haran. I'm pleased that Umit—or Demir— has brought you to us." He turned to David and added, "And you, sir. Welcome. If you would help me with the reason for your visit so I can fully serve your needs."

Rennie provided a quick summary of the "research" efforts they would like to pursue with the help of Aslan and this man Yusuf. She did not speak of any events in Italy. She mentioned Matthew's name and his relationship to David, thinking that might be a good connection. Along the way, Aslan's eyes would nearly close and he would nod as if thinking through her comments.

"Well, Miss Haran and David, I believe we can be of great assistance to you and fairly quickly. If you will follow me, I will introduce you to Yusuf. He is our chief curator and a distinguished archive professional."

As they followed the director, Rennie's shoulders lifted in eager anticipation. She happily whispered to David, "This might all work out."

They marveled at the massive scale and elegance of the building through which they were escorted. Polished marble floors, walls hung with tapestries and art, and large windows providing views of beautiful gardens all hinted at the grandeur of a sultan's life.

They turned into a short hallway that ended with an elevator and small sitting area. Aslan touched a button on the elevator console.

"Mr. Yilmaz," Rennie said with delight, "this palace or

museum is an extraordinary place. What you've done here, and I guess what you do on a routine basis, is amazing. I wish I had a week to see the entire collection."

"If you had a week, you could maybe get through much of this building. We have many others. Sometimes, I ask myself if I've seen all of it."

Everyone, even Demir, enjoyed the comment, but he became serious again. "Director, can you advise us where we are now going?"

"Yes, I am so sorry. This elevator is our primary access to the archives center. It is underground for security and environmental control reasons. Also, down there are the storage facilities we have for works coming in or leaving the museum. We have shipping and receiving access routes and freight elevators from the surface so our treasures can be properly managed in transit."

When the doors opened, and they stepped into the elevator, Rennie's excitement grew. Success was around the corner, or more correctly, a few floors below. At the level of the archives, the elevator opened to another small waiting area and several doors. The walls were painted concrete and had none of the refinements of the palace grounds above.

Aslan used a thick key from a ring with similar keys to unlock and then open a large door.

"This way, please."

The door creaked loudly as it swung wide. Aslan laughed, "I think the staff keep this door noisy so they hear me coming."

The guests absorbed every aspect of their surroundings as they moved into the main room. David and Rennie expressed delight by pointing at objects and making comments as they proceeded, while Demir held back with cautious steps. Aslan made steady strides ahead, glancing down the dimly lit aisles of storage racks.

He stopped and pointed to an area of worktables. "Usually,

Yusuf works in that area. He might be in the racks examining an artifact. If you will wait here, or make yourselves comfortable in those chairs, I'll find him."

Chetin walked into the room and discovered the group. "Oh, Director, forgive me. I did not know you had special guests today. Are these the people you were expecting?"

"Well, not exactly Chetin. Miss Haran, David, and Umit—or Demir—this is Chetin, our intern. I have learned how good he is at this craft, so I've become concerned he might take my job someday."

Chetin bowed and was clearly uncomfortable with the surprise meeting. "Director, if I may?"

Chetin motioned to the side, apparently wanting a private conversation.

After a short visit, Aslan returned to the visitors.

"Yusuf has stepped away and should return soon. Due to our being underground, it's not possible to have cell phone service down here. Now and then, staff must go up for a call. Chetin, this is Miss Haran from the United States and this is David, from England."

David put out his hand to shake that of the intern. "Chetin, my grandfather is or was Professor Matthew Justus of the British Museum. Are you familiar with the name?"

"Sir, I've heard the name 'Matthew' mentioned by Yusuf. I regret not knowing him. However, my mentor, Professor Ahmet Erkan of the Turkish Institute of Religious Studies in Izmir, he might have known your grandfather. Sadly, Prof. Erkan died, or was killed recently. By coincidence, another associate of Prof. Erkan's, a priest in Greece also died."

Rennie and David looked at each other, mouths open. She put a hand over her mouth.

"Forgive me for mentioning these things," Chetin said, noticing their responses. "I know they are graphic. May I show you around until Yusuf returns?"

Rennie, deep in thought, said, "Yes, of course. Thank you, Chetin."

Demir took David's arm and held him back. Rennie noticed.

In a course, low voice Demir asked, "What's the meaning of these deaths? Who can explain?"

Rennie stepped up. "I will. David, would you go with Chetin and keep him and Mr. Yilmaz occupied?"

As David walked away, Rennie turned to Demir. "I wasn't sure how much I should say or what you wanted to know. There's far too much to express quickly or simply."

She summarized for him the deaths and the so-called war within the Christian church and involving ancient documents, adding to what she thought he knew. She studied him. He seemed ready to pounce.

"Miss Haran, I don't care about documents. They don't hurt people. Tell me about who wants what, as far as you know."

Rennie described what happened in Italy, first in Naples and then in Rome, focused on the people. She mentioned the new information about Sfumato. She said she didn't know Yusuf or anyone else in Turkey.

"This is enough, Miss Haran. We shall learn more when Yusuf returns. Until then, we must get to know this room, access, and the people here."

XIII / 2

The museum reception clerk noticed three men enter the main doors. One man, tall and thick in a black suit with a crisp white shirt and dark red tie, took cautious strides through the grand lobby of Topkapi. He paused and motioned to those at the entry. A deeply tanned elderly gentleman, distinguished in a form-fitting light gray suit, entered the hall with an elegant attitude accompanied by a third fellow, a clone of the first.

The clerk made a brief call, then came around the desk to greet the visitors. Charles Sfumato introduced himself and the purpose of his visit. Sfumato drifted away with casual grace. He scanned the great hall with an air of satisfaction, as if he approved.

The three men met for a quiet conversation. The first man removed a phone and made a call, then made a brief comment to Mr. Sfumato. The two support men maintained vigilant positions as their boss strolled, pausing at times to study the detail on a tapestry or table. Looking at his watch, the cuff of his linen shirt displayed a gold-wrapped silver coin with an Etruscan image.

All three turned with the sound of someone entering the hall from the side. Yusuf waved a warm welcome. Ignoring the two men at the side, he went straight to Sfumato, offering his hand and bowing.

"Sir, I'm pleased to see you again. Welcome to Topkapi Sarayi. I regret we've not been able to prepare for this delightful and surprising visit."

"Thank you, Yusuf. I hope you can come to San Francisco again soon. Perhaps, our situation will work out and that your coming may be for a long time."

Yusuf eagerly nodded and humbled himself with awkward abandon. "My hopes are that our arrangements will be fulfilled to your satisfaction."

"I have every confidence in you. The product of your work will be memorable and forever secure."

Yusuf again shook the hand of his possible grand benefactor. An unusual, joyful spirit seemed to be upon him.

"And, what are the plans, Yusuf? Will we have our prize today?"

Despite the doubts showing on the face of the chief curator, he eagerly replied, "It is very possible. We have much supporting evidence, so I know the treasure lies near. Would you like to visit the archives?"

A corner of the old man's mouth moved, telling little. "It would be a privilege, my friend."

Yusuf led the way to the elevator, followed by one of the support men, then Sfumato, and finally the other assistant. All was quiet on the way down to the facility. When they reached the door to the archives, Yusuf paused, noticing the door was not entirely closed.

"Is something amiss, Yusuf?" Sfumato asked.

"I don't think so. Whoever has last come or gone failed to secure our door. Please, welcome to the treasure room, as some have called it."

Yusuf held the door for the three visitors and upon closing it, he hurried past them. "Again, my apologies for not being ready for your arrival. This is, after all, a workroom."

The sound of voices amidst the racks turned their attention toward the noise.

Yusuf called out, "Chetin, is that you? Is someone with you?"

The intern responded as he came down a softly lit aisle. "Yes, the director is here. So, also, are guests."

Chetin, Aslan, and Demir appeared from the darkness. Behind them, came David and then Rennie.

As they arrived in the workroom, Sfumato and Rennie's eyes locked onto each other. No one said anything for a deadly quiet interlude.

Aslan broke the moment open. "Yusuf, who are your guests?"

"Ah, Director, this is Mr. Charles Sfumato of San Francisco, USA. With him are his two assistants. Mr. Sfumato, this is the director of Istanbul's Antiquities and Topkapi Museum Operations, Mr. Aslan Yilmaz."

As Aslan shook hands with the visitors, he commented to Yusuf, "Are these the visitors you expected? Forgive me, Mr. Sfumato and gentlemen. Sometimes, the man at the top knows less than anyone."

"I fully understand, Director," Sfumato responded. "Ambiguity adds a consistently unique flavor to management, wouldn't you say? And, I see there are other guests here."

"Yes, also unexpected. This is —"

"Forgive me, Director. Miss Haran and I have met. It was in regard to another significant find. Miss Haran, a delightful surprise."

They maintained a stiff distance between them.

"Yes," she replied. "A surprise, indeed."

Sfumato glanced at the others. "And, Director, we have others here? I'd be pleased to meet them, also."

"Of course, this is Umit Yildirim. He's with the government and has been conducting a project, I guess we could say a research project. And, with Miss Haran, is her friend David. You might know his grandfather, a Professor Matthew Justus."

Although Sfumato's face gave no reaction, it was difficult to miss the continued look of shock in Yusuf's expression.

Finally, Aslan again took the lead. "What is the reason for your visit? It is quite remarkable we all find ourselves here in the archives. On limited arrangements, we have noted researchers participate in our work here but never casual visitors. Perhaps, we should all return to the conference room on the main level where we might be more comfortable."

Sfumato responded, "Director, it's indeed a privilege to be in this place where the hard work of discovery becomes the revelation of understanding. You and your colleagues are to be applauded. Since we are here, could we be informed of any updates and see some of the work you are pursuing? It would be a profound gift to us. We have come a great distance. Perhaps Miss Haran and the others have had a chance for that delight."

"Of course, for a few minutes, that would be fine. We welcome any distinguished visitors who are friends of Yusuf. Yusuf, we were in the old sections back there. That might be of interest to your guests."

"Yes, Director, that's a good idea. Gentlemen, please follow me and I'll be your guide to the collections."

As they passed one another, the intensity between Rennie and Sfumato remained, despite a polite handshake and greeting in passing.

When Yusuf's guests disappeared into the stacks, Chetin suggested that Rennie, David, and Demir might like to visit his work area in the storage room. Aslan agreed, but continued to study the departure of Yusuf and his arrivals.

When they had a moment alone, Rennie said to David and to Demir, "I can't believe it. He's here, now. Something's going on. This is no coincidence."

Chetin appeared wary but enthused that people would have an interest in his work. He led them into the storage room and provided a general overview of the layout and processes of how property enters the storage facilities from the freight elevators and ultimately proceeds into the archives review rooms. From there, selected pieces go upstairs into displays as needed.

Aslan entered the room. "Chetin, you've recently come upon another item. I'm sure Miss Haran will be interested."

The intern didn't move. "Sir, this is still new, it's ah, —"

"Please, go ahead. You will find them quite well informed."

With careful attention to detail, Chetin presented the work-table where he was currently reviewing items of interest. He referred to the Constantine collection of artifacts that was largely intact and not fully researched. He pointed to some obvious artifacts that caught the eye.

Aslan interrupted him, "Chetin, show them the unique items you set aside."

Chetin wrung his hands and bit his lip. "Sir, these are—"

"It is my wish."

Rennie sensed Aslan was pushing to reveal something special. *It's here!* she thought.

Conversations of the other visitors arose in the main room. Aslan made a quick pivot and left the storage room.

Rennie asked Chetin to show them what he had found. As he laid them on the table, she asked him if others knew of this. He responded that only the director had been informed.

With shaking hands, he displayed the latest find and stepped back.

Rennie and David moved closer.

David asked Chetin, "And, what did you find of interest here?"

"It mentions certain parties of significance. There's the Emperor Constantine, of course, and then a person who played a key role in the first Council of Nicaea, one Eusebius of Nicomedia."

"Interesting," David continued, "but other than the names, what's so meaningful? What do they say?"

Chetin again wrung his hands and turned toward the entry door to the storage area.

Rennie knocked her knuckle on the table to get Chetin's attention. "Excuse me, we've spoken to the director and he wants us to know everything."

Chetin stepped around the table and pointed to the plate David was closely examining. Rennie joined them as Demir held back, surveying the overall situation. Chetin used his notepad to deliver a brief, focused summary of the key points.

Rennie looked into David's eyes. "We are so close."

Chetin responded, "I agree."

Sensing a common understanding, David said, "Chetin, where did these come from? I mean, among what other materials?"

"These over here on this shelf. There are some large items, a box and then document folders used for the initial preservation of documents."

David went to the shelf. "May I?" he asked, pointing to the folders. "I have some experience with this."

Chetin seemed uncertain but agreed.

David carefully opened a folder and laid several plates on the shelf.

Rennie pointed to the box. "Chetin, what's in this?"

"I don't think it has been opened. Typically, a box will hold heavy or large items. We never find any documents in them."

David held up a plate and shifted it for better lighting.

"Yes, the lighting back here is not good. I think it's our budget. The basic needs are often cut."

As David studied the document in the plate, Rennie slid a fingertip along the joint in the box separating what looked like a cover from the base. It was sealed shut.

"Chetin, would you open this please? It's probably nothing but a vase, but while we're waiting —"

"Yes, I believe I can do that. Let me get the proper tool."

A desk telephone in the main room rang. Everyone stopped. The group in the storage room went to the door to see Yusuf answer the phone. He spoke little and with hesitation. He turned to the director.

"There are more guests."

Rennie mouthed the words, "Oh, God."

Yusuf turned to the director. "Sir, now I think it's best that we all go up to the conference room."

Aslan responded, "Yusuf, I will go and you update Miss Haran and our other visitors on the special find you have. I will return in a moment."

The group shifted in place as Aslan left the facility. All eyes went to Yusuf.

Sfumato and his men stepped away into a private conversation as Yusuf showed to Rennie, David, and Demir the document on his desk. He explained they were reviewing what appears to be an agenda item for the Council of Nicaea meeting and the purpose of this item to be testimony from women of the churches of Corinth and Rome.

Rennie said to Yusuf, "So, this means there is a letter somewhere from the apostle Paul and maybe letters from these women?"

Sfumato announced from across the room. "Yes, Rennie, that's exactly what the document indicates. The question is whether those are here in this room."

Inside, Rennie rode a wave of anger. She needed power. She hated those with it, but now she needed it. She looked at Demir.

Sfumato and his men approached the worktable. He pointed at the document. "This is a treasure in itself, but it's circumstantial. The piece that has been sought for two thousand years is hinted at."

He turned to Yusuf. "But where is it?"

"It's here, sir, somewhere. We're close. It's here."

Sfumato snickered. "My friend, it is said that 'close' only counts with hand grenades and love. We don't need close. We need results. Isn't that what we agreed?"

Demir now spoke. His low flat tone began with a gurgle and ended strong. "And, 'agreed' means what?"

All eyes turned to him.

Sfumato responded, "I'm not sure if we are fully acquainted. What again is your role or position here?"

"The question—" Demir began, and then the entry door to the main archives room opened with its screeching announcement.

Aslan entered, followed by Father Angelotti and Busca.

"Oh, dear God," Rennie said aloud. She put a hand over her mouth.

As the Vatican visitors entered the room, their smiles turned into expressions of shock.

Sfumato said with a laugh, "We're gathering quite a party here."

Aslan spoke with unusual strength. "Distinguished guests, I don't know what this is about, but perhaps you all come for what may be common interests. Is this so?"

"Thank you, Director," Sfumato answered. "And, I believe we may all know each other, or at least most of us. Am I right, Father, and Rennie?"

XIII / 3

Aslan divided the group to diminish the apparent tension among the parties. He told them he understood their shared interest in what documents might be found, and that all parties would be given the current status of any new finds. He recommended that Chetin take Rennie, David, and Demir into the storage facility while the guests from the Vatican and from California be briefed by Yusuf. After that, any added questions or suggestions could be addressed. He said he would rotate between the two groups.

Returning to Chetin's desk, Rennie's attention to the antiquities lying around them vanished. She gathered with Demir and David to discuss what ties and possible conspiracies might be in the works between Sfumato and Angelotti.

Demir answered, "Don't forget Yusuf."

Chetin gasped and stepped back.

Demir said, "And, you?"

Chetin's face twisted in fear. "No, no! In fact, Yusuf remains unaware of this last find, the letter from Eusebius to the emperor. The director told me to not say anything. I don't understand any of this!"

The eyes of Demir met Rennie's.

"How do we proceed?" she asked.

Demir pulled out his phone. "No signal. I must make a call. Chetin, is there a phone here in the storage area?"

"Yes, over by the freight elevator. Come, I'll show you."

Rennie and David could hear the mumbles of but not understand the conversation in the other room.

David whispered, "This could be history."

Rennie responded, "Yes, Mr. Justus, but consider the danger."

She gasped and pushed away from him. "What, Rennie? What?"

"You said this could be history. Maybe, it's a repeat of history."

She looked at the shelf. *That's it.*

"What do you mean, Rennie? A repeat of history?"

She grabbed his shirt with both hands. "David, your great grandfather, Matthias Justus found the letters from Jesus in an overlooked box on a shelf in the storage area of the British Museum."

They turned as one toward the unopened box.

"Could it be?" he asked.

Chetin returned. "What?"

David took the box off the shelf and set it on the worktable. "Chetin, we need this opened."

Rennie's mind raced through memories and images. The potential discoveries inside the box and the threats of those in the other room pushed her to the limits of her self-control. She felt the protection device in her pocket.

The intern took a tool from a drawer and slid the box into position.

Rennie noted how cluttered the area was.

"Is there another table we can use, cleaner and maybe near the back?"

"Yes, there's another one. Good idea."

Chetin carried the box down an aisle, made a turn and then another to find the lonesome, empty workspace in dim light.

"Do you need help with this, Chetin? When I was young, I helped my grandfather, Professor Mathew Justus, handle some of the antiquities in his care." David sounded reassuring.

"Thank you for asking, but this should be easy."

Applying the tool with a simple flip of the wrist, the box lid popped up. Rennie and David bent over, trying to see the contents.

Chetin was amused. "Yes, the air in there is probably from the fourth century. How does it smell?"

They ignored him. David touched the lid and shifted it away from the container as Chetin put on a pair of cotton gloves.

Lying in the box beneath a cut of fine white linen was a leather bag the size used by a courier or messenger bag.

"Ah, yes, as I expected," was Chetin's response. "This is not a surprise to me."

He took a brush to sweep off the tabletop and laid down a white sheet to receive the box contents.

"It is common to find things like this in boxes. Vases, small statues, various artifacts. It must have been valuable to someone. Maybe it was a gift from the emperor to his wife," Chetin laughed.

"A purse," Rennie whispered. "David, do you remember the inscription on that monument in Delphi?"

"Yes, what was it? Something like, "A purse is more valuable than the king's treasury". Yes, it was next to the treasury."

Rennie pointed to the leather bag. "Is this a woman's purse?"

They held their breaths, looking at the bag.

Chetin paid little attention to them as he placed the bag on the sheet and opened it. He peered inside and then removed folded linen cloth, similar to the piece lying on top of the purse.

"David," Rennie said, "when we laid out the letters at my house to photograph them, your grandfather instructed us to first put down a clean sheet."

Chetin seemed unimpressed. "Well, here we are. Maybe these were the king's sheets. Ha!"

Rennie's eyes were fixed on the cloth. Something had to be

in them.

Demir walked up. "What's this?"

Chetin was still casual about the find. "We don't know, but it looks like a bundle of sheets."

The sounds of other voices grew louder and nearer.

Rennie pointed at the cloth. "Chetin, it's best to put that back in the leather bag."

"Yes, I agree."

As he did, Rennie said, "Let's go," and spun around, heading for the entry to the storage area.

They were met in the aisle by Yusuf and the crowd following him.

"What's going on back here?" he demanded.

"Oh," Rennie responded, "while we waited for you, Chetin was showing us around. Wait, is that—?"

"Hi, Rennie. We keep running into each other."

"Michael! What are you doing here?"

Her arms and shoulders flexed, wanting to strike. Fury pumped through her. This last "visitor" was too much!

David rushed to stand in front her. He pointed at Michael, "You son of a b—"

"Well, David," Michael interrupted him and continued in his nonchalant attitude.

"It's nice to see you too. I work for Mr. Sfumato. We figured Rennie would be a great resource who could help get us here. He was right. You know, it's hard to keep her alive and out of prison."

Sfumato spoke up from behind. "I sense there might be something special up ahead. Let's go see."

Yusuf responded, "I agree. Chetin! Show us where you've been."

The momentum of Yusuf and those with him, forced Rennie, David, and Demir to return to where Chetin placed the leather bag into the box.

"My, this is most interesting," Sfumato said with glee. He turned to Rennie, "Your gambit of hiding this fell through. And, what do we have here? Yusuf, you might want to take a look at this."

Chetin placed the bag back on the table.

"I opened it, and it's nothing but sheets of linen." He laughed, "I told them they might be the emperor's sheets."

He removed them from the bag and set them on the table. "See, our treasure."

He waved his hand across it in dramatic fashion.

Rennie churned with anger and shock that Michael had deceived and used her. Her frustrations nearly boiled over as the focus remained on the discovered bag and he approached the table.

Yusuf turned to Sfumato and shrugged. "What do you say, sir?"

Aslan stepped forward and said with authority, "As director, I ask Chetin to open the sheets. Let's see if the emperor monogramed them."

Sfumato's guards chuckled, but everyone else tilted forward to see what was revealed.

As Chetin unfolded and overturned one sheet, Yusuf yelled, "Stop!" He pointed and followed his own finger to the linen. There, in the dim light, between the folds, parchment was stuck to the cloth.

People pushed forward, but Aslan intervened. "Please, let's have the experts here handle this."

All retreated a few steps and were quiet as Yusuf put on gloves and worked with Chetin to carefully lift the document from the cloth. It fell away with surprising grace. Other folds of the sheet were opened and another and then another document fell away. Each was moved with the utmost delicacy to a glass plate quickly placed on the table by Aslan. With another small sheet unfolded, four documents were now under glass.

Sfumato stared with wet eyes at the table. He said, "This day is beyond profound."

The moment was broken when Father Angelotti approached the table. "Gentlemen, and Miss Haran, it's nice to see you again and well. Many of us have ideas of what might be written on these sheets of papyrus. Given that, I believe it best that these return now with me to the Vatican, their proper home in Christendom. We're grateful for the diligent work and safe keeping of these here in Topkapi. It is now time they go to where they are destined."

Rennie heard a rumble in the voice of Demir, behind her.

Aslan responded to Angelotti, "Father, in due course we will decide what these are and deal with them in the proper ways."

"Of course, my friend," Angelotti began, "but—"

Sfumato interrupted. "Since we might have the linguistic expertise here to get an idea of what's on these, let's move them to a location with good light. This can do no harm, and it might solve potential conflicts."

Yusuf intervened. "This is an excellent idea. I'd like to know right now what we found."

With Aslan's agreement, the glass plates were folded into the two small sheets of linen and placed in the leather bag. It was returned to the box and Aslan carried it into the main room of the archives. As this happened, Chetin did his best to raise the lighting level and bring over a desk lamp to a cleared and clean worktable.

Two of the plates were laid open on a sheet. Yusuf studied one followed by Chetin. When they moved to the other, David and then Sfumato examined the text. They even exchanged a few thoughts about particular words.

Yusuf and Chetin moved to a quiet distance from the table to discuss what they reviewed. Then, with Chetin at his side, Yusuf announced, "Gentlemen, and Miss Haran, our brief examination of the documents indicates the first two are letters from women from the churches of Rome and Corinth. The dates will need to be established, of course. Our cursory review suggests these are not to the Council of Nicaea. They are to people in other churches, and they comment on a new revelation of the apostle Paul. They say he has recently spoken to them of this awareness."

The eyes of Father Angelotti, Busca, David, and Sfumato all grew large as they exchanged recognition of what was said.

Yusuf continued, "The signatures indicate that one comes from what appears to be Julia Livilla and Mary of Magdala. The other is from a Priscilla and another name that is not clear due to a break in the document."

David put his arm around Rennie. He whispered, "I saw the names."

Yusuf set aside the two plates in a folded cloth and laid out the other two. The same process continued, and he announced the findings with Chetin at his side.

"Here again, we have two letters. One is from a woman of the church, and it addresses the Council of Nicaea. It requests they allow her testimony and presentation of letters she brings written by leaders from the earliest days of the church. It is signed by only one person, and that name is broken in the text from deterioration of the document."

Angelotti gasped, "This is unbelievable."

"What about the other letter?" Rennie asked.

"From our objective observation," Yusuf glanced at Chetin and then around the group, "the other letter was possibly written by one known as the apostle Paul."

Rennie took a deep breath.

David grabbed her hand and said, "From the little I could see and understand, I think that's correct."

Sfumato appeared unsteady, gazing into the distance. "And,

what did it say?"

"Chetin and I agree, the text refers to Paul's visitor from heaven. In addition, it states what's been rumored in some traditions. That is, the resurrection of Jesus was to give authority to His message of love and forgiveness. It wasn't about sin. Paul wrote that as a Jew, he saw sacrifice for atonement of sin as the purpose for the Messiah, not realizing that love was the only message. As a sacrifice-focused Pharisee in the logic culture of the Greeks, he had applied those perspectives to the reasons for the life and death of Jesus. He finally realized his error."

Yusuf's chest rose as he spoke with confident power. "We found the Holy Grail."

Barely concealing his glee, he folded the plates into a sheet of linen and placed the treasure in the leather bag.

As he did, Chetin stammered and hesitated but addressed the group.

"I'm not a Christian, so I don't understand the significance of this message other than it's perhaps our only complete letter from Paul. Why is this so controversial?"

"I'll tell you why!" Angelotti shouted. His face looked puffed and red. "News of this is a threat to the very existence of the church! Rumors said it existed, and now that it's found, we must destroy it. If this message is correct, and if people believe Jesus didn't die as a sacrifice for the sins of humanity, he didn't have to be sinless, there's no need for the law, for virgin birth. There's no need for confession and redemption. Speaking of the blood of the cross is meaningless. The core of the church is empty!"

David pushed past Rennie and went straight to Angelotti. His presence was forceful as he pointed at the priest's face. "Maybe this means the church should be a community of caring and not a power structure. The church is supposed to be a place of love and refuge instead of a place of guilt. Maybe you and your religion gang should be servants instead of powerbrokers. The message of the cross is love."

Busca's face looked fierce as he stepped toward David, so Rennie hurried over, thinking she might have to physically pull David from a confrontation. It was difficult for her to not smile as she wrapped an arm around him to ease him away.

She held him closely and said, "You're wonderful."

"*No!*" Angelotti responded. He shook his fist and pointed at the leather bag. "These are from the earliest days of Christianity. They must be moved to the Holy See for full evaluation and restoration. The church is the true home of all that is our faith and we must do this now. These items come with us."

"In truth," Sfumato countered in an arrogant tone, "the finest independent facility for ancient documents is operated by the International Antiquities Foundation, of which I am CEO. For authoritative management on the validity and content of the relics, it's best this be done by an independent organization, by us. Yusuf can oversee the work."

Angelotti and Sfumato approached each other with imperious, confrontational dignity.

"Stop," Aslan ordered. "This tension must diminish here and now, or I will call the authorities. There are many who have an interest in these assets that belong to Topkapi and the Republic of Turkey. This is where they were found, this is where they were first sent by the authors, and this will certainly be where they stay until we, their guardians, decide to do something else. I thank you for your devoted interest and enthusiasm. We all agree that history is being made on this day. Knowing now what has been found, you all can return to your homes and offices and report as you wish. Chetin, put this find a way for safekeeping. Do so now."

Sfumato pointed at Yusuf and demanded, "And, what do *you* say, Chief Curator? We have an agreement. Do you plan to stay here and find worthless relics in the dim lights of this dungeon?

Or, do we leave with these documents and take them to modern facilities where you will manage priceless artifacts with modern tools and support? What do you say?"

Confused looks all around were directed to Yusuf, especially by Aslan and Chetin.

Sfumato again called him out with more power in his voice, "What is your decision? Will you stay here to be the next bureaucrat? Is that your goal? Where should the documents go? With us?"

Rennie saw Sfumato's men shoulder their way forward. It seemed no one else was aware of their potential threat. She held onto David as she eased her position back a step. Something ugly was about to happen.

Yusuf erupted in a crescendo of emotional clarity. "Director, with sincerity and respect, I have had my fill of forms and spreadsheets, policies and procedures developed by clerks who know little of our art. It is my wish to go to San Francisco to serve the foundation described by Mr. Sfumato. *And,* these documents shall go with us."

Unobserved by most of those gathered, one of Sfumato's assistants slipped a hand under his jacket.

Suddenly, Busca stepped up.

"I stand in defense of the Holy Roman Catholic Church and all of Christendom. These documents must never be seen again. All threats to the church must be terminated. So must *Porta* in all its forms!"

Sfumato sneered, "If they go with me, my friends, they might never be seen again. So, we are in agreement, correct, Yusuf, Angelotti?"

"They must go with us!" Yusuf responded.

Aslan interceded again. "Yusuf, I don't understand. You are devoted to the preservation of history. What do you mean these must not be seen again?"

"What you do not know is that I converted to Christianity long ago and am devoted to our doctrine. I've kept this hidden for years. As Father Angelotti and others in Rome know, these letters are a threat, as they've been for all of time. As an archivist, I believed the traditions of these documents were alive somewhere and their surfacing was a grave threat to the church. I was devoted to finding them so Porta and its affiliates could not use them for heretical purposes. Now, here they are."

As Angelotti and Busca moved closer to the table, Michael said, "Whoa, boys. Not so fast." He came through the group between Aslan and Sfumato.

"You could say we're on the same team with different playbooks. Let's do the right thing here and not get too excited over little differences. We'll assume responsibility for the material and get it all safely and secure back to the US. The church will face a lot of questions inside and out, but we will not. We have an aircraft ready to go, so it's time for us to take these items and go."

Busca pulled a pistol from an inside pocket.

"Stop! This argument ends now. We are taking these to Rome and will decide what to do with them there."

Busca waived the gun about, pausing for a moment with it pointing at Sfumato. The instant he lowered it, an explosion blew through everyone's ears. Busca grabbed his chest as he fell to the floor, a hole opening in his jacket. A growing pool of blood slipped from under his body as the surprised look on his face became gray and changed to the appearance of sleep.

Sfumato recoiled to the side to see his assistant holding a pistol pointed at the now fallen Busca. The other assistant drew his weapon and stood with his associate. Demir silently slid away from Rennie to a better position as he reached under his coat for a gun.

Angelotti yelled "*No!*" and fell to the floor over Busca, making the sign of the cross on the forehead of the dead man. He looked up at the stunned group.

"Why?"

David put his arm across Rennie and backed away, looking across the table at the menacing, isolated presence of both associates of Sfumato. She slipped her hand into a pants pocket and removed the mysterious device.

To a far side, Aslan commanded, "Put the weapons down!"

When he did, one of Sfumato's men pointed his gun at the director. Instantly, in silence, the two gunmen were slammed backward into the shelving racks of the Topkapi archives. They crumpled to the floor with shelves, posts, and artifacts falling upon them.

Only David knew what happened. He looked down to see the device in Rennie's hand. Everyone else was in shock and confused. Demir saw David look down and noticed Rennie's device. He kept his hand on his weapon but still in his jacket.

"Dear God, what is that?" asked Yusuf. He pointed at Rennie as she put it in her pocket.

Demir burst forward with his gun drawn. "I'm taking charge here! Rennie, keep your hands visible. You two, Aslan and Yusuf. Which of you is 'the Turk'?"

"What?" responded Aslan. "We are both Turks."

"One of you knows what I mean Which one?"

He pointed his pistol at Aslan's face. "Is it you? I give you five seconds! One, two, three, —"

"*No!* It is me." Yusuf screamed. "It's not Aslan."

"*You.*" yelled Demir. "On the floor, hands out."

Demir turned to Angelotti, again pointing his weapon at the priest's face.

"Are you the Priest?"

"Of course, I'm a priest." Angelotti placed a hand over Busca's face. "Does someone have a cloth I may use to cover this man?"

"Answer me!" Demir demanded. "Are you the priest in Rome

who conspired with Yusuf?"

Angelotti shook his head "No, I only take orders. I don't give them."

"Enough! Who gives the orders to kill people? Who? Answer me!"

Demir turned to Yusuf, lying on the floor. He placed his foot on the man's back and pushed. "Who is the Priest?"

Yusuf shook with grief. "I don't know who he is, who is in charge. There is more than one."

Swinging his pistol again at Angelotti, he placed the barrel against the man's temple. "One last time. Who is it?"

Angelotti's body shuddered and his head fell.

In a voice barely heard, he said, "It's the archbishop, the secretary of the Office of the Supreme Tribunal of the Apostolic Signatura. He's the one who gives the orders. The secretary of the supreme court of the Holy See."

Demir turned again to Yusuf on the floor.

"And, you carried out the orders here in Turkey."

Yusuf responded with a nod. He buried his face in his hands against the floor.

Aslan and Chetin whispered the name, "Yusuf."

Bursting through the entry door, seven men in black uniforms, automatic weapons drawn, stormed into the facility. They screamed in Turkish, "*Down. Now!*"

Aslan and Chetin dropped to the floor, hands out and shouted in English, "Down, down!" The others followed.

Demir raised his hand to the troops and, in Turkish, told them all was in order. The men took orders from Demir and surrounded the gathering. He directed them to tie the hands of Yusuf, Sfumato, Angelotti, and Michael behind their backs with plastic bindings as they lay on the floor.

When Sfumato attempted to turn and get up, one of the soldiers slammed him in the back with the stock of his rifle and shouted at him. The rich man groaned and slumped flat on the floor. He pleaded, "Wait, wait, we can fix this. Let's talk for a moment. Wait, please."

"Quiet!" the soldier yelled in English.

Another member of the special ops team pushed aside Busca's gun and worked through the debris lying over and around the two unconscious associates of Sfumato. As he looked for their weapons, he saw the blood sliding from their noses and mouths, so he checked them for wounds and found none. He lifted his facemask and gave Demir a quizzical look.

Demir knelt next to Rennie and David on the floor and told them they could stand. He asked her what the device was in her pocket and said he must take it.

She laid it in his hand saying, "I have no idea what it is or how it works. There are things we'll never understand."

As he inspected it, she warned him, "Don't press the button. You saw what can happen."

A cheerful voice came from a new visitor. A round, old man entered the archives as the troops spun around, pointing their guns at him.

"It's okay, boys, I'm here in peace."

Rennie and Michael simultaneously cried, "Rafael!"

"Yes, it's an old friend, and as they say, still kicking! What's going on here? Please, men, I'm no threat."

His jovial manner disarmed everyone, including Demir and the troops.

"Rennie, Michael, what happened?"

Feeling new joy, she turned to Demir.

"He's okay. He loaned me that device. It's his. I thought he was dead, but here he is. Can I go to him?"

With Demir's approval, she ran to and embraced the old man. "I'm so happy to feel you alive!"

"It's good for me, my girl. Young man," he said to Demir,

"may I have my little toy back? It can't be used for bad purposes. Long ago, a visitor left it with me and said that in the right hands, it will be good for the world." Rafael nodded at Rennie and added, "I thought it would be good in her hands, and I guess it was. She won't need it anymore."

"Who are you, old man, and what are you doing here?" she laughed.

He surveyed the scene and shook his head. "I've heard a lot of stories over the years and with all the recent terrible events, it seemed the legends could soon come true. This was the most likely place to be, and *voila*, I'm right, but what a sad scene. Will someone share with me what was found?"

Demir turned his attention to those on the floor whose hands were tied.

"In the name of the Republic of Turkey, you are all under arrest for various crimes against the state. Director, Rennie, David, and Chetin, and the old man, you remain free. We will need you to return at some point for testimony."

Rennie approached Demir.

"Dear friend, may I return the device to Rafael? It's okay. He's good."

He studied her, and then in a calm voice she didn't expect, he said, "If you say so," and gave it to her.

"There's one other thing," she said. "I need to contact someone at the Vatican. One of the conspirators remains out there, this secretary that Father Angelotti mentioned. He must be brought in."

Demir flung his hand toward the door. "Good, go."

Rennie, David, and Rafael hurried to the door. Aslan called after them, "Wait, I'll take you to my office. You can call from there. Chetin, stay here, secure the plates we found, and watch over things. You are now in charge."

As they dashed to the door, Demir directed activities in the chaos of the archives room.

On the way to Aslan's office, David asked Rennie who she was going to call.

"There's only one person I know with any authority there. For some reason, I think I can trust her."

"You mean the nun who helped us get out of the Vatican that night?"

"No, the Abbess Serena Magdalena. I don't know her that well, but my gut says she's on the right side of this. Hey, where did Rafael go?"

David looked around. "I don't know. He's probably trying to catch up with us. Maybe, he got lost."

"Yeah, maybe that. So, what do you think of him?"

"I don't know. There are dimensions beyond our under-standing, and he seems to fit in with that."

Turning into Aslan's office, the director asked, "Do you want to make the call from my phone or your mobile phone?"

"I think I'll use my phone so she knows who it's coming from. She left me her mobile number in case I need to contact her."

Aslan and David stepped out of the office and closed the door as Rennie caught her breath and made the call.

XIII / 4

Subdued lighting and soft conversations nurtured the bodies and souls of Rennie, David, Aslan, Demir, and Chetin. They raised glasses of wine and, with happy faces, offered simultaneous words of acknowledgment and blessing to one another. The mixed, overlapping voices prompted nervous laughter and extra sips from their glasses.

A server brought bottles of water, offering an opportunity for quiet and reflection. They had just witnessed the destruction of lives in body and spirit of people they knew. Awkward looks and pauses fumbled through thick emotion. Connection was needed amidst sadness and relief. Rennie's thoughts wandered in wide circles.

Demir broke the silence. "So, Rennie, your phone call went well?"

"Yes, the abbess answered immediately. She was shocked but grateful to hear what happened. This woman holds an important position in the Vatican hierarchy, and it's well deserved. I told her about Busca and Angelotti, and she said they had a recent incident that implicated these people. They were trying to contact Angelotti. I also mentioned that significant ancient documents had been discovered, and they were the basis of the war that had been going on in the church. Then, I told her who the person is at the Vatican that led the secret group conducting the killings. He's an archbishop in their supreme court."

Aslan inquired, "Did she have many questions? Do you think it will be addressed? Sometimes, large organizations have so many procedures and power structures, one can't solve a problem like that."

Rennie took another sip from her wine glass.

"She needed information which I provided to her satisfaction. Serena is a lawyer, so her questions were to the point. On the matter of dealing with the issues in the Vatican, problem solved."

Demir looked confused. "How is that possible?"

"She called me back when we returned to the hotel." A grin turned into a chuckle. "They did what we in the States call a 'sting.' The pope's security people arranged for Serena to be wired for a private conversation with this archbishop who gave the orders to their secret group to destroy *Porta*, the other group. She went in and got him to admit what he was doing. *And!* With him was another one of Angelotti's associates by the name of Scarpia. He was part of it too. So, Serena got them to talk, it was recorded, and now they're busted! They were immediately taken into custody. The pope was decisive."

Rennie gave David a light jab with her elbow.

"You've been quiet. Are you thinking about one of your physics projects?"

He didn't look up, then responded in a quiet, hesitant voice. "No, but maybe, yes. My work in physics is to know the nature of the universe, defining it and explaining how it all relates."

He lifted his water glass and set it down. He seemed to be struggling.

Aslan filled the awkward silence. "That's impressive work. I hope to someday learn how to relate to bureaucracies!"

As he and others laughed, David interjected, "I guess my insight is, the more I discover and the more I learn, what is still unknown to me grows even greater. I have a new sense of humility about that. My grandfather had it, but I couldn't appreciate it. Now, I do."

Rennie leaned against him, placed a hand on his thigh, and whispered, "Welcome to the mystery business. It's kind of scary but exciting, and I can't let go of it."

A squeeze of the thigh prompted a smirk and a nudge from David.

He said, "Then, don't let go of it."

Multiple courses of fresh exotic food came to the table. Quiet times amidst mindless conversation were frequent. Demir asked Rennie what she planned to do next. Aslan said he too would like to know, then quickly added he wants her to return to Topkapi for a personal tour.

She swirled the last ounces of drink in her glass and watched it come to a stop. The corners of her mouth stretched wide into a smile.

"I called my friends in Iowa when we got back to the hotel. They were happy to finally hear from me, and they asked if I was coming home. I told them I want to go to London for the memorial service of David's grandfather, Matthew. He meant a lot to me. David, can we still make it?"

"Yes, and I'd like to introduce you to my family and friends."

"I'd also like to meet Professor Snapper. After that, I'm ready to go home. But Aslan, perhaps we could discuss an exhibition at Topkapi sometime in conjunction with the British Museum. It would be an honor to Matthew as well as to his father Matthias, who discovered the letters of Jesus at the British Museum."

"Definitely," he quickly responded.

Demir's intense eyes scanned the people around the table. "Rennie, may I ask why you did this? This was not your fight."

"I often ask myself that question. Sometimes I think it's about stopping the bad guys or maybe finding truth. Frankly, I'm not sure."

Demir persisted. "We stopped some 'bad guys' as you call them, and I guess some new truths have been revealed. Was that enough for you? Are you satisfied with this considering the serious risks that were involved?"

"That's a good question. It's difficult to know what you want and value. There were risks in discovering what happened to David's great grandfather and finding the letters that Jesus had written. The benefits to me in my discovery were the family and friends who reconnected and came into my life. I was alone, alienated. Then, I belonged to people who are meaningful to me."

Aslan looked sad as he stumbled toward saying something. "Rennie, I don't know the full meaning of your discovery, but you've become meaningful to all of us. You are a friend."

"Thank you. Friends are what really count. I met a nun on my flight to Rome who told me that a sense of belonging with others is a key part of a happy life. That's what I appreciate now more than ever before."

David asked Rennie what the Vatican thinks of the discovered documents and their message.

"Good question, and Serena said something I treasure. She said the pope told her he was fine with the basic message of love in the letter from Paul. He said the greatest truth is to live with love as Jesus did, and added that theology is important, but it can divide people instead of invite them to inquiry and deeper understanding."

In a shy voice Chetin replied, "Miss Haran, I hope you come back to see us again. I have much to learn from you."

"Chetin, there's one more thing in this piece of history I need to learn, and your help is important. It will require a special effort to find it. I hope that would be acceptable to you, Aslan."

"Of course, if it involves our archives and another discovery of significant history, we will make this a priority. What is it?"

"This letter from the apostle Paul was given to some women who were leaders in the original church. In subsequent writings for hundreds of years, there are no references to women except for a few who were martyred. I would be grateful if you could find anything in your records that might indicate why women suddenly disappeared in the history of this significant religion. That knowledge could also be a profound discovery."

Aslan turned to Chetin who gave a quick nod of approval.

"Rennie, if the information exists, we will find it for you. We may ask you to participate in the search. You have skills in this area. Are there other topics?"

"My friend, I think we've just begun."

Rennie fell back against the plush cushion. She listened to the gentle melody of the distant piano music and breathed in a fragrant mix of perfumed scents from large bouquets of flowers, spices in the foods, and the flavor of the pinot noir on her tongue. As she learned a year ago and nearly forgot, she should savor each moment of life.

"Dear friends, this moment is priceless and there are many more ahead of us. Demir, since we are now in this great city, will it be okay for us to stay another day to discover its richness?"

"Of course, Rennie. And, I will be delighted to serve as your personal guide."

"Thank you, but first we'll need to rest. David, is that okay with you?"

An uncontrollable laugh rippled in him until he could finally speak.

"Yes. We have just enough time to make it to grandfather's memorial service."

She leaned against him. "Perfect, let's go."

He got up and took her hand to assist her from the table.

Rennie turned to the group.

"Demir, we'll leave a message for you at the hotel front desk to update you with our plans. Friends, I look forward to seeing you again. There's much more to do. Thank you, from my heart."

She wrapped her arm around David, and the two disappeared into the darkness.

Thank you for joining Rennie on this adventure.
If you enjoyed it, please let your friends
know and offer a review.

Thank you.
R. D. H.